EVEN WHEN
YOU CAN'T SEE ME

EVEN WHEN
YOU CAN'T SEE ME

Samantha Ray

WINDY CITY
PUBLISHERS

EVEN WHEN YOU CAN'T SEE ME

Windy City Publishers
2118 Plum Grove Road, #349
Rolling Meadows, IL 60008
www.windycitypublishers.com

Published in the United States of America

ISBN:
978-1-941478-69-1

Library of Congress Control Number:
2018951074

WINDY CITY PUBLISHERS
CHICAGO

This is dedicated to my first "editors:"

Dad
Shawnee
Joyce

Thank you for reading and critiquing my "book"
before it was a book.

You are the best father, daughter, and mother-in-law
a person could hope for.

ACKNOWLEDGMENTS

DARRIN
My husband and best friend for the last nineteen years.
You are and will always be my hero. Thank you for everything you
have done to help me cross this dream off my bucket list.
I couldn't have done it without you.
Day after day and year after memorable year,
I love you with all my heart, body and soul.

LISE MARINELLI
The first woman I spoke with at Windy City whose time and
honest advice will never be forgotten. From the very beginning you
have not only pointed me in the right direction, your trusted opinions
have brought me peace of mind. Thank you for going above and beyond!

DAWN MCGARRAHAN WIEBE
You have been a blessing beyond words. I can't thank you enough
for your guidance and encouragement every step of the way.
I am truly grateful for your much needed attention and patience.
Your help with my cover will always be appreciated!

RUTH BEACH
My editor whose words of wisdom made me a better writer.
Thank you for your encouraging comments and more importantly,
thank you for helping me portray Josh as a likeable guy
and for not allowing Meagan to be a complete pushover.

To those at Windy City who helped me from behind the scenes:
Thank you and you are phenomenal!

1

Certain she had never felt so embarrassed; Meagan cowered down in her bus seat. She couldn't blame the passengers for their repulsed stares, blunt comments, or even moving away from her. She wouldn't want to sit anywhere near someone with the likes of her sickly cough. She cringed when she reasoned everyone on the bus could hear her disturbing attacks, just as she could hear their snide remarks.

"People like that don't have any common sense," an irritated man grumbled from a couple rows behind her.

"She is going to get every one of us sick," an elderly woman whined when she stood up to move to the rear of the bus.

Meagan's last cough drop had long since melted away and her plastic bottle of purified water was down to less than half. Angry with herself for not bringing more than one bottle, she exhaled a grossly long sigh. "That's what I get for being in a hurry," she scolded herself when she figured she would soon have nothing left to quell her debilitating cough. Staring at the back of the seat directly in front of her, Meagan imagined what she would tell her fellow passengers. It wasn't as though she wanted to travel in her condition. Unlike the insensitive tourists condemning her presence, she had no choice. She would much rather be at home wrapped up in her cozy electric blanket and sipping green tea. However, due to circumstances beyond her control, she had to leave everyone and everything she cared about as quickly as possible.

After realizing an explanation was pointless, Meagan thought back to the last conversation she had with her mother. While it was Meagan's father who insisted on taking her to the bus depot, it was her mother who did all the talking.

"Can't you wait a couple weeks, honey, just until you are stronger and feeling better?" her mother pleaded only hours ago.

"I feel much better and the fever is gone," Meagan replied before she hugged her mother one last time. She remembered brushing off her parents' concerns by telling them she loved them and would call the moment she reached her uncle Pat's. She could still see her mother's disappointment when her father lifted her overstuffed backpack from the trunk of his car.

"Please take your cell phone, honey. Your father and I would feel better knowing you had it."

"I told you it isn't holding a charge and I will get a new one as soon as I can. Don't worry, Mom. I'll be fine. I'm almost thirty years old and it's not like I'm flying to the other side of the world." Already on the verge of tears, Meagan hurried to avoid breaking down in front of her parents. The last thing she wanted was to burden them with more grief. Forcing a phony smile, she anxiously kissed her mother and father goodbye. "I love you and don't worry," Meagan said with a reassuring wave. Then she slung her hefty backpack over her right shoulder and headed for the terminal entrance.

Meagan's recollection was suddenly interrupted by another coughing spell. This time the bout lasted longer and burned deep within the confines of her chest. The tissue she used to cover her mouth was not only filled with the usual yellow and green gunk; it was tinted with blood. "Oh no, it's coming back," Meagan whispered to herself and closed her eyes.

It felt like forever since the bus had stopped and the driver stated the next scheduled stop would be at a remote, unmanned facility. The break could not come soon enough for Meagan, who was experiencing chills one minute and sweating the next. The constricting pain in her throat was back with a vengeance and riding on a dry, stuffy bus for hours wasn't helping. Recalling her doctor's words and advice over and over again seemed to compound her aches and pains.

"You have strep throat, bronchitis, and a double ear infection. You need to rest and drink plenty of fluids, and take this prescription until it is gone. If you don't take care of yourself, it could develop into pneumonia…"

As far as following her doctor's instructions, Meagan spent more time preparing for the undetermined amount of time she would be living in Montana than in a bed. In a hurry to finish her last errands, she almost forgot to pick up her prescription and a bottle of acetaminophen. She did however manage to drink a large amount of orange juice and green tea while she finished packing.

When the bus finally stopped, Meagan was choking and picturing herself vomiting on the narrow floor. She wanted to jump for joy when the driver's mumbling and monotone voice got her attention.

"Ladies and gentlemen, we have reached our unmanned rest facility. Feel free to use the restrooms and vending machines. Due to running behind schedule and inclement weather…"

Between her plugged ears and the driver's garbled tone, Meagan struggled to make out the driver's announcement. Am I the only one who can't hear him, she wondered and gave up when she barely heard him bring up the weather. Thinking about nothing more than getting to the restroom, Meagan pulled the zipper of her double-lined, snowmobile parka up to her chin. It was only last week when she argued the expensive coat was more than she needed but her mother insisted on buying it. Recalling how she complained the coat made her feel like the Abominable Snowman, Meagan stepped into the bus's cramped aisle. She reached toward her seat, wrapped her puffy arms around her bulging backpack, and checked her area for trash. Satisfied she had everything, she began making her way to the front of the bus. Through the low, filtered lighting of the large bus, Meagan could see she was the only passenger still awake, let alone taking advantage of the break.

The instant she stepped off the bus, Meagan's face was pelted by a mixture of rain and sleet. While her initial check of the weather appeared favorable, she had no way of knowing a late April storm was changing its original course. She was clueless to the warnings detailing how the early spring storm would intensify as it bore down on the Northern Plains, including the entire state of Montana.

Once in the building, Meagan wasted no time finding the ladies' room. Without delay, she went to the sink, lowered her backpack to the tile floor, and turned on the faucet. Desperately craving a cold drink of water, she couldn't fill her plastic bottle fast enough. When the liquid spilled over the top of the bottle, Meagan proceeded to guzzle nearly half its contents. With trembling hands she retrieved her acetaminophen and prescription bottles from the side pocket of her backpack. In less than a minute she became frustrated as she fought to open the child proof cap of the amoxicillin. It didn't matter if it was her quaking hands or lack of patience when the brown, plastic bottle sprang into the air, bounced on the floor and rolled to a stop against a trash bin.

"What next?" Meagan yelled and threw her hands to the ceiling. As much as she needed the pills, she could not bring herself to put them in her mouth after seeing them on the floor of a very public restroom. One by one she plucked the useless pills from the bathroom floor, tossed the medication into the trash and retrieved the empty bottle. After taking two of the acetaminophen, she returned the bottles to her backpack and went into a stall to relieve herself. When she returned to the sink to wash her hands, the liquid soap dispenser was empty and the water felt cold enough to freeze.

"You have got to be kidding," Meagan complained and then tapped the silver button to start the hand dryer. The heat felt so refreshing on her chilled hands that she pushed the button two more times. Although she was feeling slightly better than when she stepped off the bus, Meagan knew she was going downhill fast. Ready as she could be, she zipped her parka, picked up her backpack and started back to the bus.

Leaving the warm comfort of the building, Meagan stepped into the nippy, rain-soaked air. After looking toward the bay where she left the bus, she scanned the entire surrounding area. "No, this can't be happening. Oh god… no," she said with disbelief. "Where the hell is the damn bus?" Meagan felt a horrible sense of panic and tried to grasp the fact that the bus had left without her. "How could this happen? Damn it!" She yelled as a fine mist continued to spray her exposed face. Feeling completely helpless and very much alone, she shook her head and returned to the shelter of the building. "Where the hell am I?" Tears began to fill her tired eyes and she started to cough. "Now what do I do?" She tried to say through her crying. With a soaked face, Meagan returned to the ladies room and pulled a handful of crisp, brown paper towels from the dispenser.

Overcome with anxiety and lightheadedness, Meagan removed her parka and set it on a long, pine bench. Taking a seat beside her coat, she struggled to regain her composure. Her first thought was of her mother. *I should have listened to you, Mom.* Looking at herself in a nearby mirror, Meagan repeated one of her mother's favorite quotes. "Mother knows best." She couldn't help but wonder if she should have waited and thought things through as her mother suggested.

After spending quite some time trying to collect herself, Meagan checked her watch. It was only 10:45 but she was felt so worn out that she thought it should be closer to dawn. Nothing made any sense. She wasn't thinking rationally and her mind was a whirlwind of worries and dire possibilities. *Well I can't stay here and I need to find a phone*, she reasoned. Then she looked toward the restroom door and whispered, "What did I get myself into?"

It was another jarring cough that drove Meagan to her feet. She slowly went to her backpack and took out her extra large ski hat and thick gloves. After twisting her long and thick, brown pony tail into a bun, she crammed all her hair into the hat. Next, she put on her parka, zipped it as high as it would go, and shoved her fingers into her insulated gloves. Finally, she tried to scrounge up some motivation, slung the backpack on her weak body, and headed for the main entrance.

Always taking pride in herself, Meagan refused to allow her five foot, seven inch frame to exceed 135 pounds. Although she did not work out with conventional weights, she considered herself to be in tip-top condition. She enjoyed many outdoor activities, but her two favorites were walking and jogging, especially with a dog from the shelter where she volunteered. She and her canine partner would exercise for hours. She bragged up the needy dogs and posted their pictures at her pet shop. She got a charge out of telling people there was no better work-out companion than an energetic dog that's eager to please and raring to go. It had been less than a year since doctors told Meagan and her parents that it was likely her exceptional stamina that saved her life and assisted her rapid recovery. While she would be forever grateful to her first responders and medical team, she held a special place in her heart for each one of the dogs.

Leaving the protection of the building, Meagan tried to convince herself that she was merely going for a walk. Since she knew which direction the bus was traveling, at least she could be sure of which way to start walking. A light but soaking drizzle continued to fall when she left the parking lot and began hiking along the abandoned road. It did not take long for her to learn there were countless potholes and the deeper the hole, the more water it held. Worse yet, her boots were beginning to slip thereby warning her that a layer of ice was beginning to cover the pavement.

As she began her trek, Meagan strived to focus on something positive. She had wanted to visit Yellowstone Park for years, and thanks to living and working on her uncle Pat's farm, the park was within biking distance. She recalled how she became interested in the remarkable landmark after writing a ten-page research project for her high school geography class. She was most impressed by the park's captivating history, magnificent scenery and vast array of wildlife. While she never pictured Yellowstone or Montana as being cold, rainy, and dark, she wanted to think it could only get better. It certainly couldn't get any worse, or could it?

Time seemed to crawl as Meagan trudged on, one demanding step at a time. Under constant pressure of all the things that could happen to her, she hoped to find a house or flag down a passing car. Scared and growing desperate, she wanted nothing more than for someone to stop and call her father. Although she was still quite a distance from her uncle Pat's farm, her father could get word to him and he would come to her rescue.

Please, please stop raining, she thought. Her parka was water-resistant, not waterproof, and it soon began to absorb the moisture of the freezing rain. The longer and further she walked, the harder it became to lift her water-logged hiking boots. The burden of her backpack and wrenching cough were causing her to stumble and trip. She feared it was just a matter of time before she lost her footing on an icy patch and tumbled to the ground. Thinking she must have walked a long way, Meagan wondered why she hadn't come across any buildings or cars. Still having no idea where she was or where she was going and with no sign of help or shelter, her frustration and fear escalated. "Damn it! Stop raining!" she shouted and threw up her clenched fists. Her drenched hat was nothing more than a dripping nuisance and she could feel her chilled fingers sloshing in her spongy gloves.

While her shouting did nothing to ease the freezing rain, it initiated another onslaught of deep coughing. The lengthy assault brought Meagan to tears and she thought of her mother. "I'm so sorry, Mom. You were so right." Meagan struggled to speak, but her coughing made it all but impossible. She pictured her always generous and dependable mother standing in front of her, smiling and holding her arms out as if reaching for her lost and lonely daughter.

Paying no attention to her footing, Meagan's right boot caught on a rock or chunk of asphalt and sent her face first into the hard, wet pavement. Barely conscious, her nose was bleeding heavily and a large bump formed just above her right eyebrow. She was so stunned by the sudden fall that she lay motionless and unable to bring herself to stand back up. At the moment her only desire was to lay there and wait for someone to find her no matter how long it took.

It was the terrifying howl of some kind of meat-eating animal that made her think twice. It's probably a wolf telling its pack mates to come make a meal out of me, she feared. In addition to everything else going wrong, Meagan now had to consider the dangerous animals that could be stalking her. While it offered little if any comfort, she pulled off her dripping glove and felt for her knife. She slowly closed her numb fingers around the stiletto concealed in the right pocket of her coat. The knife was her father's idea and since she opposed anything associated with violence, let alone carrying a weapon, she only accepted it to appease him.

"Knives have a lot of uses, Meggie. I'm sure it will come in handy for some-thing," Meagan's father told her, and she hadn't wanted to waste valuable time arguing with him.

The brisk and intensifying freezing rain pushed Meagan to her feet and she struggled to look ahead. For a moment she thought she could see a road branching off to the left. Could it be a driveway, or was it just another useless and deserted road? Using the little strength she had left, she gradually shuffled her boots toward the questionable path.

The harder it got to keep her eyes open, the more Meagan began to think she would never reach her destination. "I'll just take a short catnap to get my strength back," she mumbled to herself. Her eyes were no more than slits when she nearly collided with a large mailbox that resembled a barn. Startled and relieved, she latched onto the object like a three-year-old clutching their favorite toy. Feeling dazed and a profound sense of urgency, Meagan's only thought was to find shelter.

The mailbox was at the end of a narrow driveway lined on both sides by towering, mature trees. Engulfed in complete darkness, the black trees were slamming back and forth in the storm as if they were possessed by demons. At least they're blocking some of the wind, Meagan reasoned to ease her fears. Proceeding up the driveway, she followed the first winding curve to the right. Then she went down a steep hill and turned back to her left. It was not until the driveway straightened and the trees thinned that she looked up. She had been fixated on the ground for so long to avoid another fall that she failed to notice the glimmering light just ahead.

After walking nearly four hours since leaving the bus terminal Meagan saw the blurred form of a long building under the light. The mixed rain and sleet made it difficult to tell what kind of building it was, but she couldn't care less. With a security light as her guide, she managed to find the front of the out-building. She stumbled to her left where two beaming, halogen lights hung above a white, steel, walk-in door.

Frantic and not thinking, Meagan began knocking on the door as if she was being hunted by a pack of wolves. When no one came to the door, she began yelling for help. "Hello, hello...please help me!" Still no one answered her cries. "Please let me in!" Meagan fought to scream through her coughing and gag-ging. "I need help!" She put all she had into beating the steel door with her cold and wet, gloved fists, but to no avail.

Whether it was right or wrong, legal or illegal made no difference to Meagan. With no concern for whom or what was inside the building, she turned the shiny, silver knob and pushed the door. It took less than an instant for the furious wind to slam the door into the wall. After promptly stepping inside, Meagan backed herself against the door until it finally closed. When her movement activated a motion light, she was overwhelmed by its sudden brightness and had to close her eyes. Even with her eyes shut, the sweet aroma of the alfalfa hay and the smell of the horses confirmed Meagan's beliefs. She was in a horse barn. Squinting while her eyes adjusted, she cautiously stepped to the center aisle where she heard the familiar and pleasing sound of the resting horses.

The recognizable sounds and smells took Meagan back to one of her favorite times. She was a young girl again, taking English riding lessons and helping at a nearby farm. Fortunately for Meagan, her family lived in a subdivision close to Willow Creek Farm. She was remembering her favorite Quarter Horse mare, Cleopatra, when she was struck with an unusual pain. A nearly unbearable throbbing in her forehead caused her to feel faint and she longed for a place to lie down. She barely made it to an enormous stack of hay when she fell on the bottom row of the neatly placed, rectangular bales. With the barn spinning around her, Meagan pulled off her ice-covered gloves and dropped them to the cement floor. She was scarcely able to wiggle her arms from the straps of her backpack before it fell beside her gloves.

In serious need of medical help, Meagan lay in a fetal position. Dripping with sweat and trembling with chills, she fell into a delirious sleep. Her entire body shook as she was swept away, back to another place and another time.

Just a short walk from the horse barn where Meagan lay sick and exhausted, Bess Mackenzie greeted her nephew with her Irish accent. "Good mornin' to ya, lad."

"Good morning," Josh replied, just as chipper as his aunt Bess.

"How did ya sleep?"

"Like a rock until the wind started howling and beating on my window like it was trying to get in." Josh pulled a solid oak chair away from his usual spot at the rectangular kitchen table. "I bet that nasty storm didn't bother you at all, did it?"

"Not a bit. I was so tired after unpackin' and helpin' Mrs. Calhoun set up for the church sale, I slept straight away. I didn't even hear Benjamin come home."

Josh scooted himself to the table. "I didn't hear him either, but his door is closed and his fan is on, so he must be home." Josh couldn't be prouder of his older brother Ben, who was a volunteer fireman and worked in search and rescue. He figured Ben made the six hour drive home after spending the last few days re-qualifying his search and rescue dog, Molly Girl.

"Ya would be wise to bundle up this mornin', lad." Bess advised Josh then placed a pewter mug in front of him. "Tis only 34 degrees and that devil of a wind has it feelin' like 20. We're in fur a cold rain thru the day," she advised and brought Josh an extra large, steaming bowl of brown sugar oatmeal. On a normal morning, Bess was the first one awake. Without fail, she was in the kitchen by 5:00, and would start her morning by listening to the weather radio and brewing the first pot of coffee. She made it a point to have a pot ready by 5:30 so Josh and Ben could have a cup or two before heading out to start the morning chores.

"Mmm Mmm, I love your Irish coffee," Josh complimented his aunt after he cautiously took his first sip from the steaming mug. Since he could not drink any alcohol when he was on call, he always appreciated when she surprised him with an occasional mug of her non-alcoholic recipe. "I won't be long this morning, Aunt Bess," Josh declared after swallowing his last bite of the thick cereal. "I am going to feed those ungrateful beasts," he said while pointing toward the barn. "And then I'm going to make a fire and hang out in the den."

"Sounds like a fine idea, lad."

"I'm not going to do a thing all day but sit in my chair and catch up on my magazines."

"I think I'll do some readin' myself. After I put in some wash, I should be free till lunch." Bess sounded cheerful as always.

Josh finished his coffee, pushed his chair under the table and smirked. "I am going to give you my phone and if Brody or Captain Berkowitz calls, please tell them I went on a cruise."

Bess laughed with amusement because she knew Josh was joking. Anyone and everyone who knew Joshua Mackenzie also knew how much he enjoyed his work. Hell would freeze over before he would refuse any assignment.

"I love you, and thank you for the coffee," Josh said as he bent down to kiss his aunt's cheek. While he was a mere inch shy of six foot, Bess was only five foot, three inches. Ben, on the other hand, was taller than both Bess and his younger brother at a lofty six foot, three inches.

Regardless of their physical shape, the men learned at an early age that they were no match for Bess's commanding spirit. Both knew what she lacked in height, she made up for in countless other ways. Above all else, they made a conscious effort not to provoke their aunt's Irish temper. They were well aware the best way to stay in her good graces was to avoid fighting with each another. If and when a fight broke out between them, Bess never took a side. "Neither one of yas are comin' back in this house until both of yas can talk without yapping like fools. Ya can both stay in the barn until yur ready to shake hands and work on yur problems like sensible lads."

Being slow learners and having inherited some of their aunt's stubbornness, the two spent plenty of time sleeping in the barn and going without meals. However, because of Bess's firm manner as well as always showing her love for them, they not only learned to respect her, they learned to respect each other and themselves.

As was their early morning ritual, Bess replied to Josh's show of appreciation for the coffee. "Yur very welcome and I love ya." After discussing the weather, their plans for the day, and usually his fiancée, Josh would go upstairs to his bedroom and get ready to start the morning chores. Oddly enough, this Tuesday morning brought no mention of Jillian Davenport and Bess saw no reason to bring up the woman.

Once in his room, Josh closed his door and considered what to wear. Looking forward to spending the day being lazy, which didn't happen very often, he was in a slight hurry to finish his chores. Not liking to overdress, he chose an old pair of baggy blue jeans and one of his favorite cotton sweatshirts. Satisfied with what he was wearing, he sat on his bed and pulled on his over-the-calf socks. Nearly ready to brave the horrible weather conditions, he leaned to his left and slid open the drawer of his nightstand. He took out his heavy-duty, molded holster and fastened the top and bottom straps around his right thigh. Lastly, he reached back into the drawer and took out his loaded Smith and Wesson M&P and secured it in the holster.

When he started for the mud room, Josh thought about his buddy Peter. Peter, or P.D. as Josh called him because his full name was Peter Douglas Buchanan, was a corporal for the Montana Highway Patrol. Whereas Peter was due to go off duty at six a.m., Josh guessed he was likely tied up with numerous car accidents and detailed reports.

Josh peered out the window of the back door then tied his tan, waterproof, work boots and zipped his wool-lined coat. He could hear Bess starting her first load of laundry when he checked his pockets to make sure he still had his gloves and face mask. Seeing the nearly horizontal rain, he frowned, pulled his hood over his head, and ducked out the door. At a fast jog, Josh pushed his way through the wind and rain until he reached the barn. While he enjoyed training and working with the horses, feeding them in the morning always brought a smile to his face. Time after time he looked forward to how the horses greeted him without fail.

When Josh opened the barn door, he kept a tight grip on the knob to prevent it from blowing into the wall. After activating the overhead motion light, he flipped on the remaining switches. His normal routine was to check on the horses before feeding them to ensure they had not fallen ill during the night. However, before checking the first stall he thought the horses were strangely quiet. Determining the silence was odd at the very least, Josh looked toward his stallion's stall at the far end of the barn. He was wondering why the normally boisterous horse wasn't greeting him when he noticed a strange object on the hay bales. *Hmm, it must be something Benny brought home*, he thought and started to approach it for a closer look.

"What the hell?" Josh said under his breath when he saw what appeared to be a body lying on the bottom row of the hay bales. At first he wondered if Ben was trying to play a spiteful joke on him. It would not be the first time one of the brothers pranked the other. When such an opportunity presented itself, neither would refuse a good laugh at the other's expense. Having no idea what to expect, Josh kept a safe distance. After inching close enough to conclude the crumpled-up heap on the hay bales was definitely a person, he stopped cold. From where he stood, he could tell nothing more than the person was curled up and facing away from him.

It only took a moment for Josh to decide it was no joke. The person was nowhere near his brother's size, so it couldn't be him and he knew it couldn't be Peter. From the looks of the backpack and gloves, the items were tossed to the floor as if the person didn't want them.

Josh studied the person very carefully as he processed who they could be. First, he thought of all the positive possibilities such as neighbors, long lost relatives, or someone who unexpectedly showed up to see Ben. Then he focused on negative people such as an escaped convict, an escapee from a psychiatric institution, a serial killer running from the cops, a girl he dated, or the worst one of all, someone who was after him. The only conclusion he could come up with was the person had to be an outsider.

While Josh was recognized for his patience, his curiosity was overpowering his typical willingness to wait. The person in his family's horse barn was most likely a stranger. He needed to know who they were and why they were there. Eager to wake them and having no idea if they were dangerous, he rested his right hand on his pistol as a precaution. Feeling fully prepared, Josh gave a firm order. "Hey, wake up! Hey you…wake up!"

Josh was not at all surprised by the person's lack of response and yelled louder. "Hey you, I said *wake up!*" Not seeing any movement, he wondered if the person was alive. Still concerned about getting too close and not wanting to touch them, he stepped just close enough to kick the hay bales and shouted, "I said wake up!" Almost instantly the person moved their legs. It was only slightly, as though they were startled, and while this confirmed the person was alive, Josh was not yet sure if that was good or bad.

Meagan's mind was still in a state of limbo. She fought her way through a vast labyrinth of ominous pathways as she searched for any sign of reality. She tried to tell herself it was just another nightmare, but his repeated yelling proved her wrong. How did he find me? Has he been following me the entire time? He must have been watching me when I got on the bus. Meagan's heart sank when she thought all her effort was for nothing. She knew he would only scream at her so many times before he became enraged and violent.

After Josh saw the person move their legs, he took a few steps back to where he felt safe, yet well in control. Positive the stranger heard him, he was further frustrated when they continued ignoring him. "I know you fucking heard me, now stand up," he ordered, to show he was in control of the situation and it was getting serious. With a stern show of authority he repeated the command, "I said stand up and keep your fucking hands where I can see them!"

Meagan visualized what the vile man wanted her to do and began contemplating. He wants me to stand up…just so he can enjoy knocking me back down. With her psyche forever impaled by his last beating, she knew full well what his intentions were. Even armed with a knife and even if she were in perfect health, Meagan knew she didn't stand a chance. She ached for a way to even the odds, but deep down she knew she would need a miracle just to survive.

When it came to a professional matter, Josh was completely comfortable playing the waiting game. He was perfectly willing to hang tight and wait for the perfect opportunity, but he wasn't working. This was personal, and when it came to his personal life he couldn't have been more protective of his privacy. Until he got to the bottom of what was going on, he was going to treat the situation as a threat to himself and to his family. Losing his patience, Josh decided this would be the last time he tried verbal commands and hollered. "Listen asshole, this is your last warning!" Then with a show of force, he kicked the bale the unyielding stranger was resting on and shouted. "I said get your ass up!"

Meagan was preparing to give him what he wanted. She was going to stand up all right, but this time was going to be different. She was going to stand up and face him like the evil monster he was, even if it was the last thing she did. She knew he would easily and swiftly overpower her and that she was most likely going to lose her life. But one thing was for sure; she would rather die a loser that a quitter. Suddenly she pictured the automatic, stiletto knife and even though she hadn't planned on using it, her father was right when he gave to her. Like her mother, her father always seemed to be right. Thinking of her father and the knife, Meagan made the most basic of plans, which was simply to show no fear and stare into his hateful eyes as long as she could.

Preparing for the fight of her life, Meagan summoned all her remaining strength. With her energy sources depleted, she fed off her bold spirit, enduring nature, and courageous desire to face her untimely passing with dignity. As ready as she could be, she rolled on to her right side, sat on the edge of the hay bale and went to her feet. Then she stood face to face with Jeremy Constadine, or so she believed in her fever-induced delirium. But then adding insult to injury, she was unable to blink away her blurry vision and panicked. With her distorted sight and the severe pain pounding above her eyes, Meagan felt she had little time and no choice. With her right hand, she began to fumble deep within the pocket of her sodden parka for the stiletto knife.

"Show me your hands!" Josh commanded. He could see the person was reaching for something and knew he had to be ready for anything. With a firm grasp on his weapon and fully prepared to pull it out he shouted again, "I said show me your hands!"

While Meagan could tell Jeremy was shouting, his voice sounded muffled as if he was screaming under water. His words were so distorted that she couldn't understand a word he said. Plagued by the recurrence of her bronchitis and strep throat, it was no surprise that her ears were also re-filled with lingering infection. Feeling weak and sick were no longer her only problems. Unable to hear and see clearly, she felt more vulnerable than ever. Her hopes of standing up for herself and facing Jeremy were fading fast. Longing for him to see her as bold and fearless, she believed he would see her as broken and worthless.

Meagan finally found the knife buried under some folded up tissues and cough drop wrappers. With mounting apprehension she wrapped her fingers around the handle. Unsure of herself and what to do next, she clung to the knife and looked at Jeremy. Thinking he was about to attack her and desperately wanting her chance, she took out the stiletto and released the five inch blade. With a trembling hand she raised the knife in Jeremy's direction and strained to see his surprise.

"Drop the knife!" Josh yelled. He pulled out his forty-five and took aim at the person's chest. He placed his finger firmly on the trigger and fixed on his target. If the person made even the slightest move, he would have no choice but to shoot and from where he stood, he wouldn't miss. "Drop the fucking knife now or I will shoot you!" He repeated as loudly as he could. While holding his aim Josh tried to read the person but could only see a few inches of their face. With their hood down to their eyebrows and coat zipped well above their chin, he had every reason to suspect they were trying to hide their face.

When Meagan thought she heard Jeremy threaten to shoot her, she could feel the pounding of her heart. She was almost positive he was pointing a gun at her when her vision cleared just long enough to see him holding something black. She found it strange that he had come that far just to shoot her. He wants to control me and hurt me first, she reasoned. After he has finished with me and is satisfied with what he has done, then he will kill me. However, while anticipating the unspeakable things Jeremy would do to her, Meagan never guessed she would fail herself.

Everything seemed to hit her at once. The burning and tightening sensation deep in her chest was compounded by the intense pain in her throat. Feeling like her esophagus was about to close, she was overcome with the constant need to swallow. The urge to cough and gag became overpowering as she struggled to prevent Jeremy from seeing her as meek and petty. The more she tried to focus, the dizzier she felt and the harder it became to stay on her feet.

Josh held his ground and his aim. Telling himself he had no choice, he still hoped to convince the person to back down. "Drop the fucking knife! Drop it now or you're going to die!" He hoped his blunt honesty would persuade the relentless intruder to comply. But just seconds following his stern warning, his hope came to an abrupt end. *Aw shit,* he thought when the person took a few steps and closed the gap between them. "Stop, stop right there!" Josh ordered. He knew better than to allow anyone armed with a knife to get this close to him. But rather than shoot, he squeezed the trigger just to the point where he knew it wouldn't fire. *One more step,* he thought. *Just one more step and I'll…* On the brink of taking the shot, Josh noticed the person appeared drunk. They were looking at the floor and had lowered the knife to just above their waist. After quickly sizing up the thug, Josh felt confident he could take them, especially if they were off balance.

Knowing he had to act fast and there was no room for mistakes, Josh focused on the knife and made his move. In one sudden motion he holstered his handgun and leapt for his attacker. Then with perfectly timed precision, he used the edge of his left hand to karate-chop their wrist only inches away from the knife, and simultaneously struck them in the left side of their face with his right fist.

The impact of his left hand sent the knife soaring, then sliding across the barn floor. Within an instant of his first blow, Josh's right-cross landed under the assailant's left eye and broke open the skin across their cheek bone. The force of the sudden punch knocked the attacker off of their feet and they were likely unconscious before they landed on the concrete floor.

Relieved beyond words that he chose not to shoot the lunatic, Josh fumed with anger. "You crazy motherfucker, what were you thinking?" Glaring at the person he just knocked out, Josh knew they couldn't hear him. Thoroughly infuriated, he realized the unconscious person bleeding on his barn floor might actually *need* medical attention. Although he didn't punch them all that hard, he heard the impact when their body fell to the floor.

Putting his own safety first, Josh was still uncomfortable with getting too close to his aggressor. Keeping a safe distance, he was unable to verify anything about the extent of the person's injuries or condition. Due to the way they were slumped on their right side, he couldn't even determine if they were breathing. Following a brief assessment of the situation and his options, Josh decided he had no choice but to wake his brother. Ben was not only a qualified first responder, Josh could use his help rousing the intruder and convincing them to answer some questions. Keeping his eyes on the body, he backed his way to the intercom and called his aunt.

"Joshua?" Bess responded to his call from the kitchen.

Although it took a great deal to unnerve his aunt Bess, Josh always preferred not to worry her. "Could you please go upstairs and wake up Benny. Tell him I need his help in the barn ASAP."

"Are ya okay, lad?"

"Everything is fine. I will have to fill you in later."

"Okay, lad, I'll tell him straight away."

For Ben or Josh to wake the other once they assumed responsibility for the morning chores was beyond rare. The moment Ben heard Bess knock on his bedroom door and say his younger brother needed his help, he could not move fast enough.

Unlike Josh and Peter Buchanan, who were both gun enthusiasts, hunters, and always carried, Ben was quite the opposite. He had no interest in guns and did not hunt unless he had to go after a predator that threatened or killed his livestock. Nonetheless, due to Josh's unusual request for help, Ben reasoned something was wrong. He threw on his clothes and after buttoning his blue jeans, he decided to take his nine millimeter. Better to be safe than sorry, he thought, quoting Josh's philosophy, and rushed downstairs.

"What did he say when he called you?" Ben asked Bess when he crammed on his work boots but didn't take the time to tie them.

"He just asked fur ya and said he couldn't chat."

"Okay, I better get out there." Ben pulled his arms through his coat sleeves and darted to the back door.

"Be careful, Benjamin," Bess advised to Ben's back.

Ben ran to the barn hoping that he was overreacting and it was a perfectly normal morning. Once inside the barn he slowly peeked around the corner of the first row of stalls and found that was not the case. Not believing his own weary eyes he did a double take and hurried to Josh's side. "What the hell? Are you okay?"

"Yeah, I'm good now. When I came in to start chores, I found this lunatic passed out on the hay. I don't know how many times I yelled at him before I finally got him to wake up...And would you believe he came at me with that knife?" Josh explained and pointed to the green-handled stiletto on the floor.

"Is he alive? He sure the hell doesn't look good."

"He should be. I only hit him once. But I want to beat his ass." Josh paused and it was obvious that he was outraged. "I was this close Benny." Josh held up the thumb and index finger of his right hand to where they almost touched. "I was into my trigger pull and ready to squeeze off a round but something told me not to shoot."

"Okay, take it easy."

It was not like Josh to lose his temper. "Don't tell me to take it easy. I keep thinking of all the bullshit this asshole could have caused me, between my job and the publicity. You know what could have happened if I took the shot."

"Yes I get it, but you didn't. So let's see if he is okay. I am going to see if I can wake him up and you cover me."

"Okay, but watch it. Who knows what he is capable of?" Standing directly across from his brother, Josh prepared to jump in.

When Ben cautiously rolled the limp body onto their back he gestured to the cut and smeared blood on their sickly face. "I would say you hit him pretty hard. He isn't responding at all."

"You weren't here, Benny. He more than deserved it and he is damn lucky to be alive. I still can't believe I let him get that close. What was I thinking? I only backed off because I thought he was drunk and I could take him. He went down pretty hard. Maybe it was the fall."

Ben cautiously unzipped the heavily soaked coat and prepared to react if necessary. "His coat is completely drenched." Then with his left hand, Ben carefully supported the person's head while he gently pulled off the sopping wet hat with his other hand. No sooner did he tug on the hat and a wet, tangled, brown ponytail spilled across the floor.

"No way, you have got to be kidding me." Josh said with complete surprise while shaking his head.

"Holy shit, your psycho killer is a girl." Ben responded almost as shocked as Josh. "Damn, Josh, you almost took out a girl. That could be why you knocked her out so easily."

"A girl, just great. I don't even want to think about how that would have gone over." Josh got down on both knees and closely studied the woman's bruised and bloodied face. "Who the hell are you and why did you come after me?" He indignantly questioned the comatose young woman. "Can you believe this, of all the mornings I offer to let you sleep in."

"Her hand is ice cold." Ben slid up the left sleeve of the woman's coat and thick hoodie. For what felt like an eternity to Josh, Ben searched for a pulse. Finally showing noticeable relief, Ben spoke. "It's weak and slow, but she has a rhythm." When Ben leaned down to check her breathing, he noticed her nose. "There is dry blood in her nose but it looks like it's from a previous injury. I don't think you caused it." Then Ben held his face over her mouth and concentrated on her chest. After a minute of watching her chest rise and fall he added, "I don't like the way she is breathing. It's way too shallow and when I listen she sounds very raspy, almost gurgled. You said she looked intoxicated?"

"Yeah, she staggered right before I popped her."

Ben stood, put his hands on his hips and looked at Josh. "I think she has hypothermia." He paused. "Her wet clothing and being exposed to the temperatures overnight could have easily brought it on, especially if she was exposed for too long. Her slow, weak pulse and shallow breathing are just more symptoms…and her cold hands and the staggering you describe really make me think she is hypothermic. I think finding our barn and getting out of the weather when she did…I think it saved her life."

"Well good for her. She almost lost her life and maybe you are right about the hypothermia, but there is a lot more to this. Did you happen to forget she came at me with a knife?"

"Hey now, I'm not the enemy. I'm just telling you how I see it."

"I know, but I keep thinking she could have cost me everything, not to mention my reputation. I don't give a shit about her or what she's got."

"Well, *so far* everything has worked out. Since you were smart enough not to shoot her, I don't think it would be a good idea to stand around and let her die in our barn. So hear me out. Both of us have had hypothermia. You know the causes and symptoms—and treatment—just as well as I do." Ben hesitated because he knew what he was about to tell his brother was going to annoy him even more. "Being hypothermic can cause confusion."

Josh pressed his lips together and briefly turned away from Ben to prevent himself from saying something he would likely regret. He ran his hands through his hair, looked at the ceiling and took a few deep breaths to calm down.

"Damn it, Josh, for once will you listen to me?"

Out of respect and not agreement, Josh turned back around to face his older brother.

"It's obvious the girl needs help. She is in rough shape, and while I'm not sure how bad she is, we need to get her some help *now*."

"Yeah, you're right. You go ahead and call your buddies at county fire and rescue and I will call for a deputy."

"Aw, come on now. I don't need to tell you how long it will take the guys to get out here and drive her all the way to the hospital."

"And that's my fault? Confused or not, she should have picked a different barn, maybe one that is closer to a hospital."

"Wow! I haven't seen you this pissed off in a long time." Ben looked at Josh with concern and confusion. "This is not like you at all."

"Yeah, well I guess she struck a nerve when she almost forced me to put a bullet in her chest. Did she really think I was going to just stand there and let her cut me? What did she think I was going to do?"

"I know you want her arrested, but we need to get her out of those wet clothes *now*. Come on, Josh. I know you don't want her to die."

Josh looked at Ben as if he was suggesting something utterly ridiculous. "You want me to let this psycho into our house?" Before Ben could say another word Josh remarked, "Oh hell no, over *my* dead body. Did you forget we don't even know who she is?"

"All I'm asking you to do is let me revive her so she has a chance to explain herself to a deputy. Then you can have her arrested."

Josh looked baffled. "Why do you care so much about this freak, and why would you let a mentally ill stranger who just pulled a knife on me to come into our house?" After pausing for a breath he argued on, "Aren't you the slightest bit worried she could hurt Aunt Bess?"

"You know what Josh; let's finish this so I can go get some sleep. Let's call Aunt Bess and see what she has to say." Ben knew exactly what his aunt would say when he made the suggestion.

"You only want to do that because you know she would never turn anyone away, psycho killer or not."

"I'm going to call her." Ben declared on his way to the intercom. "Are you going to come with me to give your two cents?"

"Why, you know as well as I do that my side of the story won't change her mind once she hears your sympathetic bullshit."

Keeping a watchful eye on the unconscious woman while his brother went to the intercom, Josh walked over to the knife. He carefully picked it up, examined it, and closed the sharp blade. "*So far* we have both been very lucky," he spoke to the woman as though her luck was about to run out and pushed the stiletto down into the front pocket of his blue jeans. "I can't wait to find out who you are and how many other people you have used this thing on."

"Okay, Aunt Bess said to bring her into the den. She is putting a sheet on the sofa and getting ready." Ben could see the disappointment on Josh's face and his utter silence spoke far more than any words. Hoping to lighten Josh's irritation, Ben offered to help. "Don't worry, there are three of us to keep an eye on her. I will go through her things and try to find out who she is. Later this afternoon, I will call Pete and have him check her out. If he finds something, I'm sure he will be right over."

"Whatever, Benny, all I have to say is that whatever happens because of your screwed-up decision, it's all on you."

"That's fine," Ben said with a look of satisfaction and for just a moment he stood over the young woman, shaking his head.

"What, did you finally come to your senses?" Josh asked with surprise.

"No, I'm so tired after getting less than three hours sleep that I am afraid I might slip and fall on some ice and drop her. Do you think you could carry this young lady into our den?"

Josh knew Ben was trying to reach his sensitive and sympathetic side by having him carry the helpless woman.

"Sometimes you can be a real asshole, Benny."

"I'm glad to see you're coming around and thank you for your help." Ben ignored Josh's vulgarity and went to retrieve the backpack. "I think you got off easy by taking her…this thing weighs a lot more than she does." Ben joked then slung the bulging pack over his right shoulder.

Josh knelt down and slowly slid his hands under the still and silent woman. With delicate form and ease he lifted her from the cool, concrete floor and carefully walked to the barn door. He tried not to look at her battered face, but a sense of need drew him in. Although he wanted to detest what she did and loathe her existence, he was never one for hitting a woman. Intruder or not, had he known she wasn't a man and was going to be so easy to defeat, he would have reacted much differently.

Lugging the backpack, Ben rushed past Josh and held open the barn door. The rain had diminished to a cool blanket of spray when Josh left the barn and made for the house. It was only because he was looking down to avoid the fine rain that he noticed when the feverish woman moved her head. Even through her thick coat he could feel the heat emitting from her body.

"You *are* alive," Josh said quietly. Well at least she is responding to the rain, he thought. At first, he figured her troubled expressions were because of the weather, but then he could see she was experiencing pain and fear. By the way her mouth twisted and turned and her eyelids were twitching, he wondered if her discomfort was the result of a bad dream. "If you think your dream is bad, just wait until I give you a piece of my mind. And just when you think the worst is over, I am going to have you thrown in jail."

Josh was looking forward to questioning the woman when he stopped dead in his tracks. He was sure he heard her speak. He could barely hear her over the wind, but she was definitely saying something. "Hey, Benny, I think she is trying to talk. It almost sounds like she is telling me to stop." Josh placed his left ear over her mouth and concentrated. "She keeps repeating no and stop. Wait, hold on...I think she just said please. I think she is having a nightmare. She seems scared shitless."

"Okay, we need to get her inside."

Bess was watching from the laundry room window and stepped outside just in time to hold the door open. "I've set towels on the floor, lad. Just go straight for the den."

Josh carefully stepped on the towels as he walked across the kitchen floor and into the den. Once in the den, he delicately laid the woman on the sheet-covered sofa with Bess and Ben watching.

"All right, lads, could one of yas please build a fire?"

"I still need to feed the horses," Josh announced.

"Okay Joshua, go see to the horses. Benjamin, can ya please build a fire? If the lass was stuck in that storm, she's got to be chilled to the bone."

"Sounds good," Ben agreed before he picked up the backpack and carried it over to the fireplace.

Josh was in no mood to talk and simply stated, "I will be in the barn."

2

"He is fuming," Ben said when Josh walked away.

"Aye, with good reason."

"Yes, with very good reason," Ben immediately agreed.

"Let's give the lad some time to clear his head and I'll try chatting with him later." Bess knew Josh took after her when it came to his Irish temper. He rarely got angry, but when he did, he needed time and space to cool off. Having no idea what was wrong with the woman placed in her care, Bess wasted no time getting started. "I'll be undressin' her to bare skin and towlin' her dry. A warm rubbin' may help."

"No problem, I'll stay here by the fireplace and keep my back turned until you get her covered. It will also give me some time to go through her backpack and look for her ID."

Bess started by removing the lifeless woman's wet boots and socks and then placing them on a towel she had spread out on the fireplace hearth. "Her feet are soaked and chilled," she told Ben before she patted them dry with a soft towel and covered them with one of her hand-made quilts.

"She has to be hypothermic," Ben announced from across the room.

"'Tis hypothermia all right…she's showin' all the signs." Bess continued the process of removing drenched clothing, drying damp skin, and layering what was exposed with heavy blankets.

While Bess and Ben saw to their tasks in the den, Josh fed the horses and confronted his lingering animosity. Although he tended to the horses in his usual manner, his mind was elsewhere. He didn't talk to a single horse until he came to Cheyenne. "What the hell was wrong with you?" He replaced the stallion's nearly empty bucket of water with a full one. "Why didn't you warn me about the crazy bitch?" Josh patted the strong neck of the magnificent Medicine Hat Stallion, shook his head in disbelief and closed the stall behind him.

After seeing to Cheyenne, Josh sat on the hay bales where he first saw the deranged woman and began processing what had happened. While he tried to make sense of it, he still refused to accept the sick woman like his brother and aunt. It was his life and career that would have been impacted, not theirs. When he stopped trying to come up with a reason for the woman's behavior, it suddenly hit him. It was her brush with death that disturbed him, not his.

Josh was not only no stranger to death, he was far more involved with it than most. It encompassed his professional life and when it was completely necessary, he both accepted and approved of it. However, he did not want to have a hand in it at his home and on his time. What happened was unacceptable and he needed answers. But in order to get those answers, he needed to talk to the lunatic in his den. It was almost two hours since he left the house and he was eager to see if the demented woman was improving under Bess's care. *What the hell am I doing out here*, he thought then jumped to his feet to head back to the house. There was some psycho bitch in his den and he couldn't wait to confront her.

Ben was relaxing in his favorite recliner when Josh walked into the room. Before Josh could say a word, Ben pointed to what appeared to be a heaping pile of blankets on the sofa. "Joshua Mathew Mackenzie, please say hello to Meagan Rose Dawson."

Josh walked over to the sofa and looked at the thickly covered form. Between the woman's tangled hair and the obvious bandage on the left side of her face, Josh was unable to make out any of her features. "Meagan Dawson, huh… what the hell were you doing in my barn, Meagan Dawson?"

"According to her driver's license, Meagan is 29 years old, 5 foot 7 inches tall, 138 pounds and she is from Illinois."

Without acknowledging his brother Josh asked, "Why did you come at me with a knife, Meagan Dawson?"

"Josh, Pete must still be sleeping. I left a message on his cell for him to call *you* ASAP."

"Works for me," Josh said with quiet enthusiasm.

"Aunt Bess called Doctor Kincaid's office and he will be coming by late this afternoon when he finishes with his appointments."

Josh looked baffled. "I don't know why she did that."

"She is worried about Meagan's high temperature and thinks she fell before she got here."

"That's Aunt Bess for ya," Josh replied and took a hard look at his brother. Then he grinned and shook his head. "Benny, you look exhausted. I will keep an eye on…uh…Meagan so you can go back to bed."

"That sounds great. I think I will take you up on that offer."

"I will even look after Molly." Josh gestured to where Ben's retriever was contently sleeping in front of the moderate fire.

Ben stood and pushed in the foot rest of his chair. "Would it be too much to ask you to do me a couple of favors? Stay out of trouble and come wake me up when Doctor Kincaid gets here."

"Sure thing, Benny...uh, are you forgetting something?" Josh pointed to where Ben had set his holstered weapon on a table before going through the backpack. "I have my own and if I have any more trouble out of Meagan Dawson, screw it. I'll just shoot her and be done with it."

Ben offered a small smile, presuming Josh was feeling better. "I'll see you later. I better go before I fall asleep standing up."

Josh had one more thing he wanted to say to his brother. "Thanks for coming to save my ass, Benny."

"Any time," Ben said and punched Josh in the bicep on his way out of the den.

Josh was looking forward to finally chilling out. He stretched and went to his recliner less than two feet away from the end of the sofa where Meagan slept. Then, he took out his pistol and carefully set it within easy reach on a round, oak table to the left of his chair. At last, he sank into his ample recliner, pulled up the foot rest, and propped up his feet. For just a moment he wondered if Meagan was getting any better, but only a moment before he remembered his magazines.

After Bess watched Ben go upstairs, she went to the den hoping Josh had calmed down enough to talk. She was relieved when she walked into the room, handed him a large mug of his favorite non-alcoholic Irish coffee and he grinned.

"Thank you, you always know how to make me feel better."

"Yur very welcome."

Josh was the first to open up about the incident with Meagan. "I almost messed up."

"Ya have a good head on yur shoulders and everyone respects ya fur it. Seems ya had little time to make a life or death choice. I'm proud of ya fur doin' the right thing."

Josh took a sip of his hot coffee and set the cup down on the table. He slowly stood up, reached into his pants pocket and pulled out the emerald green, handled stiletto. After releasing the deadly blade, he set the knife next to his pistol and coffee mug. Then he sat on the edge of his chair and voiced his opinion. "I don't know why, but killing her terrified me more than being killed by her. I would have rather let her cut me with that damn knife than shoot her. This is my home and my safe place. I'm pissed that she came here to screw with me and my family."

"Ya know, I fur one don't blame ya fur bein' spiteful. She put ya in a tough spot. I never doubt ya, lad…or what ya do. I know I raised ya right. Ya have a good heart and everyone knows it."

Out of the blue, Meagan moaned and mumbled in her fever-ravaged sleep. "The lass seems to be callin' fur her mum. Yur brother and ya never gave me this much trouble." Bess stepped to the sofa and felt Meagan's forehead. "This one is testin' me and I don't know how else to help her. She was bitter cold this mornin' and burnin' with fever. Tis hours later and the lass is no better."

Josh walked away from his oversized chair and went to his aunt's side. While he condemned Meagan for what she did, he was impressed by his aunt's willingness to help her. "She is a complete stranger and you still treat her like she's one of your own. You are always so willing to help."

"Ya know my door and my heart are always open to those in need."

"I know, but *you* are *too* trusting and that worries me."

Bess took a cloth from a large, ceramic bowl she had set up next to the sofa and wrung it out. She placed it on Meagan's forehead and then looked up and into Josh's kind eyes. "A stranger today can be yur new friend tomorrow and a trusted ally for the rest of yur life. Ya know yur own mum is proof of it."

Josh was perfectly aware of how his mother brought him and Ben to Bess's ranch when he was eight and Ben was eleven. But he didn't mind that his aunt was about to tell him again. With a new sense of calm he said, "Yes, you know I love when you talk about mom."

"My own brother's wife, yur mum was a stranger when she came to my door in need. I was pleased to take her and both of ya lads into my home and my life. We didn't have long, but she became my best friend until the day she passed. Not a day goes by I don't miss yur mum…but I am still blessed by what she left me. To think how my life would have been without ya and Benjamin." Bess shined with love and pride.

Josh was still lost for words when he heard Bess repeat the touching story.

"Keep an open mind and an open heart. Ya never know, Joshua. This lass may be a stranger today, but she could be yur friend tomorrow. She could even become a blessin' to yur life."

Josh bent down and kissed his aunt on the cheek. "I highly doubt that. Mom never attacked you with a five inch knife."

"Tis very true, but her sons are worryin' me to an early grave."

Josh chuckled and returned to his chair and magazines while Bess fell asleep in her recliner. While he tried to concentrate on his reading, Bess's words resounded in his mind. Although he contemplated the possibility of forgiving Meagan, he had no doubt that he wanted her punished. When Josh finally relaxed, he too fell asleep, leaving no one to watch the passing time. He was into a rare, afternoon nap when he and Bess were startled by someone knocking at the front door.

Bess nearly stumbled out of her chair and said, "Tis probably Dr. Kincaid. I will see him in."

"Okay, I will go wake up Benny."

When Josh and Ben returned to the den they found the door completely closed. "I guess we will wait out here." Josh suggested knowing they had no choice. Meanwhile, Ben went to the back door to let out Molly who was dancing around and whimpering.

While the doctor seemed to be taking his time, Ben and Josh sat at the kitchen table and made small talk about how good the venison stew in the slow-cooker was going to taste. They had started discussing how much meat was in the freezers when Josh's phone rang.

Hearing the familiar air horn ring tone assigned to his almost lifelong friend, Josh thought out loud. "There's P.D." Then looking at Ben, Josh took the call. "Hey, P.D., how did your shift go?"

"Oh you know, just the usual bullshit. I just woke up and got Benny's message. I got to bed late this morning after staying to finish reports. So what the hell is going on over there?"

"Hmmm, other than some psycho named Meagan Dawson showing up in the barn and coming at me with a knife, nothing out of the ordinary is happening here either."

"No shit, that doesn't sound good. Please tell me she's still breathing."

"Yeah, but she shouldn't be. She kept coming at me and I couldn't get her to drop the knife. Anyway, I hit her and she's been unconscious since this morning. Dr. Kincaid and Aunt Bess are in the den with her now. I would say she is pretty sick, physically and mentally. It's almost like she *wanted* to die. I kept telling her I was going to shoot, but she wouldn't back down."

"Sounds like you got real lucky, Mackey. I can't believe you didn't put one in her forehead."

"Yeah, we are both damn lucky. When you get a chance can you check her out for me? I want her arrested, but I think there is a chance she is on the run and wanted for something, especially as nuts as she is."

"No problem, I'll get right on it. Go with her info."

Josh had just finished providing Peter with Meagan's information when Bess and Dr. Kincaid stepped into the kitchen.

"P.D., can you come by some time tomorrow? Doctor Kincaid is finished and I don't want to keep him."

"I'll be there sometime tomorrow afternoon and we can go over everything. Call me if you need me sooner.

"Thanks, P.D."

"No problem, stay out of trouble and I will see you tomorrow."

"Sounds good," Josh replied and ended his call with Peter.

"Well hello, gentlemen, for once I'm not here for one of you," Dr. Kincaid greeted the Mackenzie brothers, grinned and gave each of them a very firm hand shake. After a short discussion about how they were doing the doctor brought up Meagan and informed them that there was little he could do. "I wish I could do more, but I don't know her history or allergies. Call me right away if she gets any worse, especially if her temperature goes up. Right now she appears to be holding her own. When she comes around I want you to start pushing fluids. Call me after she wakes up and I will see what I can do about helping with a prescription. If she wants to see me, call for a re-check and I will swing by."

Bess was the first to show her appreciation. "Thanks fur comin' out and please give Mrs. Kincaid our best."

"You're welcome and I will do that. Goodbye, gentlemen."

"Thank you," Ben replied before Josh offered a simple, "Bye."

No sooner did the front door close and Josh began to question Aunt Bess about what the doctor had to say regarding Meagan.

"The poor lass is full of infection. Tis in her ears, throat, and chest. It could be pneumonia, but he can't be sure without more tests."

"Oh, that's not good," Ben sounded concerned.

"Aye and her fever is over 102."

"Is the den too warm?" Josh asked without hesitation.

"I don't think so. We need to keep the lass warm, but not hot. I'm worried I can't take care of the lass myself."

"What can I do?" Ben asked looking at his aunt.

"Dr. Kincaid said to watch the fever close through the night."

"Say no more, you and I can take turns checking…" Ben was offering his assistance when Josh interrupted.

"Hold on, unless I get a call or I'm in the shower, I am going to watch her until she leaves this house. I don't trust her for a minute. P.D. will be here tomorrow and I'm sure he'll charge her and take her in." Josh didn't give Bess or Ben a chance to respond before he turned away and headed to the den.

While Josh intended on going back to his chair, he stopped in front of Meagan. He noticed that while she was covered with a light blanket, she was no longer buried with quilts. Kneeling down, he was finally able to get a better look at her face. He was glad to see Bess had washed away the blood and covered the gash from his punch with a small butterfly bandage. It was her swollen and bruised face and the size of a bump over her right eyebrow that made him frown. The entire left side of her face was inflamed and marked by a deep shade of dark purple. Although she looked like a battered mess, he knew the cuts and bruises were nothing compared to the alternative.

Not long after Josh eased back in his recliner, Bess returned with a forehead thermometer and took Meagan's temperature. Without saying a word she left the room and quickly came back with a plate of food for Josh. "Tis nice and tender the way ya like it."

"Oh that looks good, thank you."

"Benjamin went out to do the evening chores and said he'll be back in straight away."

"Okay, what was her last temperature?"

"Tis finally coming down. It was barely above 101."

"Aunt Bess, since I am going to be right here watching her, I can take her temperature and you can get some sleep. How often should I take it?"

"Thanks fur helpin', Joshua. Could ya please check her every couple hours? If it goes up or ya need my help, wake me straight away. I'm expectin' her to sleep straight through till mornin'."

"We will be fine and I'll see you in the morning."

Hours passed and it was nearly 11:00 pm when Bess told Josh she was turning in for the night. Only a short time later Ben came into the den. He looked at Meagan and then stepped in front of Josh's feet.

"You know you don't have to do this by yourself. I can take a turn watching her, at least long enough for you to catch a nap."

"Thanks, Benny, but I'm good. I want to be here if she wakes up. I didn't have a chance to shower today so if you can watch her in the morning long enough for me to clean up, that would be great."

"Sure, and I'll check on you first thing in the morning. Good night and try to get some sleep. I don't think she's in any shape to try anything stupid."

"We'll be fine here. Goodnight, Benny."

The first couple times Josh checked Meagan's temperature, he was pleased to see it had dropped even further. She was also moving much more than she had all day, leading him to believe she was improving.

It was just after 3:00 am when Josh was woke up by a thud. Instantly wide awake, he saw Meagan lying on the floor near the door leading out of the den. "Where do you think you're going?" he asked as he stood towering over her.

With her overly dry and swollen throat Meagan could barely speak. "Please…let me…go."

Josh could see Meagan was scared to death. "Take it easy, I'm not going to hurt you." When he reached to help her, Meagan backed away then started to cry and cough. She was coughing so hard, Josh was unable to understand anything she said. Hoping Bess could calm her down, he called for his aunt and tried to convince Meagan to let him help her. "You are very sick. You need to let me help you back to the sofa."

"Please…let me…go," Meagan repeated and attempted to stand up, but was so dizzy and weak that she was forced to sit back down.

Bess was in the den within two minutes and found Josh standing over Meagan, who was cowering on the hardwood floor. After slowly kneeling beside Meagan, Bess softly whispered, "Tis okay, lass. I am Bess Mackenzie and this is my nephew Joshua. Yur sick and we have been takin' care of ya. Would ya like a glass of tea?"

"No…thank you…just a…bathroom…please. Then may…I go…please?"

"Tis good to see yur feelin' better. Can Joshua help ya to the bathroom and I will come with in case ya need help?"

Meagan was coughing and gagging to the point that she could only nod. Too weak and afraid to protest, she did not dare to look at Josh.

Bess disappeared and quickly returned with a glass of tea. "Joshua, help Meagan with the tea so she can see ya aren't goin' to hurt her."

Josh gave Bess a dirty look, but accepted the glass and offered it to Meagan. "Here, drink this. My aunt makes the best raspberry tea."

With no strength and a trembling hand Meagan was unable to hold the glass and Josh barely caught it before it fell to the floor.

"Here, let me help you," he offered and held the glass to her cracked lips.

"Thank...you," Meagan whispered after she swallowed several times. "What...am I doing...here? Where...am I?" Meagan looked terrified when she pleaded with Josh. "Please...let me go...Please."

"Come on, let's get you to the bathroom." When Josh slowly reached for Meagan with his right arm, his T-shirt sleeve crept up and exposed a jet black tattoo encircling his eye-catching bicep.

After catching a glance of the tattoo, Meagan made another weak effort to push herself up, but instantly failed. "Please, let me...go."

"Hush and look at me," Josh said softly. Then, he delicately lifted Meagan's chin to within inches of his face and looked into her frightened eyes. "You can trust me, I promise." While gently holding her chin with his right hand he caressed her undamaged cheek with his thumb. "Come on Meagan, let me help you. You can trust us. You are too sick to do it on your own. Let me take you and Aunt Bess will come with to help you."

Terrified but feeling she had no choice, Meagan lifted her trembling hand. Before she could change her mind, Josh gently lifted her up and carried her to the bathroom with Bess following closely behind. After several minutes of patiently waiting outside the bathroom Josh carried Meagan, who looked as though she saw a ghost, back to the den.

"I need... to find...my bus. I have...to go."

"You need to lay your butt down on that couch and get better before you can worry about some bus," Josh ordered and pointed to where he expected Meagan to go.

"Aye, Joshua is right, lass. Get some rest and we'll chat when ya feel better." Meagan lay down and Bess covered her up while Josh put a few logs on the glowing coals. Bess went to Josh and put her hand on his shoulder. "That was nice of ya to help her like ya did."

"Thanks, I'll see ya in a couple of hours."

"Sleep as long as ya can, lad. She should be out of the woods now." Bess went back to her room and Josh walked past Meagan, who finally appeared to be in a peaceful sleep.

Josh remained in the den with Meagan as the morning passed into the lunch hour and early afternoon. He only left long enough to shower and shave with Ben briefly taking his place. Even though Meagan was tossing and turning for the last few hours, she hadn't opened her eyes since using the bathroom. Josh was surprised to learn she was awake when Bess brought him a late lunch.

"How are ya feelin', lass? Can ya sit up fur some tea?" Bess asked Meagan with a smile then left the den.

After gradually sitting up, Meagan struggled to clear her eyes and head. Thinking she was alone, she tried clearing her sore throat, but was startled when she saw Josh out of the corner of her right eye. When she shyly turned to look at him and her submissive eyes met his, Meagan had to look away.

Full of countless questions and comments, Josh only held back because he didn't know where to start. While he had no problem holding his stare, he thought Meagan looked pitiful and afraid. He thought she would say or ask something, but she just sat silently with her eyes fixed on the floor.

"Here is yur tea, lass. Ya were in bad shape yesterday, but I think yur gonna be fine."

Meagan nodded and smiled, but her smile quickly faded when she tried to swallow. "Thank...you...I am...so sorry...but I ...forgot...your name." The strep throat made it painful for Meagan to talk let alone swallow.

"I'm Elizabeth...Bess Mackenzie, and this is my nephew Joshua. Benjamin is my other nephew and Joshua's older brother. Ya will meet him later."

Meagan turned to look at Josh and tried to say hello, but nothing came out. There was something about the unnerving way he glared at her that made her feel intimidated and once again she looked away. Sounding hoarse and barely audible Meagan asked Bess, "Please...may I...use a... restroom?"

Before Bess could answer, Josh was on his feet and offered to help. "I will take her. Come on, let's go." He offered Meagan his hand, but she wouldn't budge. "I take it you forgot I am the one who carried you to the bathroom last night?"

"'Tis fine, lass. Let him help you."

Not sure what to say, Meagan reached for Josh's hand and he gently eased her from the couch. But when she wouldn't move any further, he took her in his arms and carried her to the bathroom just like before. However, when they returned to the den, Bess held Meagan's hand with Josh following behind them.

When Meagan neared the sofa, her eyes were drawn to the coffee table between the sofa and Josh's recliner. She cringed when she saw her green stiletto next to a sizeable and menacing, black handgun. While the gun was in a holster, it was so large and obvious that she couldn't miss it. Thinking she was in danger, she couldn't help but freeze with fear and stare at the pistol.

Josh could see Meagan was not only fixated on his gun and her knife, it was quite obvious that she was too afraid to move. Thinking she might try to run, he stayed a few feet behind her. He also thought it was about time she answered his questions. With a stern voice, not caring if he scared her, he said, "Have a seat, Meagan."

Trembling and fearing she had no choice, Meagan did as she was told. She watched in horror as Josh walked over to the table and picked up the open stiletto.

"Joshua…" Bess said with concern.

Josh threw his aunt a look that told her to be quiet and mind her own business. When he positioned himself right in front of Meagan with the open knife, tears welled in her eyes and rolled down her bruised face.

Unable to look at the knife, Meagan's eyes wandered up his well pronounced forearm and stopped on his thick, black, armband tattoo.

"Does this belong to you?" Josh sounded annoyed.

Crying, Meagan could only nod yes.

"Have we ever met before yesterday?"

Meagan shook her head to show they hadn't.

"Did you come here looking for me?"

Still sobbing and starting to cough, Meagan once again shook her head no.

"What is your problem with me and why the hell did you come at me with this knife?"

Stunned and thinking Josh was about to lunge at her, Meagan's crying and hacking intensified. She continued shaking her head and began to plead. "Please…what do you…want…Please…let me…go."

"I want to know what you were doing in our barn yesterday morning and why you came at me with a damn knife. They are two very simple questions. You can tell me, or you can explain yourself to the police and spend some time in jail."

While Meagan was well into an all-out coughing attack and could not speak, Bess was having a difficult time watching the interrogation. Josh's concerned aunt appeared to run from the den to avoid what was coming, but within minutes she returned with a box of tissues and another full glass of tea for Meagan.

Josh closed the knife and set it back on the coffee table. "You will answer me. I need to know what you are doing here." When Josh's phone suddenly chimed, anyone could tell he was annoyed. "I'll have to call you back, Jilly. I am in the middle of a problem." He didn't give his fiancée a chance to say a word when he hung up and thought *she only calls and wants to spend time with me when it's convenient for her.* After shoving his phone in his back pocket, Josh silently stared at Meagan to show he was still waiting.

"I…don't know…I am…so sorry, but…I don't know…who you are…or where I am." Meagan was coughing so hard she was about to vomit. "Please…let me leave. I promise I… won't…ever come…back. I won't…tell anyone…I was here."

Josh felt like he was getting nowhere. He needed a break and so did Meagan. He went to the coffee table, snatched up the knife and put it in his front pocket. Still believing Meagan had something to hide and could not be trusted, he grabbed his forty-five. "Keep an eye on her, Aunt Bess. If she causes you any problems, come get me. I will be on the porch. Don't let her out of your sight."

Bess simply nodded and watched Josh storm out of the room.

Meagan sat paralyzed and weeping on the sofa.

Sympathizing with Meagan, Bess went to her side, put her arms around her and held her tight. "He's upset, lass, but he won't hurt ya. I promise ya 'tis the last thing on his mind." Bess knew it was not up to her to tell Meagan how close Josh came to shooting her. "I understand ya don't know us, but ya have my word yur safe here."

"He has…a gun…please…help me," Meagan cried. "I can't …remember… anything. I'm so sorry…I don't know…what he is talking about. Why does…he have…a gun? Please…help me."

"Try not to fret, lass. The pistol is just because Joshua doesn't know or trust ya. A trooper with the Highway Patrol is coming to speak with ya. His name is Peter Buchanan. He is a good lad and I've helped raise him most of his life. I know yur not feelin' up to it, but we should try to clean ya up before he gets here. We can clean ya up a bit now and I'll help ya take a bath after supper."

Meagan had been in no condition to care about her appearance and suddenly became embarrassed when she pictured how terrible she must look. "I'll try. Please…can you…help me?"

"Aye, we best get started." Bess grinned then went to get Meagan's backpack she had placed on the floor in front of an oak bookcase. After retrieving the pack, she set it in front of Meagan. "Here, lass, find yurself somethin' to wear."

When Meagan unzipped the pack, she recognized the hoodie and jeans she had worn the day before. They were neatly folded and right on top. Not sure what to say, she looked at Bess. "This is what I was wearing…" Meagan was unable to remember exactly when she wore the clothes.

"Ya were soaked clear thru. I needed to find ya somethin' warm and dry, so I had to go thru yur clothes. I washed and dried yur shirt and jeans and yur coat. Yur boots are there on the hearth."

"Thank you…" Meagan wasn't sure how to address Bess. "I'm sorry for any trouble…I have caused you."

"Yur very welcome and ya have been no trouble. Please call me Aunt Bess or Bess."

"I appreciate…your help…Aunt Bess." Meagan's throat was killing her and she didn't think she could talk to anyone, let alone a cop.

"Come, lass, we best get movin'. It's best we don't keep them waitin'. We don't want ya to get off on the wrong foot with Peter."

"Oh no, I'll try to hurry."

Bess helped Meagan stand then carefully held her arm as they made their way to her own private bathroom. When Bess closed the bathroom door, Meagan caught a glimpse of her reflection in a full-sized mirror that hung on the back of the door. She leaned closer to the mirror and examined her face in disbelief. It was the butterfly bandage that first caught her eye. Next was the baseball-sized, plum-purple bruise that covered the left side of her face, and then it was the yellow and green discoloration over the bridge of her nose and right eyebrow. "Oh my god, do you know what happened to my face?"

"Ya had some of the injuries when Joshua found ya…" Bess hesitated. "I'm so sorry, lass, the cut and bruise on yur left cheek are from Joshua."

Meagan turned and scowled at Bess with what looked like uncertainty and betrayal. "What? But you told me he wouldn't hurt me…and I'm safe here. I don't understand. Oh my god…he hit me…with his fist? What if he…"

Bess stopped Meagan. "Ya went at him with yur knife. He said ya kept comin' and he had no choice but to hit you. It was either that or…" Bess stopped herself just before telling Meagan how close she came to losing her life. "He is sorry fur hurtin' ya but understand he had his reasons."

Meagan felt a sudden need to sit down. "That's why he asked me about my knife…Oh my god…I really pulled my knife…on *him*?" Recalling Josh's questions, Meagan pictured his handgun.

"After he hit ya, he and Benjamin brought ya to me."

Meagan looked at the floor and asked, "The trooper you mentioned…He is coming here to take me to jail…isn't he?"

"Look at me, lass," Bess sat down on the floor in front of Meagan with a sly grin on her face. "Don't fret, I'll tell ya what I believe after years of raisin' these lads as my own. Each one has a big heart and they'll do right by ya. If my heart tells me right, ya will be here fur my stew and soakin' in a hot bath. Just be truthful to the best of yur memory…and try to look him in the eyes when ya speak."

"I'll try and I hope *you* believe me. I would never hurt anyone, never. I wish I could remember."

"I believe ya, Meagan," Bess affirmed with a reassuring smile. "Now we best get movin'. We don't want them waitin' on ya."

3

While Bess helped Meagan and Josh filled Jillian in on the recent events, Peter Buchanan pulled up to the house in his Montana Highway Patrol SUV. Peter was shaking his head when he stepped out of the vehicle and approached Josh. "What the hell, Mackey! Are you getting so bored from lack of work that you have to get into something at home?"

"When was the last time I told you that you're an asshole?" Josh retaliated and gave his friend a sly smirk.

Peter paused at the bottom of the porch stairs and took off his sunglasses. "Is she awake and willing to answer some questions, or is she being a pain in the ass?"

"Oh, she is definitely awake. I had to take a break from asking her my questions because she was getting on my nerves. She is playing the I-don't-remember game and acting like she lost her memory. I can't wait to see how she does with your nasty tactics. Benny wants to watch and said he will meet us in the den when he finishes with the horses."

When Peter took a seat on the top step, Josh took the knife out of his pocket. "Check out the blade on this thing, P.D."

"Holy shit, let me take a look at that…Ah, a five inch stiletto…lethal, but legal. I'm sure I can come up with a few charges if you want me to take her in. It sounds like you did the right thing." Peter closed the knife and returned it to Josh. "Hold on to this for now."

"I can't believe I let her get so close," Josh admitted his mistake and crammed the knife into his front pocket. "If you would have been there, you would have been yelling at me to shoot. I don't know what I was thinking. I knew what I had to do and couldn't get on the fucking trigger to save my life…literally. I got so far and it was like something told me to stop. It's not like I knew she was a woman…not that it would have been my first time."

"A woman is alive because you went by your gut instinct rather than a damn book of procedures. Personally, Mackey, I see that as good judgment—shoot because you have to, not because you can. You of all people don't need me to tell you that, and if it makes you feel any better you did the right thing. And it's not like you are used to being up close and personal. Now do us both a favor and stop second guessing yourself."

"Thanks for the pep talk."

"Any time, and strange as it sounds, I didn't find anything on Meagan Rose Dawson. There is nothing on her in Montana or Illinois. She is clear on NCIC. She had an order of protection against a guy in Illinois that expired at the beginning of the year. I got a phone number from one of my contacts and called a detective in Illinois. He was out of the office, but is supposed to call me in the morning. I'll see what he can tell me about her and let you know. Come on. Let's go see what she has to say."

"Hmm, it doesn't make sense. I thought you would find something on her. Thanks, P.D."

"None needed."

"Did you bring cuffs?"

"They are on the belt in my truck. I figured I would bring her out here before I cuff her, just in case she gets stupid. I don't want to risk breaking something in the house if she tries to fight or run."

Ben was already in the den and seated behind the desk when Josh and Peter walked in. The three men started off talking about the situation involving Meagan. Then they laughed and joked about how Ben was the one who wanted to bring her in the house and care for her like a stray puppy.

"You took a lot bigger chance than I would have," Peter declared. "Are you sure she's not robbing you blind as we speak? I don't think it's a good idea to leave her."

"I already checked on her. She is in Aunt Bess's bathroom, and if you think *I'm* a sucker..." Ben admitted to his overzealous generosity, "...Aunt Bess is probably giving the girl one of her chamomile and lavender bubble baths."

The three were still laughing and carrying on when Bess and Meagan slowly walked into the den. The laughing came to a sudden stop and each of the men rose to their feet.

Peter went to Bess and kissed her right cheek. "How is my favorite aunt?" He asked Bess the same question every time he greeted her to show his respect and appreciation.

"Hello, Peter. Will ya be joinin' us fur dinner? We are havin' Irish stew and I made enough fur an army. And don't let me forget, I have a bowl fur ya to take home to yur dad."

"You know I wish I could and how much I love your stew, but something tells me I am going to be tied up this evening."

During Bess and Peter's short greeting, Meagan returned to the familiar and comforting sofa. When she sat down and began to look around the den, she broke out with nervous perspiration. Completely thrown, she saw there were not two men, but three, and she found each one of them intimidating. Without turning her head she could see Josh was sitting practically right next to her in his recliner. A second man, whom she believed to be Josh's brother, was seated behind a large desk in the far corner of the room. She couldn't tell much about his appearance, other than he was well-groomed with light brown hair and probably in his mid-thirties. And the third man, who looked quite large, not to mention serious, was headed right for her.

In another time and place, Meagan would have thought the man walking toward her was absolutely gorgeous, but this was neither that time nor place. To her, this was hell on earth, especially when the man stopped only a few feet in front of her. It did not help any when Bess took a seat on the sofa to Meagan's left, leaving her wide open to Josh's potent stares. She reasoned the attractive, dark-haired man must be Peter Buchanan. Fearing what he could do to her, Meagan found it impossible to admire his well-sculpted, 6 foot plus body. While she wanted to look away from his smooth, flawlessly shaven face, his gray-green eyes seemed to demand her attention.

He sure looks like a cop, Meagan thought. His well-groomed, dark black hair was trimmed tightly at the sides, back and around his ears. The top was only slightly longer where it was cut into a thick, short spike. He was wearing dark gray, tactical-style pants and a black polo that had something embroidered over the left side of his chest that Meagan assumed to be a badge. And then she saw his firearm. He had a big black pistol on his right hip that reminded her of the one Josh picked up from the table. Recalling the weapon, she glanced at the table and was glad to see the gun was gone.

What is with these people, Meagan thought? *Do I really want to live in Montana? Is everyone this paranoid? And I thought I was bad.* She was suddenly drawn to Josh's brother when the giant moved closer and sat in Bess's recliner. She began to panic when she realized from where the men were located, all three could glare at her at the same time.

"Miss Dawson, is it okay for me to call you Meagan?"

After nodding at Peter, Meagan quickly looked away, but directly at Ben who offered her a sympathetic grin. She didn't hesitate to look back at Peter when he spoke.

"My name is Peter Buchanan and I am a corporal with the Montana Highway Patrol." Peter turned and nodded toward Josh. "You have met Josh…"

Meagan could feel her tears building when she looked into Josh's uneasy eyes.

"…And the man you see to my right is Ben Mackenzie, Josh's brother."

Swallowing hard, not only from the strep throat but because she was on the verge of tears, Meagan could not speak. She merely nodded at Ben and looked down at her lap.

Once the questioning started, even Bess's expression turned serious. She knew Meagan was too weak and sick to endure Peter's numerous and harsh questions.

"Meagan, do you know why I am here?"

That was all it took. Silent tears began streaming down Meagan's face. She looked directly into Josh's eyes and said, "I am so sorry…if I did something… to you." Then she looked back at Peter and cried, "You are here…to take me… to jail."

"I will make that decision *after* I talk to you. You aren't going anywhere until I can figure out what happened and why. Do you understand?"

Trying to comfort Meagan, Bess placed her hand on Meagan's left thigh. "See, lass, he just wants to talk to ya and clear things up. Try to stay calm so ya can explain yur side."

Ben exercised his sensitive side by walking over to the desk, picking up a box of tissues and taking the box to Meagan.

"Thank…you," she said and met his kind, light, blue eyes.

"You're welcome," Ben briefly held Meagan's eyes and went back to his seat.

Josh had been watching Meagan since the moment she entered the den. If someone had told him she was the same girl who wanted to stab him less than thirty-six hours ago, he would have told them they couldn't be more wrong. The remarkable difference and improvement reminded him how looks could be very deceiving. While just yesterday she appeared to be a psycho killer and ready to kill him, she now looked like any other attractive young woman. With her damp and wavy, light-chocolate brown hair reaching the middle of her back, Josh wondered how she had managed to cram it all into her hat. Even her eyes look different, he thought. They were no longer dark and callous, hateful slits, but seemed bright and full of life, with mixed shades of blues and greens.

"Josh…Josh…?" Peter asked but Josh had been staring at Meagan so intently that he missed the question.

"Yes…?" Josh immediately replied to show he was interested in the conversation.

"Josh, can you please show me the knife that you claim Meagan used to threaten you?"

"Absolutely." Josh stood up and slowly removed Meagan's stiletto from the front pocket of his blue cargo jeans.

Already beyond her limit, Meagan covered her mouth to vomit. Then she leapt to her feet, bolted past Peter, and ran straight for Bess's bathroom.

When Bess stood to go after Meagan, Josh joined her. "No, Aunt Bess, you wait here. I'll go get her, P.D."

"Take your time. I'm not in any hurry."

Ben was also standing. "Do you want me to come with you?"

"Thanks, Benny, but you can wait here. I want to talk to her." When Josh walked into Bess's bathroom he found Meagan heaving into the toilet and could see she was struggling with dry heaves. Wanting to help, he crouched down behind her and held her hair to prevent it from falling into the toilet. "Oh shit, take it easy. Stop or you're going to make me sick."

"I …can't." And with that said Meagan continued spewing the rancid bile.

Josh leaned toward Meagan's right shoulder and while holding back her thick hair, he tenderly placed his left hand on the middle of her back. "Come on now, this toilet isn't big enough for both of us."

While Meagan couldn't know the effect she was having on him, Josh had no way of knowing he was adding to her misery. She hadn't been this close to a man in over six months, let alone been touched by one. It was impossible for him to know all the ways he reminded her of Jeremy Constadine. His voice, powerful and muscular physique, controlling demeanor, and especially the threatening, black handgun around his right thigh were terrifying her. The very thing that had been used to cause her substantial physical and mental trauma now loomed so close; she could reach out and touch it. "What do you…want… from me?" Meagan asked after spitting.

"Well, right now I would really like you to move away from this gross toilet and come talk to me, just you and me."

When Meagan went back on her heels, Josh handed her a cool damp wash cloth. After sponging around the bandage and tender parts of her face, she reluctantly checked behind her. Josh was grinning and watching her as he leaned against the bathroom sink. He unfolded his arms and gestured for her to sit in an empty chair right next to him. As much as she feared Josh, there was something about his reassuring eyes and gentle expression that roused her curiosity.

"Wait here, I will be right back." Josh left and immediately returned with a glass of ice water. He carefully placed the glass in her nervous hands. "Meagan, I want you to do your best to look at me while we work through this. Can you do that?"

It was the first occasion Meagan had to study Josh. She raised her chin ever so slightly and met his eyes. She thought they were blue with a slightly green tint. His mostly straight, sandy-brown hair was trimmed shorter around the sides and back. The tighter sides went straight down and followed the shape of his ears to where they were trimmed straight across about mid-ear. While it was noticeably longer on top, she could see it had a slight wave going from back to front. The front fell straight down just barely touching the top of his forehead. But it was his warm, trusting face that was most appealing. He had sensitive and gentle features that invited her to look at him, and appreciating his softly contoured lips she longed for him to smile.

"I would like to try a different approach. I think you will be more comfortable. I want to take turns asking each other a question, and please feel free to ask me anything." Josh wanted to use the method of questioning to find out what Meagan knew about him.

"Okay…I guess."

"Ladies first," Josh said with a friendly smile.

Extremely anxious and struggling with severe throat pain, Meagan had no clue what to ask.

"Meagan, please try to see this from my point of view. I'm just trying to get some answers; after all, it was only yesterday when I thought you came here to kill me."

Meagan surprised Josh when she stared straight into his eyes and defended herself for the first time. "Don't you think *I* want to know what happened?

Don't you think *I*—?" She tried to go on but had to swallow. "I'm trying to remember what *you* say I did to you. But I can't."

Stunned by her change in demeanor, Josh stood and went over to Bess's first aid closet to find a package of cough drops. After handing one of the drops to Meagan, he spoke with calm sincerity, "Now we are getting somewhere."

"What difference does it make?" she asked, being extra careful not to bite the drop into pieces. "If *you* say I did something to you—and it sounds like I did—I am going to jail."

"You're not looking at me again."

"Why do you keep…" Meagan had to stop and briefly sucked on the drop to lubricate her throat, "…telling me to look at you?"

"Your eyes tell me a lot about you. Like whether you are being honest or telling me a line of bullshit. And to be honest with you, I'm still trying to figure out what color they are."

Is he flirting with me before he has me dragged off to jail, Meagan wondered. "They are hazel," she replied while holding Josh's gaze.

"Ah, mine too, and about you going to jail…if having you arrested was the only thing on my mind, I would have taken you myself."

Meagan could not believe her ears. She looked at Josh with complete shock and curiosity. "*You* are a cop, no wonder."

While his smile and expression suggested that he was, Josh's silence admitted nothing. He immediately changed the subject. "As you probably guessed, my friend Pete is the ultimate interrogator." Josh decided it was best to start from the beginning. "I'll admit that I was pretty pissed off at first and wanted you locked up, but getting my questions answered is more important, so I asked Pete for his help. You are doing fine. Ask me another question."

Although Meagan was feeling slightly more comfortable with Josh, she was hesitant about asking her next question. Peering deep into his patient face, she needed to know, "Did you hit me?"

"Yes, you didn't give me a choice. I repeatedly told you to stop and drop the knife, but you ignored me and kept coming. When you were practically on top of me I had to do something. I thought you were going to cut me, and to make matters worse, I thought you were a guy. Your hat was pulled down to your eyes and I couldn't see your face. I thought you were some crazy psycho or fucked up on something."

Meagan took her eyes off Josh's face and looked down at his pistol. Already predicting his answer, she softly asked, "Could you have…Did you think about…?"

Josh sensed Meagan's anxiety and answered the question she couldn't finish asking. "Yes, under the circumstances I could have shot you, and yes, I thought about it," he replied with morality. "But I didn't *have* to."

"Oh my god, I'm so sorry," Meagan gasped and covered her mouth. After going to her feet she started for the toilet, but Josh blocked her and gently set his hands on her shoulders.

"No, don't you dare barf again. Look at me. You are okay and I'm okay. We are both okay and that is all that matters."

Meagan swallowed slowly and asked, "So, you put yourself at risk by just hitting me?"

"Trust me, Meagan, I know how to handle myself."

Overwhelmed with everything that was happening and still under the weather, Meagan crunched the remaining cough drop and sobbed. "I don't know what to say. I'm sorry."

Josh could see Meagan needed someone. Although he still didn't understand her intentions, he realized he had misjudged her and felt partly responsible for her stress. After concluding she wasn't after him, he wanted to ensure her that she was safe. Believing it was the right thing to do, he delicately put his arms around her lower back. He brought her in for a hug and said, "You don't need to say anything and you don't need to be sorry for anything. We all make mistakes."

While Meagan kept her hands down at her sides, Josh held her for a good thirty seconds until she seemed to regain her composure. After he stepped away, he rinsed the washcloth with cool water and examined her face. Looking closely over her injuries, he grinned and stated, "Trust me, I have looked a whole lot worse and healed just fine. You will be back to normal in no time."

After patting her face with the refreshing cloth, Meagan realized she hadn't felt that safe and secure in a very long time. Only minutes ago she was terrified of Josh, but now appreciating his reassuring comfort, she wouldn't mind if he held her again.

"I know you feel like shit, but I think Pete has a few more questions for you. I'll ask him to take it easy on you and it shouldn't take very long. Do you think you can handle it?"

"So, I'm not going to jail?"

"Not unless Pete thinks you should. I think he'll agree you made a mistake."

"Thank you, Josh, for everything."

"You don't need to thank me. Come on, let's get back to the den and see if we can help you remember what you are doing here."

"Okay, because I feel lost."

When Josh followed Meagan into the den he smiled and nodded at Peter who was enjoying a bowl of Bess's stew.

"How are we doing?" Peter asked anticipating Josh's optimistic answer.

"I think I heard what I needed to and I told Meagan you probably have a few more questions for her."

"Great, I do have a couple more but I will be quick and painless. I think we have tortured her enough for one day."

Bess was sitting in her recliner and got up to help Meagan back to the sofa. "How are you holdin' up, lass?"

"I'm better, thank you. Josh is a nice guy."

"Aye, that he is and very understanding."

Wanting some privacy, Peter and Josh went to the far corner of the den to talk. Josh was leaning against the desk with his arms crossed while Peter stood in front of him and continued eating his dinner.

"I'll be right back, lass. Stay and rest."

"Thank you for all your help, Aunt Bess."

"Yur welcome, I'm glad I could help ya."

Meagan could not see the men since they were behind her, but she had no doubt they were discussing what to do with her.

After a few minutes Bess returned with Ben and each of them was carrying a tray with more bowls of stew. Ben took his tray back to Josh while Bess set hers on Meagan's lap. "Eat what ya can, lass, and if ya want more don't be afraid to ask."

Meagan didn't think she had any appetite, but after the first bite of the tasty stew, she was grateful for the generous serving.

After everyone finished with their meal, Peter helped Bess carry the dishes to the kitchen and Ben and Josh sat in their usual spots.

"How are you feeling now that you've gotten something in your stomach?" Ben asked as if he were glad Meagan finally had a good meal.

"Better, thank you. I had no idea I was so hungry."

"Good, you just need to take it easy and rest up. I'm sure you will back on your feet in no time." Ben knew Meagan was lucky to be alive after battling hypothermia and facing a point-blank shot from his brother, but he also knew better than to tell her so.

Rather than sitting next to Meagan, Bess went to her chair and Peter took Bess's original spot on the sofa beside Meagan.

Oh my god, the closer he gets the bigger he looks. Meagan hoped Peter didn't catch her looking at his bulging chest and arms. He must work out every day...maybe twice a day.

"First, I want to thank you for cooperating with us."

"Of course," Meagan replied.

"This conversation is completely off the record. I'm just being me, Pete Buchanan, the curious and nosey son of a bitch that I am."

"You got that right," Josh poked at his friend and Peter gave him a dirty look.

"Just two questions and then I will leave you alone."

Josh already knew what Peter was going to ask and looked forward to hearing Meagan's answers.

"So, Meagan, what brings you to Montana?"

"Oh...uh...I am going to stay and work on my uncle's farm. He has an exotic animal farm and trail rides near Yellowstone."

Peter and Josh both nodded their heads.

"Sounds interesting, what will you be doing there?" Ben asked

"First, I am going to work with the horses and train as a trail guide. In August, I hope to become an onsite veterinary assistant."

"You must be one heck of an animal lover to come all the way to Montana just to work as a vet's assistant," Ben sounded impressed.

"Yes, I love animals...more than some people."

Everyone in the room was nodding when Peter continued, "Okay, last one. You say you can't remember what happened in the barn with Josh. So, can you tell me the last thing you do remember?"

"I will try," Meagan agreed and took a much needed drink of her tea.

Everyone watched Meagan who appeared to be in deep thought. "My parents dropped me off at the bus terminal. I got on the bus to go to Uncle Pat's farm..." Meagan seemed lost.

"Where does your uncle live? Where is his farm?" Ben inquired.

"He lives in…Gardiner. The farm is in Gardiner."

Peter sounded amazed. "Well heck, you're still east of Broadus. You're in Powder River County, about 350 miles east of Gardiner. I think I know of the place. It's been a few years but I 've worked the area. It's a huge piece of property."

"Okay, so you got off the bus before making it to Gardiner and wound up here?" Josh asked to help jog Meagan's memory.

"I would say we are about six to seven hours away from Gardiner," Ben confirmed while looking at Josh and nodding.

The word Gardiner tripped Meagan's memory and she suddenly went into hysterics. "Oh no! Oh my god…my Mom and Pop!"

"What about them?" Peter asked and stood.

"Please, oh god, may I please use your phone?"

"Sure, did yours go dead? You could be having a hard time getting a signal," Peter suggested.

"I didn't bring one," Meagan said and swallowed again.

"Really?" Ben jumped into the conversation. "You are traveling alone *and* without a phone? Are you out of your mind?" He was noticeably disturbed. "I work in search and rescue and I'm a volunteer fireman." Ben was almost yelling. "You came all the way from Illinois without a phone? Do you have any idea what could happen to you?"

Meagan was about to explain her reasons for not bringing her phone or taking the time to get a new one when Peter changed her mind.

"Yell at her later, Benny; she needs to talk to her folks. Meagan, write down your dad's name and number and I'll call him for you." Peter took a pen and notepad from the pocket of his shirt and handed it to her. Then he stood up and took a cell phone from the left thigh pocket of his pants.

While she wrote, Meagan could see Josh shaking his head out of the corner of her eye. She wasn't surprised when he gave his opinion.

"I was thinking you were intelligent until I heard the part about you not bringing a phone. You are asking for trouble."

Josh and everyone else in the room became silent when Meagan began speaking to her father. "Hi, Pop."

"Meggie, are you okay?"

"Yes, I'm fine. I am at a ranch east of Broadus, Montana, and a very nice state trooper is letting me use his phone."

"What is going on, Meggie?"

"Everything is fine, Pop. I can't talk now. I don't want to tie up the officer's phone. I'm just calling to let you know I'm okay. Tell Mom I'm fine and I'll call when I get to Uncle Patty's."

"She has been worried to death about you. We were beginning to think something happened to you."

"I know and I'm sorry, Pop," Meagan apologized to her father then rolled her eyes and looked at Peter.

"Take your time," Peter whispered with a compassionate smile.

"I am really sorry, Pop. Tell Mom I only have a minute and please put her on the phone."

"Meagan, honey, do you need our help?" Meagan's mother sounded fully prepared to make a trip to Montana.

"I'm fine, Mom. My fever came back and I have been pretty sick. I had to get off the bus, but a nice woman and her nephews have been taking good care of me."

"Please tell them I said, thank you. Are you going to be staying there again tonight? You sound terrible."

"I can't, Mom. You know I need to get going."

"Don't you be walking after dark. It's too dangerous."

"I have to go, Mom. I love you and tell Pop not to worry. I will call when I get to Uncle Pat's."

"I love you too, honey. Oh, hold on a moment. Your father wants to talk to the police officer."

"Okay bye, Mom."

"Bye, honey."

"My father wants to talk to you," Meagan said with a curious expression and handed Peter his cell phone."

"Yes, Mr. Dawson, this is Corporal Buchanan."

"Can my daughter hear me?" Meagan's father whispered.

"There is that possibility sir, but I can take care of it."

"Has she said anything about the SOB who is stalking her?"

"No, sir," Peter replied and promptly walked out of the den.

"Look out, Meagan. Now you are in *real* trouble." Josh seemed to be joking, but was sternly serious because Peter wanted privacy.

Ben and Josh talked to Meagan for several more minutes about traveling alone and not having a phone until Peter returned.

"Meagan Rose Dawson?" Peter said with absolute authority and looking totally serious the second he re-entered the room.

"Yes?" Meagan looked at Peter with surprise because he obviously knew her name.

"I am placing you under arrest."

"What the hell?" Josh looked stunned. He stood up and went to stand beside Meagan. "What's going on, P.D.?"

"Meagan, I'm giving you the choice of staying here for a few days or going to our county jail. The choice is yours."

"No way, is this a joke?" Ben also stood up looking baffled.

"Do I look like I'm joking?" Peter asked and held up a set of handcuffs.

"My pop put you up to this, didn't he? What did he tell you?"

"The part you left out about why you really came to Montana."

"Please, I really need to go. I have been here too long already."

Peter looked solemnly at Meagan. "If you can give me a good reason why you shouldn't stay here, I will let you walk out right now. Look around, Meagan. You couldn't be any safer. You are with two cops and a fireman. Why the hell would you risk walking a dark and dangerous road where anything can happen to you?"

"You wouldn't understand."

"What's your decision?" Peter appeared ready to detain her.

Everyone, including Meagan, looked puzzled and concerned.

Not waiting for Meagan to respond and certain Peter would take her in, Bess appeared desperate. "Come, lass. Let's see to yur bath."

Meagan glanced at Bess then silently walked over to her backpack and hoisted it by the straps. When Ben went to help her, she tried to sound convincing. "I'm fine. I can take care of myself." Then Meagan wrapped her arms around the backpack and stormed out of the room.

Once Meagan was out of earshot, Peter made an announcement. "Just in case you haven't noticed, she is Irish and has the temper to prove it."

"Aye she is," Bess cheerfully agreed then followed Meagan to her bathroom.

"Hey, P.D.," Josh began. "All these years I have been telling you to hook up with an Irish girl and what do you do? You literally hook up an Irish girl. Nice try, but I think you are a bit confused."

"You are not the least bit funny, Mackey," Peter responded and slid his cuffs into his pocket. "I apologize for not asking before I told her to stay here."

Ben spoke first. "No problem, Pete. She can stay as long as she needs to. We have plenty of room, and I think Aunt Bess likes her company. So, are you going to fill us in on what's going on?"

"Now that she is out of the room I think that would be a good idea. Mr. Dawson practically begged me to do everything I could to keep her from leaving, including locking her up, just until he can make other arrangements. He said she is running from her ex-fiancé who put her in the hospital after she ended their engagement."

"Oh shit, that explains the order of protection," Josh added.

"And according to Mr. Dawson, the asshole hardly served any time before he was released. When Meagan got wind he was out, she panicked and made arrangements to go into hiding."

"No wonder she seems terrified. It could even explain why she went after Josh with the knife," Ben sounded confident.

"Mackey, after talking to Mr. Dawson I would say Meagan had no intention of hurting you."

"Yeah, I figured that when I talked to her in the bathroom. She definitely wound up here by accident. I don't suppose you have the asshole's name just in case he decides to pay her a visit while she is here?" Josh made it sound like he hoped to meet Meagan's ex.

"Of course, the prick's name is Constadine, Jeremy Constadine."

"It would be nice to have a picture of him just in case we see him nosing around the area or when we're in town," Ben added with genuine interest.

"I'll take care of it first thing in the morning. I am expecting a call from the detective in Illinois who handled her case, a Detective Blanchard."

Appearing deeply concerned, Josh crossed his arms. "Can you find out if this Constadine still poses a threat? Meagan may want to get another order of protection. Maybe we can help her with it."

"I will see what Blanchard has to say and let you know. But for now I better get home. I am probably too late to give my dad Aunt Bess's stew for dinner. He probably already ate."

Bess sauntered into the den and couldn't have sounded more pleased. "Okay, lads, Meagan is soakin' in my tub and sippin' a toddy."

"Watch it, Aunt Bess. If you keep treating the girl like she is a princess, she will never want to leave." Ben smiled because he knew his aunt was elated to have another woman in the house.

"Oh no, the lass is pitchin' a fit. She keeps sayin' she needs to be on her way. It seems like she is afraid of somethin', but after a couple of my toddies she will want nothin' more than a bed."

Peter, Josh, and Ben explained to Bess why Meagan was in a hurry to leave and why she appeared so nervous.

"I was thinkin' of puttin' her up in the spare room, but maybe she will feel safer and sleep better here in the den."

"I think the den would be better," Peter agreed.

"I will stay down here with her. What are a couple more nights in my recliner?" Josh offered and grinned.

"Will one of yas be able to grill steaks tomorrow?"

"I should have time," Ben promptly accepted Bess's request.

It wasn't as though Peter wanted to leave his friends. "I really need to get home. I should be back here by lunch time."

"Thanks again, P.D." Josh stood up to see his friend out.

"Hey no problem, just call if you need me to come sooner. Bye, Aunt Bess," Peter said as he bent down and kissed Bess on the cheek.

"Good night, lad, and give my best to yur dad."

"I will," Peter said and left with a large bowl of Bess's stew.

Ben opened and covered his mouth to hide a monstrous yawn. "I think I am going to go up to my room and watch some TV, not that I haven't had enough drama lately."

"I am right behind you, Benny. I need to change into my sweats if I am camping in the den again." Josh didn't seem to mind another night in his recliner.

"I will send the lass into the den after her bath, and I'll see to it she has a second toddy."

Josh got a kick out of the way his aunt was doing what she could to help Meagan unwind. "Sounds like a plan. I'll be right down and make a fire."

4

When Meagan walked into the den sipping her second hot toddy, Josh had one foot up on the fireplace hearth and was poking a small fire. She blamed it on the toddies when for just a moment she thought he looked appealing no matter what he wore. Although she was rather buzzed, it was her fear of Jeremy that pushed her to approach Josh. "Please excuse me, Josh?"

Josh could see the toddies were working their magic the moment Meagan walked over to him. "Hi, you look like you're feeling better. Aunt Bess makes one ass-kicking toddy, doesn't she?" He was glad to see the oversized butterfly bandage was gone and the swelling in her face was down.

Meagan smiled and forced herself to look Josh in the eyes. "Yes she does. Josh, I have cash in my backpack. Can you please take me to the nearest bus station?"

Josh couldn't help but tease Meagan. "Oh, that's not good. Do I look like a bum? Do I look like I need your money?"

"Please help me. I don't want to disappoint my uncle more than I already have."

"Meagan, you do know it's after nine?" Josh knew she was lying by the way she was avoiding his eyes. He tenderly placed his right hand under her chin until she met his eyes. "Are you that terrified of him? Did he hurt you as bad as I think?"

Meagan looked Josh full in his eyes and whispered, "Yes."

Suddenly disgusted, Josh had no doubt Jeremy had forced himself on her. "Please, come sit with me." Josh lightly rested his hand on the back of Meagan's arm and guided her to the sofa. With an empathetic smile he took a seat to her left so he could keep an eye on the growing fire. "I may not know you very well, but that doesn't mean I don't care about what happens to you. I care enough not to put you in danger."

"You don't know him," Meagan said with anxiety. "He will come looking for me. Maybe not today or tomorrow, but he will come after me," she affirmed, and in one large gulp drained the last of her drink.

"That's fine with me. I hope he does, because he will have to go through me and *that*." Josh turned to the right and gestured to where his holstered and loaded Smith & Wesson sat on the coffee table. "Meagan, I will not allow him the same opportunity I gave you. Do you understand what I'm telling you? If he somehow manages to get in this house, he won't get to you and he won't make it back out."

Meagan's eyes grew wide and she nodded in silence.

"You can trust me. I know what I'm doing and even though we just met, I always keep my word. Come on, you need to trust someone."

"I want to, but I just don't know what to think any more." Meagan couldn't explain how difficult it was for her to accept anything or anyone that represented violence. How something she wholeheartedly despised could be used to protect her. In addition to his incredible suggestion he was asking her the impossible; to believe in another man.

"You mean you don't know what to think of men, especially after what you went through."

First, Meagan nodded. "I don't trust any man. I can't."

Josh let out a long sigh Meagan could hear. "That's too bad. I wish you were staying long enough to see there are plenty of good guys who treat a lady the way she deserves."

"Was Pete referring to you when he mentioned two cops?"

"I don't have the same responsibilities as P.D., if that's what you're asking."

"So, you are local, like a county deputy?"

"Let's just say my jurisdiction includes the state of Montana and anywhere else I am needed in the country."

Meagan sensed Josh was being evasive and did not want to discuss his work. She thought at least he was open enough to admit to working in law enforcement, or was he?

"Will you please try to get some sleep?" Josh patiently asked, looking into Meagan's eyes.

"I am tired," Meagan said before she lay down.

"I will be right here in my awesome recliner and I will see you later," Josh declared, then took the folded blankets from the back of the sofa and covered Meagan from neck to toe.

"Josh, thank you for being one of the good guys."

"My pleasure and sleep well."

Meagan fell into a fast and deep sleep, but Josh lay there with his mind racing. He was still semiconscious when he was startled by a rapping on the window behind the desk.

The knocking was so loud that Meagan sat up. With the light from the glowing embers she saw Josh leap to his feet then stand directly in front of her. She watched him put his hand up as if telling her to stay put.

"It's okay, Meagan."

Meagan was still holding her breath when she heard Josh laughing.

"It's just Jillian."

"Oh, your girlfriend?" Meagan asked trying to catch her breath.

"My fiancée."

"Oh, congratulations."

"Thanks."

"I promise I will be a good girl. You can trust me." Meagan sounded ready for more sleep.

"I will be right back," Josh said believing that he would be.

Meagan was back to sleep before Josh left the room.

When Josh returned to the den, the fire had faded to gray coals. The chilly night air seemed to follow him in and he silently placed a few hardwood logs in the fireplace.

It was the popping and crackling of the dry walnut firewood that woke Meagan. She raised her head in time to see Josh silently sneaking past her.

"It's just me. Go back to sleep, Meagan." After noticing the time, Josh regretted sacrificing his hours of sleep to appease Jillian. He yawned at the thought of doing chores in just over two hours and decided to come back for a nap. Sticking to his plan, that was precisely what he did until almost noon. He was still reclined when he leaned to his right to check the antique cherry clock above one of the trophy cases. After blinking several times he gave his eyes a firm rubbing. "No, that's impossible," he whispered. The damn thing must have stopped right before midnight. Straining his eyes again, he could see the pendulum maintaining perfect rhythm and tossed his head back. *Aw shit*, he thought and quietly got up from his chair. When he checked on Meagan, she was in a restful slumber with her back to the front edge of the sofa. Launching into stealth mode, he swiftly and silently gathered his phone, pistol, and Meagan's empty toddy glass. He struggled to open and close the heavy, solid oak door without bothering her. When he stepped into the kitchen where Bess and Ben were adding more marinade to the strip steaks, he was still tip-toeing.

"Are ya feelin' okay, lad? Tis not like ya to sleep the day away."

"I'm fine, thank you for asking."

"Aw what's the matter, Josh? Not enough sleep last night? I thought you like sleeping in your recliner?" Ben teased Josh because he heard Jillian's car leave and knew why his brother was unusually tired. "Anyway Peter called *you*, but since *you* were still sleeping he called me."

Josh ignored Ben's ribbing. "Is he still coming by?"

"Yes, his printer is fucked up and slowing him down."

"Benjamin David!"

All the men knew better than to use profanity around Bess, but they seemed to forget more than they remembered. "Sorry, Aunt Bess. Josh, by the time you get a shower Pete should be here."

"Great, I'll be right back." Thinking of Meagan, Josh turned back around. "Meagan is still out like a light. The toddies were the perfect trick, Aunt Bess. She didn't give me any trouble."

"Ah good fur her. I was hopin' they would ease her mind."

Benny snickered and continued making fun of his brother. "Oh, Josh, I almost forgot. Jillian also called *me* because *you* weren't awake. I told her dinner will be around six."

"Thanks, Benny, some day you will make a great secretary." Josh hurried through his shower and was well into a ham sandwich when Peter walked in. "Hey, P.D., want a sandwich?"

"No thanks, after looking at this…" Peter grimaced while holding up a file, "…food is the last thing on my mind. So, how did you and your new roomy get along?"

"Not bad, other than trying to bribe me to take her to the nearest bus, I have no complaints. We talked a little bit; her ex fucked her up pretty bad. I don't think she will feel safe anywhere."

"When you see her file, you will see why."

"I think talking helped her relax, but it was Aunt Bess's toddies that got her to sleep so fast."

"Speaking of Aunt Bess, I don't want her to walk in when we are looking at this file."

"Oh shit, let's go find Benny. He should be in the barn."

Once they were in the barn, Peter and Josh found Ben winding up a rubber hose. "Hey, Benny, P.D. wants us to go through Meagan's file out here. Be prepared, he turned down a ham sandwich."

"That doesn't sound good."

After handing the manila envelope to Josh, Peter went to his horse's stall. Then he rolled open the stall door and began scratching his bay gelding behind the ears. "How's my good boy?"

Josh opened the file and studied the first photo. "He even looks like an asshole."

"Take a good look at the motherfucker. According to Blanchard, Meagan received cards and flowers from an unknown sender right after the asshole was released. It sounds like Constadine will make it a priority to find her. When Blanchard tried to find out why Constadine was released, he kept hitting brick walls. He finally found someone but wouldn't tell me their name. Evidently Constadine is cooperating in a military investigation."

Seeing more than their share of tragedy and devastation, it took a great deal to unnerve Ben and even more to shock Josh. But the brutality they saw in the photos made their stomachs lurch and their hearts ache.

Josh became angry with himself when he recalled punching Meagan. "Oh shit, *I* fucking hit her. Then I acted like it was no big deal by telling her I have looked a lot worse and…oh hell, even when Marcus beat the shit out of me, I didn't look *this* bad."

"Take it easy, Josh. You didn't know about this and you had no choice, so don't even go there." Ben not only admired Josh's decision to merely hit Meagan, he doubted that he would have spared her life.

After the first two pictures of Meagan's battered face, neck, and back, Josh could not take any more and slid the remainder of the photos in the back of the envelope. He and Ben were scanning the disturbing reports when Ben responded to the heinous crimes.

"Fuck, he pistol-whipped her and then kicked the shit out of her. Who the fuck does he think he is? Can you believe this shit? I want five minutes with this prick."

Even Josh was visibly shaken. "I can certainly see why she's acting the way she is. She doesn't trust anybody to keep her safe, and I sure the hell don't blame her. The motherfucker is damn lucky he didn't do this to anyone I know." While Ben and Josh discussed the cruel details of the reports, neither one of them could bring themselves to point out the sexual assault.

Both Josh and Ben looked toward the driveway when they heard a vehicle approaching the house.

Peter closed the stall door and asked, "Is Jilly coming over?"

"I told her dinner is going to be around six," Ben advised.

"I hope like hell it's Constadine. I want him," Josh stated while nodding his head.

"We couldn't get that lucky," Peter announced.

The three men watched as a tiny black sports car cleared the trees.

"Aw shit, it's just Jilly. She probably came early to show me some of her designs."

"Those are your copies, Mackey. I have my own. I thought both of us should have copies available in case the motherfucker shows up."

Josh took the folder and handed it to Ben. "Can you put this in the center drawer of the desk? If Jilly sees me with it, she will be nosey and start asking questions."

Peter seemed more interested in staying in the barn. "I am going to hang out here and try to scrape some of the mud off Captain. His legs are covered."

"Okay, I better get up to the house before Jilly comes to get me."

"Josh, I think I will stay and help Pete. Captain is a mess and it will go faster with both of us working on him."

"All right, I'll see you guys later," Josh said when he saw Jillian walking in his direction. He met his fiancée halfway and after a quick kiss, the couple walked back to the house.

After two hours of grooming Captain, Ben returned to the house for a fast shower, and Peter ran home to do the same. On his way to clean up, Ben crept into the den to put away Meagan's file. When he left the door open a crack, Molly Girl pushed it open with her nose. Ben was closing the desk drawer when his dog began licking Meagan's exposed right arm.

For the first time in days, Meagan woke up with a smile on her face. "Oh, aren't you a beauty," she commented to the mocha-colored dog and sat up.

"I'm sorry, Meagan. She must have pushed her way in," Ben apologized as he crossed the room toward her and Molly.

"She is beautiful. Is she a Chesapeake Bay retriever?"

"Yes, you know your breeds. She has wanted to visit you since the minute you got here, but I didn't want her pestering you."

"Oh no, I would love her company." After reading the dog's tags, Meagan appeared even more impressed. "I am honored to meet you, Molly Girl. I see she is a search-and-rescue dog."

"Yes, she is one of the best in the state and the whole northwest. Uh, it's completely up to you, but you might want to clean up before dinner. "

"Oh no, Benny, what time is it?"

"Almost four o'clock."

"Oh no, I can't believe I slept so long."

"No worries, I'm glad to see you feeling better. I am going up to take a shower and Bess is outside hanging laundry, so her bathroom is available if you want it. And Dr. Kincaid called this morning to check on you. He said he is available tomorrow if you want an appointment."

"I think I will be okay without it, but thank you."

"And, how do you like your steak?"

"Medium, thank you for including me." While Ben's blue jeans had a few dirty spots, Meagan thought he looked just fine without a shower. She found his care-free appearance, especially his messy hair, rather charming.

"It's the least I can do. I'll be manning the grill if you want to come out for some fresh air."

"Fresh air sounds so good. Maybe I will come out after my shower."

Immediately after Ben left the den, Meagan grabbed her backpack and scurried toward Bess's bathroom. Needing to pass through the kitchen she was surprised to find Josh in a heated kiss with a blonde woman she presumed to be his fiancée. The slender woman had Josh backed and pinned against the kitchen counter. The way Josh had his well-placed hands on the woman's fanny; Meagan hoped they were too preoccupied to notice her sneaking by.

Upon finishing her shower, Meagan was relieved to find the kitchen clear. When she heard everyone talking and laughing in the living room, she felt like an outsider and ducked into the den. She crammed her sweatpants and shirt into her backpack then found her maps and bus information. After refreshing her memory, she put away the material and began wandering around the quaint room.

Beginning at the fieldstone fireplace, she smiled at the photos on the mantle. One of the most recent pictures was of Josh posing with an elk. Looking up, she marveled at what she believed to be the same enormous bull in the photo. She didn't think the picture did the animal justice as the trophy's towering antlers nearly touched the vaulted ceiling. *It looks like I was lucky to get away,* she thought. While Meagan could never hurt an animal, she respected a person's choice to hunt. Taking her time, she studied the numerous mounts that included a mule deer, prong-horn antelope and even a mountain lion.

She was further impressed by the trophy cabinets. In one cabinet Josh had a few older barrel-racing trophies, but most were awarded for target shooting.

Another one of Ben's cases held countless ribbons and trophies for showing cattle. The largest and final cabinet was devoted to awards Ben had earned with his previous dogs and Molly Girl. Meagan most appreciated the grand, hand-crafted oak bookcase that covered nearly the entire wall opposite the fireplace. After glancing over a variety of books ranging from how to breed and show champion Black Angus to how to prepare and cook wild game, Meagan settled on one about Yellowstone. She was completely involved in the book when Aunt Bess greeted her.

"'Tis good to see ya up and about, lass. Ya look so much better. How are ya feelin'?"

"Much better, thanks to you." Meagan saw no reason to tell Bess that her chest still burned and her throat ached.

"Thank ya for sayin' so, but it was yur good strength and will that helped ya most. I came to tell ya we will be eatin' in five minutes and I have a spot set at the table for ya. I know ya feel like a prisoner, but in this house ya are a welcome guest."

"Thank you, it means a lot coming from you."

"Yur welcome, please come have supper with us."

Meagan couldn't explain it, but she couldn't bring herself to waltz into the Mackenzie kitchen like she lived there. Several minutes after Bess's invitation, it was Peter who came looking for her.

"There you are, are you okay?" Peter was genuinely concerned.

"Yes, thank you, I just don't feel like eating."

"I hope you aren't still pissed off at me. Please don't tell me you are going to miss out on one of Benny's steaks to avoid me?"

"No, you are just doing your job and helping my pop."

"I'm glad you feel that way. Please don't disrespect Aunt Bess by missing dinner. She set a place for you and wants you to eat with us. The only one you haven't met is Jillian and take my word for it, you aren't missing anything."

"Okay, I'll be right there."

"No you won't, please come with me." Peter held out his right hand. "I can see you are uncomfortable, but like I said, the only one you don't know is Jillian. And eating a healthy dinner will do you good."

Meagan thought Peter's gray-green eyes looked even brighter than when he questioned her. He was wearing fetching, dark blue cargo pants and a gray button-up shirt with short sleeves. She couldn't help but notice that he looked and smelled like he had just showered. By the smooth appearance of his face and chin, she guessed he also shaved. She didn't say a word when she offered her tense hand.

"That's more like it," Peter grinned and led Meagan to the kitchen. When they reached the table, Ben and Josh went to their feet. "Everything smells great," Peter remarked then moved a chair out for Meagan and took a seat to her right.

"Thank you," Meagan told Peter with a shy smile and noticed Josh and Jillian were sitting across from her and Peter while Bess and Ben sat at the opposite ends of the table.

There was one steak remaining on the pewter serving platter when Peter passed it to Meagan. She put the thick cut of meat on her plate and reached for her steak knife.

"Let me know if you need me to throw it back on the grill," Ben offered after seeing Meagan's reaction to the large steak.

Meagan slowly sliced into the flawless strip steak. "It looks perfect, Benny, thank you." Never one to stare, she only needed to glance at Jillian to see the woman surpassed attractive. Her smooth blonde hair outlined her perfectly shaped face and curled in toward her chin while the skylight above complimented her lustrous golden highlights. She had impeccable lips and her perfectly colored face led Meagan to wonder how long she spent on her makeup. She was dressed in a silky green blouse that not only matched her emerald green eyes, but exposed her significantly enhanced cleavage.

Meagan was about to take her first bite of Ben's steak when Josh addressed his lacking manners. "Meagan, I'm sorry, I would like you to meet my fiancée, Jillian Davenport. Jilly, please say hello to Meagan Dawson."

"Welcome to Montana," Josh's fiancée sounded indifferent.

"Thank you. It's nice to meet you," Meagan replied and put a piece of the light pink steak into her mouth.

"Josh, don't tell me this is the crazy psycho you said you should have shot in the barn? I would say she is lucky you decided to use her as a punching bag instead of one of your targets." Jillian made the snide remark as though Meagan wasn't even in the room, let alone sitting directly across from her. "Does she know she is lucky to be alive? That you don't miss?"

Looking down at her plate, Meagan was not sure how to respond or if she should act like nothing happened. She barely forced down the half-chewed piece of meat, excused herself, and found the back door.

All three men went to their feet, each one looking shocked and disturbed.

"Are you done already?" Jillian asked Josh, without regard to Meagan's departure.

Meanwhile, Bess cast an unforgiving glare at Josh that spoke more than a thousand words. Her tight lips were all she needed to speak her mind.

Peter, on the other hand, had plenty to say. "The steak is great, Benny. Thank you for dinner as always, Aunt Bess, but I seem to have lost my appetite." When he stepped away from the table, Peter shot Josh a defiant look. "I'll talk to you later, Mackey," he retorted then went after Meagan. When he did not see her from the deck, he recalled her appreciation for animals. He promptly walked to the barn and found Meagan sitting on the hay bales.

"Is this where I was sleeping when Josh found me?"

"Yes, right here," Peter replied and sat beside her. "While it's a good thing you don't know Jillian, I wish you could know her the way I do. She hasn't always been rude. She used to be every guy's dream. There was a time we all envied Josh."

While Meagan intently listened to Peter explain, she kept her eyes glued to the barn floor.

"I used to think he was lucky to have someone who was beautiful, intelligent, and very sociable, but the older she got, the more she changed. Now, she is a conceited, insensitive bitch. I know it and he knows it, but he refuses to admit it. She prefers to hang around her big-shot friends in Billings than to even talk to us. I don't mean to air out Josh's dirty laundry, but I don't want you to take anything she says to heart. In my position, I hear and learn things about people; sometimes things I feel morally obligated to repeat regardless of what comes of it."

Meagan looked at Peter and waited for him to specifically state an infidelity, but it never came. His hints were enough. "Pete, did Josh really say those things about me? That he should have shot me? Did he really call me a psycho?"

"If you want the truth, you needed to hear the entire conversation. I would prefer to let him explain himself to you, but I promise it was nothing like Jilly made it sound."

"I guess it doesn't matter. I will be gone soon and I don't know why I let it bother me."

"I wish I could do more to help you. I know we started off on the wrong foot, but I had no choice but to question you the way I did."

"Really, you want to help me?"

Peter had a feeling Meagan was going ask for something she already knew he would disagree with. "If it is in your best interest."

Meagan stood up and let Peter have it. "Now you sound just like my pop."

"Hang on, I know what that sick bastard did to you and I'll be damned if I'm going to make it easier for him do it again. I want what's best for you and I don't care if you like it or not. I am dedicated to protecting people, not getting them hurt or worse."

Meagan turned and looked into Peter's frustrated face. "I understand, and don't worry, I won't bother you again."

Peter exhaled, shook his head, and held Meagan's inpatient eyes. "Beginning tomorrow, I am working the next four nights or I would drive you to Gardiner myself."

"Thank you for the offer. I'm sorry I blew up."

"Can we please go back now? I have a steak with my name on it."

"I think I would rather stay with the horses. I promise I won't run away. Could you please tell Josh so he doesn't mistake me for some lunatic again?"

"Stop being ridiculous. I will take you around to the front of the house. You won't even have to look at her. Come on." This time when Peter held out his hand, Meagan didn't hesitate. The trembling changed to willing acceptance and Peter joked, "If she says anything that makes you the slightest bit uncomfortable, feel free to knock her teeth out and I will look the other way."

Once they stepped out of the barn, Peter let go of Meagan's hand but remained by her right side. When they were almost to the back deck, Meagan stopped. "Do you hear someone fighting?"

Peter held his index finger to his lips and whispered, "Oh shit, they are arguing by her car. We can use the back door."

Meagan had run out of the house shoeless, thereby leaving her socks caked in filth.

"Yuck, better you than me," Peter chuckled when Meagan sat on the floor of the mud room, made a repulsive face, and began peeling the socks from her feet.

"I think I better throw these out," she said and giggled when she stretched the sock to twice its length.

Bess was surprised and thankful to hear the two laughing. She made it to the mudroom in time to see Meagan yanking off her last sock. "Give them to me, lass...I'll wash them straight away."

Embarrassed, Meagan carefully handed the blackened socks to Bess, who was visibly amused. "Don't fret, lass; I will get them pink again. Now, both of yas go finish yur supper. I put yur plates in the oven to stay warm."

"Thank you, Aunt Bess," Peter acknowledged her generosity.

"Yes, thank you," Meagan added and smiled.

"Have a seat," Ben said, then used a couple of bulky oven mitts to remove the hot plates from the oven and remove the foil. He carefully set the first plate in front of Meagan and put the second in front of Peter. "Make sure I gave you the right steaks. I think the plate in the oven belongs to Josh."

"Thank you, Benny," Meagan said and set her napkin on her lap.

"Yes, most definitely thank you. Benny, did you say that Josh has a plate in the oven?'

"Yep, I can't believe he is finally giving her what she deserves." Undeniably pleased, Ben was trying to prevent Bess from hearing him. "You should have been here when he picked up Jilly's plate and threw the whole nine yards into the trash, plate and all. Then he told her she needed to leave and walked her out to her car. Her expression was priceless. You don't know how much I wanted to ask her for a picture."

"Sounds too good to be true, but I'm sure I'll see next week's performance."

"It wouldn't surprise me," Ben agreed. "They are on and off lately more than Aunt Bess's washer and dryer."

Meagan ate her dinner while the two men tried to outdo the other with horror stories detailing how Josh tolerated Jillian. She was nearly finished with her meal when they all heard Jillian tear off in her car, throwing gravel in her wake.

"He will be in any minute. Damn, I bet he is hot," Ben warned.

Surprising everyone, Josh casually walked into the kitchen and went to stand between Meagan and Peter.

"Please excuse my interruption. P.D., do you remember that pawn shop Brody took us to?"

"Yeah, it's been a few years, but I know where it is."

"If you're up that way this next week and you have some spare time would you mind popping in and selling this for me?"

Peter opened his hand to receive what Josh was holding. Then, he almost fell out of his chair when he saw what only minutes ago was Jillian's engagement ring.

Before Peter closed his hand, Meagan caught a glimpse of the flashy ring and reasoned it must have cost Josh a small fortune.

"Just get what you can for it. I am going to go dig through my safe for the paperwork and you can take it with you."

Ben looked at his brother with compassion. "I'm sorry, Josh."

"No you're not, you are relieved and so am I. We all knew it was just a matter of time, and it was actually Jilly's decision. I asked her if she wanted to take another break. She said if we were going to do that then we should call it quits so we can move on with our lives and see other people. Then I asked her, 'so this time you would rather be a quitter than a cheater?'"

"Holy shit, you do have balls. I bet that got her fired up," Peter claimed while nodding his head with approval.

"She let me have it. My face still stings from where she slapped me. I guess I should have seen it coming."

"She hit you?" Ben asked.

"Yeah she did, so damn hard I wanted to find my cuffs and put them on her, just to see her reaction. But then it dawned on me that she would think I wanted a piece of ass."

"Joshua Mathew Mackenzie!" Bess shouted after she returned from the laundry room.

"Now you did it, Mackey. She used your middle name."

"Sorry, Aunt Bess." Josh wasn't expecting Bess to hear him.

"Do not apologize to me; ya need to apologize to Meagan. How can ya talk like that when there's a lady in the room...*and* eating at our table? Did I not teach ya better?"

"Yes, ma'am, you did, and you are right." Josh looked down at Meagan, who was staring at him in shock, not because of his foul language but because he seemed happy with calling off his engagement. "I am sincerely sorry, Miss Dawson. Other than my aunt, I am not around *ladies* that often. Please accept my apology."

"Please excuse him, lass. I have tried to teach them proper manners so they can find a good wife someday, but ya can see how my hard work has paid off."

Ben spoke up first. "Now hold on, Sarah is a successful woman *and* I consider her to be a lady. She is a grade school teacher and doing very well for herself."

"Aye, Benjamin that she is. But I hope the day comes when she doesn't just make ya proud, she finds time to make ya a husband."

Peter was next to defend himself. "I would consider the women I have been seeing to be ladies. Rachel, Amber, Jody, and Caroline. Heck, Amber is a pediatrician and Jody is a dental hygienist. Aunt Bess, you need to realize professional women are more interested in having a successful career than committing to a relationship."

Josh saw the opportunity to support his friend while mocking Jillian. "P.D. is right, now that Jilly has found success in her career and high society, she only comes around for one thing."

"Oh, lass, do ya see what I've been puttin' up with?"

Meagan smiled and knew better than to take either side.

Still looking at Meagan, Josh gently set his hand on her right shoulder. "Excuse me, Miss Dawson, when you finish eating could you please meet a good-for-nothing ass like me in the den?"

Having ended her own engagement, Meagan knew the heartache it caused and regardless of how Josh was acting, she believed that deep down, he was upset over the breakup. With an empathetic smile she looked at him and accepted his invitation. "I will be right there."

5

When Meagan walked into the den, she gathered Josh must have already found the paperwork for Jillian's ring. By the way he was sitting in his chair and reading a magazine, she began to think he wasn't as crushed as she first thought.

"Hi, please have a seat." Josh set his reading material on the coffee table and Meagan took her place on the same sofa where she had been recuperating. Following a hefty sigh, Josh leaned slightly forward in his chair. "I don't think telling you *I'm sorry* is nearly enough for Jilly's lack of respect. I am still ticked off over the way she treated you. You are as welcome here as she is. Actually I take that back. I would say you are more welcome. She had no business saying what she did and I hope you will accept my apology for her big mouth."

Meagan stood, looked at Josh, and caught herself admiring him. While she initially thought he was slightly flushed, possibly from the argument and maybe the slap, there was something about him that roused her attention. Drawn to his bluish-green eyes, she wanted to see his smile. "You don't need to apologize to me for what someone else said, *or* for what you said." Meagan couldn't help but wonder if Jillian had simply repeated Josh's opinions. For some unknown reason she wanted to know if he had been saying one thing to her while telling everyone else what he truly believed. Still uneasy around Josh, something empowered her to confront him. "Josh, did you say those things about me? Is that what you *really* thought, to think I almost trusted you."

"Hold on, Miss. That was completely uncalled for." Josh raised his voice and left his chair without pushing in the footrest. "I am not two-faced, let alone a liar, if that's what you think." No sooner did he take two steps in Meagan's direction and she backed away. While he hadn't meant to scare her, it was Meagan's reaction that gave him an idea. "Wait right here, I will be back in two minutes." Josh didn't give Meagan a chance to reply before he left the den.

What could be so important? Meagan spent Josh's entire absence questioning his odd departure.

When he returned almost five minutes later, Josh was wearing an oversized, black zip-up hoodie. "Are you with me, Miss Dawson?" He asked and then pulled the large hood over his head.

"Oh, are we going somewhere?" Meagan asked, baffled.

Josh laughed at her question and replied, "No, I want to show you something. Point your right index finger at me like it's a gun. That is going to be your pistol, and when you are ready to shoot me, just point at me and say 'bang, bang.'"

Meagan looked at Josh as if he suggested something utterly bizarre.

"Or if you would prefer, I can go up to my room, unload my forty-five and let you use it."

"No, please…I hate guns. All they do is hurt people."

"I knew how you would feel. That's why I thought you would rather shoot me with your finger. Okay, try not to be afraid. I want you to follow through with what I'm leading up to, okay?"

Meagan looked at her finger and nodded. It seemed easy enough.

"Please stand and face me," Josh instructed and walked to the bookcase.

From where Meagan stood, she was near the middle of the den with the fireplace located on the wall behind her.

Josh zipped the hoodie up to his mouth and pulled the hood down over his forehead to where it touched his eyebrows.

"Wait, uh, Josh?" Meagan could not see any of his face.

She is going to panic. She is going to kill me too soon for this to work, he thought. Without warning, Josh removed Meagan's stiletto from his right pocket and released its threatening blade.

Meagan watched in awe. Visibly stunned, she didn't know how to feel or react. Is this some sick way of getting back at me, she wondered, and had to look at the floor.

Josh held perfectly still and let Meagan stir for a full ten seconds before he finally spoke. While he understood she could not fathom everything she put him through, he hoped she would have a better appreciation for how he felt when she pulled the knife. "Meagan, are you still with me, sweetheart?"

"I don't know. I think so," she whispered with apprehension.

"We are just doing a role reversal. Do you know what that is?"

"Oh yes, you are me and I am you."

"That's right, you are Josh and I am Meagan before we knew anything about each other."

"I don't know if I can do it. Are you sure it's safe?"

"You will be fine. You can do this. You are Josh and you have a gun, just tell me what you want me to do. Will you try?"

"Okay, I'll try," Meagan's voice wavered.

When Josh took a small step toward her, Meagan moved back.

"Miss Dawson, it's okay. Aim your gun at me and when you think you should shoot me, say 'bang bang.' It's no big deal."

"Okay."

Josh could see Meagan's index finger shaking. For every small step he took, she fell back. He began to think his approach wasn't going to work. "You are doing great, Miss. Now try to talk me into giving up."

"I don't know what you mean."

Josh thought Meagan was going to cry. "Tell me to stop and drop the knife. You need to stop me from attacking you."

"Stop," Meagan said softly and Josh took another step. "Please drop the knife." She was already backed against the fireplace whereas he hadn't even made it to the center of the room. "Please...stop."

Josh took a large step, hoping it wouldn't push her.

"Bang, bang," Meagan said and Josh fell to the floor like a corpse. "Oh shit." When she realized how she behaved when Josh found her, Meagan began to quietly cry. "I just killed you. I'm so sorry. I wasn't myself Tuesday morning. I didn't know what I was doing. Oh my god... *you really should have shot me. Why didn't you do it? Were we this close?"*

Josh closed the knife and shoved it in his pocket. Then he took off the sweatshirt and tossed it on the sofa. With both arms out, he went to Meagan. "You were closer when I decided to hit you." Sensing Meagan's heartfelt regret, he gently embraced her and softly held her head against his left shoulder. Hoping he wasn't too harsh, he turned to her ear and whispered. "Do you understand why we did this?"

"Yes."

"I thought you would better understand why I said those things if I showed you what happened. You had too many unanswered questions and I want you to know the truth. I *meant* that I *should* have shot you because you were too close and it was the normal way to respond in that situation."

"I don't know what to say, other than I am sorry. To think what almost happened. Thank you for...uh...I am glad you only hit me."

"You and me both. I hope you still trust me."

"I do, and you are at the top of my good-guy list." Meagan couldn't describe it, but the way Josh held her was different. His soft yet confident touch assured her that somehow, someday, her life would be good again.

Neither Josh nor Meagan heard Peter slip into the room until he spoke. "Excuse me, but I have Meagan's father on my phone." Peter voiced his concern when he saw Meagan dab her tears on her sweatshirt sleeve. "Is everything okay?"

Josh sensed trouble in Peter's tone. "Yeah, I'll explain later. What's going on?"

While Meagan stepped across the den to talk to her father, Peter took Josh by the arm to whisper the news. "Her uncle can't send anyone for a week. Mr. Dawson and Aunt Bess want her to stay here until someone can pick her up."

Meagan was sitting on the sofa almost yelling. "No, Pop, don't waste your time coming here. I will not come home. It's too risky for all of us. I am staying in Montana."

"You need to work with me, Meggie, and stop being stubborn."

"I'll be fine, Pop. I have been studying my maps and the bus information I have in my backpack. I figured if I leave early enough, I can hike to Broadus by dark."

"No, Meggie, you need to stay put until we can figure something out."

"I can't stay here. I love you, Pop, and tell Mom not to worry. I'll call as soon as I can, bye, Pop." For the first time in her life Meagan hung up on her father. Then, she returned Peter's phone. "Thank you," she told him with a forced smile, but avoiding any eye contact.

"Any time and I don't mean to be nosey—actually yes I do. Are you out of your damn mind?"

Meagan wanted to get the impending fight over with. "My uncle fell off a roof and broke his leg and my cousins are picking up hay somewhere. No one can come until later next week, and who knows what will come up between now and then."

Bess went to Meagan and took hold of both of her hands. "Please stay with us, lass. Ya can have the guest room upstairs."

"I appreciate your invitation, Aunt Bess, but I have to be on my way. I'll be leaving in the morning. If things were different, I would love to stay." The honesty in Meagan's voice confirmed her desire. "Please understand I have no choice. I have to get going."

Bess tenderly let go of Meagan's hands and gave her a hug. The woman's dark blue eyes looked distressed and glassy. "I understand, lass. Ya want to get on with yur plans. *Please* be careful."

"I will, and I will never forget you or your kindness. Thank you again."

Josh was not about to go unheard. "No. Hell no. Meagan, stop and think about what you are doing. We told you about the dangers. Tell her again, P.D. Maybe she will listen to you."

"No, I give up; the girl has an obvious death wish. Since *you* didn't grant it for her, she is still bent on dying. It's her life, Mackey."

Josh wasted no time and let out a sigh. "Settle down, Meagan, I will take you to Gardiner first thing in the morning."

"No, Mackey, absolutely not, don't be as stupid as she is."

"Do you expect me to just sit here knowing she is out there walking alone, and without a phone? *I* can't do it," Josh was firmly insistent.

"Yes, I expect you to do just that. You better re-think your priorities real quick. You can't risk missing a call. You know you will be too far to respond. Think about *that*."

"Peter is right, Joshua, ya must think of yur job."

"Speaking of our jobs…" Peter sounded furious. "I have seen horrific things that I will never forget, but do you know what haunts me the most?" Peter didn't allow Meagan a second to respond. "Seeing dead women thrown into ditches as if they were trash. We are all willing to help you. Josh is even willing to accept a reprimand, but you need to help yourself. If you take off on your own, you may as well go back to your ex. Both are asinine and both can get you killed."

The entire conversation took its toll on Bess. With tears in her eyes, she excused herself and went to the living room.

"Mackey, when was the last time you saw Aunt Bess cry?"

"Uh, the only time I have seen her cry was when Mom passed."

Meagan finally gave in. "Okay fine, both of you belong in Hollywood. You would both make a fortune. I will stay until next week, but not a day longer."

"Hurry, Mackey, grab her backpack and carry it upstairs before she changes her mind. You know how women are."

"You got that right. Miss Dawson, come with me and I'll show you to your room."

Peter approached Meagan and cordially covered her hands with his. "I have to get home. I am back on duty tomorrow, but I will be here on Tuesday and keep Thursday free to take you anywhere you want."

Meagan preferred looking at Peter when his face relaxed and his lips weren't contorted. "I guess I'll see you Tuesday. Please be careful and stay safe."

Josh was halfway up the stairs with Meagan's backpack when he yelled at Peter. "Don't forget the paperwork for the ring and I don't care what you get for the damn thing."

"Okay, see you on Tuesday. Call me if you need to, Mackey."

"Yep, watch your ass, P.D."

"You too," Peter shouted and headed for the front door.

Meagan climbed the polished hardwood stairs to the second floor where Josh was waiting for her. "My room is right here next to yours. I am a light sleeper, so just knock if you need anything. That's Benny's room and this is our bathroom. Your bathroom is on the other side of your room and has a huge bathtub."

When they stepped into the spare bedroom, Meagan fell in love with the antique decor. With so much to look at, her eyes stopped on a black antique weather vane topped with a galloping horse. "It's beautiful."

"It was my mother's room and she collected antiques."

Bess pulled an extra quilt out of a closet and set it on the dark walnut sleigh bed. "The dressers are empty, please make yurself at home. There are linens in the closet fur yur bed and yur bath. May I fix ya a toddy before I turn in?"

"No, thank you, you have already done too much for me. I can't thank you enough and I love the room. It is amazing."

"Did I hear someone mention a toddy?" Josh asked with wide eyes and a grin.

"Ya know yur not gonna sip it even if I put it in yur hand, so stop yur teasin'." Bess's scolding expression matched her tone.

"Yeah, but after the day I've had, I could sure use one."

"You can't have just one?" Meagan asked.

"No…oh, it's not because I have drinking problem. I can't drink when—how should I put this?"

"His job doesn't allow it, lass. It might affect his performance."

While Meagan didn't know what Josh did for a living, she knew it was none of her business.

"I best turn in. Five in the mornin' will be here before we know it."

"Good night," Josh said to Bess when she stepped into the hall.

"Thank you for taking such good care of me, Aunt Bess, and good night."

"Good night, lass," Bess said sounding more relieved than Josh could remember.

"Thank you for deciding to stay, Miss Dawson. You were about to break my aunt's heart. I think you can see we have plenty of room."

"I think I should be thanking you, especially for your patience. You didn't have to show me how everything happened." Meagan felt her cheeks glowing like an ember when she caught herself admiring Josh's contoured chest through his Henley.

"It was my pleasure. Let me know if you need anything, and I hope you have a good week. You certainly deserve it. Are you okay with sleeping in a strange room? I can keep my door open."

"Thanks, but I am so tired and I can't wait to crawl into that bed. I think I am going to sleep till noon." Meagan was glad Josh couldn't read her mind regarding their previous sleeping arrangements. She realized how much she liked sleeping in the den with him and secretly wished she could feel that safe one more night, but she knew it had to end.

"Okay, Miss Dawson, I will see you tomorrow at noon."

"Good night, Mr. Mackenzie," Meagan said with a grin.

"Sleep well," Josh smiled and disappeared after closing the door behind him.

Without pulling back the covers, Meagan lay on the tempting sleigh bed. Rather than taking in the one-of-a-kind antiques surrounding her, she began planning her strategy. She started by thinking what she should wear, when to change her clothes, and the best time to sneak out.

At first Meagan was against leaving a thank-you letter. She wanted her absence to go undetected until at least noon. But she believed it was the least she could do considering the Mackenzies' hospitality. Trying to write and avoid breaking down, Meagan visualized Bess's disappointment when she read the touching letter. She apologized countless times and described how much she enjoyed her stay. She briefly explained how it wasn't that she wanted to leave, especially without saying good bye, but she had no choice. Finally, she thanked each of the Mackenzies for their help, as well as Peter.

One thing Meagan kept to herself was her concern for their safety, even though it would have clarified her reason for leaving. It was certainly not the Mackenzies' responsibility to keep her safe, especially from someone connected to her past. She could not risk putting them in danger knowing full well that Jeremy would stop at nothing to get her back. By the time Meagan finished the letter she was unable to hold back her tears. She would never forget how the Mackenzies and Peter touched her life. Each one of them would hold a special place in her heart.

About to leave, Meagan recalled Josh saying he was a light sleeper and hoped tonight would be an exception. Constantly checking her watch, she anticipated Bess would be up at five which made her all the more eager to slip out. At precisely 2:30, Meagan put on her parka and picked up her backpack. Then, she stepped out of the spare room and silently closed the door. She was thankful for the dim nightlight in the hall when she passed Josh's room and made her way down the stairs. Once in the den, she set the folded letter on the desk. Her heart was speeding and she began to overheat when she bent over to lace her hiking boots. Struggling to stay calm, she fought the urge to bolt for the front door. That was when it dawned on her that she had never seen the front door.

After cautiously leaving the den, she tiptoed along the extended, dark living room. She continued straight through the foyer and finally found the front door and its antique brass handle. After closing the heavy, solid oak door behind her, Meagan peered toward the driveway and stepped off the porch. Don't look back. Don't look back, she repeated to herself. But right before the house disappeared behind the trees, she did just that. The emotional mistake pained her and she was still sobbing when she reached the end of the driveway. Wondering if she would be fortunate enough to see the Mackenzies and Peter again, Meagan placed her hand on the horse stable mailbox and thought it looked familiar.

Quickly cooling off, Meagan zipped her coat then put on her hat and gloves. She swung on her backpack and began hiking west. While she expected the first few hours of darkness to be the most frightening and dangerous, she told herself sunrise was coming. After barely stepping away from the driveway, she could already hear several different animals. Somewhat thankful she could not tell what they were, she tried to focus on hiking. At least the weather is cooperating, she thought, looking at the moon. Grateful it was a calm and clear morning she tried to think positive about her future and where she was going. She would be sharing a small cabin with a few other women who also worked for her uncle Pat. She hoped the people she was about to meet were at least half as welcoming as the Mackenzies and Peter.

Following almost an hour, Meagan took a left turn. It was only a few minutes later when both sides of the road became thick with magnificent conifers. Her eyes had adjusted enough for her to see a faint ditch running along the far side of the road. Bringing to mind what Peter told her about seeing dead women, Meagan felt terrible for saying she would see him next Tuesday, especially since she would likely never see him again. The best she could hope for was to cross paths with him, Josh, or Ben in Gardiner.

When she heard sticks cracking and the low growl of what she assumed to be a large bear, Meagan stopped thinking about the men and anxiously yelled, "Go away!" She hoped the alarm in her voice wasn't obvious and the noisy animal wasn't hungry enough for human flesh. Thinking it was foolish to run and could cause the bear to chase her, she slightly picked up her pace.

When she came to the next right turn, Meagan took in a full breath, exhaled, and checked her watch in the filtered light. Seeing it was ten before five, she pictured Aunt Bess starting a pot of coffee for Ben and Josh. She imagined the generous men and wondered if she could trust a man enough to date. Sleeping with any man was definitely out of the question. But if she was fortunate enough to meet someone like Peter, Ben, or Josh—especially someone like Josh—she might consider a dinner date. Josh was so caring and trusting, not to mention gorgeous, that she might try to trust a man like him, but she couldn't say for sure.

Meagan could feel her leg muscles straining when the straight and flat road began a gradual incline to what appeared to be a sizeable hill. She climbed the steep grade for a good forty minutes until it peaked and gradually sloped back down. As much as she didn't want to admit it, she was already feeling tired. Thinking how long she would most likely be awake, she was glad that she slept until yesterday afternoon.

It was just after 5:30 when Ben opened his bedroom door and Molly trotted down the stairs. He noticed the door to the spare room was closed but due to turning in early, he had no idea Meagan agreed to stay. After peeking into the empty den, he saw the empty sofa, thereby confirming his hopes.

"Good mornin' to ya, Benjamin, how did ya sleep?"

"Like a rock, thank you," Ben answered and leaned down to kiss his aunt on the cheek. "And you?"

"Very well, thanks fur askin'."

"Is Meagan in the guest room?"

"Aye, after a time of it, Peter and Joshua were able to convince her to stay. The lass is far more stubborn than she looks."

Molly was barking at the front door, which was unusual since her morning ritual was to go out the back. "I better go let Molly out before she wakes up Josh and Meagan. I don't know what has her so fired up." Ben wasn't gone two minutes before he returned to the kitchen. "Aunt Bess, did you check the front door before you went to bed last night?"

"Aye, ya know my habits."

"Hmm, it was cracked open and Molly wanted to go out."

The expression on Bess's face was pure anguish. Without a word she hurried past Ben.

Wondering what had captured Bess's attention, Ben caught up to her and followed her into the den.

"Oh no, her boots are gone. Could ya please poke yur head into the guest room and check on the lass?"

Ben took the steps two at a time and came back down even faster. Upon his return, he found Bess sitting on the sofa and reading a hand-written letter on bright pink paper.

After he scanned the depressing letter, Ben didn't wait for Bess to give her opinion. "I don't believe it, even after we told her everything that could happen. Try not to worry, she can't be far. Josh and I will go find her and I will drive her to Gardiner after breakfast."

"Ya always make me proud, Benjamin, and I'm sure the lass would appreciate yur help."

Ben kissed Bess on her cheek. "She won't be hard to find. I'll take Molly along to help. We should be back here in no time." After a good pounding on Josh's door and getting no response, Ben let himself in.

When Josh barely raised his head and saw his brother, he mumbled with disgust. "Aw, shit."

"Get up, Josh, Meagan took off and we need to find her."

"What…Oh hell no, we both know she will just leave again. I'm staying right here." Reasonably irritated, Josh buried his head under his pillow. "I'm done with her bullshit."

"Come on, after we find her I will bring you home then drive her to Gardiner."

"What, you can't…" Josh slowly rolled onto his back and looked at the ceiling. "This is your weekend to go to Sarah's."

"Sarah will understand. I will call her later and explain."

"Fine, damn it. Let me get dressed and I'll be right down."

"Try to hurry. I think she has a good head start."

Josh dressed and grabbed the baggy hoodie he used for the role reversal. After zipping the extra-large jacket he put his hands in the pockets. "Damn it," he said out loud. "She doesn't even have her damn knife." When he met Ben and Molly downstairs, Josh seemed to be the one in a hurry. "Let's go."

"I think Molly can help us get started."

"Sounds like a plan and we better get a move on. I figured it out and she could have at least a three to four-hour head start."

"Great, let's take my truck since Molly will be working."

Josh gave his aunt a reassuring hug. "Stop worrying, Aunt Bess, you know Benny and Molly will find her."

"I hope yur right and please call me if ya do."

Moving fast Josh and Ben went out the front door and to Ben's Silverado. Feeling rushed, Ben opened the driver's side back door for Molly. "We will let her ride to the end of the driveway and…Oh shit, I will be right back. I need something with Meagan's scent."

"Grab the big, brown pillow from the sofa in the den," Josh suggested.

When they reached the road, Ben opened the door and let Molly out to begin tracking. First he let the retriever take her time sniffing the pillow and then he issued his first command. "Work, Molly. Find her, Molly. Work, girl. Search, search. Find Meagan." Immediately upon hearing Ben's instructions Molly headed west at a good clip.

"She has a strong scent. As long as Meagan sticks to the road we should find her in no time." When Ben initially started following Molly, he fully expected an easy and successful search. However, after running for quite a stretch, Molly stopped going straight and turned left. Ben shook his head and followed his dog while watching for any sign of Meagan. "Wow, either she is walking fast or she left before the crack of dawn."

"I can't wait to give her a piece of my mind. What the fuck is she thinking? She won't have to worry about Constadine finding her when she is dragged away by a bear. Why didn't she listen to us? You know what, Benny, I changed my mind. When we find her, I better stay in the truck or I will go off on her. I'll let you do all the talking and you can tell her your plan."

"I'm just as pissed off as you are. Let's hope she will get in my truck. We can't force her."

"The hell we can't. Watch me. It's for her own good."

Molly had been going strong for nearly fifty minutes. "With this being a long straight shot, I would like to put Molly in the truck and drive, but I'm afraid we might miss something. If Meagan went into the trees for any reason, Molly might lose her scent."

"It's your call, Benny. I'm just along for the ride."

Meagan was surprised she hadn't seen a single vehicle in the last three and a half hours. With it being a Friday morning, she reasoned someone would pass her on their way to work or school. After conquering a couple more hills she slowed her pace, but thought she was still making good time. To her amazement, she finally heard a broken muffler approaching from the hill behind her. She peered over her left shoulder until she made out a dark green pickup coming down the hill. As the truck gradually closed the gap she could see it was older and two people were inside the cab. Feeling slightly nervous, she hoped the truck would pass her.

When the truck was directly behind her, Meagan sensed it was going to stop. Although everyone she had met in Montana was polite and friendly, that wasn't going to stop her from being cautious. She tried to convince herself that it was likely a couple ranchers and they probably knew the Mackenzies and Peter.

Meagan's apprehension went through the roof when the truck stopped a few feet to her left. The hefty male driver put the truck in park and leaned over the passenger to talk to Meagan from the open window. "Hey, darlin'." The driver spoke with an accent unfamiliar to Meagan then cleared his throat. "You need a ride?"

"No thank you." Meagan thought the man's dark, messy hair and long, scraggly beard made him look like a serial killer.

"I'm Donny and this is my brother Billy. We're from Missouri. We're here for Billy's birthday and looking for a good place to get his first elk."

The smaller and younger passenger held up a can of some kind of beer. "Just turned twenty-two." Then he downed the remaining contents of the can and attempted to toss it in the bed of the pickup, but missed. "Looks like…I'll have to try again," Billy slurred his speech and laughed.

Hoping the shady looking men would take her hint and be on their way, Meagan tried to make herself clear without sounding rude. "Well, have a good birthday." She didn't give them a chance to respond before she started walking away.

When the worn-out engine turned over, the beat-up truck lurched ahead and continued moving beside her. "Hey, darlin', what's a pretty girl like you doing out here all alone?"

Meagan did not like how Billy implied she was alone.

"I am actually walking with a group of friends for a charity called Canines Across America. We raise money for no-kill dog shelters. Some of my friends are just ahead and a few more went to get us some breakfast." It wasn't only because the men were intoxicated, something else told Meagan the two were up to no good.

"So what's your name, or should we just call you Charity?"

"My name is Anne." Whenever she wanted to give a fictitious name, Meagan used her maternal grandmother's name because it was popular enough that no one questioned it.

"Hey, darlin'—Anne—I know it's early, but you look thirsty. How about you climb in here and have a beer with us, to celebrate Billy's birthday."

"No thanks, I have to keep walking or I will miss my daily quota."

"One beer won't hurt. It's for Billy's birthday. He just turned twenty-two and we've been celebrating all night. We don't know any girls in Montana and I'd appreciate it if you would have a beer with him."

Meagan could see Donny wanted her company for his brother's sake. "I'm sorry, but I don't drink and I am going to miss my goal if I don't get moving. Take care now." After she took a couple tense steps, Meagan heard Billy's drunken words.

"I really like her and she's real pretty. I think she likes me."

The instant the truck shut off, Meagan's instinct took over. She turned and looked back just in time to see the men get out of the truck and head in her direction. Even though they were drunk, she knew she couldn't out run them with her cumbersome backpack, so she let it fall to the ground. Then, thinking the parka would impede her escape; she threw it down and prepared to run for her life.

Before the parka hit the ground, Meagan jumped into a sprint and made a mad dash for the cover of the trees. She knew better than to waste even a solitary second to look back. At first, it was navigating over fallen trees and around brush that slowed her down. She was further hindered by branches and thorns tearing at her clothes and cutting her hands. Fearing she wouldn't last long, Meagan hoped the men would think she was a waste of time.

She was sadly correct about her endurance when only a few minutes later, breathing became difficult and her chest began to tighten. When she suddenly erupted into a coughing attack, Meagan nearly tripped over a fallen limb. She made it less than a hundred yards into the woodland when she felt her body giving out. It was the terrifying sound of the men's boots breaking and cracking fallen branches that pushed her on.

Much stronger and healthier than Meagan, it took little effort for Billy to get close enough to snag her hood. "I got her, Donny! I got her!" Billy yelled back to his brother.

Meagan was kicking and slapping at Billy with all she had, but froze with dread when she saw Donny stomping toward her. The goliath didn't say a word as he walked up to her then painfully backhanded her across the mouth with his immense right hand. She instantly felt as though the corner of her lip was sliced in half with a searing knife. She tasted an all-too-familiar fluid when blood filled her mouth and trickled down her throat. Dazed and hurting, Meagan touched her bloody mouth to her shirt sleeve and struggled back to her feet.

"Please...if you just...let me go...I won't tell anyone...about this." Meagan wept because she knew her pleas were worthless.

Ben was regretting the way he allowed Molly to push hard in the beginning of the search. The highly intelligent dog had slowed to a fast walk, but was still on Meagan's scent when they came to a right turn. "She is getting tired and I am worried about her paws. I didn't think she would need her paw pads."

"Give her a break if you think she needs it. You know how long and hilly this damn road is."

"Yeah, and the hills will wear her out even faster. We were in such a hurry, I didn't bring her any water. I will give her another ten minutes then I better bring her in to rest," Benny sounded disappointed.

When Donny spoke again, Meagan looked at the ground.

"I'll make you a deal, Anne. If you will party with us, I'll give you something for your time. If you keep fighting us, I will have to hurt you. Now get on your knees."

Sobbing, Meagan refused to please the men and shook her head. Although she expected it to be bad, she was nowhere near prepared for Donny's punishment. In one swift and powerful move he swung his fist straight up, jabbing her in the pit of her abdomen. Reeling from the force of the punch, Meagan fell to her knees the way he ordered. Coughing and gasping for each and every precious breath, she felt like her stomach had exploded and broken apart. While the pain surged through her body, her lungs craved and begged for air.

Billy and Donny's attack was much different than Jeremy's. This time Meagan was in the middle of nowhere and miles from help. Donny was also much larger and forceful than Jeremy. Not to mention, Donny also seemed to be more experienced at beating people with his fists than Jeremy, who rarely used his hands. She had also been engaged to Jeremy, while Donny was a complete stranger. Although both men were extremely violent, Donny was a different kind of monster. He was the one a woman would expect to attack.

"Please lay down, darlin', don't make me hurt you."

Once again Meagan refused. This time Donny opened his hand and swung the back of his large fingers and knuckles into her left cheek. Barely holding on, Meagan was too weak to tolerate another blow. When her head snapped back, her lifeless body flew backwards and slammed to the ground. On the verge of losing consciousness, she envisioned millions of needles stabbing her face and head. She was completely paralyzed when one of the men grabbed her left wrist and dragged her across the rough ground.

"Bring her to this tree, Billy. I'll sit on the other side of it so you can take your time and have some privacy."

Capable of hearing everything the men said and still able to see with her right eye, Meagan wished Donny would knock her out. It was becoming clearer by the minute that she would never see her parents again, thereby making an apology impossible. As if her life were flashing before her eyes, she recalled Peter's honest and grotesque warning. She couldn't help but hope he didn't see her body left in the woods like a piece of trash. Thinking about her last days, she felt fortunate to have spent the time with the Mackenzies and hoped Josh would find someone who deserved him.

It was when Meagan felt Billy fumbling with the button on her blue jeans that she found her last bit of strength. "No! Stop it! Get your hands off me!" She instinctively began kicking her feet and knees to fight back.

"Take it easy, Anne. I don't want to hurt you. Please hold still for me. She won't simmer down, Donny."

"We can fix that," Donny grumbled after he reappeared from the cover of the tree. First he pulled a knife from a sheath in his boot and cut the button off her blue jeans. Then he put the knife away and impatiently told Meagan, "You are making this way too hard on yourself."

"Please don't," Meagan pleaded.

Shaking his head, Donny stood back up. Using the side of his worn cowboy boots, he kicked Meagan in her right and then left thigh. "That should do it, Billy. After we are both done with your precious Anne you can go back to the truck and I'll take care of her. Have a couple more beers while you wait. It shouldn't take me long."

After hearing Donny tell Billy to wait for him in the truck, Meagan's dire hope was that she would die quickly. Thinking Donny was going to strangle her or cut her throat, she longed to lose consciousness and feel as little pain as possible. While she believed she was in danger and feared a man would take her life, she never expected this.

Ben sounded miserable. "Damn it, I better bring Molly in before we push her too far and she's finished for the day. It sucks, but I think we better go down to fifteen-minute intervals." Ben no sooner made the tough decision to slow the search when they topped the hill and got their first look at an older model green pickup truck. "Hmm, do you recognize it?" Ben asked Josh, who also appeared stumped.

"No, take it slow, Benny, just in case. I don't want to scare anyone off or let them know we are here. If it is Constadine, he might do something to her before we can move in."

"Aw shit, out of state plates. *Missouri*? What the hell?"

"We need to move now," Josh sounded fearful. "With out-of-state plates it could very well be Constadine. Park here and leave Molly in the truck. She has helped more than enough."

Josh and Ben both leapt from the tall four-wheel drive and ran to the abandoned pickup.

"Oh shit, Benny, check out the beer cans. It looks like somebody has been partying hard," Josh remarked and then asked his brother a seemingly worthless question. "Please don't tell me you left your damn gun at home."

"Sorry, I thought we were just going down the road. Come on, you know I got your back," Ben was encouraging Josh when they found Meagan's backpack just outside a heavily wooded area. Reacting to the backpack, Ben knew they didn't have a moment to lose. "Son of a bitch, I will track until we get a visual and then you take the lead."

"Okay, let's go. Fuck, I hope we aren't too late."

Ben wasn't in the thick cover of the trees long when he stopped and whispered, "We have one set of hiking boots, should be hers, and two sets of cowboy boots. One of them is a hell of a lot bigger than the other."

"Two assholes...got it."

After warning Josh, Ben moved fast. He was far too experienced to let this simple piece of ground slow him down. He didn't stop again until he found where Meagan was hit the first time. He paused, pointed out the blood-stained leaves to Josh, and continued on in total silence. Josh and Ben were running so hard they were forced to come to an abrupt stop when they heard voices directly ahead of them. Whereas Ben hadn't planned on getting quite that close, Josh was more than ready.

"Her pants are sticking to her. I still can't get them off."

"Just cut them off Billy, she won't need them."

Without a sound, Josh drew his M&P and nodded to his brother. After Ben acknowledged he was ready, Josh made his way toward the men using the wider trees as cover. Uncertain of Meagan's condition, he paused long enough to confirm what he and Ben were up against. First, he sized up an average male who had his back to him and appeared to be straddling Meagan. Then he located a second male behind the same tree where they were holding her. Eager to help Meagan, Josh gave a thumbs-up and nodded to Ben, who was waiting directly to his left.

Ben signaled that he would take the male straddling Meagan, leaving Josh with the larger one behind the tree. No sooner did Josh give his final nod and Benny was gone. He was at a full run and didn't slow until after he buried his size-15 boot right between Billy's legs.

6

Billy never saw Ben coming. After dropping like a rock, Ben's target was in too much pain to cry out. Billy laid writhing in agony and holding his throbbing crotch.

Donny instantly emerged from behind the tree with his readied fists clenched and raised.

"What the fuck did you do to my sister?" Josh lied to affirm Meagan was important to him and he wasn't leaving without her. Then, with a firm grip on his pistol, he aimed at the center of Donny's forehead.

"She ain't your fucking sister," Donny groaned and started walking toward Josh without a hint of hesitation.

"Keep coming, motherfucker. I will drop you right here."

"Sissy, can you hear me?" Ben not only followed Josh's lead, he liked referring to Meagan as his sister. "Come on, Sissy, look at me. It's Benny. Try to look at me," Ben encouraged Meagan and took hold of her right hand.

Meagan opened her undamaged right eye and looked at Ben. "Am I...?" she could barely speak. "Am I...dead?"

"No, Sissy, you're fine. We are going to take you home, but I need you to hang on. I have to check you out before we go. I need to make sure I can move you, otherwise I will have to call for help." Ben did a quick once-over and was surprised how strong Meagan's vitals seemed. "I want you to close your eyes and try to concentrate on your breathing. Take in some nice deep breaths for me, okay?" Ben could see Meagan give a tiny nod and heard her trying to talk.

"I...need...Josh. Where...is...he?"

"Josh is right here. Now close your eyes, try to relax, and breathe." Ben left Meagan long enough to check on the guy he kicked and was surprised to find him coming around. Then he stepped over to where Josh was holding the larger male at gunpoint.

Donny was shaking his finger at Josh and appeared to be doing all he could to intimidate him. "You're fucking dead. I am going to gut you motherfuckers and your fucking sister like a pig."

Clearly unaffected by Donny's vile threat, Ben sadly updated Josh. "They fucked her up pretty bad. I can't tell much but I think we got here just in time, and she is asking for you."

"Really, she is asking for me? Shit. Take my gun and shoot this motherfucker if he moves. I want to talk to her before we finish this. I mean it. If he moves, you shoot. We might not have time for me to do it."

"Keep it. I would rather beat the shit out of him."

"Okay, but I want two minutes with her before you start." Josh walked over to where Meagan lay battered and bleeding. "I'm here, sweetheart. Are you with me?"

Meagan opened her right eye. "I...am...sorry...my...fault...I should... have...listened to you...and...Pete."

"No, it's not your fault. Can I help you sit up? I think you might want to watch this and then we will get you out of here."

"Josh...they...both...have...knives. In...their...boots."

"Okay thanks, now I'm going to help you sit up." Josh had to close his eyes when the pain on Meagan's face made him feel sick. "You are doing great," he said before he took off his jacket and carefully placed it between her and the tree bark. Relieved to see her breathing easier, Josh decided to include her. "Meagan, could you do me a favor since I am going to be busy?"

Meagan slowly nodded her head.

"I need you to cover me." Josh placed his heavy forty-five on her lap and watched her healthy eye widen. "Are you still with me? Are you sure you can you do this?"

"I...think...so."

"Excellent, I'm sure we can handle this but if something goes wrong I want you to use this. Do you understand, just point it at their chests and squeeze the trigger, okay?" Josh knew Meagan didn't have the strength to pick up the fully loaded pistol, but he wanted her to see that no one was going to get away with hurting her again. "I will be right back."

Billy was less than ten yards away from Josh and now back on his feet. He was struggling to reach toward his right ankle and cried out, "Donny, what the fuck?"

"Whenever you are ready," Josh advised Ben and the fight was on. Josh swiftly closed the distance to Billy, drilled his right fist into the man's nose and felt it crack. Ben, too, wasted no time as he connected with Donny's right cheekbone. While Billy was already down and suffering from his broken nose, it was obvious Ben was going to have more of a challenge with Donny. Josh glanced at Meagan, grabbed Billy by the back of his jeans and dragged him to her left side. "Tell her you are sorry."

"I'm...sorry."

When Billy apologized to the ground, Josh held him by the back of his shirt, smashed his bloody face into the dirt and then yanked him to within inches of Meagan's face. "Now, look the lady in the eyes and tell her you are sorry."

With blood bubbling from his nose and mouth, Billy's apology was impossible to understand.

Donny's only swing at Ben was so slow that Ben blocked it with his left forearm then used his right hand to jab Donny full in the left jaw. No sooner did Ben feel the jaw smash against his fist then Donny fell to his knees. Not usually one for cheap shots, Ben kicked Donny in the groin, causing him to collapse to the ground and clench his stomach. "Get up, Motherfucker! You weren't going to show her any mercy!" Ben bent down, lifted Donny's head completely off the ground by his hair, and punched him square in the face three times. "Are you good over there? We are taking a short break." Ben checked on Josh and wiped his blood-soaked hand on his flannel shirt.

"We're all good here." Josh was worried that Ben might be so furious that he would go too far. "We want them to need a hospital, not the morgue."

"I know," Benny still sounded unsatisfied.

Certain Billy was playing opossum, Josh kicked him in the ribs to rouse him. "Wake up, asshole!" When he saw Billy squint, Josh gripped the groaning man's left arm, pulled him up to his knees, and forced him to kneel beside Meagan. "Look at her. What would you do to me if I did this to your sister? Do you have any idea how much I want to kill you right now—how easy it would be?"

Meagan looked at Billy, whose face was covered and dripping with blood. In her entire life, she had never felt what she was feeling at that moment. Donny was not going to spare her and if Ben and Josh had not found her when they did, her parents would have lost their only child. Although she never thought she would condone violence, she completely accepted Josh and Ben's behavior.

"Look at this innocent young lady and tell me what you would do if I hurt your sister. Think real hard before you answer."

"I am sorry. I was fucked-up drunk and..."

"That's your fucking excuse." Josh took Billy by the back of his shirt collar with his left hand and with his right hand, pointed to where his M&P was still on Meagan's lap. "I say we let her make the decision." Looking at Meagan, Josh asked her opinion, "Would you like to get rid of this piece of shit, or it would be my pleasure to do it for you. Either way, he has got to go."

"No…please…" Billy begged after spitting out a mouthful of blood, then urinated on himself.

Josh saw Meagan's eye open wide, but could not tell her that as much as he wanted to, he could not shoot Billy. He knew she would agree that it was legally and morally wrong. Without waiting for her to reply, Josh expressed his disappointment. "Well damn, it's your lucky day, motherfucker. She isn't a sick piece of shit like you are." Josh holstered his forty-five and dragged Billy away by the cuff of his pants. He kicked him over and over until he was sure he broke a number of Billy's ribs. When Josh stopped, Billy was crying, gagging, and pleading for his life.

Although Josh had holstered his weapon, Meagan still wondered if he would shoot Donny and Billy. She completely believed him when he said he would have no problem doing it. Before she could think any more about it, Ben was next to her and re-checking her vitals.

"I am going to lift you up, Sissy, and I'm not going to lie; it's going to hurt like hell. I'll be as careful as I can."

Without moving her lips, Meagan replied, "Okay."

Carefully, as if she would shatter into a million pieces, Ben lifted Meagan from the hard ground. Sadly, he was right; the excruciating pain in her lower stomach and legs was almost unbearable. While she fought not to cry out, she could not stop the moans and tears.

After looking back to ensure they weren't being followed, Josh picked up Meagan's coat. Then he sprinted to Benny's truck, opened the passenger door, and got in so Benny could lay Meagan across his lap. While Josh gently held Meagan's head and body, he let her legs relax across the driver's side. Hovering only two inches above her cut and bruised face, he studied her injuries. "I am so sorry, Meagan. If there was any way I could trade places with you, I would." Josh's eyes watered as he imagined her pain. "Hold on, we will be home soon," he encouraged Meagan and turned back one last time to memorize the tuck's license plate.

Ben got into his truck, eased Meagan's legs across his lap, and turned the truck around. With one hand, he removed his phone from his shirt pocket and started making calls. First, he put in an emergency call to Doctor Kincaid's office. Then without delay, he left Peter a voicemail and proceeded to call Bess. "We are on our way home with Meagan. She is okay but she is going to need your help…She took one hell of a beating…I already called him….Okay, we will see you in a bit."

"We are almost home. Just keep squeezing my hands."

Meagan had no idea she was squeezing Josh's hands until he brought it up. "How…bad…is…my… face?" She was sure she looked as horrible as she felt. Peering into Josh's serious eyes, Meagan hoped for an honest answer.

"Well, other than some added color…"

The sensitive way Josh was examining her face filled Meagan with a sense of warmth she couldn't describe. Just looking into his hazel eyes seemed to alleviate her pain and relax her mind.

"It's no big deal; some bruising, a small cut, but nothing serious. You still look great, especially your eyes."

Meagan was starting to smile at Josh when she felt her cut lip. Feeling beholden to him and Ben for saving her life, she didn't take her eyes off Josh for the entire ride home.

Bess was waiting and propped the front door open when Ben parked his truck by the porch steps.

"I got her, Benny. Can you bring her backpack?"

"Yeah, be careful with her neck."

When Josh carried Meagan up the porch stairs looking grim, Bess knew it was no time to show emotion. "Take her up to the spare room and set her on the bed."

Once they were in the house, Josh made his way to the stairs. "We are almost there…hang on, sweetheart…you got this…just keep looking at me. I got you."

With each stair, Meagan's face tightened and her body tensed. "It…hurts." She didn't need to scream or shout. Her taut face and streaming tears were more than enough to tell Josh she was struggling.

"I know. I'm sorry, Miss Dawson, just two more minutes. Hang in there and keep looking at me." Holding tightly to Meagan's eyes, Josh carried her up the flight of stairs and into the spare bedroom. Then with all due consideration, he lay Meagan on the bed. "You will be back to yourself in no time. Aunt Bess will take good care of you and Dr. Kincaid is on his way. Okay, Aunt Bess, she is all yours."

"Ah, lass, let's have a look at ya while we wait fur Dr. Kincaid."

After setting Meagan's backpack out of the way, Ben went to her left side and told Bess the little he could about her condition. "Her pulse is good and I didn't see any obvious fractures, but she is in quite a bit of pain. I'm sure Dr. Kincaid will want her to go for x-rays."

Josh was pacing back and forth across the room until the little voice in his head told him he was not helping. Feeling the need to do something, he tenderly removed Meagan's boots and socks while Bess raised Meagan's sweatshirt to examine her torso.

Ben was taking his time checking and feeling Meagan's arms and hands. "Her arms have some nasty bruises but there is no swelling. I don't think anything is broken."

"Arms...are...fine...don't hurt..." Meagan tried to talk without moving her lips.

"Good, lass. She has deep bruisin' about the stomach and lower ribs, but I doubt if any are broken. The poor lass needs a hospital. Benjamin, ya best call the firehouse."

"No, I'm okay. I know I'm okay."

Josh, Ben, and Aunt Bess exchanged worried glances.

"I will go call Doctor Kincaid again." Ben used his still bloody hands to retrieve his phone and quickly stepped into the hall to talk.

Josh silently went to Meagan's right side and looked closely at her face. "Even with a couple small cuts, a split lip and a pretty purple and blue eye she is still beautiful, isn't she, Aunt Bess?"

Once again, forgetting her torn lip and about to smile, Meagan winced. "Ow...damn it."

When Ben returned he was speaking with someone on his phone. "Meagan, are you allergic to any medications? Doctor Kincaid is on the way and wants to know before he gets here."

"No. Morphine and...penicillin...are okay." Meagan looked at Bess and wholeheartedly apologized, "I...am...so sorry."

"Oh, lass, ya don't need my forgiveness. Ya had yur reasons fur leavin' and tis not up to me to judge ya. I'll be back after I get ya some tea."

Although Ben knew the answer to his next question, he thought it would be amusing to ask. "Kincaid is on his way and one of us needs to get to the barn. Do you want to talk to him or go do chores?"

"Hmm, that's a tough question. Let me see..." Josh faked his sarcasm and tried to sound cheerful, or at best make light of the situation. "Should I go take care of the horses, or stay here with Meagan? Um...I think I will stay here with the lady, but could you give me a minute to go wash the blood off my hands?"

Ben smiled and replied, "Absolutely and nice work."

Meagan tried to speak to Ben and Josh. "Thank you...you two saved...my life...Donny...said...he...was going...to kill me."

Ben's sorrow silently surged through his body. "Shhhh...talk when you feel better. We came looking for you and I was going to drive you to Gardiner after we dropped Josh off at home. I am so sorry I didn't offer you a ride sooner."

"Don't be...sorry...for my...stupidity."

"Hush and hang in there. I will be back after I do chores. Go wash up, Josh, and you might want to change your clothes."

Upon his return, Josh pulled the historic rocking chair up to the side of Meagan's bed and sat down on its thick mauve cushion. "I'm sorry we didn't get there sooner. If we would have moved just a little faster..."

"Josh...Jeremy...will come...for me." Meagan paused and swallowed hard, "He will hurt..."

Josh cut Meagan off. "Good, I told you I hope he does. I am saving a special Montana welcome just for him, even better than the one we gave those Missouri boys. May I hold your hand, Miss Dawson?"

When Meagan nodded with tears in her eyes, Josh reached for her right hand. "Please...tell Corporal...Buchanan...I am...sorry. He was right."

Josh leaned over Meagan's cut and swollen face. "Hey now, stop talking like that. Nobody could have known what was going to happen. Benny left P.D. a message, so I'm sure he will stop by to see you before he goes on duty."

"I wanted...to stay...really...I did...but Jeremy...."

"Okay, we will talk more about him when you are feeling better." Josh leaned over Meagan and gently moved her hair away from her face. Then he sat down and enclosed her right hand in both of his. Not one for tearing up, Meagan's situation struck a rare nerve and Josh's eyes watered. He was blinking hard and did not notice Bess watching him from the doorway.

After hesitating for just a moment, Josh's aunt stepped into the room. "All right, Joshua, let's get her somethin' to drink. Can ya please get a couple pillows from the closet?"

After retrieving two large firm pillows, Josh leaned over Meagan. "Okay, Miss, lean forward nice and easy."

Meagan was too exhausted. "I am…too tired…I can't."

Josh handed the pillows to Bess. "No problem, we will help you." As lightly as he could, Josh placed his hands behind Meagan and eased her forward while Bess slowly positioned the pillows.

"Take it slow, lass," Bess held a straw to Meagan's torn and enlarged lips.

Meagan barely opened her mouth when she felt a sting and her damaged lips threatened to rip even further.

"Excuse me," Josh said and went to the hallway after helplessly watching Meagan cringe in pain.

"Is he okay?"

"He doesn't take well to seein' people he cares about in pain."

"Aunt Bess…Benny and Josh…saved my life. You did raise…them right."

"Good afternoon, ladies, I was told someone here could use a doctor?" The moment Dr. Kincaid stepped into the spare room to examine Meagan, Josh was right behind him.

"Excuse me, Dr. Kincaid; can we talk for a minute?"

"Of course, what can you tell me about this?"

Satisfied he and the doctor could speak privately in the hallway, Josh began to explain what happened. "By the time we got to her they already beat the shit out of her. I don't think she was, um…" Josh could not say the words.

"Sexually assaulted?" Dr. Kincaid finished Josh's sentence.

"Yes, thank you. But last year another asshole, he hurt her. It was real bad."

"I understand, and I will take good care of her. Did you find out if she is allergic to any medications?"

"She said no and that morphine and penicillin are fine."

"Okay, thanks, I need you to wait out here. Better yet, go get some fresh air. You look like hell."

After finishing the morning chores, Ben waited on the front porch with Josh whose anxiety was growing by the minute. "What could be taking so long? We should have called fire and rescue. Kincaid is good, but I think she needs a hospital."

"I don't think I have ever seen you like this. Are *you* okay? I'm not a doctor, but I can tell you her vitals were good and she didn't go into shock. I think she is going to be fine…if she stays and takes it easy until she is completely healed. I think she just needs to rest for a few days."

"I wanted to kill them, Benny. And *you know* I could have done it without blinking an eye. After all, what are a couple more dead motherfuckers, right? Knowing what they were about to do to her...shit, I could taste it."

"I did too, but deep down we both know better. You take orders, and this was personal. Our lives would have ended with theirs. We aren't criminals, Josh."

"Thanks for putting it that way. For once, you are actually right."

Shaking his head in silence, Ben was not sure how to say what he was thinking, but he had to get it off his chest. "Josh, don't let yourself get attached to this girl, you hear me?"

"What the hell are you talking about?" Josh stopped gazing toward a distant stand of fir trees and stared at his older brother.

"You know exactly what I am talking about."

"No, draw me a picture because I don't have a clue."

While Ben was trying to come up with the right words, he watched Peter pull up and park his highway patrol vehicle.

"I can't leave you two alone for a minute. What the fuck is going on?" Peter's question evoked pitiful expressions from Josh and Ben.

After Ben and Josh explained the situation and how Dr. Kincaid had been with Meagan for the last hour and a half, Peter frowned and shook his head. "I will go see what is going on. Then I need to find out if these motherfuckers are wanted for anything else." Ben and Josh followed Peter upstairs and watched him lightly tap on the door. "Hey, doc, it's Pete."

Bess opened the door and let Peter into the room. Then she poked her head out and updated the impatient brothers. "She's fine, and Dr. Kincaid is about finished." With that said, Bess closed the door.

Meagan could not hold back her tears when she saw Peter wearing his full uniform and gear. "Say it...say I told you...," she paused when Peter took her left hand.

"Meagan, I don't know what you are trying to say."

"I...told...you... so," Meagan finally cried out.

"Don't you ever say that to me again. I would never think such a thing and you should know that. I couldn't get here fast enough when I got the message. I was told you *should* be fine, but I want to ask you myself. Do you want to go to a hospital? I can call for a helicopter."

Still crying, Meagan could not talk and slowly shook her head.

"I am going to notify the hospitals to watch for the men who did this. From the sound of it they will need medical treatment. I will also call for a deputy to come out and meet with you for the report."

"No," Meagan said so softly, Peter wasn't sure if he heard her right.

"I'm sorry, did you say no? I can barely hear you."

"Please…no reports…can you…keep it quiet?"

Peter was livid when he heard Meagan did not want to charge the men who were going to rape her and take her life with absolutely no remorse.

Meagan raised her left hand to bring Peter closer. When he leaned over her swollen lips and face, she voiced her concern. "Please, for Aunt Bess…Benny… and Josh. No one…can know…I am here."

Peter finally realized how important it was to Meagan to keep her whereabouts a secret. He looked into Meagan's welling eyes and gave his word. "Okay, stop crying. I understand. I won't let out what happened. Is there anything else I can do for you, anything at all?"

"No, thank you. Please…be careful. I'll see you…Tuesday."

"I will call to check on you after I go on duty."

"Thank you…for caring…and coming to…see me."

Peter leaned toward Meagan's ear and whispered, "I'll see you soon. Don't worry about anything but getting better. You are safe here. Josh and Benny will see to it." He kindly touched her left shoulder and returned to the hallway where Ben and Josh were waiting. "You are right, they really messed her up. She is refusing to press charges and wants to forget it happened. She is doing much better than I would be and she is a hell of a lot stronger. Call me right away if I can do anything to help."

"Thanks, P.D.," Josh acknowledged his best friend with a thoughtful nod.

Ben was equally grateful. "Yes, thanks for coming by."

"I wanted to see her before I left. I know I don't need to say this, especially to you," Peter said while eyeballing Josh. "Try to have someone stay with her. I wish I could stay and help, but you know how it is. I will call tonight around bedtime."

"Take it easy, Pete."

"See ya later, P.D., and watch your ass."

Not more than a minute after Peter left, the doctor came out. "I tried to convince her to go for x-rays, but she all out refused. I can't treat what I can't see and no one can force her to go. So, if at all possible, someone should keep an eye on her for a few days. If she complains about severe pain and seems to be getting worse, call county rescue. I called in a few prescriptions for pain and infection. Pick them up ASAP. If she is just bruised and sore like she is telling me, she might be able to get out of bed in a few days, but don't have her doing your chores." The doctor's attempt to cheer up Josh and Ben went completely unnoticed. "That was on the record, now between the three of us; tell me the men responsible didn't completely walk away from this."

"We made sure both of them would need a hospital," Ben said as a matter of fact but didn't see the need to go into details.

"Good, I didn't think you two would let them get away with it. I told Bess to call if Meagan needs me and please get her medication. I don't like knowing my patients are in pain and I want her to sleep through the worst of it."

Josh didn't hesitate to run the errand. "I will walk you out and go pick it up."

"I will go, Josh," Ben offered. "I need to go to the bank and gas up my truck. You stay here and help Aunt Bess. I'm sure she can use it."

"Sounds good, Benny, and thank you, Dr. Kincaid. I appreciate you coming all the way out here on such short notice. There is a steer with your name on it for this one," Josh promised.

"Thank you, but this one is on me. It was my pleasure under the circumstances. Meagan seems like a very nice girl. Please keep me posted."

After watching Ben and Doctor Kincaid head down the stairs, Josh tapped lightly on the door and peeked his head in Meagan's room.

"Come in, Joshua. She's tryin' to sleep, but the pain is too much."

"Benny is on his way to pick up her meds. Hopefully once she takes some good pain pills she will sleep for hours. Aunt Bess, I really need a shower. Can you sit with her for twenty minutes and I will stay with her for the rest of the day and tonight if I don't get a call."

"Aye, a hot shower will do ya good and take yur time."

It was impossible for Josh to enjoy his shower. The steamy, hot water running down the length of his body did nothing to rinse away his stress. He wanted to punch the shower wall when he thought how Meagan had already been through so much and now this. While he was sure they could help with her physical injuries, he questioned how much they could do for her emotional well-being. As he toweled off, dressed, and prepared to relieve Bess, Josh found himself wanting to do all he could to help Meagan.

Seeing the door wide open to the guest room, Josh went around the foot of the bed and to where Bess was sitting in the aged rocking chair. "You can go,

Aunt Bess. I will stay with her." When his Aunt smirked with visible suspicion, Josh grinned and kissed her on the cheek.

"Okay, lad, I'll be back to check on yas in a bit."

"We'll be here," Josh whispered and took Bess's place in the rocker.

Overtired and aching from her head to her knees, Meagan still managed to grin. She was delighted by how the Mackenzies were pitching in to take care of her. Even with her eyes closed she could tell Bess had left the room and Josh was sitting in the rocking chair. Bess smelled like a combination of lavender and vanilla hand lotion, fresh coffee, and fabric softener. Meanwhile, Josh's scent was completely masculine. The refreshing odor of body wash, shampoo, and a hint of men's deodorant made it obvious that he just showered. Meagan was picturing Josh sitting beside her when she unconsciously took in his appealing scent.

Josh noticed Meagan's chest rise significantly when she took the deep breath. "Are you awake, Miss?" He whispered to avoid waking her if she was sleeping.

Hearing the comforting voice of one of the men who just saved her life, Meagan opened her right eye and turned to look at Josh. Even with her lips aching and pulling in retaliation, she smiled.

"Miss Dawson, you are unbelievable. After everything you have been through, you smile like it never happened." Josh inched the chair to the side of her bed and leaned in to hear her reason.

"I'm alive...and blessed."

"Wow, I feel like such an ass. I have been so hung up on how *I* feel about what those assholes did to you that I didn't stop to think how you must feel. Anyone in your shoes would feel lucky to be alive. Damn, I can't believe *I*, of all people missed that," Josh stated, more to himself than Meagan. He could tell by the way she was swallowing and clearing her throat that she had something else to say. Trying to comfort Meagan the best he could, Josh reached for her right hand. "What is it? Take your time."

"I am blessed...to have...such good friends."

Josh was pleased and smiling because he knew exactly who Meagan was referring to.

"Aunt Bess...and Benny...Pete...and you," she said warmly, enjoying Josh's kind eyes.

At first, Josh didn't know how to respond to Meagan's generous words. He was used to getting professional compliments, but for someone to express their personal appreciation the way Meagan did made his hair stand up. "Thank you, but I am the lucky one." While cradling Meagan's right hand, Josh used the fingertips of his free right hand to softly stroke her wrist and forearm. "I have only known you four days and I am already on your good-guy list, and your friend list." Josh couldn't have been happier when Meagan smiled. "You didn't sleep at all last night, did you?"

"No…how did you…know?"

Before Josh could reply, he smiled and apologized, "I'm sorry, Miss, please excuse the interruption." He didn't skip a beat when he removed his vibrating phone from his shirt pocket with his left hand while continuing to caress Meagan. "Hey, P.D., what's going on? I wasn't expecting to hear from you until later?"

"How is Meagan?"

"Trying to rest, but she needs her meds."

"I wish there was something we could do. Has she said anything to you about pressing charges?"

"She hasn't said much of anything."

"I can't say that I blame her, but if she changes her mind call me right away. So, when I left your place I went looking for the pickup truck. Sorry to say, the motherfuckers managed to crawl out and took off. I found quite a bit of blood. Looks like they spit the shit everywhere, but the truck is gone and so are they."

"Really? That's interesting. I didn't think either one of them was in any shape to drive. If we would have known that, we would have given them a few more. As it was, I was worried Benny was going to go too far."

Meagan was listening to Josh's conversation when her eyes met his. With the charming way he was looking at her, it didn't take a minute for her to feel shy and embarrassed. Needing to look away, her gaze wandered from his smooth face to his muscular and tattooed arms. He was wearing a light blue muscle shirt that had a brilliant image of a soaring bald eagle across the front. Just above the majestic eagle and across his broad chest were the words "SUPPORT OUR TROOPS" in dark blue lettering. When Meagan saw Josh's well-rounded bicep flexing as he held his phone, and how his perfectly defined forearm affirmed his strength, she was relieved to have him on her side.

Meagan's swollen left eye made it difficult to discern Josh's tattoos. Having already gotten a glimpse of his black armband, she tried to focus on the unique tree that went from just below his left shoulder to the bottom of his left bicep. Although she had no personal feelings for or against tattoos, she was curiously drawn to the tree's bright green leaves, detailed brown trunk and dark, hollowed center. She could only reason the black crisscrossing that branched around the entire tree to below its roots where it completed a nearly perfect oval symbolized something. She was mentally tracing the intriguing tree when Josh's strong presence, calming voice, and soothing touch relaxed her into a restful sleep.

It was well after the dinner hour when Meagan opened her unscathed eye and thought she was alone. But, not two minutes later, she was touched when Ben came from the guest bathroom.

"So how bad is your pain?" Ben asked while taking a seat in the creaky rocking chair.

"I'm okay. Thank you."

"I am an E.M.T. Do you really think I believe that? We can't help you if you don't let us."

"Okay, it hurts. Everything fucking hurts. Sorry, Benny." Regardless of her pain, Meagan couldn't believe she cursed.

"For what?" Ben asked with a chuckle and stood back up. "Well, I just so happen to have what you need." Ben walked over to the nightstand on the other side of the bed. He nodded at Meagan, grinned, and picked up two brown prescription bottles. "These should help, but you need to eat something first. Can you handle a bowl of Aunt Bess's chicken noodle soup?"

"Sounds yummy," Meagan replied as she looked into Ben's generous light blue eyes.

"Now don't you dare run off. I will be right back," Ben joked.

Meagan couldn't get over how comfortable she felt with Benny. She guessed he was a few inches taller than six foot, and he didn't look to have an ounce of fat on his entire solid body. *He is so nice, not to mention nice looking*, she thought. *I bet his girlfriend adores him.* She recalled how Josh told her it was a shame she couldn't stay long enough to see how well the men he knew treated their women.

Ben didn't waste any time returning with a big bowl of soup and a tall glass of raspberry tea. "Here you go." He slowly handed over the steaming hot bowl of soup. "Meagan, do you mind if I still call you Sissy, since it worked so well for us this morning?"

Meagan seemed to be talking a little better, but was still having a hard time moving her lips to form some words. "I have always wanted a brother. Are you my younger brother or my older brother?"

"I am five years older than you, baby sister. I am thirty-four."

"Sounds perfect, Benny how do you know how old I am?"

"After Josh and I brought you in the house, I looked through your back-pack for your I.D. We needed to find out if you were dangerous. I hope you understand."

"It's okay. I was just wondering how you knew."

"Would you mind if Josh and I make a little noise in your room? We will try to hurry and don't be afraid to tell us if we are bothering you."

Meagan wondered what the men could be up to. "No, I'm fine."

Ben did little more than poke his head around the corner and Josh was there in an instant.

"Hi, Miss, how was your nap?" Josh asked.

"Great, thank you. I think it helped a lot."

"Good. You will be back on your feet before you know it."

Meagan watched with silent interest as the brothers walked around her bed. Without a word, they picked up the old wooden rocking chair and hauled it out of the room. However, once the two were outside her room, they began trying to speak over each other. Before another minute passed, they were maneu-vering a hefty recliner through the bedroom door and around her bed.

"See, I told you it would fit," Josh declared.

"Yep, you were right. And *I* was right when I told *you* that *you* would be painting the walls when we scratched them."

"It's not like I don't know how to use a paint brush."

Meagan thought she had never been so entertained while eating a bowl of chicken noodle soup. She started to laugh, but without thinking cried out in pain and reached for her lower stomach.

"Oh shit, we're sorry, Miss," Josh apologized.

"Let's get your meds," Ben said then handed Meagan two pills and a glass of tea.

"Amoxicillin and Vicodin. I will sleep for a week." Meagan washed down the two medications and set her empty glass on the mahogany nightstand. "May I please use the restroom?"

"Sure, do you need help getting up?" Ben asked.

"I don't think so. But I will need a few minutes."

"No problem, we will wait in the hall," Ben suggested, before he and Josh waited and waited in the hall almost ten minutes.

"Benny, can you come here please?"

Ben smirked and laughed at Josh, who looked completely flabbergasted because Meagan called for his brother instead of him. "You are only a friend; I am her big brother, and remember *that* because I will kick your ass if I catch you messing with her."

Josh could only shake his head when Ben went to assist Meagan.

When Ben opened the door, Meagan was sitting on the edge of the bed with her legs dangling toward the floor. She was wearing bicycle shorts that revealed the dark black and blue splotches grossly covering her thighs.

"My legs won't…"

"No worries, but if I pick you up it's going to hurt."

"I know, but I have to go, so let's get it over with." The pain wasn't nearly bad as Meagan thought it would be. When she finished, Ben carefully carried her back to bed and pulled the blankets up to her chest. "Thank you, Benny."

"Any time, and that bag is also for you." Ben pointed at a white plastic bag near the prescription bottles. "There are some magazines, cards, crossword puzzle books, pens, and notepads for when you get bored. There are also a few hunting magazines for Josh, for when he gets on your nerves and you want him to shut up."

"I appreciate *all* you have done. I wouldn't be here if…"

"Stop it. You don't have to thank us. I'm glad we could help. Josh will be back after he puts on his sweats and I will be working in my room. Just holler if you need me."

"I'm fine, Benny. I will see you tomorrow."

"Sissy, promise me that you won't make me come looking for you again. Please come talk to me before you do anything crazy again."

"I learned my lesson. You have my word. *Never* again."

"Good answer. I will see you tomorrow. Get some sleep."

Meagan was working a crossword when Josh tapped on her door.

"It's open. You don't need to knock."

"Oh yes I do," Josh was still nodding when he saw what she was doing. "Oh fun, crosswords, can I have one?"

"You can, but I have something even better for you." Meagan handed Josh the hunting magazines and watched his eyes light up like it was Christmas.

"Wow, perfect. Next month's issues. How did you know?"

"Stop playing dumb. You know Benny brought them." Meagan knew Josh was going out of his way to cheer her up and she couldn't have been more thankful.

Josh and Meagan were engrossed in their puzzles and magazines when Bess popped in to say goodnight. "Tis past my bedtime and Meagan, if yur feelin' up to it tomorrow, I will help ya with a hot, soakin' bath. Tis such a dandy of a tub, ya won't want to get out."

"Thank you, a bath sounds great. And thank you for the soup, Aunt Bess. It was really delicious."

"Yur welcome, lass, and don't let this one keep ya awake all night. Joshua can be a night owl."

"Good night, Aunt Bess," Josh said without defending himself.

When Bess turned to leave, Josh and Meagan found themselves looking at each other and grinning over her words.

"Are you warm enough, Miss?" Josh went to the closet behind his recliner, took out the last two goosedown feather pillows and a light blanket and carried them to his makeshift bed.

"Yes, thank you. You don't need to stay with me. I won't run away again."

"Oh hell no, you can't shake me that easy. If I let you get away a second time, P.D. and Benny will both kick my ass."

"I can't even make it to the bathroom, how..." Meagan stopped mid-sentence and whispered, "Josh, did you hear that?"

"Yeah, it was a car door," Josh confirmed and walked into the guest bathroom to check out the vehicle. "It's only Jillian," he advised when he returned to Meagan's side. "Damn, Miss Dawson, you look scared to death."

The bleak expression on Meagan's face seemed to ask, *do you blame me?*

"I will be right back. Don't go anywhere."

"You don't need to come back."

"Like I said, I will be *right* back," Josh grinned and left the room.

Meagan lay back, sunk her head into her pillows, and closed her eyes. She vaguely remembered Josh going to meet Jillian the night he was keeping an eye on her in the den. She speculated Jillian was there for makeup sex and did not expect to see Josh back for hours. But to her amazement and true to his word, Josh was back in less than five minutes. When Meagan saw how upset he appeared, she could not help but react to his mood and her facial expression showed it.

"Meagan, are you okay? You look like you're going to cry."

"I know how hard it is to break up. I wish I could help you feel better. You have all done so much for me and I have done nothing but say thank you."

"You don't need to do anything. You needed help and we chose to take you in. You don't have to say or do anything in return." Josh was suddenly struck with an odd thought. This situation with Meagan—it was just like what Aunt Bess told him in the den, when she talked about his mom. "A stranger today could be yur friend tomorrow. She may even become a blessin' to ya and a trusted ally for the rest of yur life." Josh could hear his aunt's words as if she was repeating them herself. How does she do it? How is she always right about everything?

"But I feel like I am taking advantage of you and your family and Pete. You have been too good to me."

"Okay, fine, being the honest lady that you are, maybe you can help me by answering some questions. Give me your honest opinion and don't worry about what I think."

"All right, I can do that," Meagan replied and met Josh's eyes.

"Okay, would you ever hit me, even if I did something that really pissed you off? Let's say I slept with your best friend or your sister."

"No, hitting you wouldn't change what any of you did."

"Okay, can you think of *any* reason why you would hit me?"

"I am higher than a kite, and tired, but I don't think so."

"No problem, I will ignore the fact that you are stoned. What if *I* hit *you*?" Josh caught himself before Meagan could respond. "Oh shit, I'm sorry, Miss. I must be the one on drugs. I did hit you. Please forget I said that."

"It's okay, we are friends now. I forgive you and I trust you."

"Aw, thank you, Miss Dawson. What if we were together and I slapped you?"

"I would *probably* leave you."

"So, should it be any different when a woman hits her man?"

"I don't think so. I wouldn't want you to hit me."

"You wouldn't have to worry about that. I would *never* put my hands on you in anger. Like I expect you to believe that. I can imagine what you must think. Just since we met I have knocked you unconscious and seriously beat the shit out of some asshole. I am on a roll this week."

"No, quite the opposite. I know you could have killed me—and them—and gotten away with it. But you chose not to," Meagan paused when her lip threatened to break open. "But the way you were acting, I thought for sure you were going to shoot Donny and Billy."

Josh continued, holding Meagan's eyes, "Only when I have no choice."

"What? Oh my god…*you* have done *that*?"

Josh instantly regretted his candor. "We are both tired, let's just change the subject."

Even worn out, Meagan was enjoying their conversation so much that she honored Josh's request. "Okay…uh…so does Jillian want you back?"

"Yeah, and she apologized. I told her it was too late to talk tonight and she could call me tomorrow, but it's over. I've had it." As if proving he wanted nothing more to do with Jillian, Josh held up a magazine that had a monstrous trophy mule deer on the cover. "Wow, he would make the record books." Josh was positive of Meagan's next answer but wanted to toy with her. "So, Miss Dawson, do you like to fish or hunt?"

"It's been years since Pop took me fishing with him, but I would never hunt. I love animals."

"Me too, there is nothing like one of Benny's tasty, elk cheeseburgers or Aunt Bess's Irish stew with marinated venison."

"Please tell me you're kidding."

"Not at all. It seemed like you enjoyed the elk stew."

"Oh no, oh my god, I actually ate an elk?"

"And look, you are actually alive to talk about it."

"Oh no, please tell me the New York Strips were beef."

"Oh yeah, that was one of Benny's prime steers. It was bred, born, and raised right here on our ranch."

"I should have known. Did you shoot the elk in the den? It's huge."

Josh couldn't help but laugh at Meagan's grievous expression. "Yes, Miss Dawson. I hunted for three days before I uh—let's just say I harvested it."

"You *killed* it."

"It did die, so that would also suffice."

"Josh?"

"Yes?"

"Can we turn the lights off? I feel like shit."

"Sure, it's been a pleasure. I'll see you tomorrow."

7

By the time Meagan woke up, she forgot where she was. It wasn't until she rolled over and saw Bess sitting in Josh's recliner that she started getting her bearings. "Aunt Bess?"

"Good mornin', lass, how are ya feelin'?" Bess asked and set her cross-stitch pattern on her lap.

"Better, thank you. How are you?"

"'Tis a good day so far. I've no reason to complain."

"Aunt Bess, what day is it? I feel so out of it."

"'Tis Saturday, about one in the afternoon. Ya will feel better once ya wake up. There's a fresh glass of ice water on yur night stand."

The ice-cold water was just what Meagan needed to appease her cotton mouth and rouse her senses.

"Benjamin is muckin' stalls and Joshua has gone out. Would ya like me to run ya a hot bath?"

"A hot bath sounds wonderful, but I don't think I can walk."

"I can help ya, lass. I'm a tad bit stronger than I look."

Once they made it to the bathroom Bess turned on the antique brass faucet and helped Meagan into the enormous cast iron claw-foot bathtub. "I'm sorry to ask ya this, but what shall I do with yur clothes from yesterday?" Bess thoughtfully asked after lugging in Meagan's backpack.

"Could you please get rid of them for me?"

"I'll see to it. And do ya have any laundry to wash?"

"Almost everything I have left is dirty. I sold all of my clothes and was supposed to go shopping once I got settled at my uncle's farm. I think I am down to one pair of underwear."

"I'll wash yur clothes and find ya somethin' to wear for now. How tall are ya, lass?"

"I am five feet, seven inches."

"Joshua is five-eleven, I'm sure he has somethin' ya can use. I will be back after I make Benjamin lunch. Would ya like me to bring ya a hot ham and cheese sandwich?"

"Yes, thank you, and please take your time. This bathtub is amazing." Meagan watched as Bess sprinkled some chamomile scented bubble bath into the tub and gathered her dirty clothes. Letting her mind wander, she soaked and relaxed for more than an hour. She thought about her jobs in Gardiner and worried her uncle Pat could not hold them for her. She thought about Peter and how she should have listened to him. She also considered calling her folks, but would need to borrow Benny's phone since Josh was out. Then she wondered what Bess meant by Josh being out and decided he was likely with Jillian.

Bess returned about thirty minutes later with a pair of dark blue draw-string sweatpants and a gray sweatshirt. "I think these will work fur ya lass. Ya will need to tie them, but they should stay up once ya do."

After filling her stomach with half a colossal ham and cheese sandwich, Meagan did a few puzzles then napped the rest of the afternoon. She was still sleeping when Bess tried to sneak into the room with her clean clothes.

"Sorry to disturb ya. It will just be the three of us fur supper, so I'm warmin' up some stew. Would ya care fur a bowl?"

"Oh…uh…is it *elk* stew?"

"Oh no, lass, we finished the last of the elk about a month ago. Hopefully Joshua will get another brute on his next hunt."

"Okay, thank you, I would love a bowl of stew." Meagan grinned when she realized Josh was most likely pressing her buttons when he teased her about eating the wild game.

No sooner did Bess leave the room and Benny knocked on the open door. "Are you awake in there?"

"Of course, all I have been doing is sleeping."

Ben stepped around the bed and sat in the recliner.

"How is your pain? You sound a lot better."

"Yes, thank you. After my bath I made it back to bed without Bess's help. But if you want the truth, my legs still ache and my head and face still hurt; oh, and I feel an occasional stabbing feeling in my stomach and sides. Other than that I feel pretty good, a lot better than I thought I would."

"Good, glad to hear it. Is there anything I can do for you? I'm done in the barn for today and don't have a hot date, so we can hang out all night."

"Thanks, Benny, I appreciate it. I was wondering if I could borrow a phone to call my parents."

"You can call them now if you want, but please let me know if Josh calls."

"Okay," Meagan said and dialed her father. "Hi Pop, I am just checking in." Considering the grief she had already caused them, she had no intention of mentioning her recent brush with death. She just wanted to let him know she was still at the Mackenzies'.

"Are you okay, Meggie? You don't sound like yourself. Are you still sick?"

Meagan couldn't tell him the truth and tears began to well up. "I got hurt, Pop." She began to sob and was unable to talk.

"Let me talk to him, Sissy."

Benny disappeared with his phone for about ten minutes while Meagan tried to calm down. "You are very welcome, sir. We will talk to you soon. Here is Meagan."

"Bye, Pop. I love you. Tell Mom I miss her."

"We love you too, Meggie. Stay put and I will call Patty."

Father and daughter said their farewells, then Meagan thanked Ben for speaking on her behalf. "Thanks, Benny, I couldn't tell him."

"Any time. Are you up for a visitor?"

"I would love a visitor," Meagan replied, wondering who it could be.

Ben whistled and Molly was at Meagan's bedside in mere seconds.

"Is she allowed on the bed?"

"Sure, she likes being spoiled. Just pat your bed and call her."

"Come here, Molly Girl." Meagan did as Ben suggested and the dog leapt onto the bed. "You are so beautiful." Meagan thoroughly enjoyed stroking the blue-eyed retriever. "So, *you* helped save me. You are my hero, Molly."

"What's going on?" Ben asked when he took a call.

It only took a moment for Meagan to confirm Ben was talking to Josh.

"She's fine. Do you want to say hi?" Meagan reasoned Josh must have said no. "Okay, be careful…Good, call me if something changes…I will, and we'll see you when you get home."

Meagan knew it was none of her business when Ben didn't elaborate on the call. While picturing Josh, she tried to convince herself that it didn't matter.

After Josh's call, Meagan and Ben played countless games of rummy. She couldn't have been more relaxed with Molly lying below her feet. "Benny, don't you have to wake up at five?"

"Five-thirty, but I have been doing it for almost twenty years."

"I'm fine, Benny, really, go to bed."

"I want someone with you one more night."

Meagan tossed back the covers and raised her sweatshirt to just below her breasts. "I have had a ruptured spleen, numerous broken ribs, a punctured lung and more. Take a look and take my word for it. I am just bruised. It looks a whole lot worse than it is. I promise."

Ben studied the olive green, ugly yellow, and dark purple blotches. "Okay fine, but we are both sleeping with our doors open."

"Agreed. Can Molly stay with me tonight?"

"Sure, but I'll warn you, she hogs the bed."

"After helping you and Josh find me, she deserves it."

"Okay, goodnight, Sissy. Holler if you need me."

"I will, and goodnight…and thank you for staying with me."

"Any time," Ben replied and left for his room.

Meagan took the amoxicillin and Vicodin then crashed with Molly snoring at the foot of her bed. She was sleeping so soundly that she didn't even notice Molly's early morning departure. Just like the day before, Meagan didn't open her eyes once before noon on Sunday.

Bess brought Meagan lunch just after one o'clock and explained that she was going to be busy baking bread. She told her to call downstairs if she needed anything and to keep resting.

Starting Sunday afternoon and into early evening, Meagan had to relieve her boredom. Among hours of playing solitaire, she forced herself to ignore her pain and paced the length of the bedroom to regain her strength and mobility. She was tickled pink when Bess, Ben, and even Molly Girl joined her for dinner. Throughout bites of meat loaf, baked potato, mixed vegetables, and fresh banana bread, the three talked about their day. It was shortly after their plates were clean when Bess got Meagan's full attention.

"So, lass, did ya like the venison loaf? After ya spoke of the elk stew, I thought ya might take pleasure in some venison loaf."

Before Meagan could choke up the right words Ben made her feel even worse. "Was that the hamburger from Josh's mule deer?"

"Aye and there is plenty of it left in the big meat freezer."

It's probably too late to tell them I'm a vegetarian, Meagan thought, ignoring her full stomach. She figured she was doomed to eating the helpless animals Josh killed or be honest and try to come up with a legitimate reason why eating wild game bothered her.

Ben left to help Bess carry the used plates to the kitchen, but quickly returned. "Sissy, you have a phone call."

"Hello?" Meagan asked, wondering who it could be.

"How are you feeling?"

"Oh, hello, Corporal Buchanan."

"Meagan, you can call me Pete."

"Okay, how are you…Pete?"

"I'm doing well, thank you. I wanted to check on you yesterday, but I used all my spare time to run an errand for Josh. I probably won't make it over there until Wednesday. I got a message from my dad and he has a list of work waiting for me."

"Sounds like you will be working on your days off."

"I'm afraid so. I also called to update you on Billy and Donny Randall. After tracking them down at a regional trauma center, I met with both of them. They both told me a bullshit story that they were involved in an ATV accident. They also tried to tell me someone picked them up. Just another line of BS since I found their truck in the emergency room parking lot. They are going to be in the hospital for several more days if you change your mind and want them arrested."

"I don't know. What do *you* think I should do?"

"After checking them out, Donny is on probation for burglary and disorderly conduct. Billy has two DUI's and his license is suspended in Missouri. So, Donny would be in quite a bit of trouble for violating his probation. Billy would be looking at some time for what he did to you."

"Have they hurt any other women, like what they did to me?"

"Not that I am aware of."

"As long as they didn't hurt anyone else, then no."

"Okay, it is *your* decision and I understand your reasons. Call if you need me, otherwise I will see you Wednesday. Feel better, Meagan."

"Thanks for calling, Pete, and please be careful."

"Thanks and *behave yourself*," Peter stressed before ending the call.

After talking to Peter, Meagan asked Bess if she could take a late-night bath since she wasn't the slightest bit tired.

"Ah, lass, ya don't need my permission to do anything in this house. As long as yur here, feel free to make it yur home."

Meagan haphazardly crawled out of bed and gave Bess a warm hug. "Thank you. I hope you know how much it means to me."

"Yur very welcome and I'll be turnin' in early. Enjoy yur bath and I'll see ya tomorrow."

"Okay, good night and sleep well."

It was only eight o'clock when Ben told Meagan that he was also going to bed early. "Unless you want to share your tub with Molly. She loves water. I am going to have to keep her with me."

"I'll be fine, Benny. You can close your door."

"All right, have a good night and don't be afraid to come get me."

"Thanks, Benny, and goodnight." After playing a few games of solitaire it dawned on Meagan that her blow dryer might disturb Ben. Knowing how long it took for her hair to air dry, she decided it would be wise to start her bath.

Immediately upon lowering herself into the steamy water, Meagan tried to relax but her mind refused to let go. She stressed when she thought her entire life hung in the balance, including her safety and well-being. She was recalling how Ben defeated Donny Randall without the slightest bit of trouble, but could only hope he never encountered Jeremy. Although she trusted Ben with her life, she could not live with herself if Jeremy did anything to hurt him.

Following her lengthy bath, Meagan towel dried her long, wavy hair and went to sit in Josh's recliner. She was thinking how comfortable she felt wearing his sweatpants when she wondered if Peter sold Jillian's ring. "Pete did say he ran an errand for Josh," she said to herself and decided the errand was likely to the pawn shop. But then, out of the blue, she wondered what difference it made. Why do I care what Josh does, or who he is with? I'll be leaving soon, so what difference does any of it make?

A giant elk on the cover of one of Josh's magazines caught Meagan's attention and she picked up the book to take a closer look. According to the cover there was an article beginning on page nineteen titled "More Reasons to Manage the Elk Population in Montana." Interested in the benefits of hunting, Meagan went to page nineteen and started reading. She was nearly finished with the article when she heard two car doors close. At first she thought Josh and Jillian were returning from a romantic weekend getaway. She was convinced they had gone somewhere to make up and now he was bringing her up to his room. "It has to be them. Who else could it be at this hour?" She whispered to ease her curiosity.

It was Meagan's barreling heartbeat and the unnerving voice in the back of her mind that told her she could be wrong. If it wasn't Josh and Jillian, why did she hear two car doors? Would Jeremy bring someone with him? Breaking into a sweat, she only knew one of two things was about to happen. Either she was going to be very embarrassed when she met Josh and Jillian sneaking to his room or—she refused to consider the second possibility because it terrified the hell out of her.

Since her door was already open she decided to simply listen for Josh and Jillian's voices, and then quietly return to her bed. But if it wasn't them, she would run straight to Ben's room. Fighting the overwhelming desire to hide under her blankets, Meagan tiptoed to the bedroom door. She remained just inside her room for what felt like hours and still heard nothing, not even the expected giggle or a whisper. She poked her head into the hall long enough to look to her right and locate Ben's door.

The odd silence told Meagan to expect the unforeseen and prepare for the worst. Almost too frightened to move, she decided she had no choice but to wake Ben and tell him someone might be in the house. Shaking, and fearing her legs would buckle, she stepped into the hallway. Curiosity got the best of her and she glanced to her left and down the stairs. Doing a double take, Meagan could scarcely see the outline of a dark figure standing at the bottom of the stairway. If not for the dim light coming from the kitchen night light, the figure would have blended into the surrounding darkness.

The person was dressed in black from head to toe and Meagan cringed when she thought they were looking her way. Concluding Jeremy had found her and broken into the house, she felt powerless. No...please...not here. She couldn't fathom how he found her so soon. Paralyzed with fear, Meagan longed to yell for Ben, but her lips remained locked. Feeling herself about to pass out, she fell back against the wall and closed her eyes.

8

"Meagan, are you okay?" With the limited light coming from the spare room, Josh could barely see Meagan leaning against the wall. He swiftly took the staircase two at a time and set his gear down at the top of the stairs. Still wearing his tactical uniform and pistol, he only needed to see Meagan's daunted expression to confirm she was beyond rattled. "Miss, Miss Dawson?" Josh gently took her hands and asked again, "Miss Dawson, are you okay? You're as white as a ghost."

Trying to grasp what happened, Meagan's mind was a chaotic whirlwind of questions and concerns. Completely thrown and avoiding Josh's eyes, she fixed on the long, rectangular case and duffle bag. While both were black in color, the colossal duffle far surpassed her backpack in both size and weight. Squinting in awe, she tried to focus on what she thought was a bulletproof vest situated over the top of the duffle bag. Across the back of the vest in white, capital letters was the abbreviation S.R.T. and directly beneath the abbreviation also in bold white letters were the words SPECIAL RESPONSE TEAM.

Josh glanced over his right shoulder to see what held Meagan's attention and concluded she was glued to his vest. He delicately lifted her chin toward him and met her eyes. "I'm sorry. I didn't mean to scare you. If I knew you were going to be awake I would have called. I thought you were sleeping with your light on again."

When Meagan's initial panic steadily turned to inner turmoil, she didn't want to talk to anyone, including Josh. She was furious with herself and wanted to sort through her conflicting feelings in private. Looking into Josh's sincere, blue-green eyes, Meagan sternly reminded herself that his life and the lives of those around her were none of her business. She needed to drive it into her thick skull that she was a mere guest at the Mackenzies' and nothing more.

Concluding he was the sole reason for Meagan's alarm, Josh wanted to show his concern by saying something positive. "It's nice to see both of your eyes again, and you are back on your feet. I can't believe how much you have improved. You are a lot stronger than you give yourself credit for. Looks like I was worried about you for nothing."

When Meagan didn't respond, Josh made a disgusted face and wrinkled his nose. "Listen, Miss, I probably don't need to tell you I need a shower. And after I wash up, I am going to make a fried egg and cheese sandwich on toast. Would you like one?"

"No, thank you." The disturbed tone in Meagan's voice made it quite apparent that she didn't want anything to do with him. Her searching eyes lowered to the eye-catching patches on both sides of Josh's chest. First, she was drawn to the intricately embroidered seven-point badge over his left side. Then, she stopped on the detailed gray and black patch over his right chest that spelled out MACKENZIE. Frustrated and disconcerted, she began inching her way to the left to move away.

Josh sensed Meagan's tension and stepped back to let her pass.

"If you will excuse me, I'm going back to bed." Meagan fixated on the floor to escape Josh's doubtful and questioning eyes.

Seeing Meagan was still not herself, Josh blamed himself and wanted to help her any way he could. "Okay, I'll just tuck you in and sit with you until you fall asleep."

"No really, you don't need to do that. I'm okay."

"Like hell you are. Anyone can see you are not okay. You're shaking like a pissed off rattle snake and it's my fault."

Further discouraged because she couldn't explain her feelings for Josh, Meagan slightly raised her voice. "I'm just tired and my legs hurt." Longing to lose herself in his enticing eyes, she fought the urge to glance back and hurried into her room.

"It's okay to tell me the truth. I would rather that you did. You're pissed off at me for scaring the shit out of you, and I don't blame you a bit," Josh announced while following on Meagan's heels.

When Meagan got into bed, Josh thoughtfully pulled the blankets up to her chest. "Can I please tell you one thing and then I'll go?" Josh paused when he thought he had Meagan's attention. "I wanted to let you know I had to leave Saturday morning but you were still sleeping and I didn't want to bother you. Oh yeah, and before I forget, nice sweatpants."

"Josh, I'm not angry with you. Honestly I'm not."

"Then why do I get the feeling you want to rip my head off?"

Meagan wanted to hug Ben when he walked into the room.

"Damn, Josh, did you just get home? I thought you were going to be home hours ago. Are you okay?"

"Yeah, I just walked in the door."

"Everything go okay?"

"They took longer to come out than we expected. There were a couple of times I thought we would need to get involved. I think we were all surprised it ended the way it did. So, at the last minute I decided to hang around for a while and catch up with the guys."

Ben quickly glanced from Meagan to Josh as if asking his brother why he was speaking so freely in front of her.

Josh nodded at Ben to show he knew what he was doing. "At the moment, other than being hungry and needing to wash the stink off of me, I'm fine. I have been in these clothes for almost forty hours so I am going to go put away my gear, get cleaned up, and make an egg sandwich. Would you like an egg sandwich, Benny?"

"No thanks, I'll see you both later. I have to be back up in about four hours."

Josh felt terrible for waking his brother. "I'm sorry I woke you up. I'll see you in the morning, and let me know if you need my help with anything. I'll be back in a little while, Meagan. That is if you don't mind?"

Finally alone, Meagan began to settle down and clear her head. Josh wasn't with Jillian after all. He was working, not that she had a clue what his job consisted of and why it was such a secret. Above all, she still couldn't understand why she cared about any of it, especially Josh. She liked and cared about each of them, but in a matter of days they would be nothing more than a sweet memory.

Less than an hour later, Meagan's eyes were closed, but she was wide awake. Like Friday, she didn't need to see Josh to know he was right there beside her. She tried to be discreet when she inhaled the rich scent of his fresh showered body and his toasted egg sandwich. It was nearly impossible for her to withhold her smile when she pictured him sitting in the recliner.

"Aw, don't be mad at me. I'm sorry I scared you."

Meagan remained silent, but was glad when she opened her eyes. For doing nothing to his hair, she thought Josh looked engaging. She adored the way he left it damp and how the top was going every which way.

While holding his egg sandwich, Josh nodded toward the nightstand. "I brought you a piece of banana bread and a glass of milk."

"Thank you. Why are you so nice to me? Is it because you feel sorry for me?"

Josh paused to chew and swallow his food. "Well, there are a lot of reasons. First of all, you haven't given me a reason not to. Second of all, you have been through hell, and I want you to know that not all men are assholes. You deserve to be happy and I know you would help me if I needed it. And I like you. I like you a lot, so I am going to do whatever I can to help you."

Meagan felt her entire face turn countless shades of red. "I wish I knew what to say. Thank you doesn't cut it."

Josh merely grinned and said, "Eat your bread, Miss Dawson."

"I'm sorry I freaked out. I had no right to treat you like that in your house."

"I don't blame you, and you can be sure I won't let it happen again. I'll make sure you know if I get another assignment. But sorry to say, I rarely know how long I will be gone."

"You don't need to do that. Your life is none of my business. I will be gone soon, so can we forget it happened? I will if you will?"

"Uh, well, after the way you saw me tonight I should explain myself. So, can you do me a favor?"

Meagan looked bewildered. "*You* want *me* to do *you* a favor?"

"Yes, please, a very important favor…not so much for me but for the others involved."

"Okay…"

"First, I need to ask you to respect my privacy. I am a private person with a small group of close friends and the fewer who know me, the better. Are we good so far?"

"Yes, of course. Only my mom and pop know I am here."

Josh smiled at Meagan's sincerity. "Thanks. So, I am part of a special team, and protecting *their* confidentiality is as important to me as my own. Are you sure you are following me? I have never had to explain it like this before. People either know me or they don't."

Meagan's eyes suddenly appeared ready to burst from her face. "Oh shit, oh my god, I promise I won't talk. You can trust me, really Josh. I won't tell anyone about you. I won't even tell my parents. I swear. Oh shit."

Josh laughed like he hadn't in quite some time. "I'm not in the CIA, Miss Dawson. I'm not some undercover op. You can tell people you trust, just don't broadcast it. After what you saw tonight, what do you *think* I do?"

Meagan hesitated. "I don't know…something with the police."

"You could say that…" Josh paused then sounded very serious. "I am employed by the state of Montana. My unit or team, as we are more commonly referred to, is a very small division of the Montana Highway Patrol. While we do not patrol like it sounds, our headquarters is located in Helena, just like MHP." Josh looked at Meagan as though he was expecting a question. Then he wondered how she would handle his next point. Focusing on her curious eyes and expression, Josh continued. "Meagan, I will get right to the point to keep it simple for you. I am a rapid response sharpshooter. You saw the S.R.T. on my vest?"

It took a moment for the information to sink in and even longer for Meagan to respond. "What...*you*? No way...but you are such a nice guy. I don't believe it...Oh shit, you are serious."

Josh grinned at Meagan's expected reaction. "Yes, so S.R.T. stands for Special Response Team. I work on a small, elite team with the best group of guys you would ever want to meet." Josh could see Meagan was having a difficult time absorbing his information. "Do you have any questions? Please feel free to ask me anything. I know it can be a shocker."

Meagan feared his answer when she asked, "Can *you* get hurt?"

"The chances of that are low, but it's always possible."

"Uh, I don't know if I can ask. What exactly do *you* do?"

"Yeah sure, for the most part we are responsible for providing support to law enforcement agencies throughout Montana, but we also have clearance to work anywhere in the country."

"Oh my god, so you...have you ever...do you...oh my god, never mind. I'm sorry, it's none of my business, forget it."

Josh took a breath and then went on to answer the question Meagan could not ask. "Yes Meagan, I have had to shoot people. I prefer not to think about how many over the years because I don't think it's important. It is the countless lives we save and protect that matter."

Meagan fell silent as she processed the extraordinary details of Josh's unique career, not to mention his shocking capabilities.

"Are you okay, Miss? Say *something*. I hope I wasn't too harsh."

"Once again, I have no clue what to say to you. Wow, you...you just don't seem like the type...oh my god."

Mindful of Meagan's substantial respect and appreciation for life, Josh imagined how she would react to his next comment. Clearly disappointed he stated, "So much for being on your good guy list now, let alone your friend list."

Meagan didn't think twice about her feelings. "Don't get me wrong, I miss my mom and pop and a few friends, but right now I can't think of anyone I would rather be with. You are one of the few people I feel like I can trust…you and Benny and Pete. Your job doesn't change that. What you do for a living doesn't change *who* you are and what you mean to me. My god, Josh, *you* saved *my* life. No wonder you were so comfortable with Donny and Billy. You knew exactly what you were doing. They didn't stand a chance against you and Benny. Now I know why you didn't shoot them…or me."

It only took a moment for Meagan to reflect upon the few men she dated and compare them to Josh. Although she knew Josh for less than a week, he was as different as fire and ice. He was far more mature and disciplined. While he was noticeably strong, he was also sensitive and incredibly patient. While making the comparisons, Meagan realized it was those extraordinary differences that made her long for the time and opportunity to get to know him better. It was his unusual traits and promising distinctions that roused something deep inside her that she could not describe in any amount of words.

"Meagan, my responsibility to my job and my team are why I couldn't drive you to Gardiner. I hope you understand."

"You aren't responsible for me. You don't need to explain."

"I want *you* to know that I wanted to take you." Josh pointed to the open magazine on the nightstand next to his recliner and grinned. "What did you think of the article?"

"I didn't get a chance to finish it, but so far I would say it's been interesting. I guess it's a good thing you are helping to control the elk population. It sounds like it is necessary for the overall health and survival of the species. Someone has to do it."

"Miss Dawson, are you trying to bullshit me?"

"Sadly I am not, unless there is some way to put an elk on birth control."

Josh chuckled at her comment. "Well I am sad to say I need to call it a night. Not that a lady like you needs it, but I need to get all the beauty sleep I can. I am going to go crawl into my own bed before I invite myself to spend another night with you."

Meagan thought Josh may have just flirted with her and hoped he couldn't see her blushing through her fading bruises.

Before Josh left her room for the night he tenderly took her left hand and smiled. "Try to get some sleep and let me worry about watching and listening for the boogey man. I will sleep with my door open. Just wake me up if you need anything."

"Thank you and goodnight."

"It was my pleasure. Goodnight, sweetheart."

For the first time in several months, Meagan felt comfortable sleeping in the dark.

It was nearly noon by the time Josh made it to the barn and Ben gave him an earful.

"Well, well, well, what's more important? Spending some time with a pretty girl or helping your brother with chores?" Ben teased because he was well aware of how late Josh got home. "All kidding aside, how did she react when you told her about S.R.T.?"

"A lot better than I expected; shocked, but not hateful like I expected. I think we might still be friends."

"I *still* hope this new friend of yours doesn't break your heart."

"You are pathetic, Benny, *and* you have one hell of an imagination. I'd like to know where you come up with this shit."

"I can see the way you look at her. I know that look, Josh. It's the same way you used to look at Jilly years ago."

"As usual you don't know what you're talking about. Get the hell away from me."

Ben was carrying a bucket of brushes back to the tack room when his phone started ringing. "Hey, Josh, can you get my phone? It's probably Mr. Dawson. I told him to try calling back after noon to see if Meagan was awake."

"Yeah sure," Josh replied then went to a nearby coat hook and removed the ringing phone from Ben's jacket. After briefly introducing himself to Meagan's father, Josh explained that he was not in the house, but working in the barn. "If she is awake, can I have her call you back in about ten minutes?"

"I wouldn't be calling if it wasn't important. If she is still sleeping, please wake her up."

"Yes, sir, I'll go up to the house now and have her call you."

"Mr. Mackenzie, I will be coming to get Meagan. Is it okay to call this number in a few days for directions?"

"Oh…yes, sir, this number is fine. I will let my brother know to expect your call."

After ending his conversation with Mr. Dawson, Josh wished he didn't have to tell Meagan about the call. He understood why she did not want to go back to Illinois and now it looked as though she would be doing just that. Once in the house he untied his work boots, told Aunt Bess to skip lunch and took his time walking up the stairs.

Meagan had just finished blow drying her hair after opting for a short shower instead of a time-consuming bath. She heard someone knocking on the bedroom door and thought it was Bess.

"Miss Dawson, are you awake?"

"Oh, Josh…yes, come in." Trying to cool down after her shower, Meagan was wearing her bicycle shorts and her only T-shirt.

Josh was so busy admiring Meagan's fresh and lively appearance that he did not notice the discolored yellow and green patches plaguing her thighs. "I can't believe how great you are doing. You look so much better. How do you feel?"

"I feel better, but I am bored out of my mind."

"I've been there a few times myself. I hate sitting around. You are more than welcome to come out to the horse barn. We always have plenty of work and I'm sure we can find something for you to do."

"Really, I don't know how much help I will be, but I'll try."

Josh was laughing so hard he could hardly speak. "I was just kidding. You're in no shape to be working with us. Actually, it doesn't matter what kind of shape you're in, I would never let you do our chores." Josh figured by the despicable way Meagan was glaring at him that they were on the verge of a gender war. Desperate to protect himself from her feminine wrath, he offered her Ben's phone. "Oh here, call your dad." Josh held Meagan's eyes as he smiled and handed her the phone. "Take your time. I will be back in a few minutes."

"You can stay, Josh. I'm sure this won't take long."

"It's okay; I need to go wash my face." Josh wished there was something he could do to change what Meagan's father was going to tell her. While washing the grime and sweat from his face, he couldn't remember a single time when Jillian offered to help him in the barn. Being the only girl with three older brothers she had been privileged since birth, which spared her from any required physical exertion. If Josh asked her to do anything in the barn, she would playfully refuse by saying she might break a nail.

When Josh returned five minutes later, Meagan was sitting on the far edge of the bed with her back to the door and facing his recliner. She had placed Ben's phone on the nightstand closest to the door. "Meagan, is everything okay?" Josh asked already certain that it wasn't.

Without turning to face Josh, Meagan tried to sound truthful. "He was just checking on me, and my mom wanted to say hi. Benny told him what happened."

"You are very lucky to have a mother and father who care about you."

"Yes, I am."

"So, why do I get the feeling something is bothering you?"

"Nothing is bothering me."

"Really, then turn around, look at me and say that."

"Oh, Josh, not again. Please don't make me do that now."

"Here, I will make it easier." Josh walked to the far side of the bed and squeezed between the front of the recliner and Meagan's knees. Then he squatted down and softly embraced her bare knees between his thighs. While he wanted to be close, he didn't want to upset her.

"Please, Josh, don't. I don't feel like…"

Josh could see her eyes transfixed on his pistol as it rested in its usual place on his right thigh. He was not sure if her staring was still out of fear, or if she was just trying to avoid eye contact, but he decided to ignore it. "I don't think I need to tell you how honest I have been with you. I will only ask you one more time. You can tell me what's really going on or you can tell me to get lost and I will go back to my chores. The choice is yours."

Meagan knew Josh had her and at the very least, she owed him her honesty. "Okay, the jobs are no longer available." Trying to sound indifferent she met his understanding eyes. "Pop will be here Sunday to pick me up, probably Sunday evening."

"What, this Sunday? It's far too risky…oh shit."

"You can stop worrying about me now. I am not your responsibility."

"Someone in their right mind needs to look out for your best interests." Josh stood up, took his phone from the front pocket of his blue jeans and then squatted back down.

"Joshua, what are you doing?"

"What does it look like I'm doing?"

"Oh no, you can't be serious. You're not calling Pop? What are you going to tell him? He doesn't even know you."

"I don't care if he knows me or not. I am going to tell him I have worked hostage situations that started out just like yours, with someone ending a relationship. And if I was a father, I would have no problem watching an asshole like Jeremy Constadine die right before my eyes. But, what I couldn't handle is watching the asshole hold a knife or gun on my daughter and hope the worst that happens is she winds up wearing the asshole's brains. And I will tell him that is exactly what can happen if you go back to Illinois. So for your sake, I hope like hell I am wrong, but if I'm not…I also hope the sharpshooters in Illinois are as good as we are in Montana, because I don't think I would make it there in time."

Josh's words shook Meagan to her very core and made her stomach turn. While she completely agreed with him, she would not admit that she cared too much about him and his family and Peter to stay. She held her breath, peered into Josh's taunt face and declared, "I'm leaving on Sunday."

Josh was so aggravated he practically jumped to his feet. He tried not to lose his temper as he walked to the bedroom door. Before he disappeared from sight, he stopped and turned to face Meagan. "Meagan Dawson, you are really something. Knowing you has been a pleasure."

Once Josh left the room, Meagan narrowly made the short distance to the bathroom, kneeled over the toilet and heaved.

On his way back to the barn Josh stopped to talk to Bess who was dusting the living room. "Please see if you can talk some sense into her. Maybe she will listen to you. We only have a few days before Mr. Dawson leaves Illinois."

"I can try, but it sounds like the lass has set her mind."

When Josh returned to the barn, he was fit to be tied. Ben had just finished trimming all of the horses' hooves and was exiting a stall when Josh went stomping in his direction. "Damn it, Benny! What the hell is with Meagan? Why won't she listen to us? After everything she has been through, why is she still so damn stubborn?" Still needing to vent his frustration, Josh kicked an empty feed bucket to the far end of the barn.

"Why don't you start by telling me what's going on." Other than concerning Meagan, Ben had no idea what had triggered Josh's unusual outburst, but it had to be serious.

"She is going back home. Mr. Dawson will be here Sunday to pick her up. Can you believe she would do that?"

"Well, we can't hold her hostage."

"This is no fucking time to be funny, Benny."

"I know that, but you don't want to hear the truth either."

Josh glared at Ben while he anticipated the answer.

"She likes you as much as you like her, and she really believes she is putting us at risk."

"Aw Benny, I already know *that*, and she already knows the three of us are perfectly capable of handling one sick motherfucker."

"Are we, do you know anything about the asshole? Just because *you* think you can take him...and I would never say that you couldn't. We don't know anything about Jeremy Constadine."

"Okay, enough said. Will you try talking to her? *After all you are her older brother.* I think she might listen to you."

"It won't do any good. She is putting our safety ahead of her own and you can't blame her for wanting to do the right thing. I told you not to get hung up on her and did you listen to me? Hell no, why listen to your older brother? What would *I* know about falling for a girl?"

"Shut up, Benny, we only have a few days. I'm sure you can come up with something good."

Just as Bess expected and explained to Josh, Meagan had already made up her mind and wasn't about to change it for any reason. "Thank you for everything, Aunt Bess." Meagan had tears in her eyes because she wanted to stay so badly, it hurt. "Maybe someday things will be better. If everything works out may I come for a visit?"

"Aye, of course ya can. I will look forward to seein' ya soon." Bess understood Meagan's reasons for leaving and feeling like she had no choice. "We're havin' baked chicken fur supper. Are ya feelin' strong enough to join us at the table?"

"It *sounds* delicious, but please excuse me; I don't think I can keep anything down."

"Ya need to eat somethin'. I'll bring ya some soup after supper." Bess went back to her household duties and Meagan wrapped herself up in her blankets as pain consumed her body.

Over Bess's baked chicken and roasted potatoes, Ben and Bess began the meal by discussing Meagan. Josh, on the other hand, remained completely silent and hardly picked at his food.

"The poor lass, no wonder she's been throwin' up all day."

When Josh finally made his way into the conversation neither Ben nor Bess expected his unusual reaction. "She's getting sick again?" Josh wasted no time jumping up and scraping his dinner into the trash can. "Damn it this sucks!" He yelled and went out to sit on the front porch swing.

"He may not have known the lass fur long, but I think he has feelins fur her."

"You and me both, Aunt Bess. You and me both. He is not himself and hasn't been in days."

When Josh returned to the kitchen, Ben was upstairs with Molly Girl and Bess was adding leftover baked chicken to a bowl of soup. Unusually grim, Josh approached his aunt. "Aunt Bess, do you still believe everything happens for a reason?"

"Aye, with all my heart."

"Then why is Meagan going back to Illinois where she is likely going to get hurt or worse when she could stay here?"

"Trust yur patience, lad, and hope fur the best. Fur now, can ya please try to get her to eat some soup? She's in a bad way."

"It's obviously a waste of time. She isn't going to listen to me."

"Joshua Mathew..."

"Yes, ma'am, I'll get right on it."

Finding the guest room door wide open, Josh initially thought Meagan was sleeping. Her eyes were closed tight, her lips were parted and her breathing was in perfect rhythm. After placing the bowl of hot chicken and potato soup on the night stand, he squatted down beside her. He was grateful to see a faint smile and gently moved her tousled hair from her eyes. "Please eat some soup or Aunt Bess is going to let me have it."

Meagan opened her gloomy eyes and gazed deeply into Josh's tense face. She wished she could memorize the way he was looking at her so she could picture him when she was too afraid to sleep. "Please don't be mad at me," she pleaded barely over a whisper.

"Don't leave and make me wonder if you are okay."

"Bess said I can come for a visit. As soon as I can get my name changed and I know it's safe again I will call."

"We both know changing your name takes time. He will find you as soon as you start the process. It could actually do more harm than good. I know my opinion isn't important, but changing your name is not going to solve anything." Before Josh said something he would regret, which was what name she would use in her obituary, he bit his tongue. "Good night, Meagan, it's been a long day and I have to be up early to help Benny. I'll see you tomorrow."

"I'm really sorry, Josh. Please try to understand."

"Try to eat some soup. I wouldn't want you to starve to death before you go home." Unable to ignore the heavy pain surging throughout his chest, Josh couldn't help but think it was going to get worse before it got better.

It was nearly two o'clock Tuesday afternoon and Bess had not seen or heard from Meagan. Naturally concerned, she decided to tap on the closed bedroom door. "Are ya awake, lass?"

Meagan forced herself out of bed and went to let Bess in.

"Ah, lass, ya look awful. Are ya still gettin' sick?"

"No, ma'am, not since late last night. I'm sorry I couldn't eat much of the soup." Meagan thought she had to look and smell god awful. "You must think I am so lazy. I have done nothing but lay around every day since I got here."

"Stop talkin' like a fool. I know ya have been too sick or beaten to get out of bed since ya got here. How are ya feelin'?"

"I'm fine, thank you." Meagan didn't tell Bess that it wasn't her battered body that hurt. Her ache festered somewhere deep inside. It was a hopeless, agonizing feeling of dread that refused to release its wrenching grip. No medication or amount of bed rest could cure her pain.

"Benjamin and Joshua will be out checkin' fences till supper. So if yur feelin' up to it, yur welcome to soak for a time and come sit with me in the kitchen."

"It won't do me much good to bathe. I am out of everything: shampoo, conditioner, soap, and worst of all, toothpaste. Pop isn't picking me up for five days and I need things now."

"The lads are busy today, but I'll see if one of them can take ya to the drugstore tomorrow. Today, use my bathroom and help yurself to whatever ya need."

"Aunt Bess..." Meagan sounded embarrassed. "I am going to need something that I don't think you have." Meagan looked at Bess as if to say, please don't make me tell you it's that time of the month.

"Aye, say no more. I'll make sure that ya get to the store tomorrow. If Joshua and Benjamin are both busy, I'll find another way."

Meagan couldn't believe how swiftly the afternoon vanished. She enjoyed her conversation with Bess so much that she didn't notice the time or the dimming sun until Bess flipped on the kitchen light.

"'Tis goin' to be dark soon. They should be home any time."

"Doesn't it get more dangerous after dark?"

"That it does, but they took Benjamin's truck instead of their horses and they're very careful." Bess retrieved four dinner plates from a lower cabinet and set them on the counter. "I hope yur feelin' up to havin' some pot roast."

As usual, Meagan wondered what kind of animal they were eating. "It smells too good to turn down," she commented then picked up the stack of plates and set the table the way she thought she remembered it. After setting the silverware and adding a thick, paper napkin, she heard Ben's truck pull up behind the house.

"They're home." Bess announced, then looked at Meagan and smiled.

9

While Ben and Josh had to stop in the mudroom, Molly Girl casually strolled through the kitchen. By the tone of their voices, Ben was giving Josh a hard time about something and it continued into the kitchen. "Hello, ladies. Wow, look at you, Sissy. It's good to see you getting around. We would have been home a lot sooner if Josh would have spent as much time working as he did talking to Jillian."

"Hey now, you heard me tell her to stop calling me every time she called. And I told you I would turn my damn phone off if I could."

"And, *I* told *you* to give me your damn phone, so *I* could tell her to stop calling and let us do our work."

Josh's silence only proved his brother's point.

Meagan didn't say a word from where she leaned against the kitchen counter. She found it bizarre the two men were carrying on a perfectly normal conversation in a kitchen while each of them clutched a camouflage backpack and Josh held what she presumed to be a rifle. But as filthy as the men were and oddly wearing baseball hats, she thought any woman in her right mind would think they were two of the most sexually appealing modern-day cowboys they had ever seen.

Bess spoke up before the brothers resumed their latest argument. "The pot roast is done, but it can wait for yas to clean up."

When Josh took a step, his phone yelped twice, reminding Meagan of a siren.

"Give me your damn phone," Ben demanded.

Rather than giving in, Josh handed Ben the rifle, pulled out his phone, and grinned. "It's only P.D."

"Tell him he just saved you from buying a new phone and don't forget to ask him if he can help me tomorrow." Ben snagged Josh's backpack and headed upstairs carrying both backpacks and the gun. "I'll put your stuff on your bed."

"Thanks," Josh replied, then turned his attention to Peter. "Okay, P.D., what's up?" While listening to Peter, Josh maneuvered his way along the counter until he was directly across from Meagan. From where he rested the only thing separating the two of them was the kitchen table.

"I need to bring you the money for Jillian's ring and I got your message about Meagan. Would it be okay if I swing by there in about an hour to bring your wad of cash and talk to her?"

"Yeah sure, we'll be here." Josh focused on Meagan. "You will just be wasting your breath. I already tried."

Even Bess could see the unnerving way Josh was staring at Meagan. He was making her very uncomfortable and now Peter was coming for a visit.

"So, P.D., what are you doing tomorrow?"

"Nothing at the moment. I left the day open to take Meagan to Gardiner."

"Benny wants to know if you can help him finish the fence we didn't get to today. I would help him myself, but I need to run to B.A.T.'s and out to the canyon. I need to shoot."

"Sure, I can use some fresh air. The weather sounds perfect. You just worry about practicing, and you might want to include a trip to the bank. I wouldn't leave this much money lying around."

"Sounds like a plan. Thanks, P.D., and I'll see you later."

"Okay, see you in about an hour."

Josh was well-accomplished when it came to watching people. Therefore, it was nothing for him to stare at Meagan throughout his entire phone conversation without blinking an eye. Meagan, on the other hand, was looking at everything from the cookie jar to her left to the calendar hanging on the wall to her right. Josh knew she was uncomfortable, but he hadn't seen her all day and couldn't take his eyes off of her.

"Joshua," Bess said firmly, trying to rescue Meagan.

Josh still refused to let up. Without looking away from Meagan, he cracked a full-size grin as if he were about to laugh. "Yes, ma'am?"

"Joshua Mathew, go get yur shower before I make ya spend the night with the horses." Bess got a kick out of the humorous way Josh was flirting with Meagan, but felt compelled to defend her.

While Meagan thought Josh looked impressive in his faded, dirty jeans and worn-out T-shirt, she wished he would listen to Bess so she could take a breath.

Josh let out a playful chuckle then gallantly tipped his hat to Meagan. "Yes, ma'am, I won't be long."

When Josh left the kitchen, Meagan was certain Bess had to notice her sigh. She pressed her sweating palms against her blue jeans and seemed completely embarrassed. "Why does he do that?"

Bess smiled and replied, "Ah, lass, ya don't need me to tell ya that."

Immediately following dinner, Meagan let out another sigh of relief then helped Bess clear the table. Although Josh looked her way countless times while they discussed everything from Ben's champion Black Angus bull to Bess's cooking, he let her eat in peace. However, something told her that with Peter coming over, she was far from off the hook.

Meagan was following Bess to the living room when Bess whispered that she hadn't forgotten about the drug store. When Meagan saw the Mackenzies' sizeable, yet charming living room, she was intrigued. As if the country atmosphere wasn't inviting enough, Josh and Ben respectfully went to their feet. Not sure where to sit, Meagan was grateful when Josh came to meet her. Whereas neither Bess nor Ben batted an eye, she was shy and blushed when Josh took her by the hand.

"Come sit with me. P.D. should be here any time." When Josh guided Meagan to a tan faux-leather sofa, he felt her trembling hand. "Can I get you a toddy?"

"Aren't you on call?"

"Yes I am, but…"

"Then no thank you, I'm fine."

"I'm glad to see you are eating again. Now if we can just find a way to help you relax."

Before Meagan could even think of relaxing, she heard Peter park his Tahoe and knock twice before stepping into the entry way. Regardless of his impending lecture, she couldn't be happier to see him. She smiled when he greeted Bess with the usual kiss on the cheek, then playfully grabbed Ben's bicep on his way past.

"Hi, you look great," Peter grinned, then crouched down and offered Meagan his hand. "I'm glad to see you're getting better. I knew it wouldn't take *you* long."

Showing her deepest sincerity, Meagan took his warm hand and replied, "Thank you, Pete. It's always nice to see you."

"Thanks and just keep doing what you're doing. You are obviously doing something right." Peter slowly released Meagan's hand then sat in the open spot next to Josh. Acting covert, he removed a manila envelope from inside his brown leather jacket and lowered his voice to avoid disturbing Bess. "Holy shit, Mackey, I didn't know the rock you had me carrying around like a cheap piece of glass cost you more than two months of my salary. What the hell are they paying you guys these days? I want your job."

"I think you forgot while I am getting paid to sit here and wait for my phone to ring, I also have to drop whatever I am doing, grab my gear, and head out the door when it does. It's only my opinion, but I don't see that working for you."

"Well my friend, spring is here. In no time your phone will ring and you will be working your ass off for every dollar."

"It's about time. It's been a long winter."

"I just can't get over you spending that much on a damn ring."

"You know, Jillian, everything has to be the best. That's probably why she wants it back."

"What, no way, if you take her back again we are done. I'm serious, Mackey. It's me or her."

"She must have called me twenty times today. She wants the ring back and asked if we are still going to the Spring Fling together."

Meagan couldn't help but overhear the conversation and nearly giggled when Peter sounded frantic.

"You're just fucking with me, right? Tell me you're just fucking with me."

"I'll spare you the bullshit and skip to the best part. When I told her the ring would cost her ten grand and assured her that I would not beat the shit out of whoever gets stuck taking her to the dance, she asked if I cared if she went with Brad."

"No shit, Brad Rutherford?"

"Yep, the same asshole you tried to convince me she was screwing around with in Billings and I wouldn't listen."

"Who could forget, but it all worked out. You broke my nose, I busted a couple or your ribs. It could have been worse."

Utterly stunned, Meagan spoke without thinking. "Joshua, you hit Pete, your best friend?"

"I sure did, but not as hard as I could have. And then *he* let me have it, right in my lower ribs. He wasn't nearly as considerate as I was."

Peter looked at Meagan and grinned. "You should have been there, Meagan, it was comical."

"Yeah it was," Josh confirmed.

"By the time we finished slugging it out, we were both rolling on the ground and whining like two-year-olds."

"We sure were," Josh agreed again. "But after we caught our breath, we talked it out."

"And apologized. It was no big deal," Peter claimed still smiling.

"That's right, no big deal," Josh said and elbowed Peter in the forearm.

Meagan was just beginning to feel safe from Peter's wrath when he stood, took off his jacket and looked at her. "What do you say we get some fresh air?"

Meagan looked at Josh and froze. She never expected to be alone with Peter.

"Put on his jacket, Miss. Take it easy on her, P.D. She's been getting sick and it's her first day out of her room."

"At least I shouldn't have to worry about chasing her," Peter teased and helped Meagan into his jacket. Then, he escorted her out the front door and helped her into the privacy of his SUV. After he got into the driver's side, he closed his door and gave her a friendly smile.

Meagan was in awe as she admired the interior of the fully loaded vehicle. "Wow, how do you remember what everything does? It would take me forever."

"It took me a few years, but I eventually figured most of it out," Peter fibbed, then started the Tahoe and set the heat on low. "Are you comfortable?" he asked and turned his body to face her.

"Yes, thank you. I'm just nervous."

"I'm sorry. You don't need to be nervous. I just want to talk to you." Peter paused, and sympathetically warned Meagan, "I don't think you are going to like what I have to say, but I think you should hear me out."

"Okay..." Meagan replied, thinking she could trust Peter.

"I brought you out here because Josh will bust my nose again if he hears me telling you his business. So, you know about his job?"

"Yes. He explained it to me Sunday night. He said he works for the state of Montana. That he is a...a sharpshooter." Meagan couldn't believe Josh's occupation, let alone say it out loud.

"Good, then let me start by saying in our line of work, Josh and I have both pissed people off and received our share of death threats. Our situations are obviously different than yours, but do you understand me so far?"

Completely absorbed in Peter's words, Meagan simply replied, "Yes."

"All right, for reasons I won't go into now, Josh is the number-two shooter in the state. His team leader is currently ranked at number one."

"Oh my god..."

"I am telling you all this because I want you to understand Jeremy Constadine does not faze us in the least. Also, on a positive note, the State of Montana needs and appreciates S.R.T., Josh's team, so they watch over them very closely.

Local deputies and troopers like me routinely patrol this area. Our friends, neighbors, and local business owners also keep an eye out. Even the internet is closely monitored for potential threats. But most importantly, we all look out for each other." Peter pointed to the semi-automatic pistol he was wearing on his right hip. "We don't wear these things around like jewelry because they are comfortable and pretty to look at. We are always careful."

"Is that why Josh acted the way he did when he found me in the barn and then called you to question me? Because he thought I was after him?"

"Exactly. He thought you might have come here looking for him. Meagan, look on the dash in front of you. What do you see?"

"Um…it looks like a file."

"It's your file, and if what I just told you about this area being patrolled night and day is not enough to convince you to stay, then look in your file and take a trip down memory lane."

Meagan's eyes welled with tears and she stared at the file.

"I am going to tell you something because I think it's for your own good and trust me, I don't like saying it any more than you like hearing it."

"Okay," Meagan said, already disturbed knowing Peter saw her file.

"Meagan, if you go home, we both know there is a chance your parents could find you like you were in those pictures, or worse. I think we can also agree it's better to have Constadine come here to Montana and go after us than to risk him going after your parents. Do you think they are capable of stopping him from hurting you? Would he hurt or kill them if they get in his way?"

Meagan spoke through her quiet crying, "He already threatened to hurt them, right before I broke up with him. He said I would live to regret it, but I don't think he expected me to survive."

"Do you see my point? Do you honestly believe you should go back to Illinois?"

"I don't know what to think. And besides, it's too late. Pop is picking me up Sunday."

"I understand this is a big decision. Pardon my language, but to say it is fucked up would be an understatement. I am only asking you to think about what I told you. I won't tell Josh you are rethinking your decision. He will just pressure you to stay because he thinks you are safer here. It's your life, your family, and your decision. Do you think you can give me your final answer by Thursday evening, so that if you do change your mind, I can call your dad?

After I explain everything to him from my point of view, I think he will agree with me."

"Okay, I will let you know Thursday."

"Perfect. If you decide to stay we will talk more about keeping you safe."

"I need a job, Pete. I won't stay without a job."

"That shouldn't be a problem. I know a nice family who could use your help. One last thing. I have heard, and even a fool can see it—Josh cares a lot about you. He will try talking you into staying until the last possible minute. If you change your mind, be sure it's what you want."

"Okay. Pete, I am so tired of being scared."

"I know. Take it one day at a time. For now, I am going to tell Josh that you have made up your mind and won't budge."

"Okay." Meagan looked into Peter's gray green eyes and shyly asked one last question. "Am I allowed to hug you?"

"Absolutely. One of the perks of my job is an occasional hug from a pretty lady." Peter raised his arms so Meagan could embrace him, then held her until she let go.

When Peter and Meagan went back in the house, Josh was the only one awake. Meagan tossed Peter's jacket on the back of Ben's recliner and hurried up to the guest room.

"What can I say, the lady is tough. She is Irish to the bone and insists on going home."

"I warned you about wasting your breath."

"Yes you did. What time does Benny need me in the morning?"

"He has a few chores, so be here between six and six thirty."

"Sounds good. Get in some good practice and I'll see you at dinner. Sorry I couldn't be more help with Meagan."

"No problem, thanks again for helping with the ring."

"My pleasure and don't you dare give in to her again."

After letting Peter out, Josh went upstairs to talk to Meagan. When he stepped into her room she was lying on top of her covers and crying. "I was hoping he wouldn't get to you," Josh said and sat on the bed right next to her. "P.D. has never been one to sugarcoat anything. I'm sorry, but I'm sure you know he was only trying to help."

"He has my file." Meagan sat up and looked down at the quilt. "Have *you* seen it?"

Wishing he had no scruples, Josh solemnly admitted, "Yes."

"Josh, you have to let me go. I am not sure how you feel about me, but I should tell you that I…I don't want…I can't ever…" Meagan struggled to make her point. "I am afraid…of men. I will never…"

"Okay stop, I get it. May I tell you what I think and feel?"

Meagan nodded.

Josh turned and lay on his back with his head beside Meagan's feet. Taking his time, he looked at the ceiling as if searching for the right words. "*I think* once you find the right guy, a guy who is patient and willing to take his time with you, a guy who deserves you, *you* will be so crazy about him that *you* won't be able to keep your hands off of him. Now, how I feel about you…I guess I won't have the unforgettable opportunity to show you since you are leaving."

"Josh…"

"Yeah?"

"I hope *you* find someone who deserves you."

Josh sat back up and peered deep into Meagan's eyes. "Aw, thank you, and don't worry about me. I am a patient guy and I'm sure my wait will be well worth it. So, I hear you need someone to take you shopping tomorrow?"

"Yes."

"Well, I can take you anywhere you need to go, but then you will be stuck with me for the rest of the day, probably until dinner, and I guarantee you are not going to like it."

"Beggars can't be choosers."

"Trust me, sweetheart, going with me tomorrow would be your last choice."

"It can't be that bad and I promise I won't complain."

"Meagan, I need to go to the bank and the gun shop. After that I need to go spend at least two hours target shooting."

"That's fine. I will bring a few crossword puzzle books."

"Okay, I have to leave here by nine."

"I'll be ready. Thanks, Josh."

Josh slowly climbed off of the bed. "Don't thank me yet. Pleasant dreams, Miss, and I'll see you in the morning."

Meagan hardly slept a wink as Peter's words bounced around her mind. Her feelings for the Mackenzies and Peter were immeasurable, but imagining what Jeremy would do to her parents brought back terrifying memories.

10

Still tired at eight in the morning, Meagan took a fast shower and dressed in her only pair of blue jeans. She pulled her hair back into a wavy and lengthy pony tail, grabbed a couple of puzzle books, and headed to the kitchen. She smiled when the aroma of fresh coffee preceded Bess's familiar kind greeting.

"Good mornin', lass, did ya sleep well?"

"Yes thank you, and you?"

"Very well, thanks, would ya like somethin' to eat?"

Josh appeared rushed when he hurried into the kitchen and cut into the conversation. "Thanks, Aunt Bess, but don't worry about us. We will find something to eat in town. Enjoy the peace and quiet and we will see you later."

"I won't be havin' any of that. Mrs. Rollins called and said she is havin' lunch for any of us who want to come by and work on our quilts. Mrs. Calhoun is pickin' me up in an hour."

"Well then, happy quilting and please give all the ladies my best," Josh smiled at his aunt and kissed her on the cheek.

"I will and I hope yas have a good day," Bess said, smiling from ear to ear.

"Bye, Aunt Bess," Meagan blurted out as Josh guided her to the front door by her left arm. Trying not to stare, she thought Josh looked amazing in his black bomber-style jacket and blue jeans, and his cologne was equally appealing. Once they stepped outside, she sounded concerned, "Did I hold you up?"

"Not at all, I just wanted to leave before Aunt Bess starts cooking us breakfast."

It was the first time Meagan saw the front of the house and inside Josh's Jeep. After he opened the passenger door for her, she climbed in and was instantly impressed by the striking black leather interior. "This is nice, what is it?" she asked after Josh started the Jeep.

"Thanks, it's a Rubicon, last year's model." Josh replied, and reached behind his seat. "It is way too warm for that coat. Put this on," he suggested, and set his black hoodie on Meagan's lap. "And before I forget, there is something in the right pocket that belongs to you."

Josh was almost to the end of the driveway when Meagan pulled on his hoodie and reached into the pocket. "Oh wow, my knife." She said and looked at him with ample surprise.

"Yes, and just to be on the safe side you can put on the hat and sun glasses in my glove compartment. I doubt you need them where we are going, but it can't hurt."

"Are you trying to hide me?"

"If I thought you needed a disguise, I would have told you to write me a list of things you wanted and left you at the house."

Meagan took notice of the white MHP lettering on the black baseball hat. Then she inched her lengthy, thick ponytail through the back of the hat. Glad it wasn't pouring rain, she put on Josh's polished black sport-frame sunglasses. "Will this work?" She asked after turning to face him.

Josh gave her a sly smile and raised his eyebrows, "I like it."

Meagan felt her face turn red and shyly looked away. She forced herself not to look at Josh all the way to the bank.

Following an unusually long delay depositing the money from Jillian's ring, Josh drove to the drugstore. "What the hell, this place is as busy as the bank." After scanning the entire area for anything suspicious Josh parked the Jeep. "Do you want me to come in with you?"

"Thank you, but I'm fine."

"Okay, I'll wait right here." Josh went around to the passenger side of the Jeep and opened the door for Meagan. "Take all the time you need. We aren't in any hurry."

"Thank you, but you don't need to do that."

"You're welcome. Come get me if you need me."

Meagan wasted no time selecting and paying for the products she needed. When she exited the store, Josh was leaning against the Jeep's driver side door with his arms and ankles crossed. He was smiling and slowly nodding his head in approval as she approached. "Josh, why are you looking at me like that? Did I do something?" Meagan sounded puzzled.

"Nope, not a thing," he replied and had Meagan set her bags behind his seat. Then, once again he opened her door and said, "Ladies first."

Meagan couldn't remember when a man had treated her so well, especially when they weren't even dating. She wondered if Jillian missed Josh when he pulled out of the drug store parking lot and likely headed toward the gun shop.

She was so elated to be outdoors and getting her strength back that she didn't care where he took her. The generous touch of spring and stimulating time with Josh was exactly what she needed to heal her mind, body, and soul.

"So, Miss Dawson," Josh said as he temporarily took his eyes off the truck in front of him and glanced her way. "What did you do back in the Land of Lincoln?"

Trying to appear serious, Meagan fixed her eyes on the same truck. "Well, to relieve some of my boredom I spent the last few years as a serial killer. I preyed on attractive men in their early thirties with light brown hair and hazel eyes, and preferably no more than six feet tall."

"That sounds like an interesting and rewarding hobby. What did you do to pay the bills?"

To Meagan, the twenty-minute ride to the gun shop felt more like five minutes. Wanting to hear more about Josh, she explained how she co-owned and operated a pet shop until right before she left Illinois.

"With you being an animal lover that must have been perfect for you."

"Yes, and when I wasn't stalking my next male victim I volunteered at our community animal shelter. I had a great time exercising the dogs."

"I am very impressed. Our society could use more caring and dedicated homicidal maniacs like you." Josh's grin faded when they arrived at the gun shop. "Why is everyone and their damn brother at B.A.T.'s…and on a Wednesday?" He nonchalantly canvassed the parking lot and stopped behind a county patrol vehicle. "I know everyone here and my buddy Timmy is driving that truck, so you can wait here if you want to."

"Oh, do you *want* me to wait out here for you?"

"I assumed being surrounded by guns would make you uncomfortable, but it's up to you."

"So, you don't mind being seen with me?"

"Of course not, and feel free to take off my glasses."

"I think I should leave them on," Meagan frowned and pointed at her face.

"I would tell you how great you look without them, but I don't want to embarrass you."

Meagan no sooner put away the glasses and Josh was opening her door.

"Just tell me if you want to come back out," Josh said when they neared the door. Feeling the urge to hold Meagan's hand, he assumed the gesture would evoke evil looks and false innuendos she didn't deserve. Even if she was leaving, he could not allow Meagan to become the scapegoat for his breakup with Jillian.

Right before Josh opened the door to the business, Meagan caught a glimpse of a simple sign that spelled out, *WELCOME TO BLAKE AND TINA'S*. Subsequent to entering the shop an electronic tone signaled their arrival. Then, seemingly on cue, everyone near the entrance turned their heads to see who came in. When each person who glanced their way nodded or smiled at Josh, his popularity was evident. Almost immediately Meagan spotted a cute young deputy leaning against a display case in the far back corner of the store. Not quite sure, she thought the deputy might have motioned for Josh.

"If you're feeling up to it I would like to introduce you to a friend."

"I'm fine, take your time." Meagan watched Josh and the blond, blue-eyed deputy shake hands and pat each other on the back like longtime friends.

"How is it going, Timmy? Are you staying busy?"

"Nothing we can't handle."

"Good for you, Deputy Ashford, I would like you to meet Meagan Dawson. Meagan, I would like to introduce Deputy Tim Ashford."

"It's a pleasure to meet you, Miss Dawson."

"Please, call me Meagan."

"Welcome to Montana, Meagan, and please call me Timmy or Tim."

"Thank you, Tim."

"So, Mackey, where the hell have you been? I haven't seen you in here for at least what, two or three weeks?"

"Just sitting around babysitting my phone."

"Have you had anything yet?"

"I got called out Saturday morning with Brody, Andy, and Shane. We took turns napping and watching the grass grow."

"Sure you did," Deputy Ashford stated with obvious doubt. "How many hours did you put in this time?"

"I think it was twelve the first watch and fourteen the second."

"I don't know if I could do your job—staying awake, let alone alert."

"Good, because you are my protection."

"You know I have to ask. Are the rumors I'm hearing true, or am I an idiot for asking?"

"Well that depends. What are *you* hearing?"

"That you called off the engagement and Jillian is not adjusting nearly as well as you are," Tim said and glanced toward Meagan.

"It was a mutual decision and I am fine with being single again."

Deputy Ashford looked at Meagan without moving his head, as if expecting Josh to understand his inference. "You aren't seeing *anyone*?"

Josh fought his urge to laugh at Tim's horrible job of implying he was romantically involved with Meagan. "Nope, I'm sorry to say that part of the rumor is a far cry from the truth. Meagan is going back to Illinois on Sunday, not that I wouldn't mind if..." Josh had his back to the door and stopped talking when someone entering the building activated the tone. By the expression on Tim's face, Josh concluded it was someone he didn't care for.

"Aw shit, Mackey, I still have twenty minutes left on my break and the closest unit is..."

"Who came in, Timmy?"

"Lucas and Collin. Mackey, try to stay out of trouble."

"Take it easy, Timmy. You know better than to worry about those two. They probably saw my Jeep and came to say hello." Josh was being so overly sarcastic that even Meagan picked up on it.

"Yeah well, I have a bad feeling."

"Relax and finish your break. I need to give my list to Blake and see if he has what I want."

"Okay, I'll be here if you need me. That doesn't mean I want you to piss them off."

When Josh thought they were a safe distance from Tim, he asked Meagan's opinion. "He is such a good kid. How old do you think Timmy is?"

"Um...fifteen?"

Josh laughed at Meagan's exaggeration. "No, he's twenty-three and started when he was barely twenty-one. The same way P.D. and I started out."

"Wow that is young. Josh, is something wrong?"

"What makes you think something is wrong?"

"Even I can tell something..."

"Nothing is wrong. Two of Jilly's brothers came in. They are just a couple of thugs with a rich daddy. I am going to get what I came for and leave." Josh rested his hand against the back of Meagan's arm and guided her to a lengthy glass display case that contained a multitude of handguns.

Meagan watched Josh single out one particular pistol and study it through the glass. In awe over the marked price of $480.00, she whispered to Josh, "I had no idea guns were so expensive."

Josh straightened back up and offered his explanation. "Guns are like anything else you buy. You get what you pay for. I could save a few hundred dollars by buying just any generic piece of crap, but I would not get nearly the same level of performance. A gun is not a pair of shoes or a purse, someone's life may very well depend on spending the extra money."

"What can I do for you, Mackenzie?" A man who reminded Meagan of her father and appeared to be about the same age approached Josh.

"I thought I would pay your mortgage for the month."

"That's mighty kind of you. I appreciate your generosity. I see you are looking at the Shield, but since when are you interested in a nine?"

"Oh, it's not for me."

"I didn't think so." The man winked at Josh, removed the smaller, black pistol from the case, and laid it on top of the glass counter. "The grip is perfect for a woman. It's compact and light, and it's easy to handle. If Tina was here and not at home babysitting our teething grandson, she would tell you this is her favorite hand gun. But I guess I don't have to sell you on the M&P. You already have the .45," Blake gestured toward Josh's right hip.

Meagan had no idea Josh was carrying his pistol. The black bomber he was wearing stopped just below his waist and did a perfect job of concealing the weapon.

"Yeah, I'm more than satisfied with both of mine. I'll take it."

"Great, do you also need the usual goodies?"

"Actually, I made you a list." Josh pulled a folded piece of paper from the upper left pocket of his bomber and handed it to Blake.

"Wow, you *are* making my house payment."

Meagan watched as Josh reached into the right rear pocket of his blue jeans, pulled out his wallet, and placed two plastic cards beside the pistol. "You know me, Blake, always glad to help out where I can."

"Yes sir, Mr. Mackenzie, I can always count on you. I'll go box everything up, and I apologize ahead of time for the wait. With Tina gone, I'm stuck doing paperwork. Oh, and I will be sure to include the Mackenzie discount."

"Thanks, Blake, and take your time," Josh told the shop owner with a nod.

"I'll be back as soon as I can." Blake turned and walked toward the back of the store as though he was in a hurry.

"Oh my god," Meagan was totally astonished.

"What is it?" Josh asked thinking it must be important.

"I didn't know it was so easy to buy a gun," Meagan whispered.

"Montana has some of the most relaxed gun laws in the country. But then again, it wouldn't be this easy for you. You have to be a resident of the state for..." Josh stopped mid-sentence when he saw Lucas and Collin Davenport approaching him with their fists balled up.

"Meagan, don't say anything to them. If they talk to you, I want you to ignore them."

"Okay," Meagan softly replied as her heart rate sky-rocketed. She watched in silence as Josh moved closer to her and stood with his left side facing the Davenports. She could not believe how calm he sounded when he initiated the conversation.

"Well, well, look what the cat dragged in. Collin, Luke, how's your life of crime treating you boys? Does your daddy know where you boys are?"

"Fuck you, Mackenzie."

Josh remained calm. "I would appreciate it if you two would watch your nasty mouths around the lady."

"You have a lot of fucking nerve, Mackenzie."

"I don't give a shit what you think, Collin, and I asked you nicely to watch your dirty mouth. I know it's hard, seeing that neither one of you are used to being anywhere near a lady."

Meagan was unable to control her shaking. The two men not only outnumbered Josh, they both outsized him.

"It's your fault, Mackenzie. Jillian has been hiding in her room and crying for days. She said you sold her ring to a fucking pawn shop and she wants it back—now!"

"What I do is none of your business. What I *will* tell you is that even though I paid for the damn ring, I would have gladly let her keep it if she wouldn't have yanked it off her damn finger, thrown it at me, and told me to go fuck myself. I'm sorry, Miss Dawson."

Meagan's tongue refused to function and she could only watch the situation escalate.

"If I was you, Mackenzie, I would give the fucking ring back." The larger man harshly demanded then slowly raised the lower left side of his jean jacket and flashed a large, black, semi-automatic pistol at Josh.

"Fuck you, Collin, don't be stupid and make *me* do something that *you* are going to regret. Cover it up now, or I will shove that gun so far up your ass

that you will piss yourself in front of your brother and everyone in the store."
Josh didn't sound the slightest bit worried, just angry. "Meagan, please go
stand by Timmy."

Meagan was terrified for Josh and her legs felt like rubber bands when she
walked away from him. By the time she reached Timmy, she was in a state of
panic and could barely speak. "Josh needs your help. They have a gun."

"Who has a gun?"

"The bigger guy just threatened Josh."

"Did he say he wants my help?"

"No, he just told me to stay by you."

"Okay, take it easy. You need to calm down before you hyperventilate."

"Why won't you go help him?"

"Meagan, how long have you known Josh?"

"Nine days."

"Okay, knowing Josh the way *I* do, he is hoping they do something stupid.
He wants to handle them his way. Take my word for it. They are just trying to
scare him, and they know better than to push him too far."

Meagan was beginning to think Timmy might be right when Collin, Lucas,
and Josh walked towards the front door. She watched Josh nod at Timmy,
briefly point at Collin and raise the left side of his coat as if to indicate where
the man had a weapon.

"Oh my god…" Meagan appeared pale enough to faint.

"Stay here, Meagan." Tim wasted no time following Josh.

Meagan was anxiously waiting for nearly fifteen minutes when Blake
returned, looking for Josh and holding a large box. "Where did Josh disappear to?"

"He is outside with Tim and two men who just threatened him."

"I see. Do you know if it was Collin and Luke Davenport?"

"Yes."

"Are *you* okay? I think you should sit down." Blake sounded more concerned
about her than Josh and Tim.

"No, I'm not okay. I'm scared and I feel like shit." Meagan rarely used profanity, but the swear word best expressed her feelings.

"Come back here and sit down. They can handle those two dumbasses."
Blake escorted Meagan behind the display case, had her sit on a wooden stool,
and gave her a bottle of water. "Just hang tight. I'm sure they won't be long."

"Thank you…" Meagan was not sure of the man's name.

"You can call me Blake, everyone else does. And you are?" The owner of Blake and Tina's reached for Meagan's hand.

"Meagan Dawson."

"I'm very pleased to meet you, Meagan Dawson."

"Thank you, Blake, and thank you for your help."

"Any time, and like I said, don't worry about them. If anything, worry about Luke and Collin. If Josh and Timmy don't do it, their daddy will beat their asses for getting in more trouble."

Blake was right. Only a few minutes after he introduced himself, Josh and Timmy came back in the store. Completely relieved to see them, Meagan could not comprehend their laughter and playful attitudes.

"All right, Mackenzie, you are all set," Blake pointed to some documents next to the box.

"That was fast. Thanks Blake," Josh continued listening to Tim and filled out the required forms.

"So, I was the only one in our group who did not fill their tag."

"It happens to all of us from time to time. You will make up for it."

"Shit, I missed it twice. Both shots were less than 200 yards."

"Maybe you are putting too much into your target. Try focusing more on your breathing and don't rush the shot. Take three good breaths then exhale all your air and stay light on your trigger."

"I really need to practice."

"I will call you next week. P.D. keeps saying he needs to shoot too, so the three of us can go together and get you straight."

"Great, and thanks, Mackey."

"No problem, and thanks for your help. That should do it, Blake," Josh declared and set down the pen he was using.

"Thank you again. Take care and watch your ass."

"Thanks, Blake, and I'll see you later. Timmy, keep up the good work and I will call you in a few days." Ready to leave, Josh slid his credit card, driver's license, and paperwork in his wallet.

"Yeah, stay safe, Mackey."

Josh looked from Tim to Meagan and grinned. "Are you still with me, Miss Dawson?"

Meagan merely nodded.

Blake and Tim said goodbye to Meagan, and then Blake told Josh he better bring her back to see him.

"It was nice meeting you, Blake, and thank you again." Meagan didn't have the heart to tell him that she wouldn't be back.

Cradling his heavy box, Josh opened the passenger door for Meagan with his free hand.

"Thank you, but you don't need to do that."

"You're welcome," Josh replied with a smile then went around to the driver's side. After setting his box in the back seat, he removed his warm bomber and placed it beside the box. Then he climbed into the driver's seat and asked, "What would you prefer for lunch, a salad, a sub sandwich, or a burger? We can get anything you want."

"Thank you, but I'm not hungry."

Josh leaned his head against the head rest and looked at Meagan with utter disappointment. "Please tell me you're kidding. Unless you robbed the refrigerator for a midnight snack, neither one of us have eaten since yesterday."

"I can wait until dinner," Meagan declared, staring straight ahead.

"Aw, please try to eat something, for me. I can't eat in front of you and I'm about to spend at least two hours prone on my growling gut. Please," Josh pleaded while rubbing circles around his stomach.

"Okay, but you pick the food because nothing sounds good." Only meaning to glance at Josh, Meagan found herself drawn to his upper body when she realized he removed his jacket. He was wearing a royal blue Henley that couldn't have fit any better around the chest and arms. She wondered how he stayed so muscular when she didn't think he had time to work out. All of a sudden, Meagan felt her face heat up when she caught herself checking him out. What am I doing, she thought. She didn't mean to do it, but after all he was sitting right next to her and she couldn't help but notice he was built.

"Thank you, Miss, I hate shooting on an empty stomach."

On their way to get a bite to eat, Meagan fought to keep her eyes off Josh while thinking about what happened at B.A.T.'s. Throughout the next twenty minutes she gazed out the passenger window. Her appreciation for the extraordinary spring day had all but vanished. Although she was pleased with the outcome at B.A.T.'s, she couldn't help but question how Josh would fare against Jeremy. She agreed with him sending her away while he dealt with the Davenports, but she would not leave him to save herself from Jeremy. One after another, she contemplated different scenarios. She hated that her decision to stay in Montana could mean sacrificing her new friends to spare her parents some grief and maybe their lives. This is awful, she thought. What am I supposed to do? What is the *right* thing to do? And how do I live with myself if I make the wrong decision?

"You are awfully quiet. What's on your mind?"

"Oh, just thinking." Meagan longed to confide in Josh. Considering his background, she believed he could help her understand the pros and cons of staying and going home. Desperately wanting his help with making one of the most difficult decisions of her life, she didn't know how to ask for it.

"Are you still upset about what happened at B.A.T.'s?"

"That might be part of it, but I can't even explain it to myself."

"You are obviously confused about something. I'll help if I can, all you have to do is ask."

"Thank you, but it's complicated, very complicated."

"Maybe it will help if you talk about it. You know you can trust me. I can't guarantee I have an answer, but I can listen."

"I do trust you. You know I do, but it has nothing to do with trust. I don't even know where to begin. I'm just confused like always."

"So just ask me something off the top of your head. Maybe I can help you work through your doubts."

Meagan took in an extremely large breath and blurted something out. "Okay, were you even the slightest bit worried at B.A.T.'s?"

"No, not at all. I have known Collin and Luke most of their lives. They don't have the balls to do what they suggested. I was pissed off at their lack of respect for me and for you. I wanted to beat the shit out of them and get away with it—just one time—like they get away with everything they do. Uh, does that help any?"

"Maybe a little, but I think it brings up another question. Another one that I don't know how to ask—I'm afraid to ask."

"Oh, a tough one, huh?"

"Yes, it's definitely a tough one."

"Take a few deep breaths, then exhale and let it out nice and slow. That is how I approach everything from taking a difficult shot to, well, asking a pretty lady to go out with me."

Surprised and impressed by Josh's answer, Meagan did as he suggested. She emptied her lungs and took her best shot. "What if you wouldn't have known them? Say they were complete strangers and they threatened you?"

"Hmm, I think I see what you're getting at. I think you are referring to Constadine. First, I must ask if we are at B.A.T.'s, enjoying a romantic dinner, or napping on my hammock?" Josh was trying to lighten the mood and knew he had Meagan's attention when his questions not only caught her off guard, but she was clearly flustered.

"I thought you are supposed to be helping me?"

"You're right, I'm sorry."

"Let's say we are anywhere he could walk right up to us, because that is what he would do. He won't care who you are."

Meagan's stern and doubtful tone annoyed Josh. He stopped and parked the Jeep near the entrance of the sub sandwich shop then turned in his seat to face her. "I know we haven't known each other long, but I thought you knew me better than this. After everything I have told you about me, you should know what I would do. Do you want the gory details since you still don't get the picture? So I can clear up any doubts you may have about my ability to keep you safe?"

Josh's voice did not sit well with Meagan. She tried to look into his eyes, but instead fixed on her hiking boots. "Never mind, let's get something to eat."

Josh refused to let her go on doubting him. "Didn't the day in the den with your knife show you what I am capable of?" Then, with his right index finger, he lightly touched Meagan in the center of her chest. "Right here, if you would have taken just one more step," Josh said while holding her wide eyes. "Right here, the second you raised your foot. I would have dropped you where you stood and we wouldn't be having this conversation. You don't know how close I came." Josh paused but only for a second. "One thing I wasn't going to tell you, but here we are—I was beginning to squeeze the trigger when I changed my mind. I didn't hesitate for you, Meagan. At the time you didn't mean anything to me, dead or alive. My problem wasn't with killing you. I only held back to save my ass—my career and my privacy."

"Okay stop, that's enough… Oh my god, I'm sorry I asked."

"Look at me, Meagan, please."

Meagan did as he asked, but quickly turned her eyes to look out his window. With his right hand, Josh lightly cupped Meagan's chin, then turned and held her shocked face. "If it would have been Constadine instead of Lucas and

Collin, your worries would have ended as soon as he so much as reached—I would have made sure he never hurt you again."

Meagan swallowed hard as her stomach turned, and it wasn't from hunger. "Okay, but there is something I need to tell you. Something I want you to know. If I am with you and…uh…like what happened at B.A.T.'s…I wouldn't leave you. I will not run away and hide like I did today. I would stay with you no matter what."

"What? You can't be serious. What the hell are you thinking?" After taking his hand away from Meagan's chin, Josh threw his head against the head rest and shook his head in utter contempt. "No, absolutely not, you don't know what you are talking about."

Meagan expected Josh to disagree with her way of thinking, but she was taken aback by his extreme reaction. "All right, all right, I'm sorry I brought it up. Please drop it. I can't do this right now."

With his head still against the rest, Josh turned to face Meagan. Then, he let out an enormous sigh and apologized. "No, Miss Dawson, I am sorry. I way overreacted and you didn't deserve any of that. I ask you to trust me and tell me what's on your mind, then I go and bite your head off. I'm sorry, please forgive me. I want you to talk to me and to know I can take care of you. I want you to feel safe and not worry."

"It's okay, forget it. Let's eat, Josh. You said you're starving."

"Hold on a minute…"

Meagan tried to guess what Josh was thinking.

"What exactly do you hope to accomplish by sticking by me, especially if I tell you to run? Can you back me like P.D., or Timmy, or Benny? Would you know what to do if there is a fight, or how to disarm him if he pulls a gun on us?"

"You know I don't," Meagan replied and found herself willfully looking at Josh.

"So you are saying you will stand by me and offer moral support, so it's easier for him to kill both of us, that's just great."

"I couldn't leave you to face *my* problem. It would be *my* fault."

"You are thinking with your heart and not your head. That's expected because you know me. Staying with me, especially after I tell you to go, would give Constadine the upper hand. He would use you to distract me and to his advantage. Having you close would only make the situation worse and harder for me to act. Is what I'm saying making any sense to you?"

"Yes, you have been a tremendous help. Thank you for helping me see things from another point of view. I honestly feel a lot better."

"Really, that was way too easy. What exactly do you feel better about? Now I'm confused. You just wanted to know I'm not afraid of him, right? That if he shows up before you leave—wait a minute—there's more to it than that."

"Josh, let's just forget it and order lunch."

Josh caught on to Meagan's elusive intent. "Hmm, hang on; I think I get it now. You are asking me questions about what I would do if Constadine was here. Oh shit, you are having second thoughts about going back to Illinois."

"No, I'm not. I was just wondering—in case he finds us."

"Aw, don't bullshit me, Meagan. I can't stand liars and cheaters. Please not you too."

"I already told you, I'm going home."

"Yes, you did. You told me you are going back to Illinois, this Sunday as a matter of fact. What was I thinking?" Anticipating Meagan's next reaction, Josh lowered his voice. "Seeing as how you won't let me look after you here in Montana, I only have three days to prepare you to defend yourself in Illinois."

"What, what do you mean by defend myself?"

Ignoring Meagan's question, Josh took his place in the drive thru. "What can I get for you, and please don't tell me you aren't hungry."

"Whatever you are having is fine, thank you."

"You're welcome, and to drink?"

"Water please." Meagan remained silent until after Josh set their bag of food in the back seat and pulled away from the restaurant. "Please, Joshua Mathew; I have enough on my mind. Can you please fill me in on what you are thinking? After all, it does involve me, right?"

"Okay, I was going to wait until we got to the canyon but since you insist. Miss Dawson, ignore how long we have known each other and even though I may never see you again, I *need* to know you are safe and can take care of yourself. I want you to have a chance to be happy, no matter where you are or who you are with, as long as they make *you* happy." Josh gazed into Meagan's wondering eyes, reached over, and sweetly took her left hand. "Meagan…"

Meagan looked at Josh with heightened curiosity.

"What you think of me is not important. What *is* important is doing *everything* we can to keep *you* safe. I mean *everything*, whatever it takes. Do you understand?"

"Um…I guess so…so far."

Josh slightly tightened his grip as if to brace Meagan for a shock. "I am giving you something to help keep you safe, as much as I hope you never need to use it."

"Oh my god, oh no, please tell me you didn't do what I think you did," Meagan was shaking her head as if she already knew what he was going to say.

Before telling Meagan his intentions, Josh hoped she wouldn't tell him to let her out of the Jeep. "Well maybe. The pistol I bought from Blake is for you. I want to help you get comfortable with it and teach you how to use it my way."

As Josh predicted, Meagan blew up. "Now *you* are out of *your* mind. I don't want anything to do with a damn gun, let alone own one! Oh my god, please don't tell me you just wasted $500.00 on a gun for me that I don't want?"

"Nope, we are good there. I get a discount and besides that, it was not a waste because I knew I could convince you to trust me and let me teach you."

"No, not this, anything but this. You know how I feel."

"Why, because the motherfucker beat the shit out of you with his pistol, all the more reason."

Meagan was on the verge of tears. "I can't…I won't…I could never…guns hurt people and worse. No, forget it."

"Take it easy, sweetheart, and don't forget who you are talking to. I don't need *you* to tell *me* guns kill. You need to realize guns aren't bad; it's the people who use them for the wrong reasons that are the problem. And that is precisely why I bought this one for you, to use it for its intended purpose. To defend yourself from one sick motherfucker because I can't do it myself."

"I couldn't do it. I couldn't go through with it. I'm not like *that*."

"You mean you are not like *me*. Believe me, there is a world of difference between what I do and what you might need to do, but we aren't going to go into that. Meagan, you know Constadine and he has hurt you. Even Benny and P.D. are on board with the idea. We all think you should be ready, willing, and able to defend yourself."

"You don't get it. I couldn't do it. I'm not the type." Meagan looked into Josh's face hoping she finally convinced him.

"The hell you couldn't and oh yes you are. I saw your instinct to survive. It's not about being cruel or vicious, it's about staying alive. And I would bet anything that day in the barn when you came at me, you thought I was Constadine.

You were ready to kill *him* Meagan. If you wouldn't have been too sick to walk, you would have kept coming at me thinking I was him."

"I don't know what I was thinking."

"Well, think about this. Are you okay with him beating you again, or worse? I for one am not. Hell, I couldn't even look at the damn pictures in your file. If someone did that to me or to the woman I love, it wouldn't happen again. I don't know about you, but I would give anything to see the look on Constadine's face when you unload on him, and better yet, the look on his face when you step back and watch *him* bleed to death. And don't you even think about calling 911. I know how you are."

"I can't even look at your gun and you want me to shoot someone, to take someone's life?"

"Absolutely, today all I'm asking you to do is keep an open mind and trust me. Just give me a chance to teach you my way. It's similar to the method P.D. uses in his classes with nervous women, but we have all day."

"I don't know anything about Illinois gun laws."

"P.D. will push everything through his connections. As soon as you are legal, I will make sure you get the pistol and fast."

"I don't know." Meagan felt herself giving in.

"Listen, I am not about to put any gun in your hands and tell you to start shooting. We are going to take it real slow and you aren't even going to touch the gun until I know you are comfortable and ready."

"Josh…" Meagan said and looked down. "I still have nightmares."

Josh tried to sound reassuring. "I can't be sure, but shooting and facing your fears might help." Still holding firmly to Meagan's left hand, Josh slowed down and took a right turn onto a gravel driveway. "Stop doubting yourself. You are stronger than you think." Hoping he gave his best argument, Josh quietly continued down a steep hill. He wanted Meagan to consider everything he said without feeling like she had no choice in the matter.

Meagan was also silent while Josh's words seeped in. She peered down to her left thigh where their hands were comfortably laced together. She wanted to believe in him, completely and wholeheartedly. After all, he never gave her reason not to. Somehow Josh sparked something deep inside her. Whether he ignited her faith in him or rekindled her desire for life did not matter. The two went hand-in-hand.

11

When Josh stopped in front of a sizeable, bright yellow steel gate and glanced at Meagan, she was staring at their hands and looked to be in deep thought. He gave her a few more seconds then released her hand and gently cradled her chin. When her eyes met his, he began tenderly caressing her soft face with his thumb. "I would never make you do something you don't want to do. I mean it."

"Okay," Meagan said feeling beyond dazed. She didn't know what to think about what he was asking her to do, let alone the caring way he was touching her face.

Still holding Meagan's eyes, Josh continued moving his thumb ever so lightly back and forth across her cheek. "Once we go through the gate, I promise I won't ever ask you again."

"Okay." Not accustomed to the chills surging down the back of her neck and spine, Meagan couldn't believe how much she was enjoying Josh's touch. Completely mesmerized, it was the way he was looking at her with his vivid blue-green eyes that roused her.

"I want you to do this for yourself, not to please me."

"Okay." Meagan didn't notice when her face began leaning into Josh's hand.

"I will be okay with whatever you decide. It's your choice."

Meagan could not explain what overcame her, but she slowly reached out to Josh and softly placed her finger tips over his lips. "Joshua Mathew, I said okay."

"Okay…? You mean okay as in you are okay with doing this?"

"Yes, before I can come up with a reason not to."

"Wow, good for you. Okay then, let's get started." Hoping Meagan wouldn't change her mind, Josh quickly took a key ring from the center console, sprang from his seat, then went to unlock and push open the heavy gate.

Meagan took note of a significant black sign with bright orange lettering that warned, NO TRESPASSING! PRIVATE PROPERTY PATROLLED BY LAW ENFORCEMENT! VIOLATORS SUBJECT TO ARREST! She immediately wondered if *she* should keep out.

Josh pulled in and closed the gate behind them. Before driving on he grinned at Meagan to show his approval. Then he proceeded down the gravel drive to a row of several picnic tables and a few scattered Douglas firs. As if he had done so many times before, he backed into a spot beside a redwood table shaded by a soaring Lodgepole pine. After parking the Jeep, Josh reached into the backseat for their lunch and handed Meagan her six-inch sandwich and water. "I hope you like tuna salad and don't mind eating in my Jeep. It's a lot cleaner than those nasty picnic tables." Josh wasted no time devouring his entire sandwich while Meagan only managed to eat a few small bites.

"I'm sorry, Josh. I'm just not hungry. I feel sick."

"I don't blame you. You will be hungry when we're done."

"Should I go sit at the table?"

"Sure, you should be out of the sun but feel free to put on my glasses. I will be there in a minute."

Meagan felt tense and jittery when she put on Josh's glasses and went to the table with her water. Remembering her puzzle books, she decided she was too shaky to write and left them in the Rubicon. Strangely curious, she watched Josh open the back of the Jeep, unload his massive nylon duffle bag, and set it on the ground next to the table. Next, he unzipped a compartment, reached inside and took out a tiny plastic package. "Here, sweetheart, you are going to need these."

"Oh, is it going to be that loud?" Meagan asked when she watched Josh hand her ear plugs.

"If it was just a few shots, I would let you cover your ears. But since that's not the case, you will be glad you have them."

Meagan continued watching Josh with subtle interest while he prepared his shooting area about ten feet away. First, he unrolled and smoothed out a rubber-coated mat and set the cardboard box from B.A.T.'s just to the right of it. Then he took out a package of rifle targets and silhouettes. She reasoned he was finished when he turned to face her.

"Do you want to wait here or ride with me? I have to go put these up." Josh asked, holding up a stack of rifle targets.

"I better wait here. I need the fresh air."

"Okay, I'll be right back. Take some deep breaths."

Feeling anxious, Meagan couldn't help but take pleasure in the magnificent rock formations. She stood in awe at the base of a spectacular canyon where she was surrounded by three mammoth rock walls. The farthest wall impressed her the most. It ascended to an extraordinary height and was topped off with a stand of unfamiliar conifers. The splendid canyon looked as though it would be better suited for a spectacular and tranquil park rather than a shooting range.

Meagan's attention shifted from the dramatic setting to what Josh was doing. She could see some giant numbers strategically posted on the ground that she assumed were used to mark the distance to the corresponding steel frames. She watched with wonder when he placed some targets too far away for her to read the numbers. From where she sat, hitting any of the targets appeared impossible. She continued watching Josh make his way back and stop to place a target every 200 yards and one at 100 yards.

After Josh parked the Jeep in its original spot, he opened the rear cargo door and went to where Meagan sat waiting. He was grinning with confidence when he looked at her and asked, "Are you still with me? It's never too late to change your mind."

"I think so. This is such a beautiful place. It's so peaceful."

"Yes, it is. It wasn't easy convincing the state to reserve it for training law enforcement." After squatting down over his duffle bag, Josh put on his polarized tactical glasses and black S.R.T. baseball hat. Then he rested his earmuffs around his neck, stood up, and set a pair of binoculars within Meagan's reach. "You can use these if you want to look around. I am really sorry, Miss, but I am about to ruin your peace and quiet."

Meagan watched in silence as Josh went to the back of the Jeep and returned carrying his long black gun case. She thought she recognized it from when he scared her Sunday night. "Josh, how far is the last target?"

"It's a thousand yards," he replied as he prudently removed a black rifle from the hard case. "That yardage is mostly for my own shits and giggles, not work. It's not as hard as it looks with this gun." Amused by Meagan's speechless and squeamish reaction, Josh had to laugh. "If you were staying, I could teach you how to shoot with this one."

"No way, don't even think about it."

"Oh why not, it's easier to handle than my forty-five. Nothing to it, you just lay there and squeeze the trigger." Josh's tone made it clear that he was getting a kick out of toying with her.

"No, and after seeing yours I just remembered Jeremy had one something like it."

"Was he in the service?"

"Yes, before I met him, but he also worked overseas. I only saw it in the pictures he sent me."

"Really, do you know what he did overseas?"

"Something to do with security. He told me his work was confidential."

"So he never discussed his duties?"

"No, only that he specialized in international security."

"That is interesting. Do you remember hearing him discuss his weapon? Did he mention any numbers like AR-15 or M-5?"

"I don't remember any letters or numbers, just that it was black. What is yours?"

"To put it simply for you, this is a M25 sniper rifle. Did he ever mention the words sniper or sniping?"

"No, I would remember that. I know what that means."

"All right, if you think of anything else let me know."

"Okay."

"Make sure you use your earplugs." Josh closed his case, carried his rifle to his mat, and methodically propped the gun on its attached bipod.

Meagan squished the plugs deep into her ear canals until she thought they were impenetrable. Her fears and insecurities seemed to deteriorate as she watched Josh with budding curiosity. She admired his diligence and self-confidence when he loaded his rifle, got into position, turned his hat backwards and put on his earmuffs. So far, each of his actions made perfect sense. Even when she thought he was adjusting his scope. It was the strange way he bent his right leg that caught her attention. With his right knee almost touching his right elbow, he reminded her of a frog.

Meagan was still wondering about the odd positioning of Josh's leg when the unforgiving discharge of his first round nearly rocked her to her feet. She not only heard the blast through her earplugs, she felt the percussion in her chest. The unexpected shot did not resemble a boom or a bang the way she imagined, but was a prolonged crack; like the continuous crack of thunder. She was still recovering when the second shot had nearly the same effect. She tried to prepare herself by concentrating on his trigger finger, but that proved useless when the sudden and subsequent gunshots continued without warning. He never moves. How does he hold so still? Meagan wondered in awe.

She was still staring at Josh and bracing for another shot when he rolled onto his left side and hung his earmuffs around his neck. When he signaled to her by pointing at his ears, Meagan removed her plugs. He was smiling at her and shaking his head. "Right about now, I bet you are wishing you would have stayed back at the house."

Meagan did not hesitate before responding, "Not at all, spending time with you has definitely been…different."

"Just wait, sweetheart, your turn is coming. You haven't even started to have fun. For now, can you please do me a favor?"

Worried about what she was getting herself into, Meagan said, "I'll try."

"Thanks, can you tell me where I hit the thousand-yard target. The sun is messing with my eyes." Josh turned his hat to the front when Meagan picked up the binoculars. Watching her tremble, he could see she was struggling to find the target. "Sweetheart, try resting your elbows on the table to steady yourself, then look for the one thousand."

"Okay, I found it."

"Good, now use the center dial to focus on the target and count the holes. You should see ten unless I missed it completely."

Not believing her own eyes, Meagan blurted, "Holy shit."

"Miss Dawson, what did you say? I thought you were a lady."

"I said, *holy shit*. You really are *that* good. You got eight in the red center and the other two are less than an inch away, just above it."

Josh knew exactly where he shot; he was just getting her involved to help her pass the time and take her mind off shooting. "I think that's the first time I heard you curse."

"Maybe you, Benny, and Pete are rubbing off on me."

"Maybe, but I think you are finally starting to relax. Well, I better get back to it; I know you can't wait for your turn," Josh teased then reloaded a magazine and slid it into his rifle. After giving Meagan a mischievous grin, he pointed at his ears.

This time Meagan was better prepared. She watched Josh return to his stomach, cover his ears, and bend his right leg. After putting in her earplugs, Meagan peered through Josh's binoculars and zoomed in on the 800-yard target. Although each decisive crack of the rifle still startled her, watching him obliterate the center of each target helped take her mind off the noise. Thinking Josh made shooting look easy, she could certainly see why he was one of the best at his profession and held in high regard.

Josh was almost finished with the 200-yard target when he stopped shooting, lay on his back, and removed his phone from his pants pocket. Meagan watched him cover his face with his baseball hat and take a call. She was surprised how quickly he finished his conversation and once again pointed at his ears.

Meagan took out her ear plugs and hoped Josh would buy her act. "Oh no, don't tell me we need to leave?"

"Nice try, Miss, but you're not getting off that easy. P.D. called to ask what time we would be home for dinner. He wants to grill his secret recipe barbecue chicken."

"Oh…" The way Meagan was feeling, food was the last thing on her mind.

"I asked if he could hold off until six. That should give us more than enough time."

"Great." Meagan couldn't have hidden her sarcasm if she wanted to.

"Don't sound so excited. You sound like you are about to have a tooth pulled or something."

"I think I would rather have several teeth pulled."

Once again Josh couldn't help but laugh. "I'm about finished with my long shots. Put your plugs back in. I hate to keep a lady waiting."

After watching Josh finish shooting out the centers of the 200- and 100-yard targets, she watched him set his earmuffs around his neck and put his baseball hat on his mat. Then he went to his feet and carefully lifted his rifle. "Now, don't you get any ideas about running or taking off in my Jeep." He joked with her as he set his M25 in the protective case.

"I'm scared, not stupid. I know I wouldn't get very far."

"To tell you the truth, I'm not much of a runner. There's a good chance you might outrun me, and I know I would poop out before you."

"You would actually *chase* me…on foot?"

"I would try. I would chase you from here to Illinois if I…" For just a moment Josh held Meagan's gaze. But when he recalled she was already running from one stalker and sure the hell didn't need another one, he felt like an ass. "I'm sorry, I shouldn't have said that."

"Don't be sorry," Meagan sounded serious, but then changed her tone dramatically. "You don't scare me, you big meany. Just who do you think you are? I'll tell my big brother you tried to scare me," Meagan smiled and lightheartedly teased back.

"See why I like you? You are so much fun to play with."

"I am *so* glad to hear you like me. I wouldn't want *you* for an enemy, that's for sure."

"I am glad *you* like *me*. What's more important is that you trust me. It's going to take a lot of trust to get you over your hoplophobia."

"Okay, Dr. Mackenzie, what is hoplophobia?"

"It is the morbid fear of guns."

"Wow, so there is an actual name for my fear?"

"Well, I might be teasing you just a little bit. You have a valid reason to fear firearms—a true hoplophobic has an irrational fear of firearms without any real threat or danger."

"Whether you are teasing me or not, I definitely prefer watching you."

"You will be fine. I have to practice with my pistol and then guess whose turn it is?"

Meagan felt as though she was waiting for a terrifying roller coaster ride, but was too far in line to turn back. When Josh hung the silhouettes just beyond the picnic table at the ten- and twenty-yard frames, her stomach began doing cartwheels. Feeling warm and nauseated she took off her jacket and set it on the bench next to her. She closed her eyes and tried imagining herself soaking in a lavender and chamomile bubble bath.

Meanwhile, Josh was acting as though he didn't have a care in the world. After putting on his hat, he rolled up his mat, picked up the box, and carried the items to the back of the Rubicon. "It's still okay to change your mind," Josh reminded Meagan again after he returned to the table then closed and latched his rifle case.

"Yes, I know, but a part of me wants to do it. A very, very small part that I am still trying to talk out of it."

"I promise I will get you through it," Josh assured Meagan before he picked up his rifle case and carried it to the rear of the Jeep. Then, after spending a few minutes doing something she couldn't see, he returned to the table with a short stack of smaller boxes in his left hand and likely the gun he purchased from Blake in his right. "So this is your cute, little pea shooter." He said with a grin and set the compact, nine-millimeter on the picnic table so that it was pointed down range. "And this…" Josh cautiously drew his pistol from his thigh holster, pointed it down range and released the magazine over the table. Then, he ejected the live round and it too landed on the table. "And this is my beast." Keeping the forty-five pointed down range, Josh ensured the gun was safe and placed it next to Meagan's nine-millimeter.

"Wow, I didn't know there was such a difference." Meagan's eyes couldn't get any wider.

"Yes, the guns and the rounds we use." Josh picked up the magazine and ejected bullet and set them directly in front of Meagan. "This one is for my forty-five and this one…" he said while taking a bullet from one of the boxes and setting it next to his larger bullet. "…this is your cute, little nine-millimeter. Aw, isn't it cute, Miss Dawson?" Josh was trying to get Meagan to smile but she wouldn't have it.

"So I take it the bigger one is better?"

"Not necessarily, size isn't everything. It's placement that counts. Oh shit, that doesn't sound good. I wonder if P.D. says that to the women in his classes. He is a certified instructor and probably a lot better at this than I am. Certainly more experienced."

"I think you're doing fine, so far anyway."

"Good, now that we have that out of the way, I am going to go poke a few holes with mine. And don't worry; your nine won't be as loud as this thing."

Having no idea what Josh was doing, Meagan watched him pick up his pistol, appear to reload it, and put it back in his holster. She was concentrating on what he was doing when he took an empty magazine from his duffle bag and loaded it with bullets from one of the boxes. "Is that hard to learn?"

"Not at all. You will think it's a piece of cake. I'll show you how when we load yours. Put your plugs in. You're going to need them," Josh smiled, put on his muffs and walked toward the targets.

Taking Josh's advice, Meagan wasted no time cramming the plugs into her ears. Only moments later she realized Josh was right and quickly became grateful for the hearing protection. No sooner did he pull his gun and aim, and she heard the earsplitting *bam, bam, bam* until he shot eleven rounds into the twenty-yard target. Then he quickly swapped the empty magazine for a full one in his waistband, reloaded the M&P, and once again fired until the gun was out of ammo.

"You were right, that was *really* loud." Meagan told Josh when he returned to the table and began to reload both empty magazines.

"You just aren't used to it like I am. I barely notice any more. Do you see where I hit, in the center of the chest?" Josh asked as he slid a magazine into the gun.

"Yes."

"No matter where *I* shoot, *you* should always go for the center of the chest. It gives you the biggest target…ready or not." Josh turned away and approached the ten-yard target while holding his gun down by his right leg. After getting into position he decisively aligned the sights and then, *Bam, Bam, Bam.* He precisely placed all twenty shots in the center of the silhouette's forehead.

Satisfied with where he was hitting, Josh approached Meagan. "Whenever you're ready, sweetheart." He politely smiled and set his empty gun and empty magazines on the table. After looking at his dirty hands, he removed a plastic container of hand wipes from his duffle bag. "I hope you don't mind getting dirty." He glanced at Meagan, scrubbed his hands, and dropped the blackened wipes on the table.

Now that it was her turn and she didn't feel anywhere near ready, Meagan was speechless.

"May I sit with you, Miss Dawson?"

"I think I'm going to be sick."

"I can honestly say that I have never had that effect on a girl before." Josh laughed and straddled the picnic table bench to face her. "Look at me. I'm going to hold your hands, okay?"

Meagan briefly met Josh's eyes and nodded.

"Good." Josh softly placed his hands over Meagan's. "So, tell me what scares you about shooting. You don't think I would let you get hurt?"

"No, it has nothing to do with you. I can't stop having flashbacks and nightmares. I keep seeing him hitting me with his gun."

"Shit, I'm so sorry, sweetheart. I wish there was more I could do. I should have realized how hard this would be on you. Let's go back to the house and I will think of something else." When Josh stood up to leave, Meagan didn't hesitate to go to her feet.

"No wait, I want to do this. I need to do this." Meagan's eyes began to water. "I am so tired of him *still* controlling me. I want my life back." Visibly frustrated and shaking her head, tears streamed down Meagan's face.

"Aw, no, take it easy. Let's take a few minutes to let you settle down. Try to focus on breathing."

"I don't think I *can* calm down. Just *make* me do it and stop feeling sorry for me. Please, don't let me quit."

"Oh no, I don't work that way. I won't *make* you do anything."

"Please, just tell me what to do and don't stop no matter what, even if I get sick. You said you want to help me."

Feeling Meagan needed him, Josh took a couple steps back and reached towards her. "Grab my wrists with both hands and hold tight."

Shy and embarrassed, Meagan slowly did what Josh suggested.

"Squeeze them nice and firm, like you mean it." When Meagan latched on hard enough Josh sounded pleased. "Good, let go for now and do that again when I tell you. Remember, nice and firm and don't let me go."

"Okay."

"Come with me, sweetheart. We can still do this my way." Holding Meagan's hand, Josh led her to where he shot the ten- and twenty-yard targets. "Wait here and concentrate on the far rock wall. Don't pay any attention to what I am doing. Find a spot on the wall and stare at it."

"Okay."

Within two minutes Josh was back and standing directly behind Meagan. "Okay, just do what I say and you will be fine. I am going to get a little closer, just stay focused on the wall."

"I'll try," Meagan could hardly speak.

"Keep your hands down until I tell you to bring them up."

Meagan nodded and from that point on everything seemed to happen very quickly. While lightly pressing the front of his body against her back, Josh reached his empty left hand out in front of them. Then, with his right hand he carefully brought up the nine-millimeter to meet his left hand and gripped the gun with both hands. He calmly whispered in Meagan's right ear, "Bring both your hands up and hold my wrists like you did before, nice and tight."

When Meagan didn't move a muscle, Josh knew it was time for something drastic. Without any warning, the nine-millimeter discharged a sudden, ear-ringing *pop*.

"Oh shit!" Meagan shouted and jumped in Josh's arms.

"See, no big deal. Let's try again. Bring your hands up and hold my wrists, tight like you mean it. Come on, sweetheart, I know you can do this." He encouraged her again.

Meagan felt bombarded with emotions. First and foremost, she could feel Josh, all of him. He was completely pressed against her and the physical contact sent countless sensations surging through her. One part of her wanted to run away screaming while another part wanted to relax in his arms and go on. And then, there was the pistol, similar to the one in her recurring nightmares. Her very own nine-millimeter that not only terrified her, but there was a good chance she might need it.

"Come on, let's finish this magazine and then we can get your earplugs. Your gun holds seven and that means we only have six to go."

Slowly, little by little, Meagan raised her hands toward his wrists.

"Come on, sweetheart, I know you can do this."

And finally, she did. Meagan brought both hands up and clung onto Josh's wrists like there was no tomorrow.

"Keep holding on, nice and tight. Breathe in through your nose…good… and out through your mouth. In through your nose…a big breath…and let it out. One more, inhale and let it out."

The instant Meagan emptied her lungs, the gun jumped and her ears rang from another harsh *pop*. Josh helped her repeat the breathing process and she began to catch on because right before she let out her last breath, she tightened her grip and prepared for another *pop* of the pistol.

"You're doing great, four to go." Josh led Meagan through the breathing exercises and squeezed the trigger four more times until the pistol was empty. After the last shot he lowered his arms and pointed the pistol at the ground, but Meagan didn't move.

"We did it, we beat him," she whispered. She slowly turned around and put her arms around Josh's neck. "Thank you for helping me. I couldn't have done it without you."

Josh adoringly placed his left arm around Meagan's back, gave her a sweet squeeze and declared, "You helped yourself. Don't thank me."

"I wish everything could stay like this."

"Not as much as I do. Have you had enough? Are you ready to go back to the house?"

"I'm okay. Can we do it again the same way?"

"Absolutely, put in your earplugs and I will load another mag."

"Can you show me how to do it?'

"Sure," Josh was impressed with Meagan's optimism.

Meagan followed Josh to the picnic table where he showed her how to press and slide each bullet into the top of the magazine and to use her thumb to push the stack down against the spring.

"See, I told you there was nothing to it. Are you ready to shoot again? You are doing great and you are past the hardest part."

"I think so," Meagan replied and pushed in her earplugs. Feeling a sense of gratification and with Josh by her side, she walked back to the same spot to shoot again.

"All right, Miss, keep both your hands down." Josh spoke patiently into her right ear as he re-positioned himself against her back. "Now remember there is nothing to it. Just relax and do what I tell you."

"Okay," Meagan agreed. But between the shooting and Josh's close body it was nearly impossible for her to relax. Her pulse and breathing seemed out of control and her entire body felt damp with perspiration. Anticipating what was coming, her heart could not beat any faster. Even more than Josh's comforting touch and encouraging words, he was helping her crush her fears. However, there was no way she could have predicted his surprising twist. This time Josh brought the pistol up and aimed it down range with his right hand and momentarily held it there. Then with his left hand he took hold of Meagan's left hand, brought it up and held it firmly around the pistol's grip.

"Josh, I..."

"Shhh...relax," Josh whispered softly into Meagan's ear. "Slowly bring up your right hand and wrap it around our left hands."

Meagan timidly followed Josh's instructions and knew to hold on tight.

"Perfect, now in through your nose...exhale..."

Within seconds Meagan found herself relishing in Josh's confidence and strength. It wasn't just the way his sound body was pressed against hers, but how his strong and steady arms safely enclosed her. She appreciated his soft breath lightly brushing by her ear each and every time he soothed and encouraged her. She not only had no desire to flee, but she no longer feared what was coming when she exhaled.

After the last shot, Josh couldn't have sounded more hopeful. "I have one mag left in my pocket and then we are all done. Can you handle seven more?"

"Yes." Meagan's soft response surprised her.

"So, Miss, are you feeling brave?" Josh asked before he stepped away from her and pushed the last full magazine into the nine-millimeter.

Meagan wondered what Josh had up his sleeve and knew there was only one way to find out. "Um, I feel much better than I did."

"Just keep following my lead."

"Okay, I can do that."

This time Josh eased even closer into Meagan's back and held his left leg and hip steadily against her to give her more support. With his left hand he pointed the gun toward the wall. Then, without saying anything, he used his free right hand and softly touched Meagan's right hand. "Take a good breath and relax this hand, sweetheart."

Meagan gladly listened to Josh and wanted to melt when she felt how sweetly he took her right hand.

"Perfect." Feeling Meagan was comfortable, Josh brought up her right hand and firmly enclosed her fingers around the gun's grip. "Don't let go. Do you hear me? Don't let go." Josh kept his right hand around Meagan's in case she panicked.

"I got it." She said, not about to let him down.

After easing his left hand away from the pistol, Josh softly touched Meagan's left hand. "You're doing great. Now take a breath and relax this hand."

Taking pleasure in Josh's sensitive touch, Meagan opened her left hand and sighed when he calmly embraced her fingers.

"Good, stay with me." Confident that Meagan was following along, Josh took his time bringing up her left hand and closing her fingers around their right hands. "You're doing great. Keep that grip and think about your breathing." Next, Josh carefully placed Meagan's index finger inside the trigger guard. "Your gun has a thumb safety," he informed her while gradually maneuvering her finger back and forth against the trigger to show it wouldn't discharge. "It can't fire when the safety is on. Now put your trigger finger back on the grip… good…you got it. If you haven't looked yet, do you feel comfortable enough looking at our hands?"

"I already have," Meagan said softly and without fear.

"Good for you. For now I want you to watch our hands, okay?"

"I'm okay, go ahead."

"That a girl, stay away from the trigger. We are going to take the gun off safety. Once we take it off safety, it can fire. Do you understand everything I am saying? Do you have any questions, Miss? If you do, now is a real good time to ask."

"No, I understand."

Josh cautiously took his right hand away from the pistol. "Relax your thumb," Josh said and had her feel the safety. "This is your safety, do you feel it? You have to know where your safety is."

Meagan nodded. "Okay."

"Good, we are going to go over this more, but for now...up is fire...down is safe." Josh instructed her while carefully working the safety with her thumb. "Up is fire, down is safe. Say it with me...up is fire, down is safe."

"Up is fire...down is safe," Meagan said with Josh as she watched her right thumb and concentrated.

"I know this is a lot to take in at once, but it will get easier very quickly. You are a smart lady, Miss Dawson. If dumb asses like Luke and Collin can get it, you will have it down in no time."

"I hope you are right."

"I know I am. Can you tell me if the gun is on fire or safe?"

"Uh...safe," Meagan said with certainty.

"Very good. Bring your thumb back down and get back into your grip." Josh assured her hands were back in the correct shooting position. "Perfect." Feeling she was ready, he placed Meagan's index finger back inside the trigger guard.

"Josh...?"

"You got this. I am going to take it off safety. You are fine. Tell me you got this. Come on now, say I got this."

"I...got this."

"Nice, I like your confidence. Look straight ahead at the wall." Feeling she was ready, Josh lightened his hold on Meagan's right hand so she could feel the trigger pull and fully experience the pistol's recoil. "Okay, it's all you, sweetheart. Keep a firm grip and breathe in through your nose, nice and deep this time...exhale out...in nice and deep...let it out...in through your nose. Now let it out and squeeze the trigger nice and slow. Just start applying steady pressure....squeeze...squeeze..."

Meagan held onto her M&P as though it was going to try to escape. She thought she was pulling against the trigger, but nothing happened. With her lungs empty she applied a little more pressure and then...*pop*. The pistol finally discharged and she was elated.

"Oh my god, I did it. You were right. It wasn't *that* bad."

"Nope, piece of cake. You were awesome. Are you up for shooting the next six the same way?"

"Yes."

"All right, that's what I want to hear. I want you to work on your breathing without my coaching. Remember to begin your trigger pull after the third time you exhale."

"Okay," Meagan said and meant it. She focused on her breathing for each shot and with each squeeze of the trigger her fears of the menacing weapon faded just like the once startling noise. When she knew she was down to one bullet, she wished Josh had more.

"You did it, Miss Dawson. So, what did you think?" Josh asked while still pressed against her.

"Wow, I don't believe it. Like you always say, it was no big deal. I was scared out of my mind for nothing. It was a little loud, but I'm not afraid of it like I was."

Josh laughed at her response. "I think you would be amazed at what you could do with an open mind and if you give yourself a chance." Implying Meagan was capable of having a romantic relationship with a man, he didn't expect her to see his point.

"I don't know how to thank you." Meagan spoke from her heart as they walked side-by-side back to the picnic table.

"You don't need to thank me. Thank you for trusting me enough to give you the lesson. Unfortunately, you have a lot to learn and we don't have much time."

Meagan watched with interest when Josh re-loaded his forty-five, holstered the gun and then put her nine-millimeter into a case with two empty magazines.

"Help yourself to some wipes." After packing his shooting glasses, hat, and spare forty-five bullets into his duffle bag, Josh gave Meagan a few more wipes.

"Thank you, is there anything I can do to help?" Meagan asked while wiping the black, powdery residue from her hands.

"For now you can hop in the Jeep. I need to pick up my trash."

"Okay," Meagan replied, wondering what Josh meant by "trash."

Josh carried his duffle bag to the cargo section of the Rubicon with Meagan closely behind.

After getting into the passenger seat, she removed Josh's glasses and carefully set them in the glove box. "You were right about more than one thing."

"Really, I can't wait to hear about that."

"I am hungry," Meagan declared and smiled at Josh.

"I wouldn't eat the warmed tuna salad sub behind your seat." Josh made a sickly face and drove toward the used targets.

"I thought I heard you mention barbecue chicken?"

"I probably shouldn't tell you it's barbecue bear."

"Sure it is." Meagan remarked and glared at Josh with a threatening scowl.

"Come to think of it maybe he did say chicken."

After looking at each target and setting the last one on her lap, Meagan had to speak up. "Wow, I can see why you are one of the best shooters in the state. No wonder only one person is better than you."

"Now how do you know that?"

"Oh…a…a…little birdie told me."

"A birdie with a vulture-sized mouth," Josh affirmed and turned the Jeep around. "Shooting is like anything else. The more you practice the better you get. And now comes my favorite part." He couldn't have sounded more pessimistic. "Picking up my mess," Josh said when he pulled up to an old wooden shed hidden behind a few choke cherry trees.

"Oh, how do we do that?"

"With a rake, shovel, and broom. I will be right back." In less than two minutes, Josh was putting the items he listed and an industrial-sized dust pan in the Rubicon.

"What are those for?"

"This part sucks, but when you play you pay. The more fun I have, the bigger my mess." Josh drove back to where he practiced with his M25. "Turn up the music, put your seat back, and relax. I will try to hurry." Expecting Meagan to wait in the Jeep, Josh grabbed the rake and metal dust pan.

Meagan had to join Josh to see what he was raking. Immediately upon stepping out of the Rubicon, she heard metal tinking and went to where Josh was collecting his spent rifle casings. Naturally curious, she looked down at the scattered brass casings and picked one up. "Oh my god, these are huge. A lot bigger than mine. Wow, they are even bigger than your forty-five. What is this?"

Josh stopped raking to razz Meagan and smiled. "That, sweetheart, is from a .762 Nato round. They make a pretty big mess."

"It looks like it. Oh, Josh…oh my god. You aren't talking about the casings, are you?"

"Now what do you think?" Josh gave her a brief, secretive smile and went back to raking the scattered brass into a pile.

Meagan dropped the sizeable casing with the rest of them and went to retrieve the broom.

"Aw, sweetheart, you don't need to do that."

"Hush, I want to help. After everything you have done for me, I owe you so much. I will never be able to pay you back."

Initially upset, Josh's tone quickly changed. "Don't ever say that again. I haven't been helping you because I expect to get something out of it. Besides that, just having you around has helped me more than I can say. I can't explain it, but you showed up just in time. I should be thanking *you* for saving *me*."

"You are such a tease. You really expect me to believe that? A girl like me, who is afraid of her own shadow, saving a strong and take-no-shit guy like you?"

"Think about it, Miss. What happened right after you showed up?"

Meagan looked confused. "I'm sorry, I really don't know."

Josh let out a sigh. "My engagement with Jillian. I would likely still be with her if she wouldn't have insulted you at dinner. I finally saw her for what she is, a stuck up snob who only cares about what she wants."

Suddenly laden with guilt, Meagan had to sit down. "Oh no, please don't tell me you are alone because of me. Don't throw away your future just because of something she said to me."

"Come on, get up." Holding the rake in his left hand, Josh pulled Meagan up with his free hand. "I should have ended it before you got here. When she disrespected you, I finally realized getting married wasn't going to solve our problems. What we had was gone long before that dinner. I mean it, Meagan. Don't blame yourself for something I should have done years ago."

"I know what it is to think you have your life all planned out; a successful career that you enjoy, the person you expect to spend the rest of your life with, and then you go back to square one."

"Considering the consequences, I don't mind going back to square one. I would rather start over than be with the wrong person. Meagan, I forgot what it was like to be with a nice girl, and having you around has shown me I was about to make a huge mistake. Aunt Bess has been trying to tell me everything happens for a reason." Josh grinned and checked his watch. "Oh shit, we need to get moving."

After Josh retrieved a five-gallon bucket from the Jeep, Meagan held the dust pan for him and dumped the casings into the bucket. The longer they took to tidy up, the faster he moved and more he talked about dinner. "If I take a few shortcuts we should still make it by six."

Meagan had no idea what those shortcuts entailed until Josh used some old trails and went off-roading. By the time he parked in front of the house, she was more than ready to use the restroom.

"I'm glad you came with me." Josh smiled and reached for Meagan's left hand. "We will have to do it again. Honestly, the sooner the better."

Meagan leaned her head against the head rest, turned and looked into Josh's warm hazel eyes. "Thank you so much—for everything. I hope you know how much I appreciate it." Then she gave Josh's hand a loving squeeze. "And I hope you know I will never forget you."

"You are very welcome and I'm not at all worried about forgetting you. I plan on seeing you again and doing everything I can to help you, no matter where you are. I think you know I am not one to give up without a fight."

"Josh, please don't waste your time on me."

"Is that how you think I feel about you? Like you are a waste of my time?"

"Please don't make me explain myself."

"Can I ask you something? You don't have to answer if you don't want to. Just ignore it and we can go inside."

"Okay," Meagan answered, still clutching his hand.

"If you weren't worried about Constadine kicking our asses, would you stay? Are you only leaving because of him?"

Knowing how much Josh wanted her to stay, Meagan met his gaze and told him the truth. "I couldn't live with myself if something happened to you because of me."

"I thought you would say that. And as long as I know you feel that way, I won't give up on you. Shit, if I knew where the hell he was, I would go find him and…"

Meagan appeared stunned by Josh's aggressive insinuation.

"Settle down, I would just tell him it would be in his best interest to move on."

"Why don't I believe you?" Meagan could barely get out the words.

"Come on, sweetheart, we better get inside before we miss dinner. We'll talk later about squeezing in another lesson. I will check the weather and let you know."

"Okay. Would you believe I would rather have another lesson than have my teeth pulled?"

"Wow, it's nice to hear I did something right," Josh said with a grin and slowly withdrew his hand.

12

Before Josh and Meagan reached the porch, Ben held open the front door and Molly ran out to greet them. "You don't need to hurry. Pete just started the chicken. I forgot I used the last of the charcoal, so we borrowed some from Mr. Calhoun."

"Works for me. I thought we were going to be late," Josh nodded with relief.

Meagan carried her parka, both of Josh's jackets, and her bags from the drugstore into the house while Josh followed, hauling his hefty duffle bag and gun case.

"Hi, Sissy, how was your day? Did Josh take good care of you?"

Smiling at Ben, Meagan could not come up with the words to describe her exhilaration. "I had a great day, Benny, and Josh took very good care of me. How about you? Did you and Pete finish all your work?"

"Oh yeah, we were back here by three. So, are you two as hungry as we are?"

"We are starving," Josh declared, carrying his rifle case and duffle into the den while Meagan stood by with the coats and bags.

"It's about time, Mackey," Peter joked from the doorway where he was holding tongs in one hand and a beer in the other. "I was going to send out a search party for you two, but I figured Benny would be more help after filling his belly."

"How nice of you to think about us. I don't suppose I have time for a fast shower before we eat?"

"I think so," Peter replied and approached Meagan. "I don't know anyone who looks as good in that hat as you do."

"Thank you, I'm hoping Josh lets me take it home as a souvenir." Meagan hoped Peter caught her inconspicuous way of telling him she had decided to go home.

"I don't know, Miss. It is my lucky hat." Josh was smiling when he winked at Meagan.

For Meagan's sake, Peter acted as though he didn't hear her and hid his disappointment. "All your hats are lucky. How did you shoot?"

"Not bad. You should have been there, P.D. Meagan did great. She sure surprised me. A couple more lessons and we will have some real competition. She already shoots better than Benny."

"Hey now, watch it," Ben warned his brother.

"Now *that* doesn't surprise me. I want to hear all about it, but I need to get back to the grill or we will be eating blackened chicken."

Meagan looked to be in a hurry when she handed Josh his jackets. "I hope there is enough hot water for both of us." Before Josh could reply, she sprinted for the stairs.

"I'm right behind you," Josh declared, chasing after her.

Meagan raced through her shower, hastily worked some hair gel into her curls, dressed and rushed downstairs to the kitchen. It was when she saw everyone seated at the table and waiting for her that she froze in her tracks. "Oh, I'm sorry." Completely embarrassed, Meagan was about to turn around.

"Yur fine. Lass, please come in and eat yur supper. I know yur starvin' like the rest of us."

The instant Meagan gave in to Bess's coaxing, all three men went to their feet.

"I was about to come looking for you," Josh whispered in Meagan's ear and politely pulled out the chair next to him.

For some odd reason Meagan pictured Jillian sitting in the chair and hesitated a second time.

Ben seemed convinced Meagan would listen to him. "Have a seat, Sissy. If we had a dollar for every time one of us was late for dinner we could all retire."

Meagan was further embarrassed by what she was wearing. Once again out of clean clothes, she was dressed in Josh's baggy sweatpants and oversized T-shirt. She was only slightly relieved to see that he was also wearing jogging pants and a T-shirt. His sandy brown hair was also damp like hers, but it was unusually messy. Thinking he looked gorgeous, she nonchalantly admired his right side until Ben handed her the mixed vegetables. While she began filling her plate, she intently listened to the family discussion. The conversation evolved from the fluctuating temperatures to Ben's cattle coming home after spending the harsh winter at a neighbor's ranch.

Ben's dedication to his prospering herd was evident. "I think we should keep them in the close pasture. Grazing should be good and they will be close if we want to toss them some hay."

"After the hard winter, I would keep an eye on the calves. Did you guys see any tracks when you were out today?" Josh asked, then took a long swallow of his tea.

"About the usual coyotes but no wolves and most of the tracks were on the other side of the campsite."

"Good. The last thing I want is to spend another spring babysitting calves. If you see more tracks let me know so we can get on it."

"You know I will."

Nodding his head, Josh turned his attention to his friend. "P.D., the barbecue sauce is perfect. You outdid yourself as always. Are you ready to share your secret ingredient?"

"Like I keep telling you: mix a little of this, some of that, add a few pinches for desired flavor, stir well, then brush a generous amount over your chicken, then grill to perfection."

"Come on, Benny, I say we force it out of him," Josh suggested.

"That won't be hard. Count me in," Ben agreed and winked at Meagan.

"You two namby pambys don't scare me. Aunt Bess, tell them to leave me alone."

"The three of yas are pushin' me to the bottle and an early grave. Yur never too old to spend a night in the barn."

Smiling with visible pleasure, Meagan was having a hard time chewing her last piece of chicken. Time after time she was impressed with Bess's strength and sensitivity when it came to handling the grown men. Meanwhile, their deep respect and love for the exceptional woman was obvious. Believing it was the same unwavering love she shared with her parents, Meagan appeared delighted.

Peter noticed Meagan's mood from across the table. "Now there is something we don't see enough. Look at Meagan."

Bess, Ben, and especially Josh all focused on Meagan.

"What...?" Meagan was suddenly self-conscious and dabbed her face with a napkin.

"You were smiling and we didn't want to miss it," Ben's comment led to Josh's compliment.

"What do you know, Miss. I am not the only one who likes your smile."

Meagan could feel her face turning countless shades of red and was too tongue-tied to defend herself.

"Let me see if *I* can make her smile." Ben set his crumpled napkin on his empty plate and looked back at Meagan. "First, I want to apologize for not asking you sooner."

Meagan looked into Ben's light blue eyes with calm curiosity.

"I know you came to Montana to hide, but you also thought you had a job. Since working for your uncle fell through, I want to offer you a job working for me, here."

"Really? Me? I don't know what to say." Meagan could not believe her own ears when Ben, Bess, and Peter all stared at her with eager anticipation.

Strangely enough, Josh was the only one who appeared unpleasantly surprised. "Would someone mind telling me what is going on?"

"It won't be easy work and don't think it's because I feel sorry for you. Josh and I will likely be getting called out more often and could use the help. A neighbor boy has been working with us for years, but he just turned seventeen and will have better things to do. You would help Aunt Bess with the house and help us with the barn and the horses, especially when we are gone."

"Hold on, am I the only one who sees the problem with this? Did either one of you think this through?" Josh blurted out before Meagan could say anything.

Peter quickly jumped in. "Meagan, Benny will take good care of you and maybe a job here could replace the one you missed at your uncle's farm. After talking it over, Benny and I thought you could help each other out."

"What the hell, P.D.? You knew about this?" Josh made no effort to withhold his resentment.

"We just came up with the idea today."

"So neither one of you could find the time to pick up your phone and clue me in?"

Meagan couldn't believe Josh didn't have something to do with the shocking plan. "You honestly didn't know?"

"Hell no, I'm as surprised as you are. No, I'm even more surprised."

Like Josh, Peter didn't hold anything back. "What the hell has gotten into you? We thought you wanted her to stay. I thought you of all people would do anything to convince her not to go back to Illinois. I would have never guessed we needed your permission."

"You should have discussed it with me. You obviously needed me to tell you the problems with your idea. Not that you two give a shit, but I will be in the den." Josh got up from the table, shoved his chair in, and tore out of the room.

"Oh no, he is so angry. Why doesn't he want me to work here?" Meagan fought to stop her watering eyes. "Should I go talk to him?"

"Don't worry about him right now. Josh is a big boy," Ben stated with certainty. "I know it's a tough decision, so take all the time you need."

Peter supported Ben's statement. "Like I told you when we talked in my truck, this is your decision and no one else's."

Bess didn't say a word and started to clean up.

"Thank you for the offer, Benny. It means more than I can say." When Meagan's gratitude got the best of her, she dabbed her eyes with her napkin. "And I'm sorry, as much as I want the job, I need to think about it." Hoping Ben understood, she pushed herself away from the table, picked up a plate, and began to rinse off the dinner dishes.

"No problem."

Peter slowly stood up, sighed with noticeable disappointment, and went over to speak to Ben. "I will be in the den *trying* to talk to Josh."

"Good luck. Holler if you need reinforcements." Ben gave Peter a considerate nod then started picking up the silverware. "Aunt Bess, what time is your appointment at the salon?"

"'Tis at nine o'clock."

"Can we leave by eight?"

"Aye, that will be fine."

"I will see you ladies tomorrow," Ben announced, and kissed Bess on her cheek. "It's been a long day. Molly and I are going to head up to my room. Sissy, I will be awake for a while if you want to talk. Just knock on my door."

"Thank you again," Meagan didn't hesitate to hug Ben.

"Anytime, and sleep well." Ben gave Meagan a brotherly squeeze, looked into her grateful eyes, and grinned. Then he left the kitchen with Molly taking the lead.

"Aunt Bess, did you know about the job offer?" Meagan helped Bess load the dishwasher.

"Aye, Benjamin asked what I thought."

"Thank you for trusting me."

"Yur welcome, lass. I wish ya would trust us the same. We would never hold anything against ya. Whatever comes our way would be our own doin'. Stop runnin' and trust yur heart." Bess lowered her voice to a whisper. "I can see it in Joshua's eyes…and yurs. I see the special way yas look at each other. Yur both smitten."

"Oh no, ma'am, it's not what you think. I'm done with men. They make me uncomfortable and I could never, you know…"

"Yur still healin'. It takes time. I've been where yur at a long time ago. Just listen to yur heart, lass…yur not as done as ya think ya are. Just give *yurself* a chance. Joshua is my patient one. He will wait fur ya. And don't worry, he will never know we talked. He wants to make ya happy, Meagan, and I can see ya want the same fur him."

"It's not like that. I just *like* him and *trust* him. He's…different. Can I tell you something that you can't tell the Three Musketeers?"

"Aye, yur secrets are *always* safe with me."

"I was thinking about staying and I would even consider Benny's offer, but I know staying will put all of you in danger. Aunt Bess, are you willing to put Benny, Josh, and Pete's life in jeopardy for me? Because *trust me,* if I stay here that is exactly what is going to happen. When Jeremy finds me, he will hurt anyone who gets in his way."

"I may not know the monster yur runnin' from, but I can tell ya we will do all we can to help ya and have no regrets fur doin' it."

"Thanks for talking, Aunt Bess. I think I will sleep on it and call Pop tomorrow. I hate to think what he is going to say when he hears his daughter is living with the Three Musketeers."

"Tell him not to fret, that I raised the lads to be proper gentlemen. Now I best turn in. Benjamin is goin' to drop me off at the salon in the mornin' before he sees to his errands. We will be gone until the afternoon."

"Okay, and thank you for treating me like family." Meagan paused, then wrapped her arms around Bess's robust back. "No matter what I decide, you will always be my Aunt Bess."

"Aye, tis certain as tomorrow is after today. Good night, lass, and try to rest."

"Yes, ma'am and sleep well." Alone in the kitchen, Meagan wasn't sure if she dare venture into the den or sneak to her room. Knowing the only right thing to do was go check on Josh, she trusted Peter had calmed him down.

After Meagan slowly tip-toed her way to the den, she could hear Josh and Peter's voices, but could not make out a single word. Hoping she was not interrupting anything important, she reached into the room and knocked on the partially open door.

"Yeah, come in," Josh called out.

"Hi…um…please excuse me. I just wanted to…"

"Meagan, sweetheart," Josh couldn't help but grin. "It's only me and P.D. You don't need to knock, just come in."

When Meagan stepped into the den both men were seated on a worn blanket in front of the fireplace, but went to their feet the instant she approached them.

"Please, don't get up for me."

"We were just talking about you," Peter casually informed Meagan with his attractive smile. "Have a seat, but sit on the couch. This blanket is gross."

Meagan went to the edge of the blanket and remained standing. After briefly studying the black and silver pieces spread around the old blanket, she guessed the men were cleaning gun parts.

"Make yourself comfortable, Miss." Josh suggested and pointed to the sofa.

"No thank you, I was on my way to bed." Meagan was drawn to Josh's soft eyes. "I just wanted to say thank you for all your help today."

"You can stop thanking me. I told you we helped each other. So, if you are still up for another lesson, P.D. asked if we want to go tomorrow. We are supposed to have one more day of good weather so we thought we would take the horses out for a ride and shoot here."

"I would love to go for a ride." While Meagan seemed interested in riding, she didn't say anything about shooting.

"Josh has barn duty, so Benny can run errands with Aunt Bess and take her to the beauty salon. She needs to catch up on the gossip," Peter informed Meagan after he handed a dirty rifle barrel to Josh.

"Can you eat an early lunch and be ready by noon?" Josh asked.

"If I am finished with my manicure, pedicure, and highlights."

"Oh, are you going with Benny and Aunt Bess?"

"Get with it, Mackey. The girl is bullshitting you."

Josh lowered his head and stared at Meagan. "Oh really, I suppose you think you're funny."

Meagan knew she was in trouble.

After casually wiping his hands off on a stained, hand towel Josh warned her. "I will show *you* what *I* think is funny." He instantly jumped to his feet and in the blink of an eye took Meagan in his arms. Then he carried her to the sofa and after gently laying her down, he began to tickle her without mercy.

"Okay, okay, I give…I give…Pete…do something." Meagan was laughing so hard they barely heard Josh's phone.

"Hey, Mackey, you're getting a call. Now that's what I call saved by the bell, unless it's Berkowitz. It's not Brody's tone."

"Aw, damn it. I hate getting called out this late. Check my phone, P.D., and see if it's Berk." Both Josh and Peter had set their phones on the rock fireplace ledge to avoid removing them from their pockets with their grubby hands.

"If I was you, I would prefer a call from Berk. It's your ex."

"No shit. Can you see what she wants so I can finish up."

"I would *love* to talk to Jilly," Peter said, faking his enthusiasm.

"P.D., don't be a prick."

"Who me? I wouldn't dream of it. Hello, Mr. Mackenzie's answering service. He is on a hot date right now. Is there something I can help with?"

Meagan sat up and smiled at Peter's all-out lie.

"No, you can't talk to him. He asked me to take a message. Yes, he is here, but his hands are dirty...I just told you, he can't come to the damn phone... He is cleaning his rifle, Jilly. Hold on a second and I will tell him...Mackey, she said to quit fucking with her brothers and stop sending the fucking cops to her house."

"What? What is that supposed to mean?"

"Jilly, Josh said that *you* are the only one fucking your brothers."

"P.D. quit messing with her before you get us both killed."

"Mackey, she said she wants the tickets to the dance since you won't be using them...You are too late Jilly...The ring and the money are both gone...Yes, all of it... He bought a new rifle and scope, and he picked up some new tires and rims for the Ruby. I guess you're shit out of luck."

Josh was putting his forty-five back together and shaking his head. "Tell her no, that I am still going to the dance and need the tickets. Tell her to call for reserve tickets and they cost more."

"Jilly, Josh said you need to get your own fucking tickets. I can't believe *you* of all people haven't heard...He is taking that model from my class...Remember the tall red head he was seeing the last time you dumped him...That's right, the tall red head with the big tits...Now why would I bullshit you? She is helping Rachel find the four of us a hotel for the night. Listen Jilly, I have to go. Good luck scoring those tickets and maybe we will see you there."

Peter paused as if he was listening to Jillian then ended the call. "Just so you know, she told me to tell you to go fuck yourself."

"P.D., you are the world's biggest prick," Josh stated, shaking his head and looking grim. "Don't be surprised if we both wind up in the hospital."

Peter suddenly sounded serious. "What did she mean by you fucking with her brothers? Don't tell me you are having problems with Marcus again? I knew I should have handled him my way, but I listened to you."

"It was not big deal. Lucas and Collin came into B.A.T.'s."

"Why is she complaining you sent the cops to her place?"

"That was probably Timmy, and like I said, it was no big deal."

"Don't bullshit me. We don't need a repeat performance. You need to tell me if Marcus had anything to do with it. I know you aren't telling me everything, but that isn't anything new."

"Marcus wasn't there, now drop it."

Meagan wondered why Josh was being so secretive.

"Why can't you just level with me? Do I need to call Timmy?"

"Well I don't know, P.D., do you? And call Blake too."

"Was Meagan with you?"

"Leave her out of this. I mean it, P.D. Don't go there."

Meagan couldn't believe how the best friends were talking to one another and wished Josh would come clean.

"If it's no big deal then tell me what happened."

"I don't need your help. I can fight my own battles."

"Not three against one. I won't let it happen again."

"Meagan, since Josh is being a pain in the ass, would you mind telling me what went down at B.A.T.'s?"

"I told you to leave her alone. Don't piss me off, P.D."

Meagan looked solemnly at Josh. "Josh, what's going on?"

"Nothing, Corporal Buchanan is making a big deal out of absolutely nothing, as usual. Don't worry about it."

Peter paid no heed to Josh's comments or threats. "Marcus Davenport jumped Josh, beat the shit out of him and threw him out of a moving truck. When we finally found him, he was unconscious in a ditch. He was in the hospital for almost a week and couldn't work for three months because of the damage to his right shoulder, arm, and wrist."

"What? Oh my god, Josh, that really happened? Marcus Davenport—is he one of Jillian's brothers?"

"P.D., have I told you that you have a big fucking mouth? Yes, Meagan, Marcus is her oldest brother and it happened after Jillian and I had a fight. She was pissed off at me and told Marcus I was cheating on her. It was about three years ago. It's ancient history." By the worried expression on Meagan's face, Josh could see she was pleading with him to tell Peter the truth. "Okay damn it, Collin flashed his pistol at me, like he wished he had the balls to use it. And like I told you, it was no big deal."

"He threatened you and you didn't bust his ass? You and Timmy both let him walk? You both know he's on probation. What the hell was his problem this time?"

"He demanded I give Jilly back the ring. When he didn't like my answer, he made his move, and I let him know he fucked up. *It was no big deal.* You know I don't like to sweat the small stuff. We will get them when the time comes."

"Damn it, Mackey, you should have called me. Collin is damn lucky none of the guys on your team were with you, especially Brody. The Davenports would be planning a funeral." Peter cut himself off and looked from Josh to Meagan. "I'm sorry, Meagan."

"You don't need to apologize to me, but I think I better say goodnight. I will see you both tomorrow." Meagan took one more look at Josh, smiled with subtle adoration and said, "Goodnight." Then before he could respond, she hurried out of the den and went upstairs to rest up for tomorrow.

13

When Meagan woke early Thursday morning she could not recall a single nightmare. The alarm clock across the room showed it was only six, but her mind took off as if it was beginning a marathon. First, she imagined Josh feeding the horses. Then, she wished she had the tenacity to join him without his invitation. Since he had asked her to be ready by noon she reasoned he was busy and didn't want her in his way. With six long hours to go before they were supposed to meet, Meagan decided to quash one hour by taking a long, hot bath.

Approximately two hours passed before Meagan looked into the hall and found her blue jeans by her door. Grateful for Bess's help, she would much rather ride in her pants than Josh's sweats. After putting on her jeans, she decided to spend some time weaving her hair into a single, long braid.

Meagan's hunger pains were nowhere near enough to push her into helping herself to the Mackenzies' kitchen. She was hoping she could take her mind off her rumbling stomach when she picked up her crossword puzzle book. While she blankly stared at the rows of black and white squares, Meagan pictured her father. She made it a point to call him that evening and hoped he would offer some advice rather than condemn her for leaving. Imagining her father's voice, she recalled how he had a top-notch alarm system installed the day before she was released from the hospital.

Despite Jeremy's unexpected parole and the anonymous flower deliveries that followed, Ken Dawson still believed he could singlehandedly protect his daughter. Meagan did not have the heart to tell him that she didn't feel safe in their home. Worse than that, she was leaving to spare him and her mother from impending danger. Meagan was still staring at the puzzle book when she found it ironic that she was likely going to jeopardize her parents' lives in order to protect the Mackenzies.

"You look puzzled," Josh said, because of what Meagan was doing.

Meagan's entire body seemed to jump off the bed. "Josh, oh my god you scared me. How long have you been standing there?"

"Oh I don't know, twenty or thirty minutes. I didn't notice."

"No, have you really? I never know when you're pulling my leg. "

While he had been watching her for a few minutes, Josh didn't want to admit it. "No, I just got up here." He casually made his way to a tall dresser across from Meagan, tilted his head ever so slightly to the right and gave her his flirty smile. He couldn't help himself nor could he explain what she did to him. He wanted to tell her that he would be perfectly happy spending the rest of the day standing there and watching her.

Meagan could feel herself blushing. "Josh, please. Why do you do that?"

"Has it ever crossed your mind that I might like what I see?" He flirted with her then quickly changed the subject. "I don't suppose you have eaten yet?"

"No, but I'm okay," Meagan replied still embarrassed by how openly Josh was showing his admiration. Not sure if he had showered yet, she found Josh's thickening facial hair oddly appealing. Letting her eyes wander, she hoped he couldn't tell she was admiring his chest, biceps, and forearms. Although she could see his entire solid black, armband tattoo, only half of the fascinating tree on his left arm was visible. She couldn't help but think his faded blue jeans and navy blue t-shirt hugged his body in all the right places. Feeling her face heating up, she wished he would say something. And, as if he sensed her discomfort, Josh came to her rescue.

"I'm going to take a fast shower, and if you don't mind, we can eat an early lunch. Aunt Bess left us sandwiches since she is gone and dinner is going to be late."

"I am always up for one of Aunt Bess's sandwiches."

"Good, I won't be long."

Forgetting her puzzles, Meagan listened as Josh walked across the hall, closed the bathroom door, and turned on the water. She found herself picturing what she could of him, which wasn't much at all, but still more than enough. Listening to the spraying water, she reflected on Bess's words. Could she move on with her life the way Bess suggested? She definitely had more hope today than before she came to Montana. She never thought she would hold a man's hand again, let alone trust one, but Josh quickly proved her wrong. Even though they wanted to be together, she still couldn't picture herself giving Josh what she believed he needed.

"Are you ready, Miss?" Josh asked fifteen minutes later.

"As ready as I'll ever be."

"Good, cause I'm starving and dinner is a long way off."

When they sat down to eat, Meagan concluded by the size of Josh's bites that he had indeed worked up an appetite.

"I hope you're okay with having lunch at ten o'clock."

"Sure, it's like eating cold pizza for breakfast."

"Really, Miss, you like cold pizza?"

"I love cold pizza for breakfast, or pancakes for dinner."

"You just keep surprising me…" Josh had to stop himself again. "I know I asked you to be ready at noon and I don't want to bore you, but if you would prefer some smelly horses over your puzzles, you are more than welcome to come out to the barn."

"I would love to see the horses."

"Great, I'll introduce you to Davey Crockett."

"Who?" Meagan asked.

"The horse you will be riding later. He is Benny's horse, and even though he isn't very happy right now, he will behave for you. I kept him and the other two knuckleheads in their stalls instead of letting them out with the rest of the bunch, so the three of them are a bit ticked off."

After finishing their early lunch and the moment they stepped off the back deck, Josh found and held Meagan's right hand.

Meagan couldn't get over how perfectly their hands and fingers seemed to lace together. She also couldn't get over how quickly she was getting comfortable with Josh's touch.

Josh was still holding Meagan's hand when they reached the wide open main door of the horse barn and Molly came to greet them.

"Yuck, watch it, Miss. Don't let her get close to you. She got into some mud," Josh warned. "Benny is going to have to hose her off."

"She is still beautiful and I bet she is very smart."

"She is awesome to say the least. She's a real lifesaver."

"I can believe it. I would trust her to find me if I got lost."

"Come on, I will introduce you to Crockett."

Meagan walked into the barn and froze in her tracks.

"What is it?" Josh assumed something was wrong.

"What is it? It's a miracle."

"I know. Who would have thought I would come out to do chores and find a pretty lady sleeping on our hay, and now look." Josh held up Meagan's hand, nodded, and winked at her.

"I meant it's a miracle I made it out of the barn alive."

"I wouldn't say that. It was more like good Irish luck." Josh tried to talk over another horse kicking the inside of its stall. "Meagan, say hello to Crockett."

"Oh he is gorgeous. I can see he is a Palomino, but what breed is he?"

"He is a Quarter Horse, but eats enough for the whole barn. He was an awesome barrel racer, but now Benny uses him for search and rescue and chasing his cattle around the place."

"I can't wait to ride him. Thank you."

"Stop thanking me. It will be nice to have you along." After another kick and a whinny Josh yelled, "Cheyenne, settle down boy. Meagan, I better take him out before he gives both of us a headache. Could you please go sit on the hay? He can be temperamental and I'm not sure what he's going to think of you. He never cared for Jillian, not that I blame him."

Meagan giggled and took a seat on the bales while Josh picked up a red nylon lead and walked to the last stall on his right.

"What are you doing down here? We have a guest and you are acting like an ass. If you don't knock it off, you are going to scare her and she won't like you."

Meagan couldn't contain her enthusiasm when Josh came out of the stall leading the most captivating paint stallion she had ever seen. "Oh my god Josh, you didn't tell me you have a Medicine Hat."

"You know about the Medicine Hat?"

"Of course. They are believed to be magical, legendary."

"Well, you can believe it. He has saved my life more than once." Josh confirmed as he attached the crossties to Cheyenne's halter.

"So you're saying it's true? That they can sense danger and will protect their rider from danger, even if they could get hurt?"

Cheyenne was scratching his hoof on the floor and swinging his head, seemingly pleased to be the topic of their conversation.

"It's true, all right. If we had more time I could tell you some stories you wouldn't believe. One involves the cougar in the den. I wouldn't be talking to you right now if I would have been riding any other horse."

"Maybe someday you can tell me. I would love to hear about it. Where did you find him? I'm sure he cost a small fortune."

"Are you afraid of him, even a little? Because he will sense it like the stink of a skunk and won't respect you."

"No, he hasn't given me a reason to be afraid of him, not yet anyway."

"Okay, would you like to come say hello?"

"Really, I would love to."

"Great, walk toward the front of the barn and come back to us. He doesn't like anyone sneaking up on him."

Meagan did as Josh suggested and then offered Cheyenne the back of her hand to sniff. "So, how did you find him? How long have you had him?" Meagan was clearly curious and interested in the magnificent animal.

"Hey, he likes you. He's putting his head down so you can scratch his forehead."

Scratching the stallion between his sky-blue eyes, Meagan felt as if she were a kid again. "Aw, look at you. Do you know how special you are? Yes you are." The powerful horse was taking to Meagan as much as she was taking to him.

"Well, he cost me about a ten thousand dollar rifle set-up and I had to buy a trailer to get him home."

"Sounds like you got the deal of a lifetime."

"I sure did. It was almost five years ago. Cheyenne is six now. Uh, let's just say I had a bad day at work and didn't want to go home. My team leader dropped me off to rent a truck. After I checked into a trashy motel I went to a county fair to clear my head. I was walking around when I saw this elderly couple trying to load a yearling into a trailer. A big stallion was already in the trailer and he kept kicking at Cheyenne. I watched for quite a while and Cheyenne wouldn't have any part of going into that trailer. The old man told me he tried to sell him, but Cheyenne was being such a pain in the ass, nobody would look at him, especially for what he was asking."

"Cheyenne was overpriced?"

"The old fart knew what he had, but needed the right buyer. He said if he had a gun he would shoot both the damn horses and go home." Josh paused and laughed. "So, joking with the old man I said, 'Funny you have a horse you don't want and I have a rifle I don't want.' He started asking me about my gun, and when I told him it was a sniper rifle and had the best scope and accessories money could buy, I knew I had him. To get to the point, I asked him how much he wanted for the horse, and when he said he would take a thousand dollars, I offered him my rifle in trade. I was going to sell it anyway. It wasn't that I didn't have the cash, I just didn't want the rifle."

Meagan was listening intently as she caressed the stallion's soft felty muzzle.

"So after we made the deal, my top-of-the-line sniper rifle for his pain-in-the-ass colt, I had no way to get him home. I didn't want to bother Benny to bring a trailer, so I bought one. It cost me another two thousand. I was lucky to find a used one at the fair."

"That is a great story and I'm sure you are thrilled with your trade. I think you lucked out. When I was a kid, I read books about the Medicine Hat and used to dream about owning a horse like Cheyenne."

"Really? That's awesome. He behaves for me now, but we had a hell of a time in the beginning. It took me over three hours to load him and he didn't want anything to do with me. Since I had the time off, I slept in his stall for over a week to get him used to me."

"Wow, that's incredible. I have never seen such bright blue eyes. I like how they have a dark ring around the outside and get brighter toward the center. The sky blue surrounding the pupil is so intense."

Whereas Josh was impressed with the attention Meagan was giving Cheyenne, he was even more surprised by how well the stallion was taking to her. "He really likes you. I think you can add him to your friend list."

"I will put him on top with you. How would you describe his color?"

"Well, he is chestnut or sorrel, and see how the color on his back lays over his white sides? He is a perfect example of an overo. The sorrel patch around his eyes seems to be getting smaller as he gets older. He has what is referred to as a shield across his chest. He has perfect markings, but I am still not sure if I want to breed him, not that I haven't had some very good offers. I can't have him acting up because he wants to get lucky with one of our mares."

"Is it harder to handle a stallion? He looks so strong."

"I don't have any problems with him, but nobody else can ride him. He is too damn picky. I'm guessing he likes the way you smell." Not thinking, Josh inhaled deeply and smiled. "I know I sure do." He and Meagan were standing shoulder to shoulder when she became embarrassed and looked to her right. "Aw, I'm sorry, Miss Dawson. I shouldn't have said that."

"It's okay. You don't need to apologize for saying something nice. It was just…different." Trying to sound convincing, Meagan was unconsciously facing the sizeable bicep of Josh's left arm. The slightly longer sleeve of his T-shirt prevented her from seeing little more than the black crisscrossing of his tree tattoo.

"I'm sorry it's different, because it shouldn't be. You're not used to being complimented and it's a shame. Do you want me to stop? I hope not, because you deserve it."

"No, I don't want you to stop, but could you please watch who is around? I might faint if you say too much and *that* would be more embarrassing."

"I'm glad you're okay with it, because I was going to do it more often so you could get used to it. And while I am at it, I like your braid. I love your long hair, especially when you leave it down."

"Oh my god, Josh, okay, I think that's good for now, but thank you." Meagan pictured her reddened face and decided to change the subject before he said something else. "May I ask you something?" she asked, and went back to rubbing Cheyenne's muzzle with her fingertips to relax.

"Anything. Ask away."

"Your tattoos, what do they mean? I know people get certain ones because they symbolize something."

"I take it you don't have any?"

"Oh no, Pop would disown me and Mom would die."

Josh chuckled. "Well, let's see, the armband on my right arm. All the guys on my team have some kind of armband on their right arm. We got them at the same time. It was almost five years ago. Mine is Celtic. It represents endurance, strength, and patience. It is supposed to symbolize the Celtic hunter and what goes into a successful hunt."

"That is so cool. I have wanted to ask you."

"You can ask me anything. I'm not shy."

"How many more do you have?"

"Right now, two. One on my left arm and one under my right shoulder. But thanks to my team leader, I will be getting another one soon. He has offered to buy my entire team a tattoo of their choice; as much as we can handle in one sitting. He said it's to show his gratitude for our hard work last year. So, I am going to spend some of his hard-earned cash."

"Ouch, that sounds painful. I saw the one on your left arm last Friday, after you and Benny brought me back to the house. It's a tree?"

"It's a Celtic tree of life. It symbolizes—oh no, hold on, sweetheart." Josh was about to explain his second tattoo when he felt his phone rattle. While he continued stroking Cheyenne between the eyes with his left hand, he slid his phone from the front pocket of his blue jeans with his right hand. "Aw shit, you have got to be kidding me." He shook his head and looked at Meagan. The frustrated and disappointed expression on his face spoke more than any words.

Something told Meagan her ride was about to be cancelled. Hoping she was wrong and not wanting to move, she went on stroking Cheyenne's muzzle.

"Yes, sir…" Josh answered his phone while he and Meagan held each other's dismal eyes.

"Mackey, how soon can you be at the airstrip?"

"About the usual thirty minutes. I just need to grab my gear."

From where she stood, Meagan could hear every detail of Josh's conversation.

"Good, you fly out in an hour. You, Brody, and Andy will meet up with Franky, Shane, and Miguel when you land. Be ready to hit the ground running, son. You will be landing less than ten minutes from the scene. To give you a quick rundown, we have at least six. They hit a bank just over an hour ago, shot a security guard, and wrecked after slamming into a squad. After the wreck, they shot at city and county units, fled on foot, and broke into an abandoned hotel. My latest info is that they are shooting at anyone and anything that moves. Watch your ass, son. Your vest might not save you this time. At least one of the motherfuckers is using AP rounds. They are wearing military gear and backpacks, and I am being told they are putting up one hell of a fight."

"I got it. Other than the guard have any officers been injured?"

"So far, just the two who were hurt when the SUV rammed their squad. Brody will fill you in on where to take position and I will be calling him with updates."

"Sounds good, sir." Josh didn't seem at all nervous as he stared into Meagan's eyes.

"I told Brody to pass it on, but I am going to tell you anyway. I don't want any of you taking any unnecessary chances. Be careful and watch your ass."

"Yes, sir."

Josh hung up with his captain and began dialing his phone. "Shit, Meagan, I am so sorry." His disappointment couldn't have been any clearer.

"It's okay. I know you have to go."

"Hey, P.D., I suppose you have already heard."

"Yeah, my phone has been going crazy for the last half hour. It sounds like you guys will have your work cut out for you on this one. What time are you leaving the house?"

"I'm going to get ready now. I'm due at the airstrip in an hour."

"Okay, see you in a few."

"Thanks, P.D."

"My pleasure."

It went without saying that Josh thought he had the best job in the world, but once in a blue moon he wished his phone would disappear. "Don't get me wrong, Miss Dawson, I like what I do. But I would much rather spend the day with you."

Meagan was speechless. She had no clue how to respond to Josh's straightforward confession. Therefore, it worked in her favor when he walked away, leading Cheyenne out of the barn.

Within a couple short minutes Josh was back. "Okay, we better get up to the house. I need to get ready."

Before they were out of the barn, Meagan spoke up. "Josh, *please* be careful. Is there anything *I* can do to help you?"

Josh sighed out loud when Meagan's words touched his heart. It wasn't necessarily *what* she said, but her heartfelt, sincere tone and genuine concern that roused him. The sensitivity in her voice wiped any remaining doubt from his mind. When her flattering words hit home, he was finally sure of one thing that truly mattered to him. Meagan *did* have romantic feelings for him. Yes, he was on her good guy list and yes, he was her friend, but *knowing* she felt more than she would allow herself to admit made all the difference in the world. Now he had the best reason of all not to give up on her. Because he knew she didn't want him to.

What Josh didn't want was for Meagan to ruin a perfectly good day stressing over him. Regardless of their hurried pace, he found her left hand and was inspired by her firm yet caring grip. Although he knew it would do little if any good, he assured her that he would be fine. "Meagan, I want you to understand something. I am not going to bullshit you and insult your intelligence by telling you that there is nothing to worry about. But I will tell you the guys on my team are the best of the best. We look out for each other in more ways than I can explain right now. My team leader, Brody—I trust him with my life. He is the best. While I don't like to brag, I want you to believe we are very good at what we do, and that is only one reason why we all go home. So, does anything I said help you feel any better?"

"No, not at all."

Forcing a thoughtful grin, Josh opened the back door for Meagan and they promptly removed their boots in the mud room. Then he fondly placed his hand on her back and guided her to the living room. "P.D. is on his way and he will pick up your lesson where we left off."

"Oh no, I can't shoot with Pete. I barely got through it with you."

Josh smiled and nodded to show he understood. "I have to get ready. Have a seat, turn on the TV, and make yourself comfortable. I'll be back in a few minutes."

Josh had barely run up the stairs when Meagan heard Peter's Tahoe come up the gravel driveway and park in front of the porch. He also seemed rushed when he walked in the house and pleasantly greeted Meagan.

"Hey there, Sunshine, it looks like it's you and me but who needs *him*, right? I am perfectly capable of filling in for him." Getting no response, Peter realized Meagan was blankly staring at the floor. "Meagan, are you all right?" Naturally thinking she would be disappointed, he was completely surprised by her hopeless expression. He thought she was about to cry.

"I'm sorry, Pete. It's good to see you. How are you?" If she hadn't been so troubled by Josh's assignment, Meagan would have been more apt to appreciate Peter's arrival. Now that she had spent more time around both men, she surmised Peter was a couple inches taller and broader than Josh. She also thought Peter appeared too hard whereas Josh was firmly well-built, had a sweeter smile, and his blue-green eyes stirred her like no others.

Josh practically ran down the stairs carrying his large black duffle bag and gun case. Dressed in his all-black tactical uniform, he seemed well-equipped right down to his thigh holster, duty belt, and combat-style black boots. By the time he stepped off the last stair, Peter already had the front door open for him.

When Josh breezed past the living room, Meagan watched him with faithful admiration. She welcomed a slight sense of comfort knowing he was so much more than a strong man wearing an intimidating uniform. Recalling how he and Benny overpowered the Randalls, not to mention the confident way he faced Luke and Collin, she knew Josh Mackenzie was a force to be reckoned with.

The second he disappeared from sight, Meagan had all she could do not to cry. But then, when she heard the sound of the door closing on the Rubicon, it was as if someone turned on a spigot. Her steady tears intensified when she realized if Josh wasn't home by Sunday, she might never see him again. The thought alone caused Meagan more pain than she could tolerate.

"Watch your ass, Mackey," Peter stated as if it were an order then closed the back of the Jeep. "If you guys are still up there tomorrow night, I will try to stop by so I can watch you kick some ass."

"I have a feeling we will be there at least through tomorrow. It sounds like these assholes don't care if they live or die. My guess is they know they fucked up and aren't about to give up."

"That would be my guess. You better get going," Peter said, glancing at his watch.

"P.D., I need you to do me a favor."

"Sure anything, you know that."

"I know you are back on duty tomorrow, but can you keep an eye on Meagan for me today? Try to get her out of the house. Are you still going to shoot?"

"I don't *have* to go, and I don't think she is in the mood to go anywhere."

"Scratch the lesson for now, but if she wants to go later, everything she needs is in the backpack on my dresser."

"Relax. I'll take good care of your girl. Now get your head out of your ass and in the game before some asshole shoots a hole through it. And that's if Brody doesn't kick your ass for missing your flight."

Josh glanced down at his watch. "I still have time. I need to talk to Meagan."

"I knew it. You're in love with her. I still don't love *any* woman and look at you." Peter was grinning from ear to ear as he poked fun at his friend.

"Shut up, P.D., and mind your own business." A second later Josh began confiding in his life-long friend. "She does something to me. I can't explain it. It started right away. I don't know what it is. I can't wait to see her, and when I do, I can't keep my eyes off of her. She makes me laugh. She makes me feel safe. She is beautiful inside and out. Is it love? Maybe. I know I'm willing to wait for her and trust her as long as it takes to find out."

"Well, my friend, no one wishes you better luck with this girl than I do. If you can find a way to catch her, she's a keeper. Meagan is the type of girl a guy likes to take home to his family and spend the rest of his life with. Benny and I will take good care of her. You know you can trust us, so you just watch your ass and keep your head down." Still grinning, Peter patted Josh on the back then followed him to the house.

14

Assuming Josh was gone and quite possibly out of her life forever, Meagan was completely embarrassed when he and Peter saw her crying.

"Oh shit, please take me with you, Mackey." Peter grimly reacted to Meagan's distress. "You know I hate to see a woman cry."

Shaking his head, Josh looked at Meagan with compassion. Whether he was moving too fast or not, he had to take the chance. "Please, come with me, Miss."

Meagan used the back of her hand to wipe away her tears then gladly went to Josh.

Josh stepped outside and ushered Meagan to the far end of the porch. He hoped he wasn't crossing the line when he delicately placed his hands on her lower back. Then he affectionately nestled his softening beard against her left cheek and whispered in her ear. "Miss Dawson, do you have any idea what you mean to me?"

Meagan's surprise was unquestionable. "Really, *me*?"

"Yes, *you*. And do you know how much I want to be with you and take care of you? That I want to do everything I can to help you?"

It was the countless ways Josh had shown his emphatic feelings for her over the past several days that encouraged Meagan's prompt reply. "Yes." At first, she was entranced by how inviting Josh's cushy face felt against her cheek. But then, her eyes began to swell and tears of mixed emotions trickled from her face onto his. "Josh, should we say goodbye now? What if I leave before you come home?"

"Do you *want* to say goodbye?" Josh calmly interrupted Meagan and explained his feelings. "I don't ever say goodbye to someone I want to see again. I tell them I will see them later."

Whether it was his sensitive touch or his encouraging words, Meagan brought up her arms and gingerly rested her hands on Josh's shoulders. "No, I don't want to say goodbye."

Josh took a few relaxing breaths and hoped for the best. "If there was a way for us to be together, would you give me a chance? Would you give *us* a chance?"

Josh's stirring proposal filled Meagan with indescribable hope, but under the circumstances she didn't see how it was possible. Thinking she would like nothing more than to have a romantic relationship with Josh, Meagan spoke from her heart. "Yes, yes I would."

"Then take my word for it, this isn't over. By no means is this over. I will get back here as soon as I can and if I don't make it before you leave, I want you to trust me. Can you do that for me?"

"Yes, I trust you and I always will."

"Aw, thank you, and don't forget I have a certain item of yours to deliver to Illinois. Are you okay with me popping in for a visit?" Josh asked, but in his heart he already knew Meagan's answer.

"Really, oh my god, you are serious. Yes, any time." Meagan was in awe that she willingly started a relationship with a man; a man she wanted to be with and genuinely believed in.

"Sweetheart, I have already told you I'm not in a hurry. If you want me, I'll wait for you no matter how long it takes. Do you understand what I am asking and are you *sure* you are completely okay with this?"

"I will miss you and it will be hard, but yes. If you are sure, then I'm sure."

"We will talk as much as possible, every day if I'm not stuck on an assignment. I will help you through it. And there is something I want you to understand."

"Okay..."

"It just became my responsibility to look after you and keep you safe; no matter where you are. I mean it, Meagan. And one more thing before I go. If you change your mind, if you ever want out, you have my word that I won't be an asshole about it. I don't ever want you to be afraid of me and if you are, I want you to tell me."

"I could never be afraid of you. Josh, do *you* trust *me*? If we have to be apart for a while do *you* trust *me*? I promise I will never hurt you."

"I have trusted you since the day I met the real you. Meagan, my mother used to tell me something and I hope it helps you like it has helped me. Even when you can't see me, I am always with you. I have to go, sweetheart, and I will call every chance I get. P.D. and Benny will keep you posted for now."

"Please be careful, Joshua. Promise me."

"Everything is going to be okay. One way or another I will see to it. And try not to cry around P.D." Slowly moving his face against the soft skin of Meagan's cheek, Josh leaned back and fondly pressed his lips to her forehead. Then, he lowered his eyes to meet hers and lovingly traced across her top and bottom lips with his thumb, paying special attention to her healing cut. Lastly, he gave her the same flirty smile that he did when she caught him staring at her. "I'll see you later, Miss." With that said, Josh turned away, jogged to his Jeep, and sped off to meet his plane.

"See you later." Meagan held her fingertips to her lips and watched the Rubicon disappear behind the trees. Still taking in everything that happened, she stood in place and wondered why she was so blessed. When the initial shock wore off, she relived Josh's kiss. "Oh my god, he kissed me. He kissed me and I want him to do it again."

When she returned to the living room, Meagan found Peter lounging in Josh's recliner and eating a ham and cheese sandwich while talking to someone on his phone.

"Thanks and keep me posted." Peter ended his call and looked to where Meagan was silently sitting on the sofa. "Are you feeling better? You don't look as pale as you did."

"Just more confused than ever. I think I will call Pop. Maybe he can help. I want to stay, especially now. But if I do, everyone here will be in danger. But if I go, that wouldn't be fair to Josh. Damn it, I am so confused! Should I do what I want or should I do the right thing? Damn it, Pete, I don't even know what the right thing is."

"You *still* haven't made up your mind?"

"I was *pretty* sure until…until Josh took me outside."

"Don't forget, staying has to be *your* choice."

"I used to believe that, but things are different now."

"Am I missing something? Why do I have the feeling you have something to tell me."

"I think Josh would want you tell you."

Peter beamed, then laughed with pride. "You just did it for him, and I'm happy for both of you. No one hopes it works out more than I do. You won't find a better guy and I'm not just saying that because we have been friends since we were kids."

"Thank you for everything, Pete. You and Benny have been so good to me."

"I have to tell you, this changes things between us."

"Oh no, why? How?" Meagan sounded hurt.

"You just became my best friend's girl and a very important part of the Mackenzie family. It's up to me to look after your best interests when Josh is gone, whether you like it or not."

"Oh, uh, the way you put it, I can't tell if that's a good thing or not."

"I'm looking forward to it. Let's call your dad and see what he has to say." Peter didn't wait to take his phone from his shirt pocket. "I have his number and a secure line. Okay, it's ringing, here you go. And I would like a word with him before you hang up."

"Please don't tell him anything about me and Josh. Well that's strange… it's his voicemail…Hi, Pop, it's me. I know you are supposed to call me later but something has come up. I'm thinking about staying in Broadus with the Mackenzies. I will call back around three." Meagan's face was pale and taut when she looked at Peter. "He always answers my calls. Something is wrong."

"You don't *know* that. You can try again in a couple of hours."

Meagan was handing Peter his phone when he got another call.

"Damn, Mackey, that was fast," Peter told Josh and grinned at Meagan.

"Evidently somebody wants us up there ASAP. It's not very often we get to cruise on a top of the line jet like this."

"I'm not surprised. My phone hasn't stopped ringing since this thing kicked off. It sounds like they need you guys in a bad way."

"Brody said we should land by two and get right to it."

"Good and I don't see us leaving the house. Meagan wants to talk to her dad and I don't want to miss any calls. I am also thinking about hanging out here tonight. I'm willing to bet there will be something good on TV."

"Yeah, the fucking news is all over this. Please do what you can for Meagan. Tell her not to worry and I will call as soon as I can."

"No problem and don't you think *you* should be telling *me* something?"

"Yeah, about that…we are uh…I don't even know what they call it these days or how to put it. We are uh, you know—help me out, P.D."

"You are dating, Mackey, that's one way of putting it." When Peter met Meagan's gaze, he rolled his eyes and smiled.

"Well, I doubt I will be taking her anywhere since she is leaving, but we are together. We are going to try to make it work."

"Good for you, congratulations. You know I will help any way I can."

"Thanks and hopefully I get back before she…hold on, P.D. Brody is getting an update."

For what felt like an eternity, Peter quietly waited for the news.

"Aw fuck. Officer down, P.D. The motherfuckers just shot a cop. Shit, I have to let you go. I'll call when I can."

"Damn it, Mackey, make sure you guys fuck them up."

"You can count on it. I'll see you later."

Meagan didn't need to hear Josh's voice to know something terrible happened. "Pete?"

"Josh is fine. They're still in the air. He can handle this, Meagan."

Meagan sounded outright miserable. "I was standing next to him when he got the call. I could hear everything. It started with a bank robbery, and then a security guard was shot, and police were being shot at. This is real bad, isn't it?"

"Try to understand, Josh has been doing this for years. He started when he was twenty-three and he is thirty-one, so eight years. Damn, time flies."

"But what if something goes wrong? He can still get hurt."

"Wait, wait, wait, stop right there." Peter was visibly upset. "I get that you are scared and this is your first time, but we don't ever talk like that."

"Oh shit, I'm sorry." Meagan said on the verge of tears. "I don't know what to think or say about any of this. He just left and I'm already a wreck. I'm so scared for him I can't think."

"Try to think about his abilities and how good he is. You watched him practice. What did you think?"

"I wouldn't have believed what he could do if I didn't see it for myself."

"Exactly, he is dead on at a thousand yards and I've seen him hit almost twice that. He doesn't miss when it counts. As awful as it sounds, Josh can easily put a round through some asshole's skull at a thousand yards. Try to think about the positive," Peter added, grinning.

"Oh my god, I definitely wasn't thinking of it that way."

I have watched him and S.R.T. handle countless situations over the years. Whether I'm right there on scene or stuck watching them on TV, like I will be doing later. They usually hang back and wait until they are needed, and they train hard for this very thing. It's their job and they all believe failure is not an option. They all have families. Brody, Josh's team leader, has a wife and little girl."

"Okay, I feel a little better. Thank you for the explanation…I think."

"No problem, if you're going to be part of this family there are things you should know." Peter stopped talking when he heard Ben's truck come up the driveway and go to the back of the house. Following a brief stretch, he offered his on-going support. "It might be hard at first, but we will help you. I'm going to help with the groceries and make sure Benny knows Josh is working."

"May I help with the groceries?"

"Sure, that would be great."

With her mind teeter-tottering back and forth between thoughts of her parents and Josh, Meagan wanted to keep busy. After following Peter through the kitchen, she stepped outside and went to Ben's truck. Then she proceeded to carry boxes and bags into the kitchen while Bess held the back door open.

Ben had a gleam in his eye and smiled at Meagan in a way that made her think he knew about her and Josh. "How are you doing, Sissy? Sorry to hear about your plans, but you can hang out with us."

Meagan had to appreciate Ben's optimism. After all, he was Josh's older brother and if anyone should come off as tense, it should be him. Wanting to share his pleasant mood, she tried to sound positive. "Josh introduced me to Cheyenne. I had no idea he had a Medicine Hat. He is so perfect and sweet." Thinking it was not her place to tell Ben about her and Josh's commitment, she decided not to mention it.

"Cheyenne, sweet? If it was possible for a horse to be stuck on himself, that would be Cheyenne. He is nothing but a pain in the ass. And by the way, I'm glad to hear you accepted Josh's bombshell. I have been wondering if he would get up the nerve to ask you."

Meagan's crimson cheeks gave away her embarrassment and Ben laughed enough to express his amusement. "He called me from his plane and you can relax, Sissy. We all know about it. Josh is a good guy and will treat you right, or he'll answer to me," Ben teased again.

After Meagan set the last box on the kitchen table, Bess tenderly took a hold of her hands. She need only see the joy in Bess's soft blue eyes to know Josh's aunt considered her family.

"I'm so happy fur yas and if ya need my help fur anything just ask."

"Thank you for all your advice and your approval."

"Tis a relief to know the lad is truly loved."

Meagan smiled then helped Bess organize another week's worth of groceries. She was so enthralled with Bess's stories about raising Ben, Josh, and Peter that she lost track of time. Seeing it was after two o'clock, she politely excused herself. "I am going to see what Pete and Ben are up to. Please let me know if there is anything else I can do."

"Thanks fur the help, Meagan, and ya should know it helps me to stay away from the TV. It can be harder to watch what happens than to wonder."

When Meagan stepped into the living room she had no intention of staying long.

"There you are," Peter said with a brief smile. "I just got a message. Josh's team landed ten minutes ago and should be taking position any time. I'm sorry to chase you off, but Josh wouldn't want you watching this."

Ben bolstered Peter's warning. "Brody won't let Cassey watch him work. He said if he finds out she's watching him, he will get rid of every TV they own. Meagan, we are taking care of Brody and Cassey's horses and their daughter's pony while their barn is built. If you were staying, you would meet them. Oh shit, there they are." Ben affirmed and increased the volume on the ample, wide screen TV.

Without thinking Meagan sat on the sofa she had shared with Josh only two days ago. Her trepidation soared when she saw six uniformed men with the white letters, S.R.T., across the back of their black bullet proof vests. All six men were running toward close and frequent gunshots. Fearing for Josh like she never expected, Meagan broke into a sweat and barely noticed the news report.

"… then after slamming into a police vehicle and losing control of their SUV, the heavily armed suspects opened fire on responding officers. The suspects then fled on foot to a nearby abandoned hotel where they were somehow able to gain access and…"

A camera crew showed Josh and his team moving fast. Once they crossed the yellow crime tape and disappeared around the corner of what appeared to be an elementary school, Meagan listened to the vigorous reporter.

"For those of you who are just joining us, what you just saw is the arrival of the state's S.R.T. unit, who has been called in to assist local authorities, as well as Montana Highway Patrol and SWAT. It is hoped S.R.T. can join in the effort and assist local agencies who have been in an intense fire fight with at least six heavily armed bank robbers since just before noon today. Several businesses in the area, including hotels and restaurants, were evacuated and an elementary school was placed on immediate lockdown. An emergency alert has been issued for the entire area, advising everyone to remain indoors and avoid…"

"Oh shit, I think I am going to be sick," Meagan held her stomach and went to her feet. "Did you see him? Was he with them?" Due to all six men wearing identical tactical uniforms and running away from the news cameras, she couldn't make out Josh.

Ben cleared up Meagan's confusion. "He was there. Andy Sullivan is the shortest on the team and then Josh. The rest of the guys are well over six feet. Josh is actually pretty easy to spot."

When the number of shots suddenly multiplied, Meagan could not pull herself away.

While Peter sounded calm, his silent turmoil was clear. "Damn, I wish I was there. Everyone is providing cover while the guys get into their positions. When the shooting finally lets up, the guys should be in place and ready to go."

Oblivious to her own actions, Meagan sat down again and watched the news crew take cover behind their van. She trusted Peter's experience when the shooting diminished to a more sporadic level within ten minutes.

"Okay, they should be good. Meagan, it's after three, do you want to try calling your dad?"

"Oh, thanks for reminding me."

"No problem." Peter stood up, found his phone, and went to where Meagan was sitting. Then, he dialed Ken Dawson and kindly handed over his phone.

"Thank god, it's ringing. Hi, Pop...Pop...are you there? It's me, Pop...Are you there?" Visibly terrified for her father, Meagan could hardly speak. "Oh my god...Pete...it's not Pop."

Peter leapt from his chair, grabbed the phone from Meagan and listened. He instantly ended the call and held his finger to his lips to signal Meagan and Ben to stay quiet. Then, he redialed Mr. Dawson's number. When someone answered and Peter heard them breathing, he listened for any surrounding sounds. Following three minutes of nonstop silence, Peter hung up.

Ben looked uneasy. "What's going on, Pete?"

"I don't know. Someone answered, but they didn't say anything."

"Oh my god. Oh shit, something is wrong."

While Peter decided what to do next, Meagan was on the verge of having a panic attack. "Try to stay calm, Meagan. Freaking out isn't going to do anybody any good. Benny, I'm going out to my truck to make some calls and I will be back in a few minutes."

"Take your time." Ben went to where Meagan was sitting on the sofa and put his arms around her. "Take it easy, Sissy. Pete is the best and will find out what's going on. Try to stop crying and breathe."

When Peter returned about fifteen minutes later, Bess and Ben were waiting with Meagan. "Police are en route to your folks' place to check on them. We should know something real soon."

"Thank you, Pete. I know it was Jeremy. I know his breathing. He used to call me and—oh my god, he has Pop's phone."

"Let's not jump to conclusions," Peter advised while holding his phone in his right hand. "If you don't mind, Aunt Bess, it looks like I will be staying here tonight."

"Aye Peter, ya know I'm always glad to have ya. I'm makin' yur favorite meatloaf fur supper. I just hope we feel up to eatin' it."

When Peter's phone chirped, Meagan bolted straight up.

"Oh no you don't, you stay right here with me," Ben told Meagan and snagged her left hand.

"Yes, this is Corporal Buchanan." Obviously wanting privacy, Peter went outside to take the all-important call.

Meagan thought Peter was gone far too long to bring her any good news. First worried about Josh and now stressing over her parents, her head ached from the pressure. The longer Peter took, the harder it was for her to think straight, let alone think positive.

When Peter finally returned, Bess gestured for him to take her place. But rather than sitting, he took Bess by the arm and whispered in her ear.

"Pete, please tell me what you found out."

The moment Bess left the room, Peter sat beside Meagan so that she would be between him and Ben. With his professional and composed demeanor, he spoke slowly and decisively. "Your parents are fine. I talked with your dad for a few minutes, but we had to keep it short. One of the officers who responded to the welfare check was nice enough to let your dad use his phone."

Bess's timing was perfect when she returned holding a pewter tray with four hot toddies. First, she handed one to Meagan. "Here, lass, take a few sips. It will help ya feel better." Then she passed a toddy to Peter, one to Ben, and even took a glass for herself.

Preparing herself for bad news, Meagan downed nearly half of the intoxicating beverage before stopping.

"Like I said, your parents are safe. When your dad got up this morning his phone was missing."

"He always keeps it on the night stand, right next to him. Oh my god." Meagan took another long swallow from her glass.

"Yes, he told me that. Meagan, your dad isn't coming Sunday. He wants you to stay here for now."

"What, why? Damn it, Pete, I need to know what happened."

Ben was shaking his head because he knew something must be terribly wrong for Meagan's father to tell her not to come home.

"After talking it over with your dad, we both agree you are safer here. Meagan, someone got in through a basement window without tripping the alarm." Peter paused again, certain that what he still had to say would be the hardest for Meagan to hear.

"No! How? You're not telling me everything. Please, Pete."

"I'm sorry, there is no easy way to put this. This morning your mom noticed a picture of you was missing. She said it's the one of you from their anniversary party that sits on the fireplace mantle."

Everyone fell silent except for Meagan, who was softly weeping.

Ben was the first to break the silence. "If it was Constadine, he didn't want to hurt your parents. He got what he wanted and left."

"Exactly," Peter agreed with Ben. "Meagan, you don't have to choose between staying here and going back to Illinois anymore. No more worrying about the repercussions of your decision. Your dad and I both think this is the safest place for you, especially after what happened today. Tell me you have finally come to your senses and are ready to stop running."

"Aw, come on, Sissy. You are part of our family now. You need to let us help you. And let *us* worry about ourselves. I have never been afraid of anyone and I'm not about to start now. I don't care *who* Jeremy Constadine *thinks* he is. None of us do."

"Okay, okay, I'll stay on one condition."

Ben seemed to read Meagan's mind. "You want the job."

"Yes, I want the job and please keep me busy. I like to work."

"Great. You can start Saturday. Tomorrow we go shopping. I'm tired of seeing my sister wearing my brother's sweatpants."

"It's about time," Peter said, referring to the news.

"Oh my god, it's him. That's Josh. Oh my god." While holding her drink in one hand Meagan pointed at the TV with the other. "I know that guy is Josh."

Peter watched the live footage coming in from a news helicopter that showed Josh prone on the roof of what appeared to be a diner. "And what makes you think it's him?" Peter wondered how Meagan was able to recognize Josh.

"His right leg, he always bends his right leg. Oh my god, isn't that the hotel where the robbers are hiding?"

"The girl is smart *and* very observant. You're right, Sissy, it's Josh and he's okay." Ben confirmed what she suggested.

After quickly finishing the last of his toddy, Peter tried to comfort Meagan. "See how he is laying? He is just taking it easy and watching for an opportunity. See the way he is resting his chin on his left hand while he keeps his right hand on his rifle? As soon as he gets the okay, he'll take his shot. The asshole Josh is watching through his scope has no clue he is a target, or what's coming."

Ben followed Peter's lead. "And the guys on S.R.T. don't shoot for the hell of it. They are sneaky and quiet. Josh won't shoot until he knows he is dead-on because he doesn't want the motherfuckers to know where he is."

Bess gathered the three empty toddy glasses and went to the kitchen, leaving Meagan with Ben and Peter.

"Will it get easier?" Meagan couldn't stop her tears. "I don't know how to do this. I feel so helpless. How did Jillian do it? How did she handle his job? Oh shit, what if I—what if I can't?"

Ben offered his opinion and advice first. "This is all new to you. You were just getting to know each other and he got an assignment. We will all help you, Sissy. For one thing, Jillian didn't live with Josh. She had her own life and did her own thing. I would act the same way in your shoes."

Hearing Ben's words and still reeling from the day's events, Meagan quietly wept. She didn't mean to cry, she just couldn't stop.

"I will be right back," Peter said and headed toward the kitchen.

"How do you do it, Benny? You are his brother and you don't seem at all worried. Besides that, I am not strong like you and Pete."

Peter was back and carrying another round of Bess's toddies.

Meagan politely refused the drink. "Thank you, Pete, but I am not much of a drinker."

"You're welcome and today you are. I am not a big fan of alcohol, but there are times I really like it." Peter smiled at Meagan, handed a toddy to Ben, and took a long sip.

Ben did his best to answer Meagan. "Because he is my brother and I love and respect him, I have to accept his choices, good and bad. It's his life and he loves what he does. It doesn't matter if he is working or at home, I worry about him day and night. He was almost killed tracking a cougar right here at home. I think my belief in him helps me the most. I know he can handle himself. And I trust his confidence in himself and his team. Meagan, I am only going to tell you this once. If you care about him like I think you do, if you want to be with him, and you obviously do, you will accept *everything* about him."

Seeing an opportunity, Peter got into the conversation. "He's crazy about you, Meagan and I think he would do anything for you, but his job...I hope you know how important it is to him."

Almost halfway through her second toddy, Meagan stood up to defend herself. "Oh no, you don't think I would ever come between Josh and his work?" Her assumption of what the men were implying triggered more tears.

"I don't think you would *mean* to do it," Peter replied.

"Well, if it makes you two feel any better, I care about Josh. So much that I want to be with him no matter where he works and what he does for a living."

"Okay Sissy, I know I've heard enough." Ben quietly walked over to a hand-crafted oak bar, went behind it and set up three shot glasses. "Aw, don't be mad. Come have a couple shots with your big brother."

Peter put out his hand and helped Meagan stand. Then he placed his right arm around her waist and guided her to a high-back bar stool.

"I really should eat first. It doesn't take much for me to get stupid drunk and I haven't drank this much in a long time."

"Don't worry about it," Ben grinned and filled the three shot glasses with tequila. "I think you have a lot to celebrate. You started a new relationship, you finally decided to stay, *and* you just accepted a job working for a great boss."

Peter raised his glass and made a toast, "To Josh and Meagan."

"Yes, to Josh and Meagan," Ben repeated with heartfelt pride.

Ben and Peter slammed the tequila and their glasses down well before Meagan finished hers. Wasting no time, she chased the shot with a good portion of her toddy. Recovering from the tequila, she failed to notice Ben and Peter nod and grin at each other.

Ben refilled the glasses and once again he and Peter downed the second round while Meagan took slightly longer.

"Supper is ready and waitin' fur yas," Bess announced before returning to the kitchen.

Peter offered his help. "Relax, Meagan, I'll bring you a plate."

"What kind of meat is it, in the meatloaf?" Meagan asked.

Both Ben and Peter ignored the peculiar question. "Go ahead, Pete, I will wait here with Meagan."

Meagan didn't think anything was wrong with Bess's meatloaf. She was understandably too upset to eat more than a few bites. After repeatedly being told that she did not need to help with the dishes, she finally stopped arguing.

"Listen, Sissy, I have to run out to the barn. Hang out with Pete and I will see you in a few minutes."

"If I were you, Sunshine, I would take it easy while you can. It won't be long before Benny will have you working your butt off."

The small amount Meagan ate did very little to curb the effects of the tequila and the Irish whiskey in the Toddies. While she was not in a full drunken spin, she was having a difficult time focusing on the 52-inch flat screen. Straining her eyes, Meagan longed to see Josh again and discern for herself that he was not in any immediate danger. At the moment, however, the news channel was televising interviews from immediately after the robbery.

One after another, bank employees and customers provided their dramatic accounts. They described how six masked gunmen burst into the bank and shot the security guard before forcing everyone to the floor. Several victims described being terrorized and told they were going to die. Witnesses outside the bank recounted alarming details of how the SUV fled from the bank and raced through the busy area at a high rate of speed, nearly hitting many helpless pedestrians.

Not long after Ben was back in his recliner, Meagan got her wish to see Josh, but all too soon came to regret it. Two news helicopters were circling the scene while in flight camera crews and reporters simultaneously broadcast the action.

The first male reporter came across as being highly ambitious. "We have just received information that authorities here are ready to use every means available to prevent this appalling situation from going into a second day. And as you are about to see, S.R.T. is strategically positioned well within range to utilize their skills to do just that."

The second male reporter jumped right in to confirm his co-anchor's analysis. "Yes, that is correct, Mitch. The entire unit has been called in and has the hotel completely surrounded. It appears all six S.R.T. sharp shooters are ready to take control of this menacing standoff. What you are seeing at this very moment is one of the S.R.T. shooters across the street from the hotel, on the rooftop of the city's firehouse."

Peter leapt to his feet. "No! Shut your fucking mouth!"

"...another is prone on the roof of the theater..."

Ben knew exactly what Peter was getting at and wanted to punch the reporter. "What the fuck is he doing? Is he out of his fucking mind?"

"There is yet another on the roof of Lizzie's Pancake House and a fourth making use of a balcony at the Northwest Apartments." As the news reporter described the places of all six sharp shooters, cameras simultaneously zoomed in on their exact locations.

Peter knew what was coming. He had seen it happen before. "His fucking mouth is going to get them all killed! He just fucked over the entire team!"

Suddenly all hell broke loose. A cameraman aboard helicopter 1 filmed the initial barrage of bullets fired at Andy Sullivan. Andy was standing at the ready, atop the firehouse when he was the first to come under fully automatic gunfire.

"Aw fuck! I fucking knew it! Get on him, Mackey! Get on him!"

Meagan's hands went to her mouth. Then, before she could catch her breath, she got her wish. A second cameraman zoomed in on Josh's reaction to the shots being fired at Andy Sullivan. Just like the first time, Meagan didn't need anyone to tell her she was watching Josh.

"Make them count, Mackey. Put them in there." Peter and Ben were both trying to remain calm as an all-out gunfight unfolded and Josh was smack dab in the middle of it.

Even Meagan could see the brass casings as they flew out of Josh's M25 and bounced across the cement balcony. Holding her breath and paralyzed with dismay, it was Peter's sudden outburst that affirmed what she could not bear to watch. In less than a millisecond Josh went from assisting his team to being in dire need of their help.

15

"Aw, fuck! Cover up, Josh! Where the fuck are you, Brody? Stay down, Josh! Cover up! Aw, fuck!" Both Ben and Peter shouted in horror as bullets pelted and chipped the cement immediately to Josh's left then shattered the glass patio door behind him.

Lying perfectly still, Josh appeared to be using his forearms to shield his black protective helmet. His lack of movement and buried face made it impossible to determine if he was hurt, let alone the extent of his injuries.

Whether it was for their own safety or because they did not want to televise Josh's demise, the camera crew stopped filming the attack.

"What the fuck? I don't believe this shit! Who the fuck do they think they are?" Peter was livid and in a tirade over the reporters' absurd behavior.

"Son of a bitch! We don't even know if he's okay! Fucking reporters! They don't give a shit about anyone but themselves!" Ben could only hope his younger brother survived the heinous assault.

"Continuing to bring you live coverage, it seems that at least one of the bank robbers has been struck by S.R.T. bullets and appears deceased." Helicopter 1 was hovering over the hotel roof, thereby providing footage of the gunman's body and a menacing rifle just beyond his reach.

Hearing Ben's agonizing words, Meagan finally succumbed to her emotions. She pressed her hands over her mouth and made a b-line for the front door.

"Oh shit!" Ben noticed Meagan was about to spew and somehow managed to beat her to the door. He swung it open with one hand then followed her down the porch steps and to a nearby patch of grass.

Meagan scarcely made it out of the house and off the front porch before she threw up. "I am…so…sorry, Benny."

"You're kidding, right?" Ben lightly wrapped his right arm around Meagan's waist then held back her braided hair. "It's okay, let it out."

Meagan stopped spitting long enough to vomit a second time. "Shit. This sucks." She bent over and repeatedly spit while Ben protected her braid. "I'm sorry, I'm so embarrassed. You must think I'm such a drunk."

"I know better than that, and don't be embarrassed. I guarantee you that I have been falling-down, puking-my-ass-off drunk a zillion times more than you, and besides that…" Ben paused before coming clean, "…we were hoping you would drink enough to pass out before anything bad happened. I'm really sorry you saw that. I shouldn't have let you watch."

"I should have known you two were up to something."

"What do you think friends and older brothers are for? Come on, let's get you back inside. You can hardly stand up."

"No, please, go ahead. I don't think I'm done yet," Meagan warned Ben while holding her stomach and wincing.

"Come on, I will get Bess's puke pail. And if you make a mess I will have our new maid clean it up in the morning."

Meagan knew Ben was teasing and referring to her as the new maid to cheer her up.

"Benny?"

"Yes?"

"I have been afraid before. I mean terrified for my life. But I have never been as scared shitless as I am right now."

"I know and I'm sorry. But I think you can relax for now. I *know* Josh is okay. He is my brother and I can feel it," Ben declared and grinned. "Seriously, Sissy, if something happens to Josh, either his captain or his team leader must notify me immediately. And not that I should need to, but if Josh needs me for any medical reason, I am to be taken to wherever he is, no questions asked. I would say it's been over ten minutes since we saw him and knowing Josh, he is right back to giving them hell on earth."

"I hope you are right. The last time I wished I could see him, well, you saw what happened. I feel like it was my fault."

"It does no good to worry. He will call me after things calm down. Brody always relieves him for a quick break. Do you want me to wake you up? It will probably be well after midnight?"

"Really, can you?"

"Yes, but you have to keep it short. He doesn't usually have much time."

"I will. Benny?"

"What?"

"I miss him."

"I know, and guess what? I bet he's thinking about you right now, so let's get back in the house and see what Pete has found out." Before Meagan could argue, Ben carefully picked her up and carried her back to the sofa.

Peter immediately confirmed Josh was alive and well. "He's fine. I got a call from the trooper parked at a pharmacy about forty yards west of him. He has been watching Mackey since he moved from the diner to the apartment balcony. He will call me if anything changes."

"See, Sissy, what did I tell you? I'll be right back, Pete. She needs the puke pail."

"Ah yes, the dreaded puke pail, that's awesome. Once you barf in our bucket, you are definitely one of us." Making the most of his amusement, Peter chuckled at Meagan's expense.

"Hurry, Benny!" Meagan covered her mouth and Ben barely made it back in time before she made generous use of the pail.

"Now that's what I'm talking about. But you know what; you will have to do it again when Josh is here. He won't believe it if Benny and I tell him." Peter's comment made Ben laugh all the way to the stairs.

"Pete?" Meagan raised her head from Bess's cleaning bucket.

"I'm right here."

"Thanks for staying with us." Meagan leaned back on the sofa and closed her eyes while the room seemed to circle around her swaying head.

"My pleasure, and for what it's worth, I think you made the right decision by staying. Try not to worry about it. No one else is."

"You don't know how much I hope nothing happens to change your mind."

"You don't know how much you mean to us. I'm sure you have noticed every one of us thinks of you as family. Funny, Benny always wanted to trade Josh in on a little sister."

With her eyes half closed, Meagan struggled to focus on Ben when he returned with a stack of blankets and pillows. She watched him hand a huge pillow and light cover to Peter and then set a quilt and pillow on the sofa next to her.

"Sissy, knowing us the way you do, do you think there is anything we can't handle, especially when we are together?"

Meagan had no doubt Ben was referring to Jeremy. "He is nothing like Donny and Billy. He is much smarter and crazier. I don't think he is afraid of anything and he thinks I *belong* to him. Don't forget he got past my parents' alarm system and took Pop's phone from their night stand, while Pop was sleeping only a couple feet away."

Peter could only imagine Meagan's fear and pain. "I have heard so much about this asshole, I can't wait to meet him."

"Now you sound like Josh." Meagan's intoxication did nothing to diminish her anxiety.

"I am always up for a good challenge. How about you, Benny?"

"You know me. I never turn down a good fight and when I get my ass handed to me, I chalk it up as a learning experience."

Meagan lay down and watched Peter carry his pillow and blanket to the large couch on the left side of Ben's recliner. The last thing she saw before passing out was Peter reaching into a gym bag, changing into a clean T-shirt, and placing his forty-five on the coffee table between him and Ben.

It was well after two o'clock in the morning when Ben finally heard from his brother. "Are you okay? You scared the shit out of us."

"A little tired but we're all fine. We were just about to take out our assigned assholes when the fucking helicopters showed up. But it won't happen again. The stupid fuckers got themselves grounded and might be out of a job."

"I'm glad to hear that. The dumbasses almost got you and Andy killed. It looked real close, Josh, too close."

"Yeah, I could hear the fucking bullets whizzing past my ear and hitting the concrete. I wanted to shoot down the fucking helicopters. Anyway, we were off to a good start until the news crews screwed us. Right after I moved to the apartment building, Brody moved to the theater. That's where they should have put us to begin with. So, about thirty minutes after we moved, one of the assholes in the hotel started shooting an antique fire truck in front of the fire house. Brody put one in the asshole's throat at five-hundred and twenty yards. I knew it wouldn't take him long once we moved."

"Wow, I bet he was happy with that one."

"Oh no, you know Brody. He thinks he hit him too low."

"That sounds like Brody."

"At least he is satisfied with the team's progress. We have four down already."

"That's definitely progress, and that's why you guys are the best."

"As long as they give us a shot we are going to take it. I was already locked on the asshole who shot at Andy, so that one was a gimme."

"You couldn't have timed that one any better. Nice job."

"Thanks. Enough about work. How is Meagan?"

"From the looks of her, she is sleeping like a baby."

"What, you are sleeping with my girl?"

"Yep, me and Pete. We had a sleepover and invited her. She is sleeping on the tan sofa and Pete is snoring away on the big couch."

"Aw shit. Tell me you didn't let her watch us."

"Well, you know. Let's just say it wasn't our plan."

"Damn it, Benny, this one was bad. I bet it made her sick."

"Uh, you could say that. *Literally sick.*"

"No way, she barfed? I told her my job was no big deal. That we just sit back, watch and wait, and nothing ever happens. And you two morons let her watch some asshole nearly put a bullet in my head. Thanks, Benny. Thanks a lot."

"Now take it easy. I think it was probably more the alcohol than you getting shot at. She was feeling like shit before it happened."

"Oh that's great, now I feel better. I go to work, nearly get killed, and my brother and best friend get my brand new girl drunk off her ass."

"Hang on. We thought we could get her buzzed enough to pass out before shit went south. The girl is immune to Irish whiskey. We had to go to tequila. Hey, shouldn't you go back?"

"No, it's been quiet since dark. Brody told me to grab something to eat and take a couple-hour nap. So I'm kicked back on a cot at the firehouse. At least I don't have to worry about leaving her with you and Benny again. If I don't make it back before she leaves, keep her away from the TV or stop watching the fucking news."

"About her leaving..."

"Now what. I'm afraid to guess."

"Josh, Meagan isn't going home, at least for the time being. She will be here when you get back, no matter how long this assignment takes."

"What, no kidding? What made her change her mind?"

"There isn't enough time to go into it, but she is definitely staying. I must say you finally got a keeper. Pete and I both think she is good for you."

"No shit, I don't believe it. I was so sure she was leaving."

"We all were, and she asked me to wake her up when you called. Do you have a sec? She really needs to hear your voice."

"Hell yeah, who says I need a nap? See if you can wake her up." Josh could hear Ben trying to bring Meagan around.

"Sissy, wake up. Josh wants to talk to you. Come on, Sissy."

Peter also heard Ben and sat straight up. "Is he okay?"

"He's taking a break. She wanted me to wake her up when he called."

"Ah okay, keep trying to wake her and I'll be right back." Peter quickly returned with a cold, damp cloth. Then he handed it to Ben, who gently pressed the cloth to Meagan's face.

"Sissy, come on. Talk to Josh. Wake up."

The sensation of the cool compress finally roused her. "Benny…oh my god, is he…is he okay?"

"Here, talk to your man."

"Really? Hello, Josh?"

"Are you with me, Miss?"

"Oh Josh, are you okay?"

"I think I should be asking you that. Are *you* okay, sweetheart?"

"I am now. Are you coming home?"

"Not yet, but we shouldn't be too much longer. I am glad to hear you decided to stay. I feel a lot better."

"Me too, I saw what they did to you and the people at the bank. Have you heard anything about the police officer they shot?"

"The last I heard he made it through surgery."

"That's some good news. Josh, are you kicking their asses?"

Josh laughed because the words didn't sound right coming from Meagan's sweet lips. "I am happy with our progress. We managed to make direct contact with a few of them." Josh laughed again, wondering if Meagan caught on to what he meant by "make direct contact."

"*Please* be careful and thank you for talking to me. I will see you when you get home. I miss you, Joshua."

"I miss you too. And remember, even when you can't see me, I am always with you."

Meagan didn't want to let Josh go, but handed Ben his phone. "Thank you, Benny." She put her arm around his neck and gave him a heartfelt and warm hug.

"You're welcome. Are you okay?"

"I'm fine now, thank you. Will he be much longer?"

"He told me they got four already, but it's impossible to predict these things. You know he is okay, so try not to worry and get some sleep."

Meagan inadvertently followed Ben's advice well into Friday afternoon. She didn't even stir when Bess checked on her periodically throughout the day. It wasn't until she heard someone coming in the front door that she raised her head and looked around.

"Good afternoon, Sunshine. Oh damn, I take it you still feel like shit?" Peter was grinning when he knelt down beside Meagan because he was all too familiar with the way she was feeling.

Meagan didn't think Peter could have gotten much sleep, but he appeared just as striking as usual. Well-built, well-groomed, and eye-catching in his impressive Montana Highway Patrol uniform. "Hi, Pete." She met Peter's kind, gray-green eyes and became instantly embarrassed. She was sure she looked awful and likely smelled even worse. "I feel like you ran me down with your Tahoe and then backed over me—more than once."

"Ouch, you really *aren't* a big drinker. Go upstairs and sleep it off. Ben and Bess are outside and I will ask her to come check on you."

"No, please don't bother her." Meagan pleaded while moving her hands from her gurgling stomach to her pulsating head.

"Hush, you need something to drink. And try to eat something."

"Pete, how is Josh? Have you heard anything today?"

"Josh and his team are fine, but the last three are just as bent on dying as the others."

"After everything they have done, anyone can see they have no respect for life."

"No, they don't. I have called in some favors and will be heading up there as soon as I leave here."

"Oh no. Not you too. Please be careful."

"I will, and I'll call Benny tonight to check in."

"Thank you. I hate not knowing anything for so long."

"No problem. I also stopped by to tell you I am going to pass along Jeremy's picture and see what else I can find out about him."

"Please don't go to any trouble."

"Hush, Meagan. Sorry I can't stay longer but it's a long drive. Before I forget, Josh and I will both be too far to help you, so I want you to stay close to Benny."

"Will we see you next week?"

"For sure. And, Meagan, please behave yourself and don't do anything stupid. I expect you to be here when I get back."

"I'm not going anywhere, Pete, not if I can help it."

"Feel better and get some rest." Peter was in an obvious hurry when he turned away and walked out the front door.

After watching Peter leave, Meagan intended to brush her teeth and take a shower. However, after struggling just to make it to her room she had to lie down. Her throbbing head and lingering dizziness were still making her queasy. Deciding to take Peter's advice, she covered up and closed her eyes. Hung over and mentally drained, she wasn't surprised when Bess showed up with a glass of tea, two slices of dry toast, and two ibuprofens.

"Here, lass, have some toast and tea then sleep till mornin'."

"Thank you, Aunt Bess. Will you please ask Benny to wake me if Josh calls, or if he hears anything?"

"I will tell him. Now put some toast in yur stomach so ya can take the pills."

Meagan inadvertently followed Bess's advice and slept until four the next morning. After struggling to read her clock, she immediately thought of Josh and wondered if he called. "Oh shit," she said when she realized it was Saturday morning and she was supposed to start working with Ben. Following a cool shower, she rushed downstairs and into the kitchen by five after five.

"Good mornin' to ya, lass, how are ya feelin'?" Bess smiled with empathy.

"My head and stomach are much better, but I feel very stupid."

"Tis not yur fault. I fixed the toddies hopin' they'd help ya relax and sleep."

Meagan grinned with understanding. "Well, they were very good and thank you for thinking of me. Do you know if Josh called? Benny didn't wake me up."

"No, but Benjamin knows to get me day or night if he needs me. And ya should know, Joshua's job is usually peaceful. But peaceful or not, he loves his team and his work."

"You aren't the first to tell me that and don't worry. I would never do anything to hurt him."

"I don't doubt yur feelin's fur him, but ya must see to yur happiness too, so ya don't resent him fur yur misery."

"Good morning, ladies." Meagan was impressed when Ben went over to his aunt and kissed her on the cheek, but she was truly elated when he gave her a compassionate hug.

Bess smiled with immense pride, then gave her morning weather report. "Dress warm, Benjamin. We are barely over forty and tis gonna shower all day. Tis well into May, but spring is barely teasin' us."

"Sissy, when I am the only one home and Pete is also gone, I want you to stay in the house and help Aunt Bess. The weather sucks and everything is caught up, so I won't be out there long."

"Okay, did Josh call? Is he okay?"

"Yes, he called after one and told me to let you sleep. There is nothing new and SWAT might go in sometime today. Pete also called and said he is parked at a drugstore next to Josh."

"That makes me feel better."

"Me too, and since the helicopters are grounded I don't see any reason why you can't watch the news with me. If it looks like it's going to get bad...well, let's just hope it doesn't."

"Thanks, Benny, and please let me know if I can do anything else."

"I will, and I will have my phone with me if anyone calls."

Keeping busy did little to help Meagan. While she took her time cleaning the men's bathroom and vacuuming the entire first floor, not a minute went by when she wasn't thinking about Josh. Picturing him and recalling how he expressed his interest in her made her miss him all the more. It seemed to take forever and a day before Ben finally called her to join him in the living room.

"Don't worry, I won't offer you a drink." Ben joked with Meagan when he sat back in his recliner, pulled the lever for the foot rest, and laced his hands behind his head.

"I think I drank enough for the whole year." Eager to hear anything new concerning S.R.T. and the bank robbers, Meagan was quickly disappointed. Reporters kept showing the usual buildings and police vehicles while informing viewers that unlike the previous two days, Saturday had been quiet.

It was almost time for dinner when Ben nearly leapt from his recliner. "Oh shit, that didn't sound good. Then again maybe it did."

"What, did I miss something?" Meagan had no idea why Ben was on the edge of his seat.

"I'm not sure but I think I heard a couple shots. Did you hear two shots?"

"Were those shots? They were so quiet."

Ten minutes after Ben and Meagan were discussing the possible shots, his phone rang.

Hoping for the best, Meagan held her breath and watched Ben take the call.

"Hey Pete, what's going on?"

"I only have a second. We heard two shots about five seconds apart and SWAT is going in now. I will call when I know more."

"We were right, Sissy. There were two shots. It might be over."

"Really? How...oh, I hope so."

Within the hour and before the news channel reported the final outcome, Peter called Ben. "SWAT just found them. They took the easy way out. Josh should be home late tonight or early tomorrow."

"All right, thanks for calling. Be safe and take it easy."

"No problem. You too, and I will see you guys next week."

Meagan looked as though she was waiting for life or death information. "What is it, Benny?"

"Pete said the last two took the easy way out and Josh should be home tonight or early tomorrow morning."

"Oh thank god, I mean that it's over and he's coming home."

"I know what you mean and I won't tell you what *I* think."

"Look, Benny, isn't that Josh's team? They must be exhausted." Meagan and Ben watched as the six men formed two groups, boarded two Suburbans, and were swiftly driven from the scene.

"I will pick Josh up when he lands so he doesn't have to drive home."

"Can I go with you? If I sleep down here can you wake me up?"

Ben laughed at Meagan's enthusiasm. "Let's see how you feel when he calls."

It was several hours after dinner when Ben's phone rang again. Meagan was trying to rest on the smaller sofa when she assumed Ben was talking to Josh.

"Nice work."

"Thanks, Benny. How is everything there?"

"Just the usual. What time should you land?"

"Captain Berkowitz doesn't want any of us to drive. So when Timmy called, he insisted on picking me up at the airstrip."

"Okay, call if anything changes. Do you have a minute to say hello to your lady? She has been dying to talk to you."

"Sure, but I have to make it quick. We are in the middle of a meeting with Captain Berkowitz and taking a short break. Go ahead and put her on."

"Josh, is it really over? Are you finally coming home?"

"Yeah, sweetheart, it's over. I should be home by four and don't wait up. Are you feeling better?"

"I am now. I miss you and I will see you tomorrow."

"I'm looking forward to it. Pleasant dreams, Miss Dawson."

Meagan blew out a significant sigh of relief. Her newfound hope and promising future with Josh allayed her heart and soul. "Benny, I think I will go to my room and try to unwind."

"Good for you. And if you sleep with your door open I wouldn't be surprised if Josh pops in to check on you."

"I hope so. I can't wait to see him. Thanks, and I'll see you in the morning." Meagan stopped at Ben's recliner, reached down, and gently hugged his broad upper back.

"You're welcome and take the morning off. I won't need you."

"Okay, wake me up if you change your mind."

Once she was dressed for bed, Meagan's sole intention was to greet Josh. Nevertheless, her intense desire and countless games of solitaire were not enough to fend off her fatigue. All the hours she spent keeping busy since five that morning had caught up with her. I will just take a catnap; she supposed, and put her cards away. Thinking about Josh and her parents when she dozed off, it was a few hours later when her subconscious told her she was dreaming.

"Miss Dawson, are you awake, sweetheart?"

"Josh?" Hardly cognizant, Meagan squinted and saw Josh standing next to her bed.

"Yeah, it's me." Still donned in his heavy, S.R.T. uniform, Josh wearily lay on the empty side of Meagan's bed. "I'm sorry about what happened at your parents'. I know you are probably more worried now than you were, but I think you can breathe easier. Pete and I agree that if it was Constadine, at least he doesn't seem interested in hurting your folks."

After all his threats, I can't believe he didn't hurt them just to get back at me."

"Well for now everyone is fine, so go back to sleep. I will be back after I grab a shower."

This time it was more than Josh's reassuring voice that comforted Meagan when she met his hazel eyes. His loving and promising gaze attested to his commitment to keep her safe from any and all harm. A renewed wave of euphoria spread throughout her body when she watched Josh's eyes submit to his exhaustion. A daring, yet minute part of her longed to invite him to join her under the covers—to welcome him and hold him close like he deserved. At any rate, her lingering apprehension would not release its dreadful grip and she soon fought to stay awake. She wanted to cherish every minute he slept safely by her side, but like Josh, she was worn out; certainly not in the same ways that he was, but the unending stress in her life had become a tremendous burden.

16

The midday sun was pouring in from under the closed bathroom door when it seemed to be Josh's turn to watch Meagan. She had been sitting on the edge of the bed and staring at the sunlit floor for at least ten minutes. He was perplexed when she wiped her eyes and appeared to be crying. "Miss Dawson, what is it, sweetheart? I'm sorry if I offended you. I meant to get a shower and go to my room when you fell asleep, but I..."

"No, no. It's not you. It's me."

"Oh no, here it comes. It's never good when a girl tells her guy that."

"You have done so much for me and I...I am so selfish just thinking about myself, about what I want and about what I need. What about your needs?"

"Now I'm confused. What are you talking about?"

"Look at us. We haven't seen each other since Thursday and I can't even...I should be...you know...taking care of you...and I can't even."

Josh could not leap out of bed fast enough, leaving Meagan to wonder if he was more hurt or angry. "Is that what you think about me, about us, why I wanted to get to know you better—for a good time?"

"Please don't yell."

"I am not yelling. Just what did you think I would be doing after you went back to Illinois? You said you trusted me."

"I do trust you, completely. I'm sorry I said it. I just know what you're used to."

"If you will excuse me, I am going to take a quick shower and go see if I can find a piece of ass, since *that* is what I need."

By the time Meagan showered and hurried downstairs to talk to Josh, he and Ben had left the house.

Seeing Meagan's disheartened face, Bess offered her a sympathetic smile. "Don't fret, lass. Benjamin took Joshua to get his Jeep and they'll be back straight away. Can I fix ya somethin' to eat?"

"No thank you, I didn't mean to make him angry."

"Ah, tis not all yur fault. The lad is not himself; once he gets some rest and home cookin', he'll be the man you know and love."

"I missed him so much. I couldn't wait for him to come home and now he doesn't want anything to do with me."

"Now yur talkin' foolish. Is that truly what ya think? He needs yur patience as much as ya need his. Joshua has been with Jillian fur so long, the lad has forgotten how to court."

"I never know what to say to him and this time I should have kept my mouth shut. Aunt Bess, what do you mean he has forgotten how to court? Courting is dating, right?"

"Aye, he wants to please ya, lass. Ya might think he's brave and strong, but yur a challenge fur him."

"*Me*, a challenge for *him*?"

"Aye, indeed ya are and I'm goin' to tell ya somethin' I shouldn't."

Meagan looked at Bess with eager curiosity.

"Pleasin' Jillian was easy fur him." Bess lowered her Irish tone to a whisper. "Fur quite some time I haven't seen much between the two but makin' love, not that I would call it that. They haven't been *in love* fur quite some time."

Meagan's eyes were wide and her mouth was hanging open.

"Please keep this between us, lass. Joshua would not be happy."

"My lips are sealed, and thank you for telling me."

After hearing two car doors close, Bess looked toward the front door. "They're home and I think it would be best if ya let him make it right."

"I will, and thank you again." Meagan thought Bess's secret information made perfect sense. It would explain why Josh lost his temper with her and made the off-the-wall comment about having sex with any random woman. She just wished he would confide in her.

The front door no sooner opened and Molly Girl trotted into the kitchen as if to see what she was missing.

"Good afternoon, ladies," Ben winked at Meagan and pulled open the refrigerator.

"Can I help ya, Benjamin?" Bess asked with her accommodating nature.

"Yes, ma'am, thank you. I need two ham sandwiches to go."

Meagan's hope of speaking with Josh vanished the moment she heard Ben request the sandwiches to go. She was further crushed when she believed Josh was staying away from the kitchen to avoid her. However, she found out just how wrong she was when he snuck in behind her. She was so amazed and thankful to see him that she unexpectedly met his eyes, but then felt so awkward she had to look away.

Oddly nervous and unsure of himself, Josh placed his hand on the back of Meagan's smooth arm and smiled. "Excuse me, would a forgiving and sweet lady like you consider going for a ride with a low-life ass like me? And if you won't do it for me, please come along for Cheyenne. I think he likes you."

"You are asking *me* to go riding with you?"

"Well yeah, you can't possibly think I would rather go with Benny?"

"Hey, watch it. Seeing as how you are going to the camp site, could you please help with my coyote problem? It sounds like there are more and more of them over there every night. I would do it myself, but you are so much better at it."

"Aw, come on, Benny. I don't feel like *working* on anything. Besides that, you know Miss Dawson is an animal lover. She won't want anything to do with me if she thinks I exterminate puppy dogs. Go ahead Benny, you ask her."

"Sissy, they are nothing like puppy dogs. They are vicious killers and can spread some nasty diseases. To make matters worse, they have pups right now and are extra hungry. We are bringing my herd home on Thursday and the damn things will kill and eat every calf they can catch."

"Don't worry about me. I will just close my eyes."

"Aw, Miss, you say that now," Josh moaned then pointed at Ben. "You owe me. Bring me your recorder and best baiting cassette. I want to call in as many as possible. And just so you know, I was told to rest and relax and I always do what I'm told." Josh seemed to be making fun of his recent orders.

"Thanks, Josh, I'll get a few more Wednesday night."

"No problem and when you see Sarah, tell her I said hi and I'll see her Saturday."

"I will, and call me if anything comes up."

"Oh shit, Benny. Saturday isn't even a week away. What am I supposed to do? Will you ask her for me?"

"Stop being a wimp Josh, and you better hurry."

"Did you already forget you owe me?"

"Oh no, not this. You are on your own."

Meagan looked at Bess, who was smiling as though she comprehended the conversation. Hoping she could help, Meagan expressed her generosity. "Is it something *I* can help with?"

Josh, Ben, and Bess all looked at Meagan and replied in sync, "no."

"Miss Dawson, meet me here in twenty minutes and bring your heavy coat, since we will be out after dark," Josh stated and briefly glared at Benny before returning his attention to Meagan. "You might also want to change your pants."

Wearing Josh's sweats again, Meagan replied, "My only pair of jeans are dirty again. I think I barfed on them. Are these okay?"

"Sure, seeing as how I don't have any jeans that will fit you. I will see you in twenty minutes."

Meagan's heart raced more from excitement than sprinting up the stairs. She was elated to know that not only was Josh over their disagreement, but he wanted to take her riding. Not about to keep him waiting, she quickly twisted her ponytail into a bun, grabbed her sweatshirt, and tied it around her waist. After snatching her parka from the closet, she dashed down the stairs and returned to the kitchen.

Ben was taking a large lunch cooler from the refrigerator when Meagan hurried into the room. "Slow down, Sissy. He isn't going anywhere without you. Make him wait."

"No way. I already ticked him off once today."

"Aw, don't worry about that. I talked to him. He needs to kick back in his hammock, take it easy, and spend some time alone with you."

Meagan felt herself blush. "I have hardly done *any* work."

"No worries, after I bring in the horses I am leaving to spend a few days with my girl, Sarah. For now, just help Josh with chores and help Aunt Bess around the house. Since you will be riding with us Thursday, I suggest you spend some time on a horse."

"Okay, Benny. Have a nice time and I will see you Wednesday."

"Thanks. We better get going. I told Josh I would bring out your lunches."

After Meagan tied her hiking boots and stepped outside, she thought she was in heaven. Josh was raising the stirrups on Crockett's saddle and Cheyenne was impatiently stomping the ground

"I will check them again after you get on." Sounding lighthearted, Josh grinned at Meagan.

"Josh, is it okay if I say hello to Cheyenne?"

"Sure, I told him you were coming with us."

Feeling obligated to Meagan, Ben voiced his cynical opinion. "Be careful, Sissy. He hates strangers. Actually, he's not very fond of anyone but Josh. Like I told you, if a horse could be a stuck-up snob that would be Cheyenne."

"He likes *her*, Benny. He took to her right away. Watch him."

When Meagan stepped in front of Cheyenne, the stallion lowered his head and softly placed his forehead against the center of her chest. Using her fingertips, she lightly rubbed the horse's forehead and scratched him behind the ears. "You are such a good boy and so handsome. Yes you are. Josh is lucky to have you."

"So he likes her today. Don't trust him for a minute, Sissy. Why anyone would waste a dime on a pain-in-the-ass horse like him is beyond me."

"I traded a rifle for him…that I didn't want. The money was for the trailer… that we still use. Don't forget I wouldn't be standing here if it wasn't for this stuck-up pain in the ass."

"I didn't say he is all bad. Enough about Cheyenne. You two have a good time and Josh, I expect you to take good care of my sister. I mean it, behave yourself or you will…"

"Benny, don't you have somewhere to be? You go take care of your girl and I will see to mine."

Meagan was stunned with delight. After hearing Josh openly declare that she was his girl, not even the warmth of the sun could prevent her from breaking out in chills.

"I'll see you two Wednesday night," Ben said with a grin.

"See you Wednesday," Meagan fondly replied before Ben turned away.

"Okay, Miss, hand me your coat." Josh took Meagan's parka, folded it, and stuffed it into one of the leather saddle bags behind her.

It had been years since Meagan rode a horse and she was reasonably nervous. It wasn't necessarily falling that scared her. It was Josh seeing her fall and thinking she was an incompetent rider that worried her.

"That should do it, sweetheart. Hop up and I'll check your stirrups." Josh watched with admiration as Meagan mounted the tall Palomino and found the stirrups.

Meagan didn't dare complain when she thought the saddle felt way too big for her bottom. This has to be Benny's saddle, she thought.

"Okay, I think we are ready. Do you have any questions?"

"Not yet, but I'm sure I will."

"You will be fine. Crockett has perfect manners. Just keep your heels out of his sides or he will take off." Josh untied Crockett's reins from the hitching rail and gave them to Meagan. "All right, Miss Dawson, he is all yours." After slipping on his backpack, Josh put his reins across his saddle horn and without using his stirrups, leapt smoothly onto Cheyenne's back. "If you need anything or want to stop, just say so."

"I will, thank you."

When Josh looked back and saw Crockett was still at the hitching rail he spoke with calm sensitivity. "Meagan, are you okay?"

"I think so. I'm not sure how hard to kick or squeeze him. I don't know what he's used to."

"Just tap him with your boots while you turn him to the left."

"Oh, okay." Meagan turned Crockett's head and lightly placed her boots against his sides. She was next to Josh before she knew it.

Josh smiled when she caught up. "So, how long has it been since you rode?"

"Should I include the occasional trail ride during a vacation?"

"How fast did you go?"

"Honestly, we walked."

Josh laughed at Meagan's comment. "I need to know how experienced you are so I don't get you hurt."

"Well if you put it that way, it's been thirteen years. But I rode all the time when I had Cleopatra."

"Good, it will come back to you. We will just take it slow today and let you work on your confidence."

"Okay." Meagan was so captivated by Josh's alluring appearance that she hardly noticed his words. The confident way he was sitting on Cheyenne, not to mention the way he was wearing his cargo jeans with a matching dark blue and gray flannel shirt over a black tank top, she thought he looked positively gorgeous. His sleeves were rolled up to just above his elbows, allowing her to take in his flawlessly shaped forearms. Right down to his black baseball hat with silver MHP lettering and tan hiking boots, Meagan was awestruck by Josh's engaging impression. If she could have read his mind, she would have known he was expressing his fondness for her enticing good looks when he complimented her riding style.

"You have great form." With a genuine smile Josh added, "I like the way you hold the reins and you have perfect posture. I can tell you rode English. Did you ever ride Western?"

"No, only English for four years."

"That explains it. You look like you know what you're doing, but don't be afraid to hold on to the horn. The time will come when you need it."

"I'm sure I will."

"Meagan, I am really sorry about what I said this morning. I was a real asshole and I didn't mean any of it."

"It's okay. I shouldn't have said what I did either."

"You didn't say anything wrong. You should be able to say *anything* to me. I want to know what's on your mind."

"Okay, and I am sorry I ticked you off. I didn't mean it the way it sounded."

"Forget it. I know you meant well. I also owe you an apology for the lousy way I asked you…to uh…to give *us* a chance. You deserved more than my ten minutes of rushing you."

"You don't need to apologize for going to work."

"If I knew you were staying, I would have waited until I could take you for a nice dinner. I would have asked you the right way."

"You're kidding, right? I knew you had to go and we both thought I was leaving. I…um… I don't care *where* you did it. I am just glad you did, and thank you for not giving up on me."

"Aw, see why I like you? I felt like I had to do something before you walked out of my life. I couldn't let that happen without letting you know that…that I wanted to be with you even if it had to be long distance for a time."

"Oh my god, *seriously*…why *me*?"

"Why not you? Not that I can explain what you did to me. I am always so careful. I don't jump into anything, let alone a relationship. Don't get me wrong, I am no angel. When Jillian and I would see other people, I did my thing. But that was years ago, right after I started with S.R.T. and back when Brody and I were young and stupid. But you, you do something to me. You are different."

Slightly uncomfortable, but since they were discussing their feelings for each other, Meagan opened up. "What about what *you* did to *me*? I told you I was done with men and I meant *all men*. Yet here I am riding alone with you to god knows where and I am not the slightest bit afraid. Should I be afraid?" Meagan joked. "I can't believe any of this."

"Me neither, but I am glad we finally got some time alone. Oh that didn't sound good. I mean so we can get to know each other without any more interruptions."

"Me too. I know you are thirty-one, but when is your birthday?"

"October twentieth and yours is June sixth. Wow, to think I found out your birthday when we were running your background check. So, Miss Dawson, how does it feel to be turning thirty?"

"Please, don't remind me." Wanting to learn more about Josh, Meagan asked about his favorite food.

"Believe it or not, my favorite food is lasagna. Since Bess has never made it, I order it every chance I get. What about you?"

"I don't think I have a favorite. I like everything from Italian to Mexican and oriental to seafood, especially lobster bisque."

Completely engrossed in their conversation, the time flew by for both Meagan and Josh. They discussed everything from their favorite color, movie, and music to their interests, fears, and pet peeves. Meagan was fascinated to learn why Josh wore a baseball hat rather than a cowboy hat.

"I was eight when I had to quit my little league team and we moved here. I missed my friends and refused to take off my team's hat."

"That must have been hard, especially at that age."

"Yeah, but it only took one time on a horse to help me get over baseball and my friends, but not the hat. To this day I have never owned a cowboy hat. Neither does Benny. We also prefer hiking boots over cowboy boots." As they talked on, Josh was surprised to hear although Meagan did not share his interest in hunting, she did enjoy the outdoors.

"I like to hibernate during the winter, but I want to be outside during the spring, summer, and fall—jogging, mountain biking, swimming, hiking—and I haven't gone for years, but I also like camping."

"Then maybe you will like where we are going. It doesn't have a pool or any fun activities like mini putt, but it's our personal campground. I usually come out here after I get home from an assignment to decompress. I can't get enough of the peace and quiet."

"I can see why."

"We will be there in a few minutes. It's just on the other side of those trees," Josh explained.

"You actually bring a tent and camp out here?"

"Sometimes we bring tents, but when I'm alone I prefer sleeping in my hammock. That's one reason I came out here today."

"You sleep *out here…in a hammock… in the middle of nowhere…by yourself?*" Meagan forgot who she was talking to. "Aren't you scared, especially at night?"

Josh laughed out loud. "No not at all. There isn't anyone out here, and it better stay that way."

"What about the animals? I thought there were bears and coyotes, and aren't there wolves?"

"Animals are usually more afraid of people than we are of them. If anything gets too close Cheyenne lets me know, and so far he has done a pretty good job of keeping us alive."

"Josh…uh…we aren't staying out here…all night…are we?"

"No, I told Benny I would do the morning chores so he could spend some time with Sarah. But we will be here after dark." Josh chuckled, evoking a nasty glare from Meagan. "Wow, you should have seen the relieved look on your face, but anyway here we are."

Meagan had spent the entire ride admiring Josh. It wasn't until they arrived at their destination that she had any interest in looking elsewhere. The first thing that caught her eye was the wide opening to a well-established cluster of pines and cottonwoods. The thick, monumental trees seemed to form an elongated horseshoe.

"I haven't been here since early December. It looks like I need to bring my saw. What a mess."

"Were all these trees hand-planted?"

"When we were kids a man named Clay Fontane worked for Aunt Bess and helped look after me and Benny. He is also the one who got Benny into tracking and me into hunting and shooting. Mr. Fontane told us this was the site of the original homestead and the cabin burned down almost a hundred and fifty years ago."

"Really? That is very interesting. I love American history."

"Nice. Something else we have in common. He said the cabin was right where we have our fire pit. It makes sense, seeing that is where we found all the stones to build the fire pit."

"Unbelievable. What does Aunt Bess say about owning a piece of history?"

"I don't think it ever interested her. I'm not sure what you know about my aunt, so I'll start from the beginning. From what I have been told, which isn't very much, Harold Grant, who is Aunt Bess's father and my grandfather, was an American businessman and cattle rancher. While he was working some business deal in Ireland he met and fell in love with my grandmother, Eileen Mackenzie. He went back and forth to Ireland and carried on with my grandmother. She got pregnant with my father—a real son of a bitch—and then Aunt Bess. My grandmother refused to leave Ireland so they never married. When my grandfather died and Aunt Bess was barely old enough, she inherited this ranch. Her older brother, my piece-of-shit, worthless, womanizing father inherited a very large chunk of change, which he blew rather quickly. First my father, and then Aunt Bess, left Ireland to check out America. Today, Aunt Bess will tell you she planned on selling the place, but after falling in love with Montana she had to stay."

"Oh wow, that is so cool. You really are Irish."

"I thought you knew that."

"I did, I just didn't realize how much. I am also Irish on my father's side, but not nearly as much as you. If your father was half Irish, that makes you a quarter."

"Your math is good, but I am nothing like my asshole father. Everyone says I am just like my mother. So much for the history lesson. We can stop here." Josh swung his right leg over Cheyenne's rump, then eased himself off the horse and lowered his backpack to the ground. "Crockett is a big boy. Do you need help getting down?" Josh asked after Meagan rode up to one of many log hitching posts.

"I'm fine, thank you." Meagan slowly slid down the left side of the tall gelding. Feeling refreshed, she stepped in front of Crockett and began rubbing the brilliant, white star on his forehead.

"It looks like you made another friend." Amused, Josh watched Meagan out of the corner of his eye while he removed Cheyenne's bridle and attached a lead rope to the stallion's halter.

"Is there anything I can do?"

"Just relax and look pretty, and hang out with me."

The flirty grin Josh gave Meagan when he began removing Crockett's bridle made her feel weak in the knees. Although her undeniable appreciation for Josh's attention inspired her to respond, she could not think of anything worthy to say or do.

"Come on, sweetheart, we better eat our sandwiches before they get warm." After picking up his backpack, Josh tenderly took Meagan's left hand and led her to a group of sawed-off tree stumps. "Please, have a seat, Miss, and make yourself comfortable."

Meagan sat on one of the stumps and thoughtfully smiled at Josh. "I can see why you come here. It's so beautiful. Thank you for bringing me, Josh. I think it's just what I needed."

Josh held Meagan's gaze and spoke with touching sincerity. "You don't need to thank me for anything." Smiling, he took a whopping ham, turkey, cheese, and lettuce sub sandwich from the lunch box and handed it to Meagan. "I should be thanking you. I usually come here alone because P.D. and Benny are busy or working. So, thank you."

Once again Meagan found herself at a loss for words. She looked down and began to peel the plastic wrapping away from her sub. "Oh wow, there is no way I will be able to eat all this. It's huge."

"I know it, Aunt Bess and her king-sized sandwiches. Just eat what you can and wrap up the rest. I will get rid of what you don't eat when we get home. Make sure you save some room. We have carrot sticks and blueberry muffins for dessert."

"Really, the sandwich is too much for me."

"I know. Me and Benny are surprised we don't look more like his heifers."

About fifteen minutes later Meagan had nearly two thirds of her sandwich left on her lap, unlike Josh, who somehow finished his. "Well, that does it for me, sweetheart, and you are welcome to my muffin."

"You are very funny. Where did you put all that food?"

With a satisfied smile, Josh patted his firm abs. "Don't forget that sandwich was my breakfast, lunch, and probably my dinner. I am going to go hang my hammock, so feel free to put your leftovers in the cooler. It's in the open section of my backpack."

"Okay, I don't think I can eat much more." Feeling stuffed, Meagan watched Josh get his hammock from one of his saddlebags and carry it to several lofty tamaracks. Unable to eat another bite, she wrapped up her leftovers and found the cooler. When she saw the carrot sticks untouched in the cooler, she immediately thought of the horses. "Josh?"

"Yeah?" Josh asked as he finished spreading out the dark green, heavy canvas hammock.

"May I give the carrots to Davey Crockett and Cheyenne?'

"Sure, just watch your fingers when you feed Cheyenne."

When Meagan went to put the cooler in the backpack, she saw boxes of bullets and an older cassette player. Whereas she understood why Josh needed the ammunition, she had no idea what he would be doing with the cassette player. Instead of asking about something that didn't concern her, she decided to wait and see if he used it.

Feeling more relaxed than she had in a long time, Meagan walked over to the horses. One by one, she began plucking carrots from the plastic baggie and offering them to Cheyenne and Crockett. "Aw, look at you two. You are such good boys. Yes you are. You are so handsome and sweet, and you have gorgeous eyes." Meagan was well into praising and feeding the horses when Josh walked right up to her and tenderly squeezed the back of her left arm.

"If you keep spoiling these two, they are going to like you more than me and Benny. Did you feed your horse carrots?" After becoming uncomfortably warm, Josh had shed his flannel shirt and was down to his black tank top. Not thinking twice, he took a carrot and when he offered it to Crockett, his strong, right arm brushed against Meagan's forearm.

For a moment Meagan went back in time. She pictured Jeremy wearing a tank top, shouting obscenities and threatening her. She could see the swollen veins in his bulging arms and neck like it was yesterday.

"Miss Dawson, are you okay? You look scared to death."

"What? Oh, I'm sorry."

"What's wrong? Do you need to sit down?"

"No…I'm fine." Meagan's tone and expression told Josh something was on her mind. "I'm still getting over my hangover."

"You *were* fine until I came over here, so what did I do?"

"Really, it's nothing. Please Josh, I don't want to spoil our time together."

"That's not going to happen, unless you have decided to go back to Illinois. Meagan, I can't help you if you don't let me."

Meagan exhaled a long and heavy breath. "Okay, please don't take this the wrong way." She looked at the ground and meekly lowered her voice. "It's…it's your shirt."

"Well that's easy enough. I'll just take it off, no big deal."

"No, don't."

Meagan's snappy reaction puzzled Josh even more as he tried to connect the dots. It didn't take him a short minute to conclude there was nothing wrong with *his* shirt. "Damn, sometimes I am so slow. Sweetheart, did Constadine wear shirts like this?"

Without looking at Josh, Meagan nodded her head. She wasn't about to tell him that it was seeing his robust upper body that caused her initial reaction. "I'm fine. It was just another flashback, but it passed."

"I thought so, and I'm really sorry. Was it like the one you had at the canyon?" Josh asked.

"It was kind of like that, but different."

"Is there anything I can do to help?"

Meagan smiled when she recalled spending the entire day with Josh. Especially the sensitive way he comforted her throughout her first-ever shooting lesson. "I will never forget how you took your time with me. You were so patient."

"It was all you, sweetheart. As terrified as you were, you didn't quit. You pushed right through it."

"Only because of you. As crazy as it sounds, I wouldn't mind doing it again."

"No kidding. Do you want to shoot again or just watch me?"

"Both."

"Wow, that's awesome. Okay then, we will try to go back this week." Josh shoved the empty bag into his pants pocket then fondly lifted Meagan's chin to where her eyes met his. "I am nothing like him, Meagan. I know I remind you of him because I am a guy, but he is not a man and never will be. He is an animal. Let me help you again, like I did at the canyon. The last thing I want is for you to be scared shitless of me, for any reason."

Meagan stared into Josh's captivating eyes, hoping he would believe her. "I wouldn't be here if I was afraid of you. You have to *know* I trust you."

"Prove it right now. Grab my arms like you did at the canyon."

Meagan couldn't explain why, but she couldn't bring herself to do it.

"Are you more afraid of touching me than shooting?"

"I can't explain it, but it's not you."

"Well guess what, Miss, I have helped you with your fear of guns and now I want to help you get over your fear of men, especially me, because I am yours. I am your guy, Meagan and I want you to understand that. I am the one person you can count on no matter what. I don't ever want you to be afraid of me. Do you understand?"

"Yes, but I don't think I'm afraid of you. I think I'm…nervous." Eager to prove herself, Meagan reached out and softly held Josh's hands.

"That's all I need to hear. Are you with me, Miss? Just say no or tell me to stop if I make you uncomfortable."

Meagan indulged in Josh's trusting blue-green eyes and affirmed, "Yes, Mr. Mackenzie, I am with you."

"Good, when we were on my porch last Thursday did I do anything or touch you in any way that bothered you?" Josh could see by her expression that she was taking her time and thinking back.

"I can't think of anything."

"Good, I have been wondering." Josh gave Meagan a comforting smile and lightly rested his hands around her lower back. Then he gently drew her in and little by little pressed himself against her. Feeling his entire body touching hers, he thought they were even closer because he wasn't wearing his gear. Still smiling, he leaned back and affectionately asked, "So this is okay?"

"Yes," Meagan replied with visible content.

Satisfied with her answer, Josh laid his freshly shaved, left cheek against the side of Meagan's face. Then he ever so slowly nuzzled back and forth across her pleasing skin. "Miss Dawson, do you like to dance?" Josh quietly whispered in Meagan's ear.

With her eyes closed, Meagan was enjoying Josh's smooth face. She wondered if he could feel her heart racing against his chest and hoped he didn't notice her increased breathing. "I used to."

Josh had his own reasons for being nervous when he took a deep breath and slowly exhaled. "Miss Dawson, will you do me the honor of being my date to the Spring Fling this Saturday?"

"You want to take me to a dance?"

"Yes I want to take you, very much."

It took all Meagan had to control her excitement. "Oh my god yes, I would love to go with you. Thank you for asking."

Josh grinned and just like he did four days ago, he lightly kissed Meagan's forehead. "No, it will be my pleasure, and thank you."

Meagan was inundated with emotions. "I think I'm going to faint."

"Don't worry, I'll catch you." Josh was grinning when he began to caress her lips with his right thumb. "I can't wait to take you out and show you a good time."

Only minutes ago it was Josh's muscular body that made her so uncomfortable she had a flashback, but now Meagan didn't want him to stop. She couldn't get over how his patient touch made her crave more. A very small part of her was wondering just how far she would let him go and when he would stop on his own. Her answer came sooner than she expected when he kissed her on the forehead one more time, stepped back, and smiled. "Okay, that wasn't all that bad, now was it?" Normally well-practiced at reading people, Meagan's disappointed face confused Josh and he thought he went too far. "Aw shit, oh no."

17

"Please…don't let go…not yet." Meagan's eyes pleaded with Josh when she slowly, but surely, reached out for his left hand. "I don't want you to stop."

"Oh…uh…I don't think that's a good idea. I don't know what you want, and I don't want to scare you. I would never forgive myself if I went too far."

"I trust you to stop. Please try."

"Wow, okay. I'll try." Sensing Meagan's need, Josh reached for her right hand and loosely wrapped her fingers around his left forearm. Cautiously moving on, he guided her hand up his arm to his well-defined bicep and along his tree of life tattoo. Searching her tempting eyes for any hint of protest, he found nothing but her desire for more. Confidently embracing her hand, he moved it up his solid arm to the top of his thick shoulder. It was Meagan's intense breathing in the light afternoon breeze that encouraged him to lean his face against the back of her hand.

Neither of them spoke as Josh held Meagan's doting eyes and lightly kissed the back of her hand. Seeing her pleasure, he gradually eased her hand down his chest to his waist then placed it inside his shirt. Feeling her hand open as if she wanted to touch him, Josh pressed her warm palm against his bare, rippled abdomen. With their eyes locked and hands together, he delicately guided her open fingers up his stomach to the center of his broad and ample chest. Then, he slid her willing hand ever so slightly to the left and held it against his excited heart. While Josh never expected to lose control, it was no secret that he was fighting a losing battle.

For just a moment Meagan thought Josh was finished when he brought her hand down and subtly moved it from his shirt. Although he was clearly taking his time, she was spinning from his heated advances. It was when he erotically kissed the back of her hand while staring into her eyes that Meagan realized he wasn't done. A million thoughts were whirling through her mind when he placed her hands just above the back pockets of his jeans. She released a deep breath when she felt his warm hands rest on her hips and bring her body against his. This time when Josh settled his smooth face against her cheek,

Meagan could feel his warm, deep breathing against her ear. She sensed he was becoming aroused and couldn't believe she was right there with him. Her urge to cower seemed to fade with each of his motivating breaths.

Josh was brushing his cheek against the side of Meagan's face and stroking the inviting skin of her lower back when he got his first wake up call. Convinced she was fine, he pushed his limitations and went on ignoring his growing excitement. Finding himself drawn to her neck, he began lightly kissing and nibbling just below her ear. Meagan's increased breathing assured him that she was pleased, whereas he was struggling. It became apparent that her neck was having a profound effect on him when his delicate and soft kisses became increasingly more passionate.

Josh was fully aware that a part of him wanted to keep going and had he been with another girl, he wouldn't have thought twice. But Meagan wasn't just another girl. In fact, she was nothing like the girls he had known. Suddenly recalling what Meagan meant to him, Josh became furious for putting his own needs ahead of hers. Clearly angry and shaking his head, he raised his hands and took two steps back. "Son of a bitch! What the hell was I thinking?"

Looking utterly confused, Meagan was too stunned to speak.

"I am so sorry, Miss. I know we agreed to stop, but there is a certain member of this team who wants to go to the finish line, if you know what I mean." Appearing repulsed, Josh briefly glanced at his crotch leading Meagan to peek between his legs.

"Aw shit, don't look at him, Miss. Damn it, I should have known better. I am so sorry. Are you okay?"

Meagan was smiling like she hadn't in a long time. "I'm fine."

"I don't know what got into me. I can't believe I did that."

"You didn't do anything wrong. I practically begged you for more. I'm sorry I led you on."

"Trust me, you didn't lead me on. If I promise to behave, will you please come here?" Josh reached out and when Meagan went to him, he placed his hands on the middle of her back. "You are really something," he remarked shaking his head in awe. "Even if it's not what I want—and please don't take this in a bad way—you definitely still got it."

This time it was Meagan who stepped back looking completely puzzled. "What, what did you say about not wanting it?"

"Well, as crazy as it sounds, I want a break from sex. You, my lady, have something I want over and above a good time. That's just one reason I stopped when I did. I don't want to blow my chances of having something special with you."

"So there is nothing wrong with me? That's not why you stopped like you did?" Meagan asked.

"Is that what you think? Aw, no, no. You couldn't be more wrong. Didn't you see how hard it was for me to stop? It's because of what you do to me. When the time is right I hope I'm your guy. I do want you, more than you can know, but not now, sweetheart, not now."

After hearing Josh openly admit that he wanted to make love to her, Meagan was almost too mesmerized to move.

"Come on. Let's go put our feet up. I know *I* need to chill out." Josh confessed and glanced at his crotch with noticeable resentment.

Meagan couldn't help but giggle at the way Josh handled his embarrassment. "Josh, I should probably warn you, I have only used a hammock one time and I was alone."

"No worries," Josh said then leisurely led Meagan to his new two-person hammock. "I will hold it while you get in and scoot to the other side. Just watch your step," he warned and gestured to where he had placed his cell phone and pistol on his neatly folded shirt.

Once Meagan seemed situated, Josh went to her feet and began untying her boots. "Miss Dawson, what do you expect from a guy? What's important to you?"

Having never been asked the question, Meagan commenced thinking out loud while Josh eased in next to her. "Well, I like you. You are everything I want in a guy. Someone I can trust, someone who is patient and makes me laugh, someone who makes me feel important. And wanted."

When he rolled on his left side to face Meagan, Josh was humbly blown away. "Wow, I do all that for you?"

"You do a lot more than that for me. To me, you worked a miracle. I would have never dreamed of doing what we just did. I don't know how to thank you for helping me, again."

"Stop thanking me. I can't thank you enough for coming into my life and giving me a chance to get to know you better."

"Josh, what do *you* want from me? What's important to *you*?"

"Now don't laugh, for now I want us to be friends."

"Seriously, you just want to be friends?"

"I would say more like very close friends. Someone who wants to spend time with me and respects me. Someone I can trust and talk to. So you see, sex isn't as important to me as you thought. Jillian and I may have been sleeping together but we lost most of the things that mattered, like trust and honesty—and intimacy. You and I were just more intimate then Jilly and I have been in quite a while, without the sex."

"Wow, I never thought I would hear that come from a man."

"I am getting older, sweetheart. I won't deny I enjoy sex, but I have other things on my mind." Josh looked directly into Megan's eyes. "When *you* are ready I will be ready and willing, but until then don't worry about it. I am perfectly happy with the way we are."

"So, does this mean no touching, like what we just did?"

"Oh hell no, I have P.D. for that friendship. I am a touchy-feely guy. Feel free to touch and grab anything. It's all yours."

Meagan's face turned countless shades of red. "Um, today was great. Better than great. But um…I am not ready for anything more."

"Like I said, I'm in no hurry. Do you have anything you want to talk about or ask me? I have some questions for you, so don't be shy."

"Oh okay…well let's see…I don't know if I am supposed to ask you about certain things, let alone how. I mean I don't know if you want to discuss certain things or if I should avoid talking about them. Oh, never mind."

"We just discussed making love easily enough, so tell me what's on your mind."

With tense hesitation, Meagan began her explanation. "I think I have a good example. My pop has been a plumber and owned his own heating and air conditioning business since I can remember. Damn, how should I put this? So when Pop gets home my mom always asks how his day went. Oh forget it, I give up."

Josh grinned and brushed a stray curl from Meagan's face. "It's your choice, sweetheart. If you are comfortable with it, I have no problem discussing my job. Jillian and I hardly ever discussed our work with each other. She designs clothes and purses, so I think you can see why we didn't talk about our jobs."

Meagan wanted Josh to know she was interested in everything about him. "If something is important to you, then it's important to me. I just don't know what to say or how to ask?"

"You don't need to treat what I do any different than heating and plumbing. I will clean it up when I talk to you and save the nasty details for Benny and P.D. Just ask how I am or how did it go?"

"Okay then, are you *sure* you are okay? It looked so bad."

"Other than needing to catch up on my sleep, I couldn't be better."

"How often does that happen?"

Josh paused too long before evading Meagan's question. "I would rather go without sleep than Aunt Bess's cooking."

"Josh, you know I mean the close call."

"Damn, I can't get anything past you. What happened Thursday is rare, and when it does, it doesn't last long. I told you my team is the best and you saw one reason why. We all look out for each other. They have my ass and I have theirs."

"I was horrified. Watching you get shot at and then not knowing if you were okay."

"As hard as it was for you to watch, I knew I could rely on my team. If one of us gets in trouble the rest of the team eliminates the threat. I'm sure you saw what they did to the asshole on the hotel roof when he shot at me."

"Yes, but I didn't know he was the one."

"So, I need to ask you to do something for me before my next assignment."

"Okay..."

"I don't want you watching me again. I will make sure you get word if anything happens. I can't worry about you freaking out every time I get a call. And the last thing I want is for you to see me get blasted on national TV."

"Oh my god, don't say that. I am worried enough. What should I do if Benny and Pete are watching?"

"If you want to watch TV, go to the den or my room. Please, Meagan, do it for me. I can't focus if I am worried about you watching me."

"I would do anything to keep you safe. Please be careful and don't worry about me. Please, Josh, I can't lose you."

"Settle down, I'm not going anywhere. Things are just getting interesting."

"Promise me?" Meagan asked peering deeply into Josh's teal, blue-green eyes.

"Yes, Miss, I promise. Now can I ask *you* something?

"Yes." Meagan could not believe a man of Josh's stature had an interest in her and fearlessly accepted the dangers of being with her.

"Since moving to Gardiner didn't work out, do you plan on going back to Illinois once we know it's safe?"

"I never thought that would happen. I left so fast that I barely took time to say goodbye. All my friends thought I was overreacting, especially my business partner, Trish. I don't think she will ever forgive me for selling out and leaving her the way I did. Thanks to my decision, we didn't part on good terms. I have no reason to go back except to visit a few friends and my parents."

"Well, if it makes you feel any better, we couldn't be happier to be your family and friends and we will do all we can to help you."

"Thank you, that means a lot."

"My pleasure, but, sweetheart…" Josh's tone turned more serious, "…while I think you should stick close to one of us for the time being, I would never keep you here or hold you back."

"What do you mean?"

"When you are safe again, and it's just a matter of time before that happens, you can do what you want. Be your own person, buy a car, and get a job you like. Don't ever think I want to control you. I just don't suggest doing any of those things now."

"Oh no, you think he is coming for me?"

"Did I say that?"

"Yes, in so many words. Please, Josh, tell me what you think."

"Aw, don't look at me like that. Okay, after P.D. and I discussed the details of the break-in at your parents', we think Jeremy had a hand in it. We also think it's possible he will figure out you are in Montana. Especially if he has the right help and is determined like Detective Blanchard explained to P.D."

"No, damn him."

"Try not to worry. Montana is a big state and if he starts nosing around, we will catch wind of it and find him."

"Thank you for telling me the truth. I'm so tired of feeling helpless. What can I do?"

"For now, I want you to do what we tell you even if you don't like it. I am going to make sure someone is with you twenty-four-seven. If P.D. and I are both gone and Benny has to leave, Timmy has offered to help and I have a couple others lined up."

"Oh no, absolutely not, I will not be a pain in the ass."

"Did you already forget what I told you, that you are my responsibility? I will only leave you with people I trust."

"I didn't know you would take it to such extremes. That is too much."

"Believe me, nothing would thrill me more than seeing him walk over that hill right now so I could…" Josh was suddenly interrupted by the familiar chirp of his phone.

As Josh rolled over to retrieve his phone, Meagan let out a disappointed sigh and carefully rotated out of the hammock. Without a word, she proceeded to pull on and tie her boots.

"Hold on, Brody. Is something wrong, sweetheart?"

"Don't we need to get back?"

"No, it's just Brody." Josh was touched and chuckled. With a reassuring smile, he reached for Meagan with his left hand. "Please come back, I'm sorry you got up for nothing."

Notably relieved, Meagan inched her way into the hammock and lay on her right side to face Josh. She was appreciating his peaceful eyes when he took her hand and began stroking the back of it with his left thumb.

"Okay go ahead, Brody. Meagan thought you were going to put me to work."

"You didn't tell your girlfriend you have the week off?"

Meagan overheard Brody's question and eyed Josh with eager anticipation.

"I figured P.D. or my big-mouthed brother told her, but evidently she just heard it from you."

"Oops, I hope I didn't spoil anything."

"No, it's no big deal."

"Listen, Mackey. I'm just making my usual calls. If this is a bad time, you can call me back."

"No, I can talk. I brought Meagan out to the camp site to talk and chill out with me."

"No shit, it's about time you found a girl who wants to come out there with you. I take it she is nothing like Jilly?"

"No, she is a complete opposite and she's hot."

Meagan's scolding glare told Josh he said too much.

"She sounds like a nice girl. I can't wait to meet her."

"Yeah, speaking of nice, hot girls, how is Cassey?"

"She has been putting my ass to work on her latest honey-do list."

"Ah, you are a lucky man, Brody Nichols. We both know you have it way too good."

"Hell yeah I do. After I finish doing everything Cassey wants, I get to do everything I want. And I bet you can guess who will be helping me with that."

"Oh yeah, and I bet you are going to enjoy doing everything on your list."

"You better believe it. So, getting back to why I called and since you know the drill, I will keep this short and sweet."

"I'm good, Brody. I don't *need* the time off. How are the rest of the guys, especially Andy? This one was pretty hard on him."

Meagan was gawking at Josh as if he just lost his mind for turning down the time off.

"You know Andy; he's good to go. Shane and Franky said they are perfectly happy getting paid to sit around. Miguel, on the other hand, is having second thoughts about S.R.T. We all figured as much. He thinks we should have…oh, how did he put it…we should have brought in a negotiator and their families to reason with them. He kept referring to them as messed-up kids."

"What the fuck is that supposed to mean? Since when are we supposed to check IDs before we get involved? I don't know about you, but carding and counseling are not in *my* job description."

"Take it easy, I am just repeating Miguel. And since you don't watch the news, I will assume you have not heard about us."

"I can just imagine."

"S.R.T. shot and killed five young men ranging in age from seventeen to twenty-two."

"Aw shit, that's just great. Too bad those young men didn't give us a choice. Regardless of their ages, I wouldn't change a thing I did."

Feeling sorry for Josh, Meagan's gaze turned empathetic.

"Relax, Mackey. Miguel is the only one with regrets, and I don't know what the fuck he's so messed up about. It's not like he was any help. So now for the good part…"

"Oh sweet, it gets better?"

"Seventeen-year-old Corey Sherman was the piece of shit who shot at you from the hotel roof. He was one of mine. Too bad the kid didn't want to put his shooting skills to good use."

"Damn it, Brody, what were they thinking? That kid should have been ready to graduate. He could have been somebody."

"I'm guessing he was a drop-out. His older brother Kyle was the nineteen-year-old who shot at Andy. He was one of your two."

"Nineteen, huh? Do you remember what you were doing when you were nineteen? I was working on my degree and enjoying life."

"Don't sweat it, Mackey. Berkowitz said we did an excellent job and they got what they deserved."

"Good, they did the crime like grown men; they can assume the consequences like grown men. I'm sure the bank guard and cop they shot aren't second guessing us."

"One last thing. Be extra careful until this blows over. We both know the outstanding young men who tried to kill us have ties to someone who didn't approve of our tactics. And before I forget, I told the guys I expect them to get in some good practice and plan on training hard early next month."

"Perfect timing. Meagan and I were just talking about going back to the canyon. She actually wants another lesson."

"Good for her. Cassey wants to come see Penelope and I need to shoot. We should get together like we used to."

"Yeah, it's been too long. P.D. and Tim Ashford both said they could use some practice. And Timmy would get a kick out of you giving him some pointers."

"Sure, I can do that."

"Any day but Thursday works for us."

"How about we go riding Tuesday or Wednesday morning then drive out to the canyon after lunch. Just let me know what day works."

"Sounds good. I will call you tomorrow. Benny asked me to get rid of some coyotes while we are here and I need to get set up."

"Ah, good luck, and I'll talk to you some time tomorrow."

"Yeah, thanks for calling." After setting his phone back on his shirt, Josh looked at Meagan with a somber expression. "I should have told you I have the week off, my mistake."

"How did you get the week off? Are you on vacation?"

Josh was so amused by Meagan's excitement that he laughed as if she told him a good joke. "No, Miss, we don't get vacation time. I think I told you I am usually on call March thru October. It depends on weather conditions and when we are needed."

"Oh, okay…" Meagan still seemed confused.

"I have never explained this before so bear with me. My team is on a form of administrative leave. We are off until at least next Monday."

"So you *can't* work, even if you are needed?"

"We have to be cleared first. The nice thing is we still get paid even though we are off."

Meagan thought back to the conversation Josh had with Brody. "Josh, are you in some kind of trouble? Oh shit, I can't believe I asked you that. I'm sorry, that's none my business. See what I mean? I don't know when to keep my mouth shut."

Josh laughed with utter amusement. "It's okay. I said you can ask me anything and no, no one is in trouble. My time off is normal procedure under the circumstances. My team just took five lives, and regardless of being authorized to shoot, there has to be a thorough investigation. My captain, Captain Berkowitz, is in charge of S.R.T. You will meet him at the dance. He is a retired military sniper and always looking out for us, especially our mental well-being. When we are involved in a fatality, he prefers we take a week off. When that happens I usually come here."

"You came out here to clear your head and I keep bugging you with questions. I am so sorry, Josh. You should have left me at home."

"Did you forget I invited you? Stop being ridiculous. I want you here. Jilly would never ride out here with me. She always said she was too busy to come out here for nothing."

"Please tell me if you need some time to yourself. I will understand."

"I like having someone to talk to. Talking to my mom helps me even if she can't...hold on, Miss, something is bothering Cheyenne." Josh pointed to where Cheyenne was swaying his head up and down and stomping his front hooves. "It's still early, but it could be coyotes. If one of the bigger packs caught wind of the horses..."

"Oh no, please tell me they won't go after the horses."

Josh chuckled and left the comfort of his hammock. "Don't worry, we'll be ready." Still smiling, he picked up his phone and slid on his boots. "You might want to put on your sweatshirt and I'll get your coat."

After shoving on her boots, Meagan watched Josh quickly button his shirt and fasten his holster around his right thigh. Imagining a pack of hungry coyotes, she helped him fold the hammock then nervously followed him to the horses.

"Sweetheart, can you please put on Crockett's bridle?"

"I am not as fast as you, but I can do it."

Once Josh finished buckling Cheyenne's bridle, he untied the stallion and led him a few feet away. "I will be right back," he assured Meagan before he leapt on Cheyenne.

Meagan watched Josh reach down from his saddle, scoop up his backpack, and nudge Cheyenne into a full run. Once he reached the entrance to the site, he came to an abrupt stop and dismounted. After setting down the tape recorder, he jumped back on Cheyenne and returned to where Meagan was anxiously waiting.

Josh removed his backpack, tethered Cheyenne, and took a moment to scratch the stallion's plush muzzle and forehead. "Okay, Miss, we should get ready. The tape will bring them in pretty quick." Appearing completely calm, Josh reached into his saddlebag for Meagan's coat. "Lay on this for now. You will get cold pretty fast lying on the bare ground."

"What is that horrible sound?" Meagan asked when she took her parka and tried to determine the squalling coming from the recorder.

"It's supposed to be a rabbit in distress," Josh replied before he went to the right side of his saddle and eased his rifle from a protective leather case. After hurrying back over to Meagan, he grabbed his backpack, slung it over his shoulder, and gave her a comforting smile. Then, he placed his free left hand against the middle of her back. "Come on, let's get this over with."

The sun's heat was dwindling with its light when Josh spread out Meagan's parka in the same spot where they ate lunch. Looking slightly concerned, he had her lay on the coat and move onto her stomach. "I'm sorry, Miss, I should have brought you a blanket. I will try to hurry." Josh sat on Meagan's right side, removed a box of bullets from his backpack and set them within arm's reach. "Oh shit, I don't use earplugs when I hunt. I will tell you when to cover your ears. I'm really sorry."

"I'll be fine," Meagan insisted with her comforting smile. "I don't suppose this gun is any quieter than the one you use for work?" Meagan asked, noticing Josh's rifle was camouflage. "It is a different gun, right?"

"Yes, it is." Josh smiled and nodded. "This is an AR-15."

"Oh, even I have heard of that."

"I prefer this one for hunting smaller animals, especially coyotes. I bought Benny the same thing for his birthday last year, not that he ever uses it. If you want, you can lay on your back so you don't have to watch. Try to understand it's them or Benny's calves."

"I understand. How many do you have to shoot?"

"As many as I can before they catch on and run off. Are you *sure* you won't be mad at me for exterminating *puppy dogs*?"

Recalling Josh's previous conversation with his team leader, Meagan offered her support. "If you are okay with it then so am I."

"Good, because they are moving in."

Meagan could see several coyotes in the distance, evilly trotting toward the recorder. She glanced at Josh when he turned his hat backwards, brought his right knee up, and inched toward his scope. While she thought he was squeezing the trigger, it was obviously not enough to shoot.

"Come on…come on… I need a couple more…Okay, Miss Dawson, cover your ears."

Meagan instantly shielded her ears. She was focusing on the recorder when Josh fired four times and dropped four coyotes as fast as she could count. She had forgotten how loud the unforgiving crack of a rifle was and pressed harder to block out the shocking noise. Then she watched him go to his right knee and aim toward two more animals that were fleeing to his right. No sooner did she hear the ear-ringing *crack, crack* of Josh's rifle and they too fell to the ground. She was wondering if he was finished when he went back to his stomach.

"Are you okay?" He asked, anticipating her displeasure.

"Yes, will there be more?"

"Hopefully the pups will come in looking for the pack, but we can't wait long. I don't want to be here when the wolves show up."

"Did you just say *wolves*?"

"Listen, do you hear the howling and barking to the northeast?"

"Oh my god, now I do."

"They likely smell the blood and think they can score an easy meal. Okay, cover your ears. This should be it."

Meagan barely had time to protect her ears from the mighty shots before she heard three more blasts.

"Okay, Miss, you are my witness. We got six adults and three pups." Josh swiftly refilled his magazine and pushed it into his rifle.

After watching him reload the gun, Meagan tensely asked, "Are those for the wolves?"

"I hope not, but they are for the ride home. Put on your coat so you don't have to carry it."

Before Meagan knew it, Josh had whisked her to the horses and they were riding among the dead, scattered coyotes to get Benny's recorder. It was only a couple minutes into their ride when she noticed Cheyenne was throwing his head, whinnying, and stomping all four hooves. Before the stallion came to a stop, Josh dismounted then grabbed a lead rope from one of his saddlebags. "Hop down, sweetheart."

Meagan silently watched Josh attach the red lead to Crockett's halter and tie the end around Cheyenne's saddle horn.

"Can you put on my backpack? It's not heavy."

"Yes," Meagan quickly replied, thinking Josh wouldn't ask her to do this without good reason.

After helping Meagan put her arms through the straps of the backpack, Josh hopped back on Cheyenne and reached for her hands. "Miss Dawson, now is not a good time to tell me you can't ride double."

Meagan didn't say a word before putting her left foot in the empty stirrup and letting Josh pull her up behind him.

"Hold tight…hear me…get against my back and stay there."

Meagan squeezed her arms around Josh's waist and inched against his body until she didn't think she could get any closer.

"Good, we are going into a full run. Are you ready?"

"I'm ready." Not sure what to expect, Meagan heard Josh whistle right before Cheyenne launched into a mighty gallop. No sooner did she look forward after checking on Crockett and she saw four huge wolves race out of the trees. She watched in horror as the wolves approached them head-on and Josh drew his forty-five. Although he looked prepared to shoot, he didn't fire a single shot when the monstrous pack tore past them and continued toward the campsite.

Meagan clung to Josh and pressed her upper body against his back for the entire ride home. While the remainder of their trip had been uneventful, she didn't breathe easy until she set eyes on the back of the house.

Immediately upon reaching the back deck, Josh slid off Cheyenne, helped Meagan dismount, and held her against his chest. "I am so sorry for scaring you. It was a long, hard winter and everything is hungry. Please say something, Miss." Josh tensed, thinking Meagan had every reason to criticize him.

"Mr. Mackenzie, you have one amazing horse," she declared with her kind-hearted smile.

"Yes I do, and you are one special lady. I can't thank you enough for spending the day with me." Josh rested his face against Meagan's left cheek and swayed with her as though they were dancing to a slow song.

"Was that your favorite song?" she quietly asked when he looked into her content eyes.

"Every song is my favorite when I'm with you. And as much as I hate to ruin a good thing, I need to see to the horses."

"I can help you."

"Thank you, but I won't be long. I will find you later and we can get something to eat. I think I'm hungry for an egg sandwich."

"Mmm, that does sound good."

"Okay then, why don't you go take a hot bath? You deserve it after the hell I put you through."

"Okay, a bath and an egg sandwich *both* sound great." Feeling completely comfortable and committed to Josh heart and soul, Meagan reached for his protective hands. "Mr. Mackenzie," she whispered while peering into his attentive eyes. "Do you know how much I care about you?"

"Yes, I do." Josh grinned when he recollected how he asked Meagan nearly the same question only four days ago.

"Do you know how much I want to be with you?"

"Yes," Josh replied thoroughly satisfied.

"Good, I want you to know it is my responsibility to take care of you. I mean it, Joshua Mathew. I am here if you need me." Before she lost her nerve, Meagan rose onto her toes and gracefully kissed Josh's left cheek. Suddenly embarrassed and not sure what to do next, she turned away and went in the house.

18

When Meagan and Josh agreed to get together for a bite to eat, neither would have guessed it wouldn't be until Monday morning's breakfast.

"Good mornin' to ya, lass." Bess was handing Josh a cup of coffee when Meagan stepped into the kitchen.

"Good morning."

"Good morning, Miss." Josh stood and smiled when Meagan looked his way. Then he pulled out the chair beside him and gestured for her to join him.

"Thank you and I'm sorry for missing the egg sandwich," Meagan said when Josh placed his hand on her lower back and guided her into the chair.

"No problem, you looked so peaceful I couldn't wake you up. I turned off your light and closed your door."

"After my bath I thought I would lie down for a few minutes. I didn't mean to fall asleep."

"My guess is all that Montana fresh air caught up with you. It happens to all of us."

Bess was so happy to see Josh and Meagan together that she hesitated to interrupt. "Aye, she didn't sleep but a wink while ya were workin', except when she was two sheets to the wind."

"Next time should be easier, especially since she won't be watching the fucking news."

"Joshua Mathew…"

"I'm sorry, ladies, but they couldn't care less if they get us killed."

It was obvious Meagan was still haunted by Josh's brush with death. "I couldn't wait to see you, to know you were safe. And just when I knew it was you—I can't describe how bad it was, Aunt Bess. Be glad you were too smart to watch."

"Ya had to find out fur yurself. I learned tis better to wait and wonder than to watch and worry all the more."

The casual conversation suddenly roused Josh's curiosity. "Which big mouth told you it was me, P.D. or Benny?"

"*I* could tell it was you."

"Really, how?"

"You are the only one who bends their leg. You did it again yesterday."

"Wow, leave it to you to notice that."

"Why do you lay like that?"

"Oh…uh…for balance…for balance and…comfort."

"Joshua, do ya think the lass could hear somethin' different?"

"No." Josh shot Bess a tense look but it didn't get past Meagan.

"It's okay, you don't have to tell me."

"It's just something I do. It makes it easier and faster to pull my pistol."

Meagan looked at Josh and Bess with undeniable confusion. She couldn't understand why Josh would need his handgun.

"So, Miss…" Josh said, still glaring at his aunt. "I only have a few chores and I was thinking we could go shopping after my shower."

Meagan knew he wanted to change the subject. "But I thought you hate shopping?"

"I will do anything to get you out of those baggy sweats. Oh, don't take that the way it sounded. Uh, I mean you would look better in your own clothes."

"Thank you, and if it's no trouble, could you take me to a bank? I have some money, but I don't have enough to get everything I need."

"You need *everything*? I have a feeling I'm going to like shopping with you."

Meagan gave Josh a rollicking kick in the leg when she realized he was referring to her unmentionables.

"There is a decent mall about two-and-a-half hours away. It should have *everything* you need," Josh continued, in spite of Meagan's warning.

"I take it yas won't be home fur supper?"

"No, Aunt Bess, I have a feeling this is going to take the whole day."

"Okay, lad, call me if ya change yur plans."

Meagan was imagining her day with Josh when she suddenly panicked. "Oh my god, what do I need for the dance? Is it formal?"

"Ya will need a gown," Bess replied with delight. "Catherine's has the best, but yur likely too late fur an appointment."

Josh quelled Meagan's doubts. "I'll call as soon as they open and try to get you in on Wednesday."

"I hope they can squeeze me in. I have less than a week to get ready."

"Don't worry, and you should know, I always take care of my date. That means everything—your dress, shoes, and jewelry. Bridget is the best and will likely be helping you. If you like something, get it. I don't care about the cost and neither should you."

Meagan was stunned by Josh's generous offer. Thinking he already shelled out the money for Jillian's expenses, she tried to refuse. "Thank you, but I have plenty in…"

"Excuse me, Miss, I don't mean to be rude, but this is not up for discussion. Aunt Bess, she hasn't eaten since yesterday's lunch. Could you please help her find something to eat?"

"I'll see to it straight away."

"Thank you." Josh downed his last gulp of coffee, stood up, and affectionately gripped Meagan's shoulder. "Take your time and come find me when you are ready to leave."

"Okay, thank you."

"You are very welcome, and you don't need to thank me."

Meagan didn't think her Monday could get any better until Josh pulled off the highway and parked at a gas station. At precisely nine o'clock she was elated when he called Catherine's Bridal and Boutique.

"Good morning, Chelsea, it's Josh. Do you know if Bridget has wandered in yet? Thanks, sweetie." Less than a minute later Josh was speaking with a woman Meagan assumed to be Bridget. "Good morning, Angel…no, Jillian and I broke up but I am seeing someone…I'm fine, are you behaving yourself? Good for you, one day at a time…Yes, it was my team…Yes, we're all fine, thanks…You are the best and I was hoping you could help me…I am taking a very special lady to the Spring Fling this Saturday and I would appreciate it if you could take care of her…Yes, Meagan is a very nice girl…Do you have any openings on Wednesday? Three o'clock will be perfect, thanks, Angel…Yes, whatever she likes…That's fine. I will drop Miss Dawson off on Wednesday just before three…You too, Angel." Josh ended his call and smiled at Meagan. "You are all set, Miss."

"You dated her…Bridget?"

"Uh, was it that obvious?"

"You liked her. She meant something to you."

"Yes, we were pretty close for a couple months, until I found out she was using again. I have never told anyone why we stopped seeing each other."

"I'm sorry for prying. It's really none of my business."

"Sure it is. I want to know everything about you. I told you I have nothing to hide and so far, I don't think you do either."

"I thought Jillian was your only serious relationship."

Josh sighed out loud. "No, but she is the only one I wanted to marry. I want to be with one girl. I just haven't had much luck finding the right one. They are either hiding something or I feel like I can't trust them."

"If it helps you feel any better, I don't have any secrets and I think your luck has changed."

"I think my luck has not only changed, I have hit the jackpot."

Throughout the nearly three-hour drive, Josh held Meagan's hand as if they were devoted soulmates. His gallant behavior continued after they reached the mall and he escorted her from store to store. In addition to collecting her purchases after she paid the cashier, he held and carried her various bags and boxes.

From one end of the crowded mall to the other Meagan adored how Josh's dedication extended beyond his chivalry. While he remained close enough to ensure her safety, he stayed just far enough to let her browse in peace. Each and every time she paused to check out Josh's alluring good looks, Meagan was surprised to see him studying everyone but her.

"What I wouldn't give for some time alone with *him* in the dressing room," a daring woman who appeared to be in her late thirties declared to Meagan. "Look at that body...mmm, mmm. He looks and moves like a bodyguard. I would double his pay to take care of me. He is hot."

Meagan's face couldn't have been a deeper shade of red when she looked over the clothes racks and across the aisle at Josh. When her eyes met his and he flashed his mischievous smile, she knew at the very least, he guessed they were talking about him.

"Oh look, he is coming this way." The woman sounded excited and hopeful when Josh started walking in their direction.

"Excuse me, ladies," Josh focused on Meagan. "Would a mind-blowing lady the likes of you ever let a guy like me take her to dinner?"

Josh's seductive tone gave Meagan butterflies. "I do not consider myself a lady, but a woman like me would love to join a guy like you for dinner and dessert." Meagan took hold of Josh's empty hand and smiled. "I guess it's just my lucky day," she told the astonished woman before she and Josh walked away.

Josh seemed desperate to talk to Meagan. "Seriously, Miss, can we stop shopping long enough to go eat and come back when I'm not starving?"

"Only if we can get Italian."

"You read my mind. I could go for some lasagna right now."

They weren't even halfway to the entrance they came in when Meagan felt uncomfortably warm. She reasoned Josh had to be downright hot wearing his long-sleeve shirt and bomber, not to mention he was toting all her bags. Thinking he could use a break, she suggested they rest. "Can we stop for a few minutes?" Meagan asked and pointed to a wooden bench next to a soda machine.

"Sure, are you okay?" Josh asked before he set down the numerous plastic and paper bags and took a seat on the bench.

"Yes, thank you. I am going to get a water. Would you like something to drink?"

"Have a seat, Miss. I got it." Rather than remaining seated and handing Meagan the cash, Josh stood up, stepped over to the vending machine, and bought two bottles of water.

"Thank you," she said after he opened and handed her one of the bottles.

"You're very welcome." Josh replied, then downed his entire bottle of water without stopping.

"Josh, I know you're hot. Please let me carry a few bags."

"I'm fine, just hungry."

"Okay then, let me carry your jacket to the Jeep so you can cool off."

"No thanks, I'm good, sweetheart."

"Why are you so difficult? Just because I'm a girl doesn't mean I…"

"Meagan, I can't take off my jacket." Josh's expression told her something should click. "I'm carrying something."

"What? *Oh*, I didn't see it." Trying to appear inconspicuous, Meagan reached inside Josh's bomber and carefully inched her left hand toward his right hip.

"It's not there, sweetheart, but feel free to frisk me all you want." Josh grinned, then took Meagan's hand and guided it up and across the left side of his chest to just below his left armpit.

"Oh," Meagan's eyes got wide when her fingertips touched the well-hidden pistol. "No wonder I didn't see it, and you are burning up."

"You're not supposed to see it and I'm okay. I'm used to it."

"I think you should take a break. Wait here and I will be right back."

"No way, not here."

"Five minutes, Josh. I promise I'll hurry."

"Aw, Miss, let me come with you."

"Joshua Mathew, it's not up for discussion."

Shaking his head and noticeably grim, Josh watched Meagan walk away and disappear around a corner.

When she returned twenty minutes later, Meagan understood Josh's harsh reaction.

"Don't do that again, Meagan. I need to see you."

"Let's get out of here." Meagan suddenly snagged a handful of her bags and added them to her recent purchase. Without a word, she turned away and headed for the exit.

"Hey now, let me get those. What do you think you're doing?"

Meagan didn't stop or acknowledge Josh again until she reached his Jeep.

"Damn, don't ever ask me to race you. I wouldn't stand a chance."

After they piled all the bags but one in the back seat, Josh smiled and helped Meagan into the passenger side of his Jeep.

"Thank you."

"My pleasure." Once inside the Rubicon, Josh removed his bomber and tossed it in the back seat on top of the bags of clothes. He started the engine, switched on the cool air, and relaxed his head against the seat rest. Acting worn out, he turned to look at Meagan. "I love your energy, but I thought we were shopping, not working out. Next time I'll wear my tennis shoes."

"I don't know if you can use these now." Meagan set a plastic bag of clothes on Josh's lap. "If you don't like them or they don't fit, you can wait here while I return them."

"You bought all this for me? Wow, thank you." Josh peered in the bag and nodded, "Oh yeah, I can use them now."

"I wasn't sure about your size."

Josh checked the tags on two short sleeve shirts. "Yep, these are right." Then he reached into the bag, removed a package of tank tops and smiled from ear to ear. "Perfect, thanks." He reached into the plastic shopping bag one more time and pulled out a midnight blue windbreaker. "Aw, Meagan, this is too much. Let me pay you back."

"After all you have done for me, absolutely not."

"Thank you, sweetheart, now I just have to find a place to clean up a bit and change. I don't want to use the restroom here."

"Can you use a park?"

"That's a great idea. Why didn't I think of that?" Within twenty short minutes Josh was parking the Rubicon in a secluded conservation area. "This is perfect. I'm glad you suggested it. I wasn't sure if I could remember how to get here."

"You have been *here* before? I should have known."

"It's been years." Josh appeared to be thinking back. "I was still with the county, so I would have been…twenty-two. P.D. and I hunted the far-back when they still allowed public hunting."

"*You* were a deputy?"

"Uh, almost nine years ago. Wow, it doesn't seem like it's been that long. I started out doing Timmy's job. Why are you so surprised?"

Meagan chose her words carefully. "I don't know. I guess I'm wondering why you gave it up."

Josh grinned and opened the center console. He found his knife and a handful of hand wipes. "It wasn't what I thought it would be. By the end of my first year, I didn't like going to work."

Meagan watched Josh open the large hunting knife and use the razor-sharp blade to cut the tags off of the shirts and jacket. "But with your personality, I'm sure you were good at it."

"I like to think so, but I always felt like something was eating at me." Josh put away the knife and set the shirt and jacket up by the windshield. "I got tired of dealing with idiots and hateful people. I was either thinking no one had any common sense, or I was frustrated with the day-to-day bullshit. I didn't want it to change me and yet I wanted to do more. It's hard to explain."

Taking a minute to put her thoughts into words, Meagan realized how grateful she was that there were people like Josh who could handle his job. She understood his profession was a necessity for the protection and greater good of society.

"You must think I am just another hypocrite. Here I am talking like I give a shit only days after ending two young lives." Josh removed his shoulder holster and turned to place it on the back seat, forgetting there was no room.

"You can set it on my lap."

"Thank you. It sounds even worse when I admit I like working for S.R.T."

Meagan looked at Josh to emphasize her support. "Honestly, I was thinking how fortunate people are that there are people like you who can do your job and…"

"And, dare I ask?"

"And I know how you feel about the news, but after watching and listening to what the people at the bank went through, I see why we need you. What if your team wouldn't have been there? How many more people would have been hurt? If you are good at your job and enjoy what you do—and you are obviously one of the best at what you do. Who is anyone to judge you? The day might come when that person needs you."

"You always know the right things to say. I wish I could explain things as well as you do."

"Believe me, there have been plenty of times I wish I would have kept my mouth shut." Meagan's stomach suddenly growled, confirming her hunger.

"Sounds like I better shut my mouth and get moving." Josh grabbed a couple wipes, stepped out of the Jeep, and pulled off his Henley. After throwing his warm shirt on the floor mat, he washed up with the wipes and air-dried. Feeling much better, he reached into the Rubicon for one of his new shirts and turned his back toward Meagan.

It was the first time Meagan saw the midnight blue S.R.T. tattoo below Josh's right shoulder. While she could see the bold initials, she was unable to read the words that came down from each of the three letters. She was about to ask about the tattoo when he slipped on the much cooler shirt, unzipped his blue jeans and tucked the shirt neatly inside his pants. Lastly, he re-zipped and buttoned his jeans and climbed back into the Jeep.

"I like the color, and thanks again for thinking of me."

"You're welcome. The powder blue reminded me of Cheyenne's eyes."

"Aw, that's nice." After turning in his seat to face Meagan, he leaned in close. "I've been thinking you are going to make this a lot harder than I thought."

Having no idea what Josh meant, Meagan liked how the sun enhanced the short red tips of his light brown hair. "I am making something hard on you?"

"Please don't think I'm an ass for saying this."

"I would never think that."

"I hope not. I never thought taking a break would be this hard. But I care about you and I like being with you, so I will wait as long as it takes."

"I'm glad you told me and I never thought I would say this, but I will do my best not to keep you waiting." Meagan didn't know how to tell Josh the affect he had on her, but wanted to try.

"You look like you have something else to say. It's okay, take your time."

"At first, I thought you helped me feel something that was dead and gone. But I don't remember ever feeling this way with Jeremy. I think I loved him in the beginning, but now, with you, there is a connection. But I—how should I put this?"

"Just say it."

Meagan blushed with embarrassment. "I have never been easy, Josh. I don't sleep with someone unless…We have to *really* know each other. I want to be with you, but I need more time, and I need something from you first."

Josh knew what Meagan was insinuating. "I get it and I don't blame you. That is just one thing that makes you so special." He knew she needed to hear he loved her before they could make love. "Like you, I will try not to keep you waiting and also like you, I have to be sure." Josh took hold of Meagan's hands and stared into her faithful hazel eyes. "I think I do, but when I say it, I want you to know it's forever. I guess we're even, sweetheart. You have made me feel something *I* thought was gone and also like you, I need to be sure."

Meagan was quietly smiling when her stomach rumbled.

"I think the only thing you need from me right now is a good dinner." Josh slipped back into his shoulder holster, handed Meagan his new windbreaker, and went looking for an Italian restaurant.

After getting their fill of Italian cuisine followed by two more hours at the mall, Josh started driving home. "Now I know what it means to shop till you drop." He turned on the Jeep's stereo and found Meagan's left hand. Then, he laced his fingers with hers and held her hand on her left thigh. "Feel free to recline your seat and take a nap. We should be home around ten-thirty."

"Thank you for taking me and I'm sorry I took all day."

"No worries, I had a good time. I will go shopping with you anytime."

"I'm glad to hear that. I was worried I ruined you for life." After leaning her head back, Meagan turned in her seat so she could face Josh. The last thing she wanted was to doze off when she could simply look over and see him. However, it didn't take long for the humming of the Rubicon's tires to lull her into a peacefully enjoyable sleep. Slightly more than two hours later, Meagan was still dozing when the Jeep's tires hit gravel and startled her. When she first opened her eyes, she thought they were on the ranch's gravel driveway, but then she heard Josh's voice.

"Hey Timmy, where are you?"

Alerted by how unusually fast Josh was driving, Meagan hung on his every word.

"Good, I could use your help. Some prick is riding my ass and I don't want to stop when I have Meagan with me."

Meagan was forced to close her eyes when she looked in her rearview mirror and directly into the dangerously close high beams.

"If all goes well I will see you at the bridge. Thanks, Timmy."

Meagan leaned over and peered at the Jeep's speedometer. She was focusing her still-blinded eyes on the numbers when she thought she saw seventy-five. Then, she unknowingly bit her bottom lip when Josh cut the headlights, looked left and right for approaching cross traffic, and jetted through the four-way stop. In awe, she gasped when she saw how closely the vehicle was still following them. Feeling the Rubicon accelerate, she was only slightly relieved when Josh switched on the headlights. This time when she checked the speedometer, Meagan was certain she saw ninety-five.

"Sweetheart, can you take my phone and find Tim Ashford's number? Call him and put him on speaker."

Meagan was astounded by Josh's incredible self-control. While she struggled to call Tim with her trembling fingers, Josh was notably angry but all together composed.

"Okay, Mackey, I'm about six out."

"Tell Timmy we just crossed Butte Creek Road and will be at the bridge in five minutes."

"I heard you, Mackey. What's your speed?"

"Oh my god, we're doing a hundred and five," Meagan announced, clutching Josh's phone.

Tim calmly offered his encouragement. "Hang in there, Meagan. Help is on the way. Can you guess how close the vehicle is behind you?"

Josh immediately replied, "About twenty yards, Timmy."

"Shit, I'm going to pick it up, Mackey, but you are going to have to back off or I won't make it in time."

"Screw it, Timmy, I'm going to stop and beat his ass. I don't give a shit who the fuck he is."

Meagan spoke without thinking. "No, please, not by yourself. We don't know if he is alone."

Already letting up on the gas pedal, Josh sighed. "Okay, we are coming up on Red Rock Road, doing ninety." Like before, Josh killed his headlights to ensure there was no approaching cross traffic.

Shielding her eyes and looking back, Meagan tried to study the vehicle. "It looks like a blue or black SUV."

"Thanks, Meagan. I'm less than two out, Mackey. I have requested more units and MHP has been notified."

"Shit, he's right on my ass, Timmy. We should be there in less than two. Sit back against your seat, Miss. This bridge is rough enough going thirty."

"You're good, Mackey. I'm backing in now. You and Meagan head for home and I'll call you as soon as I can. Okay, I can see your headlights."

"Be careful, Timmy. I would stop if I could."

"You and Meagan get to the house. I will have all the help I need."

"Here we go," Josh warned Meagan with seconds to spare.

No sooner did Meagan make out the obscured bridge and she was jolted against her seatbelt. The Jeep's tires impacted the edge of the crossing with such force that she thought they went airborne. Then, as quickly as they were on the bridge, they were off. Meagan peeked over her left shoulder and was terrified to see the SUV still keeping pace.

"He's yours for now, Timmy. Call me right away if he's my guy."

"Later, Mackey."

As Josh expected, Timmy activated his red and blue lights and began pursuing the SUV. "Follow us now, motherfucker." Josh checked his mirror, pressed the gas pedal to the floor, and turned on his bright lights.

When they began pulling away from the SUV, Meagan was drawn to the telephone poles whizzing past them in the Jeep's headlights. Whereas she was somewhat relieved to see red and blue lights converging from different directions, she suddenly felt nauseated. "Oh no," she moaned and reached for her queasy stomach. "Josh, I think I am going to be sick." Grasping Josh was still driving over a hundred miles per hour; Meagan knew it wouldn't be long before she threw up her chicken parmigiana.

"Hold on, sweetheart, and stop watching the telephone poles. Close your eyes and take some slow, deep breaths. We will be home in about ten minutes and I don't want to stop if we don't have to."

The way Meagan's stomach was cramping, ten minutes may as well have been ten hours. Thoroughly convinced Jeremy was in the SUV behind them, she could not close her eyes to the danger. Thinking nothing of her own safety, she feared for Josh. While she knew he would not hesitate to shoot Jeremy on sight, she also believed Jeremy would be obsessively prepared. Like Josh, he would be armed, and he would show no mercy. If Jeremy had the nerve to follow them to the house, she would have no choice but to do all she could to spare Josh. If saving his life meant leaving with Jeremy, she wouldn't think twice.

No sooner did the Mackenzies' mailbox come into view and Meagan cringed. What if Jeremy didn't come alone? What if Josh is outnumbered and can't fight back? She was dreading every horrific possibility and looking over her left shoulder when Josh made the right-hand turn into the driveway. Regardless of who was after them, Meagan wholeheartedly trusted and believed in Josh. She knew he was a man of his word and would always be there for her.

ABOUT THE AUTHOR

SAMANTHA RAY is a romantic at heart. A proud mother and wife, she believes in chivalry, passion, and enduring love. Samantha's appreciation for her family and the great outdoors is reflected in her writing. *Even When You Can't See Me* is her debut in her upcoming series of romantic fiction.

For more information on Samantha Ray and
Even When You Can't See Me, visit:
samantharayauthor.com
Facebook.com/samantharayauthor